Return to Sender

Return
to
Sender

Zoë Barnes

PIATKUS

PIATKUS

First published in Great Britain in 2009 by Piatkus

Copyright © 2009 by Zoë Barnes

A CIP catalogue record for this book
is available from the British Library

ISBN 978-0-7499-0859-1 [HB]
ISBN 978-0-7499-3920-5 [TPB]

Typeset in Sabon by Action Publishing Technology Ltd, Gloucester
Printed and bound in Great Britain by CPI Mackays Chatham, ME5 8TD

Papers used by Piatkus are natural, renewable and recyclable
products sourced from well-managed forests and certified in
accordance with the rules of the Forest Stewardship Council.

Mixed Sources
Product group from well-managed
forests and other controlled sources
www.fsc.org Cert no. SGS-COC-004081
© 1996 Forest Stewardship Council
FSC

Piatkus
An imprint of
Little, Brown Book Group
100 Victoria Embankment
London EC4Y 0DY

An Hachette UK Company
www.hachette.co.uk

www.piatkus.co.uk

Acknowledgements

With sincerest thanks to Canon Brendan Alger, Michael Condon, Anna Hemy, the Isle of Man Department of Tourism and Leisure, and the Falcon's Nest Hotel, Port Erin

Prologue:

London – The Offices of Payne, Rackstraw and Bynt

A champagne cork hit the ceiling and everyone cheered. Everyone except Holly Bennett, who just sat at her desk and stared blankly at the telephone. Mechanically she replaced the receiver on its stand as words screamed silently inside her head: This is not happening, and I'm not going to believe it. This is not happening to me.

A spent party popper floated down, draping its blue tendrils over Holly's computer monitor. She barely noticed. Her mind was a hundred miles away in Cheltenham, where her mother was slowly, almost imperceptibly, dying. And it wasn't fair. It just wasn't fair. Maureen Bennett was only fifty-six, for God's sake! People didn't die at fifty-six any more, everyone knew that.

Don't leave us, Mum. Please, you can't leave us.

Holly's hands clenched into tight fists of anger and grief. Motor neuron disease: if she hadn't heard the diagnosis from her mother's own lips, she would never have believed that a woman so full of life could suddenly have so little of it left. How long had the consultant said? A year, maybe eighteen months; and with each day that passed she would find it a little harder to walk, to talk, to express the effervescent personality Holly and her dad and sisters had loved

1

for so long. At the end, the doctors said, she wouldn't even be able to breathe by herself any more. That's when the family might have to take the decision to ... to ...

A single tear welled up in the corner of Holly's eye, and she wiped it away on her sleeve. This was no time to fall apart. Her head was swimming, but she forced herself to think about practical things. Of course when she'd asked about getting help in, Mum had told her not to worry, that she and Dad were managing fine on their own; but that was just typical Maureen, trying not to be any trouble to anyone.

Holly knew Mum was going to need help and plenty of it, but where was it going to come from? Dad was a wonderful husband and father, but he was nearing retirement age and he couldn't do everything on his own; and on a postman's wage he certainly couldn't afford to pay for round-the-clock private nursing care. Holly's two younger sisters both lived in Cheltenham, but Grace was recovering from a miscarriage, and as for Jess ... Well, Jess was seventeen and something of a loose cannon; she was having enough problems just trying to avoid being kicked out of hairdressing college.

So there was only one solution.

Deep in thought, Holly started as someone laid a hand on her shoulder.

'Hey, you've gone awfully quiet,' said Murdo in his soft Scottish burr. 'Are you all right?'

Holly swung her chair round to look up at him and saw genuine concern on his lean, handsome face. Tall, dark, considerate and loaded, Murdo Mackay was every young girl's dream. He and Holly had been together for almost three years – virtually ever since she arrived in London to try her luck in advertising – and although they had had their ups and downs like any couple, he had never once let her down.

2

'No, I'm not all right at all,' she confessed. 'I just had some bad news. Really bad. Mum's ...' She halted, unable to say the words out loud and choking on a sob.

'Something's happened to Maureen? Holly, what is it?'

'Do you mind if I explain later?' She forced down the beach-ball-sized lump in her throat. 'Look, do you think Bill Rackstraw would see me right away? This afternoon? Only I ... I think I'm going to need some time off work. Quite a lot of time, actually.'

Murdo shrugged. 'He's a decent enough guy, you know. I'm sure a couple of weeks won't be a problem.'

'Not a couple of weeks, Murdo,' she said with a sad shake of her head. 'I'm talking about a year. At the very least.'

One

'It's got a very pointy head,' hissed Auntie Gladys from the second pew on the right, leaning out into the aisle to get a better look at the star of the christening. 'Are you sure it's quite ... normal?'

As she stood by the font, lighted candle in hand, Holly averted her eyes from Auntie Gladys's towering purple hat with the bobbing peacock feather and battled to maintain a straight face. Corpsing in the middle of a christening would never do. Luckily, eighteen-year-old Jess, Holly's sister and baby Aimee's mother, was too busy juggling the yowling infant to have heard her aunt casting aspersions, and her partner, Kev Hopkins, looked as though it was taking every ounce of his concentration not to be eaten alive by his uncomfortable new suit. Aspiring singer-songwriter that he was, Kev was not really a suit person.

Bless him. I do love my family, thought Holly with a sudden, enormous surge of godmotherly affection. Even Auntie Gladys, and that's saying something.

Strictly speaking, the Bennetts weren't actually Holly's family. Or rather they were, but in a legal rather than a biological sense, since Holly had been adopted as a tiny baby after being abandoned

5

on the steps of the local hospital. That didn't make the slightest difference to her though; as far as she was concerned they were her family – always had been and always would be. If anything, the fact that she was adopted made everything more special, because her parents hadn't just been presented with a pink, sticky bundle in the delivery room and told to get on with it: they'd actually *chosen* her.

At the thought of her parents, Harry and Maureen, a little pang of sorrow twisted Holly's heart. If only Mum could have been here today, she thought. She'd have been so proud of Jess and Grace – her two younger daughters – having their babies properly christened in church. Proud – and just a little surprised, mused Holly with a smile and a flick of her chestnut hair, recalling the almighty family row there'd been a few years before, when Grace and Steve were getting married and Grace had been her usual emphatic self, refusing to entertain any thoughts of a church wedding on the grounds that it 'costs a bomb and it doesn't mean a thing if you don't believe in God'.

And here they were today, all gathered around the font in their cost-a-bomb christening outfits, watching Grace and Jess's children being inducted as miniature members of the Church of England. Obviously parenthood makes you see things differently, mused Holly. Maybe one day in the not-too-distant future I'll find that out for myself. And she wished with all her heart that Mum hadn't been taken away from them so soon, before she even had a chance to hold her grandchildren in her arms. If God does exist, and I ever get the chance to meet him, Holly thought grimly, he's going to have a few hard questions to answer.

It was a typical mad March day on the optimistically named Bluebell Estate. Outside the church, rain was hammering down on the unappealing, concrete egg-box roof while the wind whipped up a miniature twister of old chip wrappers and crisp packets, but at least the sound of two healthy babies yelling their heads off drowned out the din of a metal dumpster blowing over in the gale.

Holly couldn't help smiling at the thought of upwardly mobile Grace and Steve in an unlovely place like this. They could have gone to a picturesque old church somewhere more posh, like Prestbury or Leckhampton, and ended up with much nicer christening photos. But as Jess had pointed out to Grace, this was where Mum and Dad were married all those years ago, and if it was good enough for them, it was good enough for their grandchildren too. So the concrete egg box it was.

As the ceremony came to an end with the closing prayers, and the rain turned to the clatter of hail, an elbow in the ribs jolted Holly back from her reverie.

'Psst. Auntie Holly.'

'Uh?'

Jess thrust something soft and strangely moist into her arms. 'Take her for a minute, will you?'

'W-what?'

'I'm bursting for the loo. Just hang on to her for a mo and I'll be right back.'

Jess legged it down the aisle to the toilets at the back of the nave, leaving Auntie Holly and her three-month-old niece to sort themselves out as best they could.

Holly wrinkled her nose. 'Pooh, you smell,' she commented with a grimace that turned into a grin. 'Are you sure you haven't done something nasty in your nappy? Must be great being a baby,' she added thoughtfully. 'You can be really antisocial and everybody still loves you.'

As Holly was pondering the wonders of life as a three-month-old, Grace materialised at her side, looking impossibly slender in close-fitting designer separates.

'Did you notice?' she asked.

'Notice what?'

'Your poor little sister couldn't even afford a hat to go with her outfit. *And* I bet it all came out of a catalogue. She and Kev are really struggling to make ends meet, you know.'

It wasn't the first heavy hint Grace had dropped, and Holly wasn't slow on the uptake. 'Are you suggesting I ought to help them out?'

'Well, it wouldn't hurt.' Grace wasn't one to mince her words. 'And I know for a fact you haven't touched a penny of the money Mum left you.'

'Just because you've spent all yours—' began Holly.

'Some of us have family responsibilities,' cut in Grace, quick as a flash.

'Yes, and some of us are loaded – and I'm not talking about me. Face it, Grace, you and Steve aren't short of a penny or two. I'm more than happy to help Jess out, but I think you should divvy up your share as well. These days I'm just a humble post-lady, remember; you and Steve are on your way to your first billion!'

Grace looked embarrassed. 'Yes, well, business isn't booming every week of the year you know, and Steve has to keep back enough to reinvest in the business. And as for you delivering the post instead of doing a proper job, when's that going to end?'

Holly coloured slightly. 'You know why I do it. I came home to look after Mum, and Dad found me a job down at the local sorting office.'

'Mum passed away a year ago, Holly. A whole year. How come you're still here? Why aren't you back at your desk in London, dreaming up killer adverts, instead of just picking up the odd bit of freelance work here and there?' Grace's gaze fixed on the sleeping bundle in Holly's arms. 'Or if you're tired of being a success, you could marry Murdo and become a yummy mummy. Either way, you can't spend the rest of your life shoving junk mail through people's letter boxes.'

8

'I . . . I'm just not ready to go back to London,' stammered Holly, not enjoying this interrogation very much. 'Not yet.'

'Like I said, you can't play at being Postwoman Pat for ever.'

'I know.' Holly stroked Aimee's tiny hand, and the fingers instinctively curled around hers. A thrill of warmth and love passed through her. You're my god-daughter and my niece, she thought. And I'm going to do everything in my power to give you a happy life. At least that's one thing I'm certain about in my topsy-turvy world.

'You know,' remarked Grace with a twinkle in her eye, 'you look rather good with a baby in your arms. Motherhood kind of suits you. And I bet Murdo agrees, don't you, Murdo?'

Holly had been so lost in her conversation with Grace and her own infatuation with Aimee that she hadn't noticed Murdo silently striding through the remnants of the congregation to join them.

'What's this that I'm agreeing to?' demanded Murdo, sliding an arm round Holly's shoulders.

'I think she'd make a great mum, don't you?'

Holly swallowed hard as Murdo looked deep into her eyes and answered: 'Oh, absolutely.'

'Well, don't leave it too late,' said Grace with a laugh as she swept off to find Steve. 'You're not getting any younger.'

But I'm not even thirty yet, Holly protested silently as she picked at the buffet in the church hall. OK, so maybe I will be before the year's out, but for now I'm twenty-nine and holding, and it'll be years and years before I have to start thinking about ticking biological clocks.

All the same, she admitted to herself, I would dearly love to have a baby. Not right now, perhaps, but some time soon. I really, really would. The question is, do I want to have one with Murdo? It's a big question, she thought, and whatever other people might

9

think, I don't have the answer. Not yet. And I'm not going to be one of those people who get pregnant and then think about it later.

As she speared a midget sausage roll with a cocktail stick, she caught sight of her reflection in the glass-fronted cabinet where the church football team kept its one and only trophy. The young woman who gazed back at her was no dazzling beauty, but could have been pretty if her nose hadn't been too long. The dark eyes were large and long-lashed; the shoulder-length chestnut hair rebellious but shiny. She was neither tall nor willowy, but there was a certain instinctive grace in the way she moved. Holly wondered, just for a second, if she'd got that from her mother. And if so, which one: her adoptive mother, who'd loved to dance ... or her biological one, who remained a total mystery?

It wasn't the first time Holly had wondered about where she came from, but seeing Adam and Aimee come into the world, and being a part of their lives as they grew, had made her think more and more about becoming a mother herself. And, as what had begun as a vague inclination grew into a real yearning, Holly also longed to know who had given birth to her. It wasn't that she didn't love her adoptive parents; on the contrary, she adored them with all her being. But the fact remained that some unknown woman had given birth to her, and then, for some equally unknown reason, had abandoned her on the hospital steps.

I have to know, she thought. Because whoever that woman is, bad or good, she's a part of who I really am. But ... what about Maureen? What about the wonderful woman who brought me up? How would she have felt if I'd told her I wanted to find my birth mother? Am I deceiving myself if I say she'd have given me her blessing?

'What's up, love?' asked a familiar voice beside her. 'Why on earth are you standing over here, all on your own?'

She turned round. 'I'm fine, Dad. Just, you know, thinking.'

'About your mum?'

She nodded. 'She'd have loved today. She'd be so proud of Grace and Jess.'

Holly's father ruffled her hair, the way he had done when she was a little kid. 'She'd be proud of all of you. She always was. Now, come back and join the others. It's not the same without all my girls together.'

At the other side of the hall, Holly's two sisters were deep in conversation.

'. . . and that's why I worry so much,' confided Jess to her sister, in a hushed yet urgent whisper.

'You think I don't?' Grace stroked Adam's soft curls as the baby boy slept on her shoulder. 'Every time I look at this little one, I think what if—'

It was at that moment that Harry Bennett bore down on them with Holly in tow: 'Well, well, if it's not my other two favourite daughters!' Harry looked from one to the other with slight uncertainty. 'Not butting in, are we?'

'No, Dad,' said Grace, in a voice that suggested the opposite. 'Of course you're not.'

'Is everything all right?' asked Holly.

'Of course it is,' replied Jess, switching on a smile. 'So, are you two enjoying the do? Not bad, is it?'

'You've done a great job,' agreed Holly.

'Mind you,' mused Jess, 'I never want to see another seafood bloody canapé as long as I live.'

'Where's Aimee?' Holly asked.

'Kev's taken her to the loos to change her nappy,' explained Jess. 'It's his turn.'

Harry chuckled. 'You've got that lad well trained.'

11

'Of course I have,' replied Jess smugly. 'Start as you mean to go on – that's right isn't it, Grace?'

'Absolutely. And if all else fails, ban sex for a week. It never fails.' She grinned. 'Mum taught me that one.'

Harry turned crimson. 'Oh look, isn't that your Auntie Gladys over there?' he cut in. 'Why don't I just pop over and have a quick word?'

And with that he fled, intent on nabbing Auntie Gladys by the vol-au-vents.

'Grace, that was wicked of you! I don't think I've ever seen him so embarrassed,' remarked Holly.

'Sorry, couldn't resist it.' Grace yawned. 'I mean, it's just so easy.'

'Mum always said that,' reminisced Holly. 'She once told me that when they were first dating, he accidentally wandered into the women's changing rooms at the swimming baths and you could hear the screams for miles – not the women's, Dad's!'

There was laughter and a brief silence. Then: 'Mum never told me that story,' said Grace, making it sound like an accusation.

'It was soon after I came back from London,' Holly explained. 'She still talked a lot then.'

'To you, anyway.'

'Well, yes. But then I was the one who spent the most time with her,' Holly pointed out with mild irritation.

In the space of a second, her mind replayed all the days, hours and minutes she had spent with her mum during her illness. Yes, there had been a lot of talking in the beginning, but at the end, only silence. Because the disease had taken away almost everything, even her voice. Everything but the light in her eyes, and at the end even that went, too.

After a moment, when the pain had gone from her chest, Holly continued: 'She'd have revelled in all this.'

Grace scanned the room, taking in all the aunts, uncles, big hats, posh dresses and profiteroles, and sighed. 'Wouldn't she just. And to think I kicked up all that fuss about not getting married in church. I'd hire Westminster Abbey and do it all over again if only it would bring her back.'

Holly stroked Aimee's peach-soft cheek as she gurgled in her mother's arms. 'I know she'd have adored this little one,' she remarked to Jess. 'She really is beautiful; I've never seen anything so perfect.'

'Well, she does ... seem that way,' replied Jess, warily.

Holly felt her heart plummet in her chest. 'Is there something wrong with her? You've never mentioned anything before.'

Grace laid a hand on Holly's arm. 'No, no, everything's fine, at least we think it is; same as it is with Adam. Jess just means ... because of Mum's illness, we can't ever be sure, can we? We can't be sure if something's been passed on. And even if we did know, what could we do about it? There's no cure for motor neuron disease.'

A nasty chill raised all the hairs on the back of Holly's neck. 'But I thought Mum's specialist said it wasn't hereditary.'

'In eight or nine out of ten cases,' Jess corrected her. 'In the tenth one, there's a chance it might be.'

'That's a pretty small risk,' ventured Holly.

'Not if you turn out to be the tenth case,' retorted Grace.

'I'm sorry, I didn't mean—'

'Of course you didn't,' said Grace. 'But you see, Jess and I probably won't know until we're in our forties whether or not we're going to get MND, by which time Aimee and Adam could have kids of their own – unless they're too scared to have them, not knowing what they might be passing on.'

'Actually, Kev and I were thinking we might try for donor eggs some time when I accidentally got pregnant,' revealed Jess. 'It was one hell of a shock, wasn't it Grace?'

'Donor eggs! You never said ...' Holly's brain reeled. It was as though someone had just torn up all her family certainties and scattered them out of the window. 'My God, yes, you're right; I had no idea ...'

She was dumbfounded. And it hurt, knowing that Jess had chosen not to confide in her. Why was that? She must have talked it over with someone: Grace, probably. All of this was going on in my own family, she thought, and I knew nothing about it. Not a thing. Am I exceptionally stupid? Or don't they feel like they can confide in me any more? Have I become an outsider?

For the first time in her life she was truly aware of an invisible division between herself and her sisters, and it didn't feel good.

'What about you and Steve?' she asked Grace. 'You must have agonised about having a baby, too.'

'We decided it was just about worth the risk. But it wasn't easy.'

Holly recalled the morning of their mother's funeral. Stony-grey faces and a sky to match. Holly was so absorbed in her loss that she'd barely noticed Grace having to rush out to be sick. Later, she'd admitted that it wasn't a stomach bug at all; she was expecting a baby. She'd wanted to say so before, but the council crematorium seemed a grotesque place to announce the imminent arrival of a new life. With hindsight, it felt curiously fitting. As great-uncle Bill had put it, with his usual tact: 'One in, one out – that's life for you. 'Spect I'll be next.'

'I'm sorry, I ... I just didn't think,' stammered Holly. 'I guess I was too wrapped up in missing Mum.'

'At least it's not a problem you'll ever have to worry about,' remarked Grace with a hint of coolness.

Holly didn't get it straight off. 'What isn't?'

'Having a baby!' Grace tossed her immaculately highlighted locks impatiently and spelled it out. 'With mum and you not being – you know – related.'

For one short moment, Holly could have hit her. 'She was my Mum just as much as she was yours!' she protested.

Jess intervened. 'Of course she was. I'm sure Grace didn't mean it like that.' Her gaze locked with Grace's. 'Did you, sis?'

There was a fraction of a second's hesitation, then Grace smiled and said, 'Of course I didn't, Hol. Trust you to be so oversensitive. All I meant was that if you have kids you won't have to worry about passing on MND to them, because we're biologically related to Mum and you aren't. And whichever way you look at it,' she breezed on before Holly could get a word in edgeways, 'it's not quite the same thing, is it?'

Two

It was Wednesday – Holly's precious day off from delivering the post. But you'd never have known it.

Instead of sleeping in until she felt like ambling downstairs to make herself some toast, she let the six o'clock alarm shriek her into consciousness, levered herself out from underneath the duvet and staggered zigzag fashion to the bathroom.

Normally she'd have squandered half the day being lazy, and the rest catching up with the freelance advertising projects she took on to keep her hand in and her brain active. Not today though. Today, she was driving her sister to the back of beyond to pick up a load of frocks. Why? Because it was all for charity. And you couldn't say no to charity, could you?

She cursed the word as she exfoliated herself into life. Why had she let Grace persuade her to go and fetch the designer outfits for her charity fashion show? It wasn't as if she was even being very nice to her at the moment – not that she'd been particularly nice to anyone who wasn't rich since she and Steve moved up in the world. Why did I agree to do it? she lamented. I must have been off my head. Just my luck that Dad has to work today. I'm sure I could've wheedled him into doing it instead.

Mentally deranged or not, by seven she was on the road in her dad's old ex-post office van. I'm sure Grace could drive this thing herself if she wanted to, Holly grumbled to herself as she rattled along Whaddon Road. She just doesn't want to be seen driving a battered, rusty-red Transit in her designer heels.

Over on the posh side of town, at 5 The Avenue, Holly could see Grace waiting in her lounge, behind the floaty voile curtains that kept prying eyes off her extensive collection of Swarovski crystal animals. As the rust-heap on wheels squealed to a stop, Holly could almost feel her sister's mortification. She couldn't help smiling to herself. Chances were, nothing quite this ghastly had been spotted in the area since the night all the lead was nicked off the local church roof.

Head down, Grace scuttled out of her brand-new Regency-style town house and made a dash for the horrible rusty-red thing that dared to call itself a van.

'Let me in before somebody sees!'

'Too late, they already did.' As Grace scrambled in beside her, Holly pointed to the twitching blinds at number seven.

'Does it really matter?' she enquired as they headed out of town on the A40.

Grace stared at her. 'God, but you've gone downhill since you left the great metropolis. The sooner you let Murdo rescue you, the better.'

'What if I don't want him to?'

'Then you're even dafter than you look.'

They looked at each other, held defiant eye contact for a couple of seconds and both burst out laughing, just in time for Holly to swerve out of the way of an oncoming Mercedes. At least the tension was gone.

'So tell me exactly what we're doing today?' demanded Holly.

'I told you, we're picking up some outfits for the charity fashion show. You know Tammy Hyde-Cooper?'

'Er ... no.'

17

Grace shook her head in disbelief. 'Yes you do. She's the one who writes that column in the *Telegraph* – the one who's married to that guy who presents *Mighty Motors* on Channel Six.'

Holly registered a brief flicker of interest. 'The one with the nice bum?'

'No, the fat one.'

'Ah.' The flicker died.

'Well, her best friend is this really trendy couture designer, and she's only talked her into letting us have some of her frocks and stuff for the show. Isn't that amazing?'

'It'd be more amazing if I didn't have to drive you all the way to rural Hampshire on my day off,' Holly replied candidly. 'So how did you meet this Tammy what's-her-face, anyway?'

'I recognised her at a charity dinner, so I went up and told her how wonderful her column is,' Grace replied proudly. 'She asked about my charity work, and we got along like a house on fire.'

'And is it wonderful? Her column, I mean.'

Grace shrugged. 'No idea. I've never read it. But that's not the point, is it?'

'Isn't it?'

Grace's eyes shone with fervour. 'Not when it's all in a good cause. And you can't overestimate the value of good contacts.' She leaned closer. 'Your Murdo's well heeled. Don't suppose he knows anyone useful? Didn't you say his mum met David Beckham once?'

Holly laughed. 'Yes – at a bus stop, and he was five years old at the time. Somehow I doubt that he'd remember. Now come on, girl, get reading that map! I hope this isn't going to take all day. I'm on baby-sitting duty tonight.'

Ten and a half hours later, a rather smart red Mazda two-seater drove slowly onto the Bluebell Estate and parked outside Crocus

House. Holly winced as she eased herself out of her beloved car – the one luxury possession she'd retained from her life in London – stretching her aching back, then heaved herself up the stairs to Jess and Kev's second-floor flat.

As Jess opened the front door, a look of relief spread across her face.

'Holly! Where the hell have you been?' Jess slid a pink diamanté hairgrip into her two-tone hair. This week it was dark brown underneath, with a top layer of peroxide blonde, rather as if someone had poured vanilla sauce over a chocolate pudding. Holly had never known Jess to have the same hairstyle two weeks running. 'The band's on in twenty minutes and it's ten minutes' walk to the pub. We were beginning to think you weren't coming!'

'So was I,' replied Holly darkly, stripping off her fleece jacket and throwing it over the back of Jess and Kev's lived-in sofa. If truth were told, an evening's babysitting for her sister was not exactly what she felt like after a day trapped with her other sister in a Transit van – she'd far rather have been strangling Grace – but a promise was a promise, and Holly was a woman of her word.

'What happened?' asked Kev, emerging from the bedroom in his best going-out T-shirt and ripped jeans, his light-brown dreadlocks tied loosely in a ponytail. 'You look exhausted.'

'What happened? Grace happened. She's had me driving all over the bloody south of England, trying to find that designer friend of hers.'

'And did you?'

'In the end. But not until we'd driven past the village five times. There were no bloody signposts, and you know what Grace's map-reading is like.'

Jess giggled. 'Do you remember that time she navigated Dad onto an army firing range?'

'How could I forget? And of course when we did get to the

19

house, it turned out that the actual dresses were stored in this ware-house fifty miles away.'

'Bit of a communication problem then?' Kev offered Holly his can of Carlsberg and she took a grateful slug.

'You could say that. Oh, and here's the really good bit: her friend forgot to mention that she only designs kids' clothes, so now Grace has to go grovelling all round Cheltenham to every parent she knows, coercing their little angels into modelling these amazing kiddie creations at the fashion show. They're hideous, by the way,' she added as an afterthought. 'Little Miss Muffet meets the bride of Dracula.'

'Sounds like you've had quite a day. I don't know what Grace gets out of it all, you know,' remarked Jess, slipping on her coat and adeptly transferring a drowsy Aimee into her sister's arms. 'What with her full-time nursing job, and Steve's business.'

'I do,' retorted Kev. 'Power.'

'Kev!' chided Jess. 'She's doing it for charity!'

'That doesn't stop her getting a rush out of it, does it? That, and she gets to feel as if she's way posher than everybody else because she knows all these celebs.'

Holly was tempted to agree, but seeing the look Jess was giving Kev, she thought it better to keep her opinions to herself. There was no doubt about it, though: since Steve had started up his own IT business, Grace had developed a streak of ambition she'd never displayed before. At one time, she'd just been happy to nurse sick people; now she was eyeing up ward sister vacancies as if they were mere stepping stones on her path to world domination. It was all very odd, thought Holly. At one time she'd have said that she knew Grace inside out, but now ...

'There are bottles of breast milk in the fridge, and there's half a steak pie on top of the stove if you're hungry,' Jess called out over her shoulder as she and Kev set off for their rare evening out. 'Phone me if there's anything wrong – even the tiniest thing.'

20

'I will.'

'And if she gets a temperature or a rash or anything—'

'I'll be straight on to the doctor, don't worry. Now go!'

As the door of the flat clicked shut, Holly gave a sigh of relief and let herself sink slowly down onto the sagging settee, the baby nestling in the crook of her arm. A warm glow of satisfaction stole over her as she looked down into her little niece's face and a pair of blue eyes gazed back at her. They seemed to say, 'Tell me about the world, Auntie Holly. I want to know everything.' The steak pie can wait, she thought. This is quality time for you and me, kid, and nothing can beat that.

The only sounds disturbing the silence were the tick-tock of the Coca-Cola clock on the kitchen wall, and the soft, regular snuffle of Aimee's breathing. Holly bent down to inhale the scent of her skin. It smelt like nothing else in the world; the sweet smell of freshly bathed, perfect newness. And once again, the yearning swept over her, carrying her heart and soul away.

You really do want a baby, don't you? whispered a treacherous voice in her head. Forget about trying to be a career woman; that's not really for you. Only a baby can make you complete.

I wonder if that's true, she thought, stroking the baby's soft blonde curls. I mean, I'm not exactly incomplete now, am I? I have a close family, a job I like and as much freelance work as I want, a nice boyfriend who's handsome and well off ... But the more she thought about it, the less sure she became. Perhaps there was some-thing missing – a certainty, a direction. Grace was right; she ought to be pitching for jobs in top London ad agencies, not hanging around Cheltenham with a bag of mail and a bicycle. And if she really was contemplating having a baby with Murdo, shouldn't she be thinking of him as something more than just 'nice'?

Do I love him? she pondered. I like him a lot, and I do fancy him, well, quite a bit. And we have fun together. Does that count? Is that

what love is? Or is there something more out there, something amazing that I might experience if I was with somebody else?

Perhaps I could live without that, she mused. Lots of people do. But if I'm ever going to have a baby, there are two questions I have to have answered: Who gave birth to me? And why did she give me away?

Holly suddenly realised that she had spent years not thinking about her birth mother, subconsciously blocking her out, virtually denying her existence. What need was there for her, when Holly already had a mother, a family who loved her, a place to belong? But her recent conversations with her sisters had made her realise that the past was part of her, whether she liked it or not. A part to be passed on, in time, to her own children.

She looked down into Aimee's questioning blue eyes. 'I want to know who I am,' she whispered. 'Do you think I'm crazy?'

By the time Holly arrived home it was almost midnight and the house was in darkness – all except for a single light in the kitchen at the back.

She found her dad in his pyjamas, busy making his special cocoa in the microwave, complete with a fortifying splash of whisky.

'Long day?' asked Harry sympathetically.

'Unbelievable.' Holly searched the bread bin for something to eat, and came up with a few slightly stale digestives. 'If Grace ever persuades me to do anything again, please have me committed.'

Harry smiled. 'You never could say no to anyone, love. Just like your mother.'

Holly opened her mouth to say something, then thought better of it.

'At least you've come home to a nice welcome,' Harry went on. 'These were delivered while you were out.' He went and fetched the enormous bouquet of red roses which he'd temporarily stored in the larder to keep them cool.

Holly's jaw dropped. 'But ... who'd send me flowers today? It's not my birthday or anything, is it?'

'Have a look and see.'

She felt for the card nestling among the scented flowers, and read out the message: 'To my darling Holly, on the third anniversary of the day we met. All my love, Murdo.'

Harry's eyebrows lifted. 'Well, well. You've certainly got yourself an attentive young man there. It took me all my time to remember your mother's birthday, God bless her.'

'Wow.' Holly scratched her ear, not quite sure whether to be delighted or slightly worried. Were normal boyfriends supposed to remember things like the anniversary of the day they met their beloved? On the other hand, were normal girlfriends supposed to forget? Suddenly she felt slightly guilty. 'I'd better call and thank him.'

'This late?'

'You know Murdo. He never goes to bed before one.'

She reached for her mobile and then hesitated, a horrible, guilty reticence overtaking her. She wanted to be thrilled, but for some reason it wasn't quite happening. She wanted to fit into Murdo's perfect, fairy-tale future too, but that wasn't quite happening either. She wanted to thank him for being the most wonderful, kind, devoted boyfriend any woman could ask for, but ...

Flipping shut her mobile, she dropped it back into her handbag. 'You're right, Dad, it's late. I'll call him tomorrow.'

Three

It was only four-thirty in the morning, but Cheltenham sorting office was already buzzing with activity. Long, overflowing 'coffins' filled with letters and packets stood waiting to be emptied and sorted, and Nesta O'Hare the duty manager – all five flame-haired feet of her – was keeping a watchful eye out for slackers from her tiny office in one corner of the enormous covered space.

Holly hummed to herself as she sorted the mail for her walk, deftly firing envelopes into a rack of alphabetical pigeonholes. She enjoyed sorting. It was pleasantly monotonous and it gave her time to think – although on this particular Thursday morning the same things kept going round and round inside her head, refusing to be resolved.

Holly and Nesta had been firm friends ever since the day they first sat on adjoining potties at day nursery, but Holly had no problem taking orders from her childhood best mate, which was just as well since Nesta had no problem dishing them out. Nesta was just one of those people who are born to tell other people what to do. She'd been queen of the Wendy house at six, and things weren't about to change now. It was a pity her love life didn't run as smoothly as her career, thought Holly. Nesta had dated almost every man in Cheltenham, but seemed destined to remain perpetu-

24

ally single. Holly supposed that it took a special kind of guy to click with a girl whose flatmate was a six-inch Amazonian spider called Ronnie.

'Good weekend?' enquired Julian, a lanky youth whose rack of pigeonholes stood next to Holly's.

'Not bad. You?'

Julian's face lit up with evangelistic enthusiasm. 'Went tomb-stoning in Cornwall with the lads. Wow – there was this one totally amazing eighty-foot drop, straight down off the cliffs into the surf.' He shot a letter into a pigeonhole as if to illustrate. 'One metre to the left and you'd be skewered on these rocks. Like needles they were, unbelievable. Fancy coming along next week?'

Before Holly had a chance to answer that on balance she'd rather saw her own ears off, one of the other postmen tapped her on the shoulder. 'Boss wants a word.' The squat, scowling individual known as Welsh Dave nodded towards Nesta's office. 'Rather you than me, kid. You know, that bitch reckons she's going to dock my pay for being four minutes late.' He sniffed. 'We'll see what the union has to say about that.'

Oh bugger, thought Holly as she walked across the sorting-office floor, wondering what she'd done wrong this time. Whether it was unauthorised uniform shorts or a sausage roll that had gone missing from the staff canteen, Nesta was nothing if not a perfectionist: the sort of person who spent idle moments arranging elastic bands in order of size.

The door to Nesta's office was ajar. Holly gave a brief knock and walked in. 'You wanted to see me?'

Nesta was sitting at her desk in the cramped and rather dingy office, staring morosely at her computer screen. The wall behind her was adorned with an official Post Office clock (broken), a pinboard groaning with yellowing memos and an out-of-date charity calendar featuring semi-naked postmen.

25

'You're good with words,' said Nesta, looking up. 'What rhymes with "kitchen"?'

'Er – sorry?'

'No, not "sorry", "kitchen",' repeated Nesta, with some urgency. 'I'm trying to do the verse for this bloody greetings card, and I can't find anything that rhymes with "kitchen". Shut the door, will you?' she added. 'Don't want the whole office to know I'm skiving.'

Holly pushed the door shut with her foot. 'I thought you'd hauled me in here to give me a bollocking for something.'

Nesta grinned wickedly. 'I will do if you don't come up with a rhyme for this bloody card.' She raked a hand through her mop of wild auburn hair. 'Poet? Me? I don't know why I bother.'

'Shove over then, and let's have a look.' Holly grabbed a spare chair and sat down next to her friend and boss. Everyone at the sorting office knew about Nesta's poetic aspirations: she'd even done a couple of local shows once, billed as 'The Next Pam Ayres', but nothing had come of it. Nowadays, she mostly wrote person-alised verses for greetings cards as a favour to friends. 'What's this one for?'

'Ken Roberts' mum's birthday. Apparently she's the Nigella Lawson of Leckhampton, and being an idiot I said I'd have this ready by tonight.'

'Ah – a cook. Hence the kitchen.' Holly skimmed the embryonic verse. '"You're a wizard in the kitchen" – is that it?'

Nesta threw her a black look. 'I told you, I'm stuck!'

'OK, OK, I'm thinking.' Holly scratched her head. 'How about . . . "lichen"?'

'She's a cook, not a botanist!'

'Stitching? Twitching? Itching?'

'Now you're just being silly.'

At last, inspiration struck. 'I know!' declared Holly. She took over the computer keyboard then sat back in her chair with a flourish. 'There you go – perfect!'

Nesta peered at the screen. '"You're a wizard in the kitchen, your casseroles are bitchin".'

'Genius, isn't it?'

'No . . . but I guess it's a start.' Nesta reread the couplet and burst out laughing. 'The poor woman's seventy-three. She probably won't have a clue what it means! Thanks anyway,' she added. 'You're a mate. Fancy a coffee?'

Holly glanced at her watch. 'Do I have time?'

'Statutory fifteen-minute break remember? Union rules.' She got up, switched on a battered kettle and hunted out a second mug from somewhere in a desk drawer. 'I know you usually give it a miss so you can finish your round early, but I could do with the company today.'

'Feeling a bit down?'

Nesta nodded.

'Didn't things work out with the lovely Leonard then?'

Nesta scowled. 'Lovely my arse. We were supposed to be going to the theatre, but he cancelled at the last minute – he got called away to investigate suspected bluetongue disease in Middlesbrough. I told him not to bother coming back,' she added. 'I'm never dating another Ministry vet as long as I live.'

Oh dear, another one bites the dust, thought Holly. 'You should've told me, I'd have come round.'

'I thought you'd be off doing something gorgeous and sexy with lover boy, seeing as it was your Wednesday off.' Nesta poured out the coffees and sat down.

'Fat chance. I spent most of it sorting out Grace and her bloody fashion show.' Holly paused, feeling a compulsion to go on but not sure if she should. 'Murdo did send me some flowers though. For the third anniversary of the day we met.'

27

'Aah, that was romantic,' commented Nesta. 'What did you send him?'

'Er . . . nothing. Actually I had no idea it was any kind of anniversary.' She cradled the mug of hot coffee. 'And now I don't know what to say to Murdo.'

'How about "Thank you, darling"?' Nesta watched Holly's face closely. 'Or am I missing the point? Is there something wrong between you and Murdo that you've not been letting on about?'

'No, no. Everything's all right. Scarily all right.' Holly turned the mug round and round in her hands, its contents so hot that they almost burned her flesh. 'I think that may be the problem. I mean, when everything's all right there's no excuse to hold back, is there?'

'And that's what you want to do? Hold back on Murdo?'

'Yes . . . No. I honestly don't know.' Holly took a sip of scalding-hot coffee and felt it trickle down her throat like a trail of molten lava. 'One day I'm completely sure how I feel about him, the next . . . Well, I know that I love him, it's just I'm not sure if I love him in, you know, the right way. The wanting-to-spend-your-whole-life-together way. Does that sound lame?'

'A bit,' admitted Nesta.

'And there's more to it than that,' Holly added rather woefully.

'Oh dear.' Nesta unlocked the top drawer of her desk and brought out the emergency HobNobs, then slid the opened tin in her friend's direction. 'Like what?' Light dawned. 'Hey, you're not . . . pregnant, are you?'

'Heck, no!' Holly laughed. 'But that's kind of the problem.'

'You're . . . infertile?'

'No! Stop jumping to conclusions. It's just that since Adam and Aimee were born I've been getting really, really broody. And I've got a feeling that Murdo's starting to feel that way too.'

'Ah! But you're not sure you want to rush into having babies with Murdo, in case he turns out to be the wrong alpha male?'

Nesta could see from Holly's expression that she'd hit the target this time. 'But sooner or later you'll have to make a decision, won't you? Everybody does. Some of us make the right ones, and some of us don't, but most people end up glad that they took the plunge and had a family. I'm sure I would – if I ever got the chance.'

Holly nodded. 'That's why I think I need to make up my mind where I'm going, so I can get on with my life.' She bit into a biscuit. 'But there is one other complication.'

'Dear God, Holly!' Nesta held up her hands in mock disbelief. 'This isn't *The Jeremy Kyle Show*, you know.' She sighed. 'Go on then, spit it out.'

'You know I'm adopted?'

Nesta nodded. 'Yes, of course I do. I've always known. But that's never been an issue for you, surely?'

'Not till my mum died and I started wanting to have a baby. The thing is, well, before I start my own family, I think I need to know where I came from; who I am, if you like – who gave birth to me and then abandoned me.'

'So you want to find your birth mother?'

'If that's possible.' To her surprise, Holly found herself looking to her friend for approval, the way she had done when she was a timorous toddler in playschool. 'What do you think?'

'I think,' began Nesta slowly, 'I think that … you're walking into a minefield, and that you should think really hard about this before you go ahead.'

Holly was taken aback. 'But … But loads of people try to track down their biological mothers, don't they?'

'And loads of people end up causing a whole lot more unhappiness than they ever bargained for,' retorted her friend. 'Look, this may sound harsh, but it's something I know a bit about. There was this lady my mum knew … Nobody had any idea that she'd had a baby when she was thirteen, and put it up for adoption. Not until

29

eighteen years later, when the girl suddenly turns up on her doorstep wanting them all to be one big happy family.'

'So what happened?' asked Holly, heart in mouth.

'When the woman's husband found out, he called her a slag and gave her a black eye and a broken arm. She called the police and charged the husband with assault, they got divorced, and things didn't work out with the daughter either. So you see ...'

'Oh no,' breathed Holly, as the vaster picture began to open up before her eyes. 'I wouldn't want to do that to anyone. But ... But it doesn't have to be like that, does it? And I don't want to barge into this woman's life, only find out a little bit about her – about why she gave me up. I mean, don't I have that right?'

'Maybe,' acknowledged Nesta with a shrug. 'And maybe not. And sure, it might work out fine for you. All I'm saying is, think about it very carefully before you start digging up the past.' She paused for a moment. 'Speaking of which, where does your father fit in to all of this?'

'Dad? I haven't talked to him about it yet.'

'No, not your dad, I mean your biological father. The man who so kindly supplied the sperm that went on to make up half of your DNA. Don't you want to track him down too?'

Holly was aghast. She hadn't thought about it from that angle at all. 'Him? Why the hell would I want to do that?'

'Well, like I said, it takes two to make a baby,' pointed out Nesta.

'Maybe it does,' conceded Holly, 'but he's still no father of mine. A father is someone who looks after you, protects you from bad stuff. And I've already got one of those, thank you very much. No way do I ever want to set eyes on the kind of callous bastard who lets a woman down so badly that she has to give her child away.'

Holly was still thinking about what Nesta had said when she

finished her mail round and went home for a sandwich and a shower.

There was no sign of Dad; he was probably still out in the Post Office van, delivering his cargo of parcels. Most of the depot's drivers had a reputation for careering round Cheltenham with their right foot on the floor, intent on getting home in time for elevenses. But Harry Bennett belonged to a gentler, more relaxed era, and would far rather have a quarter-mile tailback behind him than break the speed limit or jump a red light. That's my Dad, thought Holly with an affectionate smile, and no one could ever replace him.

There was a red light on the answering machine, announcing a message – doubtless from Murdo. It's no use, Holly told herself; I can't keep putting it off, I'll have to call him. The truth was that she didn't really know why she hadn't called him already; the poor guy must be wondering what on earth the matter was.

His office phone rang twice before he picked it up. 'Murdo Mackay.'

Holly took a deep breath. 'Hi, darling, it's me. I just wanted to thank you for the beautiful roses.'

'Glad you liked them.'

'They're perfect. They must have cost a fortune.'

'Not a penny more than you're worth, sweetheart.'

A tide of relief washed over Holly as they chatted. Now she was actually talking to Murdo there was no tension at all; everything was perfectly fine. She really couldn't figure out why she'd been so bothered about calling him. There was nothing wrong between her and Murdo, she told herself firmly, and there never had been. Like everybody said, they were made for each other.

'To be honest,' said Murdo, 'I was a wee bit worried when you didn't call me last night. I thought the flowers might have gone astray, or that maybe you didn't like them.'

31

'It was only because I got in really late,' Holly lied. 'Grace had me driving all over the place picking up outfits for her fashion show, and then I had to babysit for Jess and Kev. By the time I got home it was far too late to call you.'

'Really? Must've been well after one then.'

'Er ... yes. There was a band playing a late session at the Two Pigs.'

There was a pause. 'I really miss you,' said Murdo softly.

'I miss you too.'

'And if you ask me,' he went on, 'Payne, Rackstraw and Bynt misses you too. A lot.'

'Murdo—' protested Holly, wary of his repeated attempts to coax her back to London. 'I'll come back when I'm ready, not before.'

'That airhead Leonie doesn't have a clue how to handle an account,' he insisted, playing the card that always touched a nerve with Holly. She'd never liked Leonie at the best of times, and the thought that she had inherited her job wasn't a happy one – particularly since the little witch made no secret of the fact that she fancied the pants off Murdo. 'She's already lost us at least one important client.'

'Which one?' asked Holly, instantly interested in spite of her determination not to be.

'Billingham Industries.'

'No!' The colour drained from Holly's face.

'Oh yes – and after you put in all that work to bring them on board. We need you, Hol. I need you.'

She could feel his arms reaching across the distance between them, gathering her up, taking charge, spiriting her back to London to be what everybody said she was meant to be. And sometimes that felt desperately tempting; but at other times it felt like being slowly suffocated by a well-meaning, well-stuffed giant teddy bear.

'Can we talk about this some other time?' she pleaded. 'It's not that I don't appreciate what you're trying to do, but—'

'Yes, sure,' cut in Murdo. 'Of course we can. In fact I promise not to mention it when I take you for our weekend away.'

'What weekend away?'

Murdo chuckled. 'I think all anniversaries should be celebrated properly, don't you? With at least a couple of days away, somewhere romantic. What do you say? Just the two of us and a soft bed and a really big bottle of champagne ...'

'It does sound lovely,' she admitted. 'But I'm not due another weekend off until next month.'

'Throw a sickie.'

'I can't! We're really short-staffed, and if I just don't turn up—'

Murdo's tone changed. 'So, spending some quality time with me is less important than delivering a few bundles of junk mail, is it? How very flattering.'

'You know that's not true!'

'You've got to admit it's a pretty feeble excuse for not wanting to see me.'

'It's not an excuse!' insisted Holly, exasperated. 'It's just my work rota. I wish you'd take my job seriously, the way I do.'

'How can I, when you spend most of your time either ramming gas bills and leaflets through people's letter boxes or being bitten by semi-rabid chihuahuas? Come on, sweetheart,' he pleaded, 'it feels like for ever since I held you in my arms.'

Holly sighed, half won over, half annoyed. 'You wouldn't take time off from your job just because you felt like it,' she countered.

'I would if it meant I could be with you.'

She knew it was true. There was no combating Murdo's war of attrition. 'OK, OK! I'll try to get the time off,' she capitulated. 'But absolutely no promises.'

*

Early April sunshine spilled in through the stylish stained-glass panels on either side of Grace and Steve's front door, lighting up the kind of nouveau-rustic charm that only serious money could buy. It was later that same afternoon, and Holly and Grace were preparing to take Adam to his very first Baby Music session at St Jude's church. Music, however, was not uppermost in Grace's mind.

'You have to admit Murdo has a point,' she reasoned, reaching down her beautiful Italian leather jacket from a hook by the door.

Uh-oh, here we go again, thought Holly, playing peek-a-boo with her little nephew and trying to pretend she hadn't heard. Another lecture from my little sister.

'You're completely wasted you know, working at that grotty sorting office,' Grace went on. 'It might be OK for Dad, but he doesn't have an honours degree in media studies, does he?'

Holly opened her mouth to interject, but Grace didn't even pause for breath. 'And yes, I know you take on freelance projects, but it's not the same as having a proper job, is it? And sooner or later you'll have to get one, whether you like it or not.' She turned and eyed Holly over the rims of her Prada spectacles. 'Unless, of course, you're planning on settling down with Murdo and becoming a full-time housewife?'

'Don't be silly,' Holly protested. 'Can you really imagine me in a pinny, whisking perfect soufflés out of the oven?'

'I'd never have imagined you lugging a mailbag round the streets of Cheltenham, but you're doing it anyway,' Grace pointed out.

Holly scooped Adam up and manoeuvred the wriggling bundle of arms and legs into his pushchair. She was getting rather good at it. If only she was as good at fending off her sister. 'I told you, I'm still reviewing my options. I just haven't quite decided where I want to go with my life.'

'Well, you'd better get a move on,' replied Grace archly. 'A nice guy like Murdo won't wait for ever, you know.'

'So you keep telling me! Are you sure you wouldn't like to marry him yourself?'

'I wouldn't say no!' replied Grace, buckling Adam into his pushchair. 'But I expect Steve would have something to say about it.'

Holly laughed. At six feet five and fifteen stone, Grace's rugby-playing husband was a gentle giant, but he certainly cut an imposing figure. When he said something, people tended to listen – or run away and hide.

Adam was getting bored with all this grown-up talk, and started to grizzle. Holly retrieved his favourite pink rabbit from where he had last thrown it, and waggled it at him enticingly. 'Shall we go out, little man, and then maybe Mummy will stop lecturing poor Auntie Holly?' Adam made a grab for his rabbit, giggled, and blew a few bubbles. 'I'll take that as a yes. Come on, sis, or we'll be late.'

On the way to the church, Grace explained the virtues of Baby Music to her sister. 'It says here in the leaflet,' she quoted solemnly, 'that it "helps babies and toddlers to attain an enhanced experience of the world within a creative and stimulating environment",' she said.

'Whatever that means,' muttered Holly, who – despite working in advertising – loathed meaningless twaddle.

'Well, Penny Greenberg up the road is married to a child psychologist, and she says that if you expose babies' minds to music and rhymes from an early stage, it really helps to increase their vocabulary. I'm sure it must stimulate their neurological development.'

'Sounds reasonable,' agreed Holly.

'So when I saw this leaflet pinned up on the staff notice board at the hospital, I thought it sounded just right for Adam. After all, he's so creative already,' she added proudly.

'I know,' replied Holly with a smile. 'I saw what he did to the bathroom floor that time you left your make-up bag open!'

Grace ignored the jest. 'Now tell me – how old do you think he should be before we start him on playing an instrument?'

'Good God, don't ask me!'

'But you're the musician of the family – that's why I asked you to come along today.'

'Me, the family musician?' Holly nearly fell over laughing. 'I don't think scraping through grade three piano exactly qualifies me as a musical expert, do you?'

'Well, seeing as the best Jess ever managed was "Three Blind Mice" on the recorder, and I can't even hold a tune in a bucket, yes, I do. Besides,' she added, lowering her voice as they neared the church, as if its Cotswold stone walls might have ears, 'I need you there so you can tell me if I'm being ripped off.'

'What?'

'Some of these so-called professionals can be charlatans, you know,' she said with great seriousness. 'They can't tell a crotchet from a croissant. I need you around to tell me if I'm getting proper value for money. I've no intention of being ripped off.'

'But, it's only four pounds fifty a session,' Holly reminded her.

'That's not the point. Besides,' Grace said, as Holly helped her to hoist the pushchair into the church porch and through the heavy wooden door, 'Adam always behaves better when Auntie Holly's around. Oh bugger,' she added, the expletive echoing damningly around the cavernous nave of St Jude's, 'I think it's already started.'

Inside the church, several rows of front pews had been removed to create a space for concerts and other performances; once a week, this space was taken over by the Baby Music class.

Sitting in a circle on multicoloured velvet beanbags, a dozen or so mums, aunties, grannies and a lone embarrassed dad were doing their best to control their overexcited offspring. It wasn't easy, not with Tina the Facilitator (dressed in a baggy clown suit that made her look like Ronald McDonald) handing out all kinds of fascinating things to bang, prod and tinkle. But somehow she managed to lead everyone in a rousing chorus of 'The Wheels on the Bus' without anyone having a screaming fit or getting poked in the eye with a drumstick. Clearly she'd done it before.

Holly sat with Adam on her lap, bouncing him in time to the music. She could tell that he was loving every minute of it: hardly surprising, seeing as this was a chance to make lots of noise without anybody telling him off. Grace seemed more preoccupied with watching Tina's every move; while most of the other mothers seemed happy just to have somebody else entertaining their kids for forty minutes.

This is fun, thought Holly, laughing along with Adam at the glove puppets and helping him to do all the actions to the songs. I'm certain I could get used to being a mum instead of just an auntie. I wouldn't even mind if I had to put my advertising career on hold for a bit longer. I could be that woman over there in the green, so completely wrapped up in her twin toddlers that she hasn't even noticed her T-shirt is on inside out.

Adam felt heavy and warm on her lap. The feeling of him there, in her arms, seemed to answer a deep, primitive need that she could no longer deny. This is going to be me, she told herself. It has to be. Maybe not this year, or next year, or even the year after that, but soon.

Then again, she thought, am I just fantasising about getting pregnant because it's easier than facing up to reality, easier than making decisions about my work, about my life in general? About Murdo?

And how can I even think about becoming someone's mother when I still don't know who I am?

At tea and apple-juice time, halfway through the session, Holly almost told her sister about her plan to track down her birth mother, but Grace had to rush off suddenly to the mother and baby room to change Adam, and when she came back, she was full of the fact that she'd just 'networked' with a mum who was an office manager and who might have some work for Steve's company. She was far too full of her own thoughts to notice that her sister had gone very quiet.

Just before the recess ended, Grace drew Holly to one side. 'Well?' she demanded.

'Well what?'

'Well, is this a rip-off or am I getting what I paid for?'

'I think it's a lot of fun, and Adam loves it,' replied Holly evasively, knowing that this was not what her sister wanted to hear. 'But Adam's your son. What do *you* think?'

Grace bit her lip. 'I think it's a lot of money to pay for half an hour of pom-poms and a woman in a clown suit.'

'Four pounds fifty a week for Adam to have some fun?' Holly raised an eyebrow. 'That's just pocket money for you and Steve, surely. And if it's good for Adam's development—'

'It'd certainly be good for Aimee,' cut in Grace. 'I mean, stuck on that appalling estate, what chance does she get to mix with the right sort of children?'

Holly stared in disbelief. 'The right sort of children? You mean ... rich children?'

'No, not rich exactly, but nicely brought up and—'

'Grace, how the hell is a three-month-old child supposed to tell the difference between a rich baby and any other baby?'

'Not consciously, of course,' admitted Grace. 'But I'm sure that sort of thing sinks in without them realising. A sort of, you know, osmosis.'

'Grace.'

'What?'

Holly lowered her voice in deference to their ecclesiastical location, then hissed: 'That's the biggest load of bollocks I've ever heard. You know something? Since you and Steve moved onto The Avenue, you've turned into a total snob.'

Grace sniffed. 'You can scoff. But I'm sure Aimee would have far better chances in life if she could make friends with well brought-up children, right from the very beginning.' She sighed. 'But there's no chance of her and Kev affording luxuries like Baby Music. They barely managed to pay the electricity bill last month. I can't imagine how they're ever going to get off the Bluebell Estate unless someone gives them a helping hand.'

Holly was painfully aware of her sister's meaningful look. 'I've told you, Grace,' she said in exasperation, 'I'm more than happy to help them out all I can, but if I'm the musician of the family, your Steve is the business tycoon. And I think you two ought to pay your share, too. Don't you?'

'Well ... y-yes,' agreed Grace, a quiver of hesitation in her voice. 'In principle ...'

'But not in practice? Don't you think that's a bit mean?'

'Oh look,' said Grace weakly, forcing a smile, 'Tina's got her pom-poms out again. I think they're about to start.'

'Dad,' said Holly that evening, as she was clearing away the plates after dinner, 'can I ask you something? Something very personal?'

Harry Bennett glanced up from his copy of *Model Railway Enthusiast*. 'You know you can, love. What's up – boyfriend trouble?'

'Not really.' She smiled. 'I, um, just wanted to ask about what happened on the night you found me; you know, when I was a baby and somebody left me on the hospital steps.'

'Oh.' Harry laid down his magazine, took off his glasses and

39

polished them on his sleeveless pullover: his habitual reflex action whenever something knocked him for six. For a moment, Holly thought she had upset him, then he smiled his familiar, crinkly smile. 'Well, I don't believe it. Do you know, your mum and I waited for the best part of thirty years for you to bring this up, and you never said a word. I'm not complaining, love, but why now?'

Where to begin, thought Holly. All these years she'd been content to know the scant details and push them to the back of her mind, perhaps subconsciously hoping that they would eventually fade out of existence, leaving her to be as much her parents' daughter as her sisters were.

She sat back down at the dinner table, next to her dad, and squeezed his hand tight. 'I don't know really. It's a feeling I've had since Mum died, and since Grace and Jess had their babies. I just can't stop wondering where I came from.' She looked into the face she loved more than life itself; the face of the man she had always regarded as her father, and always would. 'Do you mind going over it all, Dad? Or would you rather not?'

Harry looked at her and chuckled. 'Of course I don't mind. In fact your mother and I always hoped you'd want to talk about it – after all, the story of how we found you is a part of who you are, isn't it?'

Holly nodded. 'It is. But I didn't really want to know before. It's funny, I always knew I was adopted, and I was proud that you chose me, but a part of me hurt to think about it,' she admitted. 'At the back of my mind I think I was sort of afraid that you and Mum might love Grace and Jess more than you loved me because they were your flesh and blood and I wasn't.'

'Holly, love, I never knew you were quite that daft! Have you any idea how proud of you your mum was? Or how proud of you I am now?' Harry got to his feet and wrapped his arms around his daughter's shoulders. She buried her face in the familiar warmth of his favourite jumper. 'You're my daughter, Holly,' he said quietly. 'My daughter, and that's all there is to it. It's non-negotiable.'

Holly felt the prickling of tears behind her eyelids, loving her dad so much that it hurt. 'No matter what happens, Dad, you and Mum will always be my real parents, you know that, don't you? Nobody in the world could ever, ever replace you.'

Harry drew back and looked at his daughter quizzically. 'And do you think someone might try?'

Holly shook her head. 'No, of course not. It's just ... oh, Dad, this is really hard to say.' She couldn't look him in the eye. 'The thing is ... I think I've decided I want to trace my birth mother.'

She held her breath, waiting for the edge of disappointment in his voice as he responded, some sign that she had failed him.

'Oh, Holly, love, did you think I'd be upset? Is that it?' There was a world of warmth in Harry's voice. 'I told you, you're my daughter and nothing can change that. And all I want is for you to be happy. Your mother wanted exactly the same.'

'You really and truly don't mind?'

'I don't mind at all.' There was a twinkle in his grey eyes. 'Why don't I make us a nice cup of coffee and we can chat about it over a big plate of chocolate digestives?'

Holly laughed. 'Any excuse to get the chocolate biscuits out.'

'Too right. If you do decide you want to try to track down the woman who gave birth to you, I'll help you all I can. The trouble is, it won't be easy,' he reflected. 'There's practically nothing for you to go on.'

Four

'So you talked to your dad last night, then?' Nesta took a big bite out of her bacon sandwich. It was breakfast break time, and she and Holly were sitting in the staff canteen, on the first floor above the sorting office. 'How did he take it?'

'He was great, he really was.' Holly took a sip from an enormous white mug of coffee. 'He said he'd support me every step of the way, and that Mum would have said exactly the same thing. I can't tell you how relieved I am.'

'It's a big step in the right direction,' agreed Nesta. 'So, did he tell you anything you didn't already know?'

'Not really,' admitted Holly, her enthusiasm muted a little by reality. 'In the end, all it comes down to is this: one night in December, Dad found me in a carrycot on the hospital steps, wrapped up in a travelling rug with a little silver necklace lying next to me. That's it. Oh – and the nurses in the hospital decided to call me Holly because it was nearly Christmas.'

'Could've been worse,' remarked Nesta. 'They might've called you Rudolph. Didn't the police try to find your mother?'

'Oh yes, I'm sure they did. But after a few months had gone by and they'd had no luck finding her, they had to close down the case. To be fair, it must have been incredibly hard, trying to track down someone who basically didn't want to be found.'

42

Nesta swallowed the last of her breakfast and wiped her hands on her paper napkin. 'But you still want to give it a try? After all this time?'

'I have to,' replied Holly softly. 'I just have to.'

'Hmm,' said Nesta.

A knot of tension formed in Holly's stomach. 'You think this is a really bad idea, don't you?'

Nesta shook her fiery auburn head. 'Not if it helps you. You're my best friend and I want to see you happy. I just worry that this might not go the way you want it to. But, hey, who am I to judge?' She rubbed her hands together, businesslike and positive. 'Right, where are you going to start then?'

'That's the trouble,' Holly admitted. 'I haven't got a clue.'

'I don't believe it!' laughed Nesta. 'You must have read every detective novel ever published, and you're the only person I know who can recite whole *Inspector Morse* scripts off by heart. You must have some idea.'

'Well ... I guess I could try the local library,' mused Holly. 'Or phone the *Cheltenham Courant* and ask to see their archives.'

'For old newspapers, you mean? Good thinking. See? You're thinking like a detective already.'

Holly felt more like an interloper than a detective as she and Nesta climbed the steps of Cheltenham's public library. How many years was it since she'd been here? Not since school. Not, in fact, since the embarrassing time she'd dropped her library book when she was reading in the bath, and had to pay an enormous fine to replace it.

She barely recognised the place. Instead of the fusty, musty little foyer she remembered, bedecked with ancient notice boards and leaflets about the local German Circle, everything was open-plan and bright, with almost as many computer terminals as there were books.

But the reference section was still easy to find. Holly's heart pounded with needless anxiety as Nesta nudged her towards the ginger-haired youth behind the desk. His name badge read: Terry. Information Assistant.

'Go on then! He won't bite.'

'All right,' protested Holly, feeling flustered. 'Just give me a minute ...'

But Nesta wasn't one for hanging around. 'Excuse me,' she said loudly, making the man behind the desk jump. 'My friend would like to see some newspapers.'

Terry pushed his spectacles back up his nose. 'Today's papers are next door in the lending section. Or did you mean old newspapers?'

'The local papers from thirty years ago,' explained Holly. 'Do you keep them as far back as that?'

'We certainly do,' replied Terry, sliding open a drawer containing row upon row of microfilm reels. 'Do you know the exact date you're looking for?'

'Only that it's December, thirty years ago. Sorry, I can't be any more specific than that.'

'No problem.' He selected a reel of film and slid the drawer shut. 'You can scroll through the microfilm until you find the bit you want. Follow me, ladies,' he said with a wink, 'I'll show you how to work the microfilm readers.'

'That's OK,' said Nesta, divesting a disappointed Terry of the film. 'I've done this before. Come on, Holly.'

Within the space of what seemed like seconds, Nesta had Holly installed in front of a microfilm reader and the reel of film securely in place. She clicked on the machine, which began to hum as a light illuminated the first page of the film.

'December the second,' mused Nesta. 'What day did you say you were found?'

'The ninth.'

'Let's take a look at the tenth, then. Go on, wind the film through.'

The film screeched through until it reached the tenth of December, overshot by a couple of days and spooled back slowly.

'Oh my God,' whispered Holly, her hand shaking on the controls. 'That must be . . . me.'

And sure enough, it was. There, on the front page of the *Cheltenham Courant*, the tiny baby who was to become Holly Bennett was shown cradled in the arms of a nursing sister. Not just any nursing sister, thought Holly with a shock. Sister Maureen Bennett. My mum.

She reached out and touched the fuzzy black and white picture on the screen, as if some kind of magic might transport her back to that cold, dark night in December, thirty years ago.

'Look, Nesta,' she said shakily. 'It's me and my mum.'

'Sure is.' Nesta laid a hand on her friend's shoulder. 'I don't suppose she realised she was going to be your mum when they took that picture,' she observed.

'She didn't think she was going to be anybody's mum. She and Dad had been trying for a baby for ages. Years. Then I came along, and they decided to try to adopt me.' Holly sat back on her chair and contemplated her mother's sweet, smiling face. 'It took months and months, but that didn't put them off. They just persevered. And then guess what: Grace and Jess came along without them even trying.'

'You're going to have to persevere too if you're going to stand a chance of finding your birth mother,' pointed out Nesta. 'Your dad was right; it won't be easy. Is there any useful information in the article?'

Holly pulled herself together and scanned the columns of tiny, slightly yellow-tinged print. 'Nothing I don't already know,' she replied, disappointed. 'Except . . . it does give the name of the police officer dealing with the investigation.'

'Jot it down. He might be a useful contact.'

'I guess,' acknowledged Holly. 'Though he could've retired and moved away by now.'

'That's what I like about you,' said Nesta wryly, 'you're a born optimist.'

They searched every local and national newspaper for the week Holly was found, but there was little difference between the articles; most were little more than photo opportunities, big on cute pictures but short on information.

'Where do I go from here?' Holly wondered aloud.

Nesta rewound the last reel of microfilm and popped it back into its box. 'If anybody knows, you should,' she replied. 'What with those detective novels you're always reading.'

'Why? What's that got to do with anything?'

'Come on. What do people in detective stories always do when they want to track someone down? Who do they always call in?'

The penny dropped, and Holly laughed in disbelief. 'A private eye? You're not serious, are you?'

'Why not?'

'Because . . . Because for one thing I could never afford it and, for another, I bet there's no such thing in a place like Cheltenham.'

'Well, I bet there is. Wherever there are messy divorces, there's always a private investigation agency within screaming distance. And you've still got your inheritance money,' Nesta reminded her. 'You've got to admit it's worth considering.'

Holly allowed the idea to sink in. 'I suppose it might be,' she admitted. 'But I'm getting a bit ahead of myself – I haven't even told Jess or Grace yet. I thought I might mention it when we have our get-together on Sunday. What do you think?'

'The sooner the better,' replied Nesta. 'You don't want them feeling excluded – especially since you've already talked it over with your dad. Besides,' she added, 'they might have some suggestions of their own.'

Every month, regular as clockwork, the Bennett sisters descended on the family home and made lunch for themselves and their dad. It was like reliving old times, thought Holly, recalling the days when Grace and Jess had brought home their cookery creations from school, and she and Mum and Dad had had to eat them – with a smile on their faces.

These days, the food was a little more sophisticated. Instead of carbonised meatballs and soggy sponge, they had Grace's baked sea bream and Holly's peach pavlova to look forward to. They always delegated the starter to Jess. Even she couldn't damage a slice of melon and a bit of Parma ham – well, not much. Left to her own devices, alas, Jess would quite happily have turned up with four Pot Noodles and a family bag of Doritos.

As she set the table for lunch in the big old family kitchen, Holly thought of all the memories the house held for her. Everything she looked at seemed to look back at her and remind her of some event in her childhood.

Over there, by the window: that was where Dad sliced the top of his finger off, cutting tiles for the back-splash. And Grace – clever little girl that she was – put it in a bag of frozen peas, so the surgeon could sew it back on. And there, on the window sill, was the souvenir snowdome Holly had brought back from the school ski trip to Austria. Maureen had loved edelweiss, and Holly managed to find her a snowdome with some inside it. Never mind that half of the water had evaporated over the years, or that the edelweiss was only plastic: Mum never could bring herself to throw it away. And that wood basket with the newspapers in it: that was where the tiny orphan kitten slept – the one Jess found by the roadside and brought home. She always did love animals; filled her heart

47

with them and would have filled the house too, if Mum and Dad had let her. She cried for a week when that kitten died. And so did I, thought Holly.

She was still lost in thought when the doorbell rang.

'I'll get it,' Harry called out from the lounge, and Holly heard her sisters' voices from the hallway. They didn't usually arrive together; Jess's car must have broken down again.

'I nearly didn't get today off,' announced Grace as she entered the kitchen, bearing a hot, foil-covered platter in oven-gloved hands. 'Sister Rose is off with flu, and we're desperately short of qualified staff.' She kissed her father lightly on the cheek. 'But I couldn't let you down, could I, Dad?'

'Of course you couldn't.' He grinned, patting her on the back in his usual semi-embarrassed, fatherly way.

'Or you, Holly,' Grace added with a smile in her direction. 'Pop this in the oven for ten minutes, would you, sis?' The foil-covered platter found its way into Holly's hands. 'Oh, and I really did appreciate you helping me out with those frocks the other day, you know. You're one in a million.'

'Seventy million,' Holly corrected her. 'And next time, we're buying a satnav. My mental health's far too fragile to take another session of your map-reading.'

'Oh, don't forget to remind me,' Grace went on breathlessly, completely oblivious to Holly's insults, 'I've reserved a pair of front-row seats at the show for you.'

Holly made all the right enthusiastic noises, but her eyes were on Jess, who was trailing behind her elder sister and looking downright miserable. 'You OK, Jess?'

'What?' Jess nearly fell off her platform shoes. 'Yes, sure,' she snapped, 'why wouldn't I be?'

'Oh, no reason. You just looked miles away that's all.'

'She's probably stressing over Kev looking after the baby,'

opined Grace. 'That boy doesn't know one end of a feeding bottle from the other.'

'Kev's a good dad!' protested Jess.

'I never said he wasn't,' replied Grace, in a tone that implied the opposite.

A boy, thought Holly. A boy with a head full of dreams: that's what Kev is. And Jess is barely out of school, without a qualification to her name. And suddenly all this responsibility is thrust upon them and they have to make the best job they can of being parents. It can't be easy for either of them.

'Let's have some wine,' suggested Holly, hoping to lighten up the atmosphere.

'Not for me, I'm driving,' said Grace.

'Not for me either,' said Jess.

'Just a little bit?'

Jess shook her head. 'I've had a tummy upset,' she said, looking more miserable than ever.

'Ah well, looks like it's just you and me, Dad.' Holly filled her father's glass, and then poured herself a large one. I think I'm going to need it, she thought, hoping that she wasn't. 'Now, who's for orange juice?'

Things lightened up as the meal progressed. Jess's marinated prawns on sticks were really not bad at all, and Grace's sea bream was – as ever – done to a turn.

'Has Dad told you all about *Tarzan and Jane – the Musical*?' Grace asked Holly.

Holly's eyebrows arched skywards. '*Tarzan and Jane* the what?'

'The musical.' Harry wiped his chin with his napkin. 'Sorry, love, I forgot. Didn't you notice the twelve-foot purple crocodile sticking out of the shed door?'

'Grace has got herself involved in another charity show,' explained Jess. 'Up at the hospital this time. It's mostly nurses and doctors, but the director's some big cheese from London who's got a house just outside Cheltenham. He's big mates with the guy who wrote all the music, and he's managed to wangle the rights to do a charity performance.'

Grace politely chewed and swallowed before elaborating. 'Granville Manleigh, he's called,' she went on. 'You must have heard of him. He's a really famous stage director. Don't you remember *Three Camels to Zanzibar*?' Blank faces gazed back at her. 'You Philistines! Anyway, just for fun he's agreed to direct us, even though we're just a bunch of useless amateurs.'

Jess aimed a forkful of fish in her sister's direction. 'And guess who's auditioning for the part of Jane.'

'Oh, er, good luck,' said Holly, toasting her in Chilean Sauvignon Blanc. 'I look forward to seeing you swinging through the vines in a leopard-skin bikini.'

'Then you'll wait a long time,' retorted Grace. 'Our production is going to be much more faithful to the book.'

'Are there any purple crocodiles in the book?'

'Oh, we blagged that from a production of *Robinson Crusoe* at the Bristol Hippodrome,' Grace explained. 'Dad's renovating it for us and giving it a fresh coat of paint so it looks a bit more, you know ...'

'Crocodiley?' suggested Holly.

'Yeah, crocodiley. It has remote-control snapping jaws ... if Dad can get them working again.'

'If anyone can, Dad can,' declared Jess. It was the first real sign of animation from Jess since she arrived. 'Dad can do anything, can't you, Dad?'

Harry laughed. 'I wish I had your confidence.'

Grace prattled on happily about Tarzan and the charity fashion show, while her lunch got cold and everybody else ate theirs – although in Jess's case, 'ate' was something of an exaggeration.

Lapsing back into her own silent world, she picked at the food like a disconsolate sparrow. I must get her on her own and talk to her, thought Holly. Something's obviously wrong. Maybe she and Kev have had another of their silly arguments about nothing. Or maybe it's just the lack of money that's getting her down. Either way, I need to winkle it out of her somehow; try and help if I can. But she'll never let on with Grace around ...

It had always been that way. On her own, Jess had a bright, sparky personality, but put her in a room with Grace and it was as if someone had turned the lights off.

Holly was still trying to concoct a cunning plan to get Grace out of the way for five minutes when her father said something that caught her completely unawares.

'Holly, didn't you have something you wanted to tell us?'

She stared at him. 'S-sorry?'

Harry smiled at her encouragingly, coaxing her gently, the way he had when Holly was six years old and frightened of getting into the swimming pool. 'I thought they might like to know what we were talking about the other evening.'

'What was that then?' asked Jess, looking from Holly to Dad and then back again.

A neat cube of sea bass quivered expectantly on the end of Grace's fork. 'This all sounds very mysterious. You're not planning something big for Great-aunt Minnie's ninetieth, are you?'

'Er, no. It's not that.' Holly swallowed hard, suddenly stricken with inexplicable terror. Somehow, knowing her better than she knew herself, Dad must have sensed that she might chicken out and made the first move for her. Ah well, thanks to him there was no going back now. She took a deep breath and went for it.

'Remember at the christening, when you two were talking about Mum, and how worried you were in case Adam and Aimee got ill because there was something genetic about Mum's MND?'

51

'We'd hardly forget,' Grace replied dryly.

'Well, what you were saying kind of set me thinking, and I realised that when it comes down to it, I haven't the faintest idea who I am.'

'Yes, you have,' objected Jess. 'You're our sister.'

'Yes, of course I am, and I'm glad you feel that way. Holly Elizabeth Bennett: whatever happens that's what I'll always be, over and above anything else. But it's more complicated than that. The thing is, I ... um ... might want a baby of my own sometime, and—'

'I knew you and Murdo were going to move in together!' Grace declared, triumphantly spearing another cube of fish. 'And it's about bloody time.'

'Actually, we're not,' said Holly. Grace's face fell, and Holly felt really bad about disappointing her. 'At least, not yet,' she went on, softening the blow. 'But because I might want to be a mum sometime, I'd really like to know more about where I came from. As things stand, all I know is that I was found one December night, thirty years ago. I don't even know when my real birthday is. Or where I was born. Imagine that.'

Jess looked puzzled. 'What exactly are you saying?'

'I'm saying ... that I've thought a lot about it, and I want to try to track down my biological mother. I know it won't be easy; I just feel I have to give it a try.'

Holly held her breath. Right on cue, the cube of fish fell off Grace's fork, landing soundlessly in the mashed potato. Grace's expression changed from curiosity to contained fury. Jess's eyes grew round as marbles in her thin, white face.

Grace slammed her cutlery down onto her plate. 'So what you're saying,' she said coldly, 'is that you want to trace the woman who gave birth to you and then casually dumped you on the hospital steps for somebody else to look after?'

Holly sighed. 'If you want to put it like that. Though I doubt there was anything casual about it. Can you imagine making that kind of decision without agonising about it over and over again?'

'No,' snapped Grace, 'because I'd rather die a thousand times over than ever abandon any child of mine.'

'Anyway,' interjected Jess, much to Holly's relief, 'how are you going to find this woman when you don't know anything to start off with?'

'Good question,' replied Holly. 'At first I thought I might be able to do the whole thing by myself – go through all the old articles, pick up some clues and follow them . . . then I realised there weren't any clues. Not one – at least, not that I could see. And then it hit me just how impossible it was going to be. I talked about it with Nesta—'

'But not with your own sisters,' remarked Grace, icily.

Holly ploughed on, beginning to wish that she'd never had this idea in the first place: '—and we both agreed that what I really need is some kind of professional investigator – if I can find one round here, that is, and if I can scrape together enough money.'

There was a long silence, heavy with unspoken criticisms. Then Grace spoke. 'Ah. Now I get it.'

'Get what?' asked Holly.

'Now I know why you were so evasive when I asked you to help out Jess and Kev. I'm right, aren't I? No wonder you didn't want to spend your inheritance on your sister, not when you were planning to use it to buy yourself a brand-new mother.'

'What!' Cold horror ran down Holly's spine. 'Grace, what the hell are you on about?' she spluttered. 'That's not how it was at all. I told you, I'll gladly help them out as long as you pay your fair share too. And what's all this rubbish about buying myself a new mother?'

Grace's eyes were bright with anger. 'You had a mother, but now she's gone, so you thought to yourself, I know, I'll get some back-street investigator to scrabble around in the dirt and find me a new one. And of course the best bit is that you're going to pay for it with the money Mum left you. How can you look yourself in the face?'

'No!' protested Holly. 'No, that's not it at all. You're not listening to me—'

'Grace,' interjected Jess, 'don't you think—'

Her sister rounded on her. 'Oh shut up, Jess, what do you know about anything?'

'Girls,' pleaded Harry, as if this was a childhood game of Monopoly and they were squabbling over the little silver racing car. 'There's no need for all this ...'

'I'm sorry, Dad,' said Grace, getting up and laying her napkin on the tablecloth. 'I came here for a nice family lunch, but suddenly I don't have an appetite any more.'

She turned to her little sister. 'I'm leaving, Jess. You'd better get a move on if you want a lift home.'

Holly's dark eyes were so red and swollen from crying that she could hardly see the bread she was throwing for the ducks.

She and Nesta were standing by the edge of the lake in Pittville Park, feeding the remnants of the Bennetts' abortive family lunch to the park's denizens. Somebody might as well enjoy it, thought Holly gloomily.

'Chin up,' said Nesta softly, slipping an arm round her friend's shoulders. 'Things are never as bad as they seem.'

'No,' agreed Holly, listlessly tucking a strand of chestnut-brown hair behind her ear. 'Sometimes they're worse.' A sizeable chunk of bread bounced off a mallard's head, giving it the surprise of its life. It flapped off in a flurry of feathers and quacking, taking most of its mates with it. 'See? Now even the ducks aren't speaking to me.'

Nesta's eyes narrowed. 'Holly Bennett, just you listen to me Your sister does not hate you, and if she did, she'd be an even sillier cow than I already think she probably is. If that makes sense,' she added, thinking over what she'd just said.

Despite herself, Holly laughed. It was hard to resist Nesta's determined efforts to cheer her up: first taking her to see the fluffy bunnies in the children's petting zoo, then feeding the ducks. Now Nesta was marching her in the direction of the refreshment kiosk, as though Holly was a troublesome toddler who could only be pacified by the promise of an ice-cream cornet.

'You're wrong though,' Holly insisted as the two of them sat on a wooden bench in the brisk April breeze, eating their ice creams and trying to pretend it was July, 'Grace does hate me. And if you'd seen her turn and walk out on me, you'd think so too. I tried to get her to listen, but she wasn't having any of it. When I phoned her up last night, Steve said she wasn't there, but I could hear her talking to Adam in the background.'

Nesta nibbled thoughtfully at the edges of her cornet. 'What about your dad? What does he think about it all?'

Holly shook her head sadly. 'He's baffled, bless him. He had no idea this was going to blow up into a huge row – neither did I, come to that.'

'And if you had, would you still have gone ahead with it?' asked Nesta.

Holly paused. 'Yes. Yes, I would actually. I don't want to upset my family, of course I don't, but it's not as if I'm doing anything wrong, is it?' She looked at her friend. 'I'm not, am I?'

Nesta's eyes rolled skywards. 'Of course you're not, you idiot.'

The two of them sat there in the cold, side by side, for a long time. They didn't say much, but Holly was profoundly glad that Nesta was there to put everything into perspective. Mind you, it was hard to feel like a great tragic heroine when you were sitting on a park bench with your best mate, eating a Cornetto and watching two ducks shagging on the lake.

'I don't see why I should apologise,' said Holly after a while.

'I suppose it depends on whether you want Grace never to speak to you again,' observed Nesta.

'Well,' said Holly with the ghost of a smile, 'it's really, really tempting but I suppose we'll have to talk to each other occasionally or Dad'll get upset. So I guess that leaves me making the first move.'

'What about Jess?' enquired Nesta.

'What about her?'

'You haven't really mentioned her, that's all. Was she cheerleading for Grace, as usual?'

'No, she wasn't,' replied Holly, thinking about it for the first time. 'She pretty much stayed out of the argument. I think she had something on her mind. In fact,' she revealed, 'I was wondering how I could get her to open up to me when Dad dropped his little bombshell. And when Grace did her dramatic walkout, Jess had to go too because her car's out of action again and Grace was giving her a lift home.'

'Hmm,' mused Nesta, huddling down inside her anorak. 'Do you think maybe she didn't want to go with Grace?'

'I couldn't tell,' admitted Holly. 'But it was pretty obvious that Jess was miserable about something before I breathed a word about tracking down my birth mother.'

'Maybe you ought to find out what,' murmured Nesta.

'Yes, maybe I should.'

In the daylight, Crocus House looked more unappealing than ever. At least night-time softened its harsh 1960s lines, making it look a little less like a giant chest of drawers fashioned out of concrete and bricks. Daylight did it no favours at all.

In her idle London days, Holly would have made heavy weather of the stairs that wound their way up to Jess and Kev's flat; nowadays, she hardly noticed them. Delivering the mail had turned Holly Bennett, super-slob, into a sleek young woman with leg muscles of steel. Who needed the gym when there were stairs to climb and pavements to walk all over Cheltenham?

Holly paused on the landing outside Jess's flat; not to get her breath back, but to ask herself if this was a good idea. Maybe she'd read Jess all wrong, and she was going to tell Holly to mind her own business. Maybe she was going to say that Grace was right, and refuse to talk to her. Ah well, she reckoned, it was a risk worth taking.

At her second knock, the door with the peeling grey paint opened a couple of inches, revealing one eye and a security chain.

'Oh!' said Jess. 'It's you.'

The security chain rattled and the door opened the rest of the way. Jess looked a mess, her T-shirt and tracksuit bottoms hanging off her scrawny body. In the back room, Holly could hear Aimee crying.

'Come in,' said Jess, raking lank hair back from a face that was too pale to be healthy, Holly thought. 'But you'll have to make the tea yourself; I need to feed the baby.'

As she boiled the kettle, Holly watched her sister carefully measuring out baby formula. 'I thought you were still breast-feeding,' she remarked.

'I was. But my milk started to run out.' Jess sounded almost ashamed of herself. 'The health visitor said I'd have to supplement it with this.' Her dark, worried eyes sought out her sister's. 'Do you think Aimee will be OK on it?'

'Of course she will.' Holly followed her sister into the bedroom, where Aimee was lying in her cot, making fretful sounds. 'Millions of babies are brought up on formula.'

57

'But it's not as good as breast milk, is it?' Jess leaned over and gathered the baby up in her arms, carried her over to a chair in the corner and began feeding her. Instantly the crying subsided.

'She'll be fine,' Holly repeated. 'She's had three months of breast-feeding to give her a good start. And she has you and Kev to love her, and that's more important than anything, isn't it?'

Jess nodded silently but looked away. 'I've been thinking,' she said, 'and I think you're right.'

Holly perched on the edge of Jess and Kev's bed. 'Right?'

'About trying to find your birth mother. I rang Dad and he thinks the same as me.'

'He does?'

'Mum would have wanted you to try to get in touch, I'm sure she would.' Jess gazed down at the baby in her arms and smiled at her. 'OK, so she gave you away, but maybe she had her reasons. Whatever she did, there's still something between you, and Grace ... Grace is just plain wrong.' Jess shook her head sadly. 'I don't know what's got into her lately.'

'Me neither,' confessed Holly, reaching out and stroking little Aimee's hand. The baby responded by seizing her finger and clutching it tightly, as if to say, 'You've got the right idea about finding your mother, don't let it go.' A ray of love as warm as the summer sun shimmered through Holly, making her smile.

'Grace never used to care about what other people thought or said,' Holly went on. 'Or did, for that matter. It was live and let live. She just cared about taking care of people. But since she and Steve went up in the world ...'

'I suppose people change,' said Jess, her voice quavering ever so slightly.

'Look at me, Jess,' ordered Holly. 'Please look at me. There's something wrong, isn't there?'

Very slowly, Jess turned her head in Holly's direction. Her eyes were very bright, with the wetness of unshed tears. 'J-just about as wrong as it could be,' she replied.

Holly felt her heart plummet seventeen storeys. 'Tell me,' she pleaded.

'I'm pregnant again, Holly,' gasped Jess through a sudden veil of tears. 'I'm pregnant again, and Kev doesn't love me any more.'

Five

Sheila's Café would never win any prizes for its decor or its cuisine, but it was the heart and soul of the Bluebell Estate. Once Holly had bundled her tiny niece into her buggy, and her sister into the warmest coat she could find, it was the natural place to head for.

Everyone who needed to talk about anything ended up at Sheila's Café. It offered an oasis of calm for the harassed, a neutral zone for feuding couples and a damned good latte for friends who simply wanted to share the latest gossip.

'Two cappuccinos and two bacon rolls please, Sheila,' Holly ordered, slapping a tenner down on the counter.

'I hope they're both for you, because I'm not hungry,' protested Jess.

'Oh yes you are,' Holly corrected her. 'I can practically see your skeleton through that parka. It's no wonder you can't feed Aimee if you're not feeding yourself.'

She wanted to pick her little sister up and kiss away her pain, the way she had when she was small, but the best she could do right now was ply her with bacon sandwiches.

Jess managed a weak smile. 'You sound just like Mum.'

Holly shrugged. 'I can think of worse people to sound like. Come on, let's get you sat down.' She steered the buggy into a corner and pulled out a chair for her sister. 'Sit.'

Jess sat. It seemed as if all the fight had drained out of her, leaving behind a frightened little girl. Sitting there in her oversized parka, with her hair scraped back in the classic 'Croydon facelift' ponytail, she looked about twelve years old and late for lessons. Certainly late for a lesson in life, thought Holly, followed by the swift afterthought: Who am I to talk? Sometimes it feels like my entire life is one big lesson in how not to do it.

The coffee and food arrived. Holly added three sugars to Jess's cappuccino, then made her drink half of it. Jess wrinkled her nose in disgust: 'This is gross!'

'Shut up and drink it; it's doing you good. Right,' Holly went on, checking on Aimee and finding her blissfully asleep, 'what's all this about you being pregnant again? Are you sure?'

'Of course I'm sure!' A spark of the old Jess reignited behind the sad brown eyes. 'I'm not a total moron, you know.'

'I'm sorry, I didn't mean it to sound like that. But there are such things as false positives, you know.'

'I know,' replied Jess. 'That's why I did three tests.'

'Oh. I see.' So much for my next bit of advice, thought Holly. 'So Kev wasn't too pleased when you told him then?'

Jess laughed humourlessly into her coffee mug. 'You could say that.'

'So what exactly did he say?' Holly prompted.

Jess looked up. Holly was startled to see real, ice-cold anger on her sister's face. 'He said,' Jess replied in measured tones, 'that if I don't get rid of it he's going to leave.'

'Get rid of it!' Holly's heart skipped a beat. 'You mean—?'

Jess's eyes stared deep into her sister's. 'I mean, he wants me to kill our baby.'

It was only then that Jess's defences crumpled and she began to weep again, her tears falling silently onto her untouched bacon roll.

Holly sat in shocked silence for a few moments, not quite sure what to say. Whatever she'd expected, it wasn't this. She'd always liked Kev a lot, thought of him as a decent lad even when everyone else was calling him a loser. But this . . .

'Why?' she demanded. 'I don't understand. Why does Kev want you to have a termination?'

'B-because he says we c-can't afford another baby,' sobbed Jess. 'And he's right.'

Holly's head was spinning. 'Are you saying you agree with him? That you're going to have the abortion?'

Jess's eyes flashed fire. 'Are you crazy? I'm not aborting this baby for anything. And I'm not giving it away for adoption either. And Kev's just going to have to get used to that, or . . . or . . .'

Holly reached across the table and gently squeezed her sister's hand. 'Or what, Jess?'

Jess wiped tears and snot from her face with the sleeve of her parka. 'Or he can ship out and good fucking riddance.'

'Would it make any difference if you had a bit of money?' asked Holly.

'But we don't, do we?' pointed out Jess.

'That's what I was trying to explain at lunch the other day, when Grace blew me out. I want you and Kev to have half the money Mum left to me.'

Jess blinked. 'But you can't. You need that money for the investigator.'

'Not that money,' Holly corrected her. 'I'm going to sell my car and use the proceeds from the sale to pay for the investigation.'

Her sister was aghast. 'Your Mazda? But you love that car!'

'Not as much as I love my family.'

'But it's our own stupid fault we don't have any money left. If we hadn't wasted my inheritance money on that holiday and buying Kev all that recording equipment, and if I hadn't got myself chucked out of hairdressing college—'

62

'Shh!' Holly put a finger to her sister's lips. 'That's ancient history. What I want to know now is will my money make any difference to you and Kev?'

'Yes.' Jess hung her head. 'And no. I mean yes, of course the money will help – a lot! But I'm not sure about me and Kev. After what he said – you know, about getting rid of the baby – I'm just not sure if I feel the same way about him any more.'

Holly's Mazda sped along the A40, swung up Glenfall Way and purred to a halt in The Avenue. Steve and Grace's modern four-bedroom detached, overlooking untouched woodland, was a far cry from a crummy second-floor flat on the Bluebell Estate.

Steve and Grace Neville had gone up in the world. In fact, Steve Neville's meteoric ascent from humble shop assistant in a computer store to the owner of a burgeoning IT-support business was the stuff of TV soaps.

Heart in mouth, Holly took the first few steps towards Grace and Steve's front door. Perhaps I'm not good enough for her any more, she thought ruefully. Maybe a sister who delivers the post is an embarrassment. She rang the doorbell, half hoping there would be no one at home, but after a few seconds she saw a fuzzy figure bearing down on her through the stained-glass panels on either side of the door.

Moments later the door opened a couple of inches.

'If you're selling anything, we're not interested.' Pause. 'Oh, it's you.' Longer pause. 'I suppose you'd better come in.'

At least this was better than having the door slammed in her face; perhaps it was an encouraging sign. But after closing the door behind her, Holly turned round to find Grace standing alarmingly close, with folded arms and her foot tap-tap-tapping impatiently on the solid oak parquet floor. 'I take it you want something? If it's an apology, you can forget it.'

Bad start, thought Holly, her heart sinking. 'I was hoping we could have a chat about what happened the other day.' Grace didn't move, so she added, 'Any chance we could sit down?'

'Adam's in the back room, having his nap.'

'I wasn't planning on shouting.'

Evidently deciding at last that her sister wasn't going to give in and go away, Grace spun round on her chic pink mules and stalked off into the sitting room, complete with brand-new chocolate-brown leather sofas and a home-cinema system complete with sixty-inch flat-screen television.

It was pretty clear that if Holly waited for an invitation to sit down she'd still be waiting two hours later. So she took the initiative and plonked her bottom on one of the sofas.

'Not there. You know Bruno sits there.'

Holly glanced down at the carpet and, sure enough, saw two beady, malevolent eyes glaring up at her out of a face so wrinkly and flat, it was a wonder the creature could breathe. A growl began at the back of the pug's throat and grew gradually louder; Holly hastily slid along to the other end of the sofa.

'You'll have to lift him up,' said Grace, almost gleefully. 'He can't get up there on his own.'

Holly resisted the urge to reply: 'Of course he can't, the vicious little short-arse.' With extreme reluctance – given Bruno's known fondness for drawing blood – Holly bent down, swiftly scooped up the pygmy pooch and installed him in his favourite spot. 'There. Now can we talk?'

Grace lowered herself onto the sofa opposite with the air of a prosecuting counsel. 'I still can't believe what you said yesterday,' she began.

'And I can't believe what you said.' With difficulty, Holly reined in an impulse to add 'you bitch'. 'All I wanted to do was—'

'It's all you, you, you, isn't it?' snapped Grace.

Taken aback, all Holly could muster was 'What?'

'All you care about is what you want, and you don't give a damn how it affects anybody else.'

'That's crazy!' gasped Holly. 'I've always thought about you and Jess and Dad, and—'

'Oh really?' sniped Grace. 'Well, have you any idea how hurtful it is to hear your own sister say she's going to use your dead mother's money to go off and find herself another mother – the one who cared about her so much she abandoned her like yesterday's rubbish?'

Put that way, it sounded like a hanging offence. Holly tried to focus on what her dad had said, that she wasn't doing anything wrong and that her mum would have approved, but it wasn't easy with Grace acting as judge and jury. It wasn't easy at all.

'Thanks, little sis. Putting it like that really makes me feel like part of the family.'

'You're the one who started this.'

Suddenly, Holly felt incredibly weary. 'Grace, I didn't – and I don't – want to start anything. All I want is to know who I am, can't you understand that? Who I am and where I came from. You already have that. You already know exactly where you come in the family tree and where you swim in the gene pool. If someone had abandoned you outside a hospital, wouldn't you want to know why?'

Grace looked down at her feet and said nothing. The pug continued to glare at Holly with its beady eyes and pant its foul breath all over her.

'Whatever searching I may do, it doesn't change the fact that you and Jess are my sisters, or that Mum and Dad will always be my proper mum and dad. Nobody else could ever take your places.'

Grace looked up. 'It's easy to say that, but what happens when you find this "birth mother" of yours? What happens when she

65

wants you to be a part of her family? Will we still be your sisters then? Will Mum still be your mother, or—' She broke off, and Holly saw that she was holding back tears. 'Or will you just conveniently forget her?'

The idea shocked Holly so much that for a moment all she could do was stare blankly. Then she got up, walked across the room and sat down beside her sister. 'Grace, listen to me. Nobody, nobody and nothing could ever make me forget Mum, or you, or Jess, or Dad. You are my family and my life, can't you understand that?'

'I thought I did,' replied Grace.

'Then you still do. Because nothing has changed.'

'Yes it has,' replied Grace, a note of steel returning to her voice. 'If Mum really is your only real mother, how can you think of using her money to find this other woman? Money you'd half promised your sister,' she added, pushing the knife further in.

'That's what I was trying to explain, only you refused to stay and listen. I'm selling my car and using that money to pay for the search. Half of the inheritance money is going to Jess, and the rest I'll keep for a rainy day.'

'Oh,' said Grace, startled. 'I didn't realise.'

They sat side by side in silence for a while, the only sound the regular rasp of Bruno's breathing. In the end it was Holly who spoke first.

'So you see, I never meant to hurt you. And the more I think about it, the worse I feel.' Now she had begun, the words came tumbling out, fuelled by a great surge of emotion. 'But deep down ... Well, it's not really the point, is it? I could use every penny Mum left me to pay for an investigator and it still wouldn't make me love her any less. And if you think it would, then you're not the sister I've always known and loved.'

Holly paused to draw breath, her anger subsiding as suddenly as it had arisen. 'Oh for God's sake, Grace, if it upsets you so much ...'

66

She smoothed a weary hand across her aching forehead. 'Maybe you're right and I should just forget about searching altogether.'

Grace drew back and stared at her. 'What – really?'

'Really.' Holly smiled feebly. 'Just call me the queen of crap ideas.'

Grace was clearly shaken. 'Do you mean that? Are you saying you'd really do that – forget about the whole thing – because it hurts me?'

'Of course I would,' Holly replied simply. 'You're my sister.'

Grace gazed ahead of her for a few moments, thinking. Then she turned back to Holly. 'Now I feel like the worst person in the world.'

Holly shrugged. 'Join the club.'

For one night only, the hall of St Dunstan's High School had metamorphosed into the venue for a glitzy fashion show, complete with runway and pounding music.

By the time Holly and Jess arrived, the audience was already filtering into the hall in ones and twos, and people were being ushered to their seats by pupils wearing outfits designed by students on the year twelve fashion course. Alas, not all the students were as talented as Tammy Hyde-Cooper's best mate, and Holly really felt for the spotty beanpole of a lad who'd been made to wear the orange spandex jodhpurs and the oversized shirt printed with pink poodles.

'Grace is backstage,' one of the teachers informed them. 'She's done an incredible job, organising this fashion show practically single-handed.'

Yeah, apart from me driving Dad's old van halfway to the moon and back, thought Holly as they went in search of her sister. They found her in a makeshift dressing room, rushing about and barking orders at a collection of amateur models while trying not to swallow her mouthful of pins: 'Come here! No, not you! Turn round and let me pin you, it's gaping at the back.' Grace deftly made running repairs to the back of a model's flamenco-style outfit. 'Emily, where's your tutu? You can't go on without your – What in God's name are you doing, Rosalie? You're wearing it back to front! Yes, I know it's deconstructed, but it still has a front and a back ...'

Holly and Jess hung back, reluctant to interrupt. While Holly was preoccupied trying not to laugh at some of the designs, she was suddenly pounced on from behind a clothes rail by an extremely camp middle-aged man with bouffant grey hair.

'At last – perfect! Grace darling, I've found you that last-minute replacement you needed! Curvy, great hair, nice legs ...'

Grace paused in mid-tirade, turned to look, and burst out laughing. 'Charles, that's my sister!'

'She'll do though, won't she?' Charles ventured.

Grace frowned. 'I guess she'll have to,' she said doubtfully. 'Assuming we can get her into it.'

'Do for what?' demanded Holly, beginning to wish they'd just gone straight to their seats.

'The final tableau,' Grace explained. 'The ensemble was put together especially for Tammy, but she went on holiday to South America and now a revolution's broken out, she can't get back. So we need somebody who can fill her shoes. Literally,' she added. 'You are a size eight, aren't you?'

'No, I'm a—'

'Never mind, we can stuff paper in them.'

'Hang on a minute,' squeaked Holly in alarm, 'I did not come here to be a model! And—'

'Don't worry, Charles has twenty years' experience in couture. He'll teach you how to walk, won't you, Charles?'

'Of course, darling.'

'Can't Jess do it?' protested Holly, her heart pounding in terror.

'No bloody fear!' Jess skipped two steps backwards.

'Don't be silly, she's half your size,' snapped Grace with her usual tact. 'Now come on, it's all in aid of MND research. So you can't really refuse, can you?'

Holly knew when she was beaten. She gave a heavy sigh. 'What do I have to do?'

'Just be our pièce de résistance, darling,' enthused Charles, 'our finale – a gorgeous autumn bride, in yards and yards of ivory organza and vintage lace, with little Cupids as your pageboys. So romantic.'

'A bride!'

'You'll be stunning. Oh, and by the way,' Grace informed her brightly, 'you'll have a little fan club watching you from the audience. I thought you might forget, so I asked Murdo to come along. Won't that be nice?'

Two days later, as she lay on her bed reading, Holly still felt like wringing her sister's neck. Dropping heavy hints about her marrying Murdo was one thing, setting her up in full bridal regalia, right in front of him, was something else. Talk about putting ideas into his head ... What on earth would she say if he suddenly turned round and proposed? What on earth would she do?

Shouldn't she feel all excited and fluttery at the prospect? So why did it just make her feel like running for the hills?

She put down her magazine, rolled over onto her side and gazed across at a poster of Humphrey Bogart kissing Lauren Bacall. Holly's bedroom wasn't just an oasis of girliness: it was a shrine to a more glamorous age. Framed posters adorned the walls, advertising classics like *The Maltese Falcon* and *The Thirty-Nine Steps*, and in one corner the six-foot-tall bookcase had proved unequal to its task, spilling piles and piles of detective novels all over the carpet.

Some of the novels were the modern adventures of trendy detectives like Morse, or modern whodunnits set in medieval times or ancient Rome, but most were vintage tales from the 1920s to the 1960s, which Holly had accumulated as she trawled through every second-hand bookshop in every town she visited. She loved the artwork on the covers of these old books, redolent as it was of a time when women wore bright red lipstick and veils on their hats, and men were rough, tough, smart-talking guys who never, ever used deodorant.

Holly reached across and stroked admiring fingers over her ancient copy of *Black Mask* magazine; a prized possession she had dug out of a pile of old *Woman's Weeklies* at a flea market in Weston-Super-Mare. The smell of its yellowed pages filled her with a sense of well-being. There was nothing like a hot bath and a gory detective story to drive away the blues.

Everything about old-time crime fiction was so fair: the villain was always punished, the hero either got the girl or took it like a man when he didn't and, best of all, in the end everything returned to normal, exactly the way it had been before the crime. Sometimes, Holly wished that real life could be more like that. These last few days had been painful, contemplating the prospect of doing something that was sure to hurt at least one of her sisters. But then life hadn't been the same since Mum died. Even if she abandoned her plans to search for her birth mother, she couldn't make life fair, or put things back the way they had been.

A print of an old 1940s book jacket proclaimed: 'Tec for Hire!', and Holly wondered if people like that really still existed – and if they did, whether they plied their trade in sleepy, genteel Cheltenham.

Maybe she was about to find out – if she decided to go ahead. But for now, she was going to try to get some sleep. Perhaps in the morning things would look clearer. But she severely doubted it.

*

The following evening, just as Holly was starting dinner, Harry seized the potato peeler from her hand and announced that he was taking her out for a meal instead.

That was an hour ago. And even a man as laid-back as Harry was starting to get impatient.

'Are you ready, madam?' his voice boomed up the stairs. 'Your carriage awaits. In fact it's been awaiting for the past half-hour!'

Holly giggled as she leaned over the banisters and called back: 'Promise I'll be down in a minute, Dad.'

'That's what you said a quarter of an hour ago.'

'Ah, but women's minutes are longer than men's,' she retorted with a straight face. 'And they're stretchy. Just let me finish my make-up, and I'll be ready.'

Ten minutes later, she danced down the stairs in her best red frock and the Louboutin heels Murdo had bought her for her last birthday, her chestnut mane twirled up into a neat chignon and her soft, full lips glossed into a perfect crimson bow. A tad overdressed for Giorgio's Pasta Palace, perhaps, but she wanted to do her dad proud.

'What's the matter, Dad?' she asked as he looked away.

'Nothing, love. It's just ... dressed like that, you're the spitting image of your mum when she was young.'

A strange frisson ran up Holly's spine. Was it possible for a child to grow up to look like its adoptive parent? she wondered. She had never really considered the idea before, but now she knew that she desperately wanted it to be true. And if she thought about it really hard, she could see the odd resemblance in some of Mum's old photos. That thought warmed her as she bounced around in the passenger seat of Harry's old rusty-red, ex-Post Office van, cursing its knackered suspension.

Like Harry's van, Giorgio's Pasta Palace was no oil painting – at least on the outside. Cursed with a pug-ugly exterior, it was

71

one of those restaurants which depend on word of mouth for survival. The food might be sensational – authentic yet imaginative – but the restaurant itself was housed in a small, narrow building which seemed to lurk unattractively between its bigger neighbours, like a bit of gristle stuck in a diner's teeth. Quite frankly, from the exterior it looked more like a coffin-maker's workshop than a restaurant. So it was fortunate for all concerned that the interior was a complete revelation: decked out like a Roman villa, with terracotta-coloured walls, marble pillars, a faux-mosaic floor and even a small fountain; and presided over by tastefully draped waitresses and a small, rotund, pink-faced man in a toga.

Giorgio greeted them at the door, wreathed in smiles and looking as if he had just stepped out of the classical frieze on the wall behind the bar. 'Miss Holly, you are more beautiful every time I see you. Mister Harry, you are a very lucky man to have such wonderful daughters!'

'I most certainly am,' agreed Harry, breaking into a grin and slapping his old friend on the back. 'How's Maria? And the twins?'

'Oh fine, fine. They spend my money all the time, of course, but that's what it is to be a father.'

Holly kissed him on the cheek and chided him for being an old chauvinist. 'Where's Benito, Giorgio?'

'There he is, Miss Holly – over there by the dessert trolley. Cleaning up. My Benito is a very conscientious dog.'

Contrary to every health and safety regulation known to man (and dog), Benito the Jack Russell terrier was on the payroll at the Pasta Palace, patrolling the aisles between the tables and acting as a kind of mobile waste-disposal unit. Nobody seemed to mind that he was there, not even when he farted, and some of the diners were so fond of him that half of their dinner went straight into Benito, saving Giorgio a fortune in dog-food bills. Consequently Benito was a very fat dog; so fat in fact that his belly almost scraped the mosaic floor.

Giorgio showed them to their table, screened by an immense potted palm, and left, winking at Harry as he went.

'What was that for?' asked Holly.

'What?'

'Giorgio winked at you.'

'Perhaps he fancies me.'

They looked at each other and both burst out laughing.

'I expect he had something in his eye,' said Harry. 'Now, what are you having?'

Benito had already decided what he was having, and was waiting patiently beside Holly's chair for a breadstick. While he crunched, Holly looked around her. Tonight the place was nearly full, but Giorgio always found room for his friend Harry.

'Thanks for this, Dad,' said Holly as they tucked in. 'You didn't have to, you know.'

'I know I didn't,' replied Harry with a smile. 'Can't I take my daughter out and show her off if I want to?'

'Oh, Dad, that's really sweet.' She paused, slightly puzzled. 'Dad ...'

'Hm?'

'Why did Giorgio give us a table for four, when there are only two of us?' She pointed. 'There's a table for two just over there.'

'Oh, I expect he just wanted us to have somewhere nice and private.' He paused, looked down and fiddled with the buttons on his shirt cuffs. 'Didn't he, Jess?'

Holly was about to correct him when a figure emerged from behind the potted palm. She couldn't have been much more surprised – or delighted – if it had been Humphrey Bogart himself.

'Jess!' She leaped to her feet and embraced her sister. 'Oh, Dad, why didn't you tell me?'

'Because he didn't know if I would come,' replied Jess simply. 'Things have been difficult with Kev; I didn't know if could get away.'

'And when Jess phoned me this afternoon to say she was coming, I thought it would be nice to keep it as a surprise. Giorgio hid Jess in the kitchen until we were sitting down. That was what all the winking was about.'

'So Giorgio doesn't fancy you after all then, Dad,' laughed Holly as Jess sat down at the table. 'Oh, Jess, it's really good to see you. I've been so worried about you since you told me about … you know.'

'It's OK,' said Jess. 'Dad knows I'm pregnant again. And what Kev thinks about it.'

'And Jess knows what I think about *that*,' said Harry darkly.

'Did you tell him about me giving you half my inheritance money?' Holly demanded.

'Of course I did.' Jess looked down. 'But he says it makes no difference. A few thousand would only keep us going for a little while, and he's not ready for another baby anyway.'

Harry cursed under his breath. 'To think I thought that lad was good for you.'

'He is – was.' Jess pushed her plate away, the food uneaten. 'Actually, I've got some news I ought to tell you. About me and Kev.'

Holly prayed it would be good news even though she knew instinctively that it wasn't. Even Benito the dog looked up at Jess with round, wondering eyes, as if he could sense the drama of the moment.

'We had a big talk last night,' Jess began.

'That's good,' said Holly cautiously. 'And—?'

Jess mustered up a wan smile. 'And Kev's moving out.'

*

74

A tunic-clad waiter fussed around the table, sorting out the red, spreading stain where Harry had upset his wine glass. They all held their breath, nobody wanting to say anything while the waiter was still in earshot.

At last he went away, promising to give them plenty of time to 'think about dessert'. Holly guessed that dessert was not uppermost in anybody's mind. Harry was as white as a sheet, looking every inch the careworn, middle-aged widower he tried so hard not to be. Worried, she squeezed his hand.

'Are you all right, Dad?'

'What? Me?' He seemed to emerge from some kind of waking dream, took off his spectacles and started cleaning them frantically on his shirt. 'Yes, I'm fine, Holly, I just ...' His face crumpled into anguish. 'Oh, Jess, love, you're just a kid; do you realise what you're doing? What Kev's doing? What about poor Aimee?'

'Aimee's got me, Dad. And I won't let her down.'

Holly looked at her sister. For once she didn't look like a terrified teenager. In fact she looked almost composed. She may not bother to look after herself but she'll do anything to protect her kids, thought Holly, feeling a sudden burst of admiration for her little sister.

'I'm really sorry it upsets you, Dad,' Jess continued, her voice steady. 'But Kev and I agreed it's the best thing to do. It's only a temporary thing,' she added on a hopeful note. 'Just until we can be in the same room without swearing at each other.'

'Is this still about the baby?' asked Holly.

'More or less. That and the fact that Kev doesn't trust me.'

'What!' Harry's kindly expression changed to one of anger and disbelief.

'Of course he trusts you!' scoffed Holly.

'Oh really? So why is he so convinced that I got pregnant deliberately?' asked Jess.

'He never is!' gasped Holly.

'Oh he is, all right. In fact he even suggested that it might not be his baby!' Jess bit her lip to fight back a tear. 'Have you any idea how much it hurts when the person you love thinks you're a liar?'

Holly's heart ached for her sister. At that moment she would have done anything in the world to spare her this pain. 'Let me talk to him,' she said. 'Maybe I can make him see sense.'

'I've got a better idea,' snarled Harry. 'Tell him to go to hell.'

'I can't, Dad, he's the father of my children,' Jess reminded him. 'He's a part of my life, and Aimee's. And the fact is, I still love him,' she added with a sigh. Then she shook back her hair and reached for the dessert menu. 'Right, that's enough miserable stuff. Can we start enjoying ourselves again?' She waved her napkin at a distant waitress. 'I'm pregnant and I want pudding!'

'It's for the best, I know it is,' repeated Jess as the last mouthfuls of dessert were scraped off the china plates. 'And we'll manage somehow, with what Kev gives me and my part-time job at the salon. But I'll tell you one thing,' she went on, waving her spoon for emphasis, 'we're not moving back in together again until Kev grows up. Which probably means never,' she murmured sadly under her breath.

Holly drummed her fingers on the tablecloth, deep in thought. The mists were starting to clear. 'That settles it.'

'Settles what?' asked Jess.

'You can have all the money Mum left me. You need it.'

Harry choked on his panna cotta, and all the blood drained from Jess's face. 'But, Holly, what about keeping some for a rainy day? You can't just—'

'Yes, I can,' Holly corrected her. 'You're the one who said I had a right to do whatever I wanted with it. And I want to give it all to you, to help you out. Simple!'

'We're not starving, you know,' said Jess firmly. 'Like I said, I'll have my money and Kev's, and tax credits and ... and I'll budget really carefully, honestly I will.'

'Take it. Please.' Suddenly it meant a lot to Holly. 'And promise me that whenever you need something – and I don't just mean money, I mean anything – you'll come to me for help.'

'You've already done more than I deserve.'

'Promise.'

Jess nodded. 'OK.'

Harry grabbed his youngest daughter's hands and squeezed them in his big bear's paw grip. 'You've got us, Jess. Money's not everything.'

'Grace thinks it is,' commented Holly.

'Yeah,' agreed Jess. 'She's was bloody delirious when she got that new fitted kitchen.' Then something struck her and she looked meaningfully at Harry. 'Dad. About Grace.'

'Oh gosh, yes. I almost forgot.' Harry let go of Jess's rather squashed hands, sat up and started patting the pockets of his favourite old jacket. 'I know it's here somewhere.'

'Grace wanted to come tonight but she couldn't,' said Jess while Harry hunted feverishly.

Holly almost laughed. 'Yeah, right.'

'No, really she did,' Jess insisted. 'She was all set to come, then Adam got poorly. Really poorly,' she emphasised. 'The doctor said it might be chicken pox. So she sent Dad a—'

'Ah! Here it is.' Harry withdrew a crumpled white envelope from one of his myriad inside pockets and held it out to Holly. 'For you. From Grace.'

'What is it?' asked Holly warily.

'Open it and find out,' said Harry.

Holly stared at it as though it were a time bomb, certain there must be something horrible inside.

'She told me to tell you that she understands now,' said her father.

'Understands what?'

'If you don't open it you'll never find out, will you?' declared Jess in exasperation, snatching the envelope from her sister's fingers and ripping it open. Inside, she found a single sheet of white paper, which she scanned and handed to Holly with a little laugh. 'I don't believe it!'

'Oh my God.' Holly looked down at the paper. I don't believe it either, she thought, her hands trembling. Her hand flew to her mouth. 'It's a list.'

'Of what?' enquired her father.

'Agencies. Detective agencies in Gloucestershire.'

Six

Late that night, when everyone else was asleep, Holly took the sheet of paper from her handbag, unfolded it and laid it on her bed.

All these detective agencies; so many to choose from. Who'd have thought it? And who'd have thought it of Grace? Holly's pulse was racing. It was pointless trying to get to sleep until she'd done something about this, taken some kind of symbolic first step along the road. But with the best will in the world, there was a limit to what anyone could achieve at two o'clock in the morning.

Perhaps there was one thing though ...

There's only one way to do this, she told herself, prising a drawing pin from the pinboard on her bedroom wall. And with that thought, she closed her eyes, took a deep breath and stabbed the pin into the list.

When she opened her eyes and looked down, she saw that the pin had landed plumb in the middle of a modestly sized advertisement, about one third of the way down the page. It read:

BLOODHOUND INVESTIGATIONS
We never lose the scent.

And underneath, flanked by two line drawings of bloodhounds wearing deerstalkers, came the part that interested Holly more than all the rest put together:

Reasonable rates – Terms negotiable.

The following afternoon after work, Nesta came round to Holly's house and they drank endless cups of tea while Holly put off doing anything.

'I wish I'd never told you about the bloody list,' she complained as Nesta plonked the phone down in front of her and then sat back at the kitchen table, eyes firmly fixed on her.

'You're the one who stuck the pin in it,' Nesta pointed out with growing exasperation.

'I'll do it in a minute.'

'Chicken.' Nesta flapped her arms and clucked.

That did it. 'Oh for goodness' sake!' Holly grabbed the phone and dialled the number from the advertisement. 'Look – I'm doing it now!'

She took deep breaths to overcome her silly, childish nerves. What was there to be afraid of? Failure? Or success?

Ring-ring. Ring-ring. The damned thing seemed to go on for ever. And if Holly hadn't had Nesta's beady eyes on her, she might have been tempted to give up and try a different agency. But at last an answering machine kicked in and a silky female voice informed her that she had reached the offices of Blood-hound Investigations.

Suddenly the message was cut short by a man's breathless voice: 'Hello? Hi. Just a minute, don't ring off.' The voice grew slightly fuzzy but still audible, as though a hand had been loosely placed over the receiver. 'Where's that bloody pencil? Dweezil, will you stop chewing that? Ah, there it is.' The voice returned to normal volume. 'Sorry about that. Bloodhound Investigations, Phil Connell speaking. Can I help?'

Holly had been reading crime fiction since she was tall enough to reach the shelves in the local library, but at the sound of a real live private detective, she froze.

Nesta mouthed, 'Go *on!*' and kicked her in the shin.

'Ow!'

'Sorry?' asked the voice on the line.

'Nothing.' Holly threw Nesta a look that would have turned molten lava to ice. 'My name's Holly Bennett. I, um, saw your advert and I was wondering if I could, er, make an appointment sometime. Just to, you know, have a chat.'

'Yes, of course.' He sounded rather nice, thought Holly, though he was probably fifty with cross-eyes and a paunch. People never looked like their voices, did they? 'Can you give me some idea of the type of case?' he enquired. 'Is it matrimonial? Corporate?'

'No, no. I'm trying to find someone.'

'Right. That's fine. How about tomorrow afternoon? About three thirty?'

'Tomorrow!' Holly couldn't prevent a squeak of panic entering her voice. Somehow she hadn't envisaged things moving quite so fast.

Phil Connell, meanwhile, completely misread her reaction. 'If it's urgent I might be able to fit you in today ...'

Holly looked across the table at Nesta. Nesta glared back at her and mouthed: 'Get on with it!'

But still Holly hesitated.

'Hello? Are you still there?' asked the nice male voice.

Nesta leaped up from her chair, grabbed the phone from Holly's hand and said: 'She'll be there tomorrow. Bye.' Then she slammed down the receiver with a triumphant clunk.

Holly stared in mounting terror at the silent telephone. 'You just—'

'Made you an appointment for tomorrow, yes. What time did he say?'

'Th-three thirty. Why?'

81

'Because I'm going to follow you every step of the way, madam. Just to make sure you don't chicken out.'

Bloodhound Investigations was situated in the part of Cheltenham tourist guides seldom bothered to mention: the tatty end.

Still, reasoned Holly as she and Nesta walked past the Lower High Street's assorted small shops, some frankly decrepit, some gaudy and new, what would be the point of shelling out vast sums for a glitzy office on the Promenade if what you were selling was essentially the ability to lurk in dark corners and not be noticed?

If camouflage was the aim, Bloodhound certainly took it seriously. They managed to walk past the office three times before Holly finally spotted the bell and a small name plate, beside a door which was set into such a deep recess that it looked as if it was trying to escape from the street. The blue paint had probably been quite smart a year or two before, but neglect had left it distinctly scruffy round the edges, and a half-eaten cheeseburger had been posted halfway through the letter box.

'Hm,' observed Nesta, gazing at the depressing facade. 'Not quite what one might expect of a company that's hoping to relieve you of large amounts of cash.'

Holly felt half inclined to agree. On the other hand, she told herself with a quickening heartbeat, it might just be the sign of a rough, tough detective who had no time for frills and fripperies: a man of the streets who never stepped out of his office without his faithful Colt .45 in a holster under his jacket ...

Well, sort of.

She felt quite excited as she pressed the bell and waited breathlessly. This was almost like stepping into the plot of one of her beloved detective novels. She could imagine the office already, all dark wood and art deco fittings, behind a door with PRIVATE

INVESTIGATOR etched into the glass, and a coil of cigarette smoke winding up towards the ceiling fan.

A crackly voice from a nearby entryphone told her to 'wait for the buzz, then push hard'.

'I'm coming up with you,' decided Nesta. 'He might be an axe murderer.' She glanced uneasily around her. 'Besides, I don't fancy hanging around out here with the druggies.'

One good shove of the door and they found themselves in a narrow hallway, facing a steep flight of steps up to the first floor. A cardboard arrow Blu-tacked to the wall indicated RECEPTION UPSTAIRS.

In a brief moment of panic Holly thought about turning tail and running away, but the heavy door had clicked shut behind her, leaving only one way left to go, and that was up.

Nesta seemed to read her mind. 'Get your arse up those stairs,' she ordered, prodding her best friend in the buttocks. 'There's no escape now.'

'Hello there. One of you must be Miss Bennett.'

'Er ... that's me, but I prefer Holly, actually,' she heard herself say to the tall, clean-shaven young man with the friendly face, the soft brown eyes and the shock of golden-brown hair that curled boyishly over his collar. He didn't look like an axe-murderer; but then again, how could you tell? 'This is my friend Nesta. We're looking for Mr Connell?'

'And you've found him.' Phil Connell stuck out a hand to shake, realised it was holding a dish of cat food and offered the other one instead. 'Do come into the office. Sorry about the slippers,' he added, with a glance down at his feet. 'Dweezil did something unmentionable in my shoes.'

The plot was thickening already. 'Dweezil?'

'My cat – well, the office cat. Wandered in off the street one day, decided he liked it and stayed. He's an anarchist, I'm afraid. Sows disorder wherever he goes. Anyway, do come in.' He gestured towards the open door, which was disappointingly short on 1930s etched glass and big on magnolia-painted plywood. 'I'll make us some coffee and you can tell me all about your missing person.'

The Bloodhound Investigations office had the air of a place that had once been rather well organised, but had recently given up the ghost. There were piles of paper everywhere, and everything looked as if it could do with a thorough dusting. On the other hand, the furniture was modern and the computer looked almost new, so maybe the firm wasn't a complete shambles after all. It's a good job Grace isn't with me though, thought Holly with a smile as she imagined her house-proud sister's reaction. She'd have me out of here faster than you can say, 'MRSA.'

At the sight of its approaching lunch, a truly gigantic black and white cat clambered off the computer keyboard, leaving a trail of fluff in its wake, and homed in on the dish of cat food with a mighty meow.

'Dweezil, meet Holly,' said Phil, rubbing the monster's head, 'and Nesta.' Dweezil looked up, growled menacingly, and dripped saliva from his yellowed fangs.

'I don't think he likes us,' said Holly.

Nesta eyed the monster warily. 'Correction: he hates us.'

'No, it's OK, really,' replied Phil earnestly. 'In fact I think he's taken to you. If he hadn't, he would've bitten you by now. Do you take milk and sugar?'

'Just milk for me, thanks,' said Holly, maintaining a safe distance from Dweezil, just in case Phil was wrong. 'And one sugar for Nesta.'

'I keep trying to give it up,' confessed Nesta. 'Then I think: Why bother? And start again.'

Holly looked around for somewhere to sit, and Phil magicked up one chair and whisked a pile of papers off another. 'Sorry the place is so disorganised,' he apologised as the kettle boiled. 'Only my, um, business partner is, er, overseas at the moment, on a big assignment, and I'm not that great with paperwork.'

'So I can see.' Holly sat down, wondering what she'd got herself into and how quickly she could extricate herself if need be. Not that she had anything to worry about with Nesta around: Nesta was a legend at the sorting office for having once single-handedly hurled a burglar out of her bedroom window. No man had ever got the better of her. Maybe that was why she was still single: they were all terrified of her.

Anyway, for all the tousled eccentricity there was something instantly likeable about Phil Connell, the same natural warmth Holly had sensed over the telephone. Then again, she mused cheerfully, Nesta could be right about him being an escaped axe murderer and I'm just a really bad judge of character.

'This is all a bit different from what we expected,' Nesta remarked pointedly. 'A bit ... well ... scuzzy.'

Holly nearly died of embarrassment. Phil's face fell ten storeys. He looked, thought Holly, like a schoolboy who'd been caught smoking behind the bike sheds. Not really axe murderer material at all.

'I know. I'm really sorry about that. My business partner Sita was – is – astoundingly well-organised. As you can see, I'm not. And as I said, I'm afraid she's away on a long-term assignment at the moment.'

'So when is she due back?' enquired Holly.

'I'm, um, you know, not one hundred per cent sure.' Phil avoided her gaze as he brought across three mugs of coffee, pulled up another chair and sat down at his desk, opposite Holly and Nesta. 'Oh dear, I don't think I've made a very good first impression, have I? You must think we're a bunch of clowns.'

'Well ...' began Nesta. Holly glared her into silence.

'Believe it or not,' Phil went on seriously, 'I'm actually very good at my job. Seven years in the police force, three of them as a firearms expert, five doing this, and a one-year specialist training course. You can ask any of my other clients,' he added. 'Most of them are happy to be contacted. And any of my former police colleagues will vouch for me.'

'Thanks,' replied Nesta. 'Can we have a list?'

Holly ignored Nesta and cut to the chase. 'Look, Mr Connell, the reason I'm here is that I don't have a great deal of money and you say your rates are reasonable.'

Phil nodded emphatically. 'And so they are. It makes sense when you're starting small and trying to grow a business. There's a lot of competition out there.' He was cradling his coffee mug in his hands, but Holly could just make out the words 'World's Greatest Boyfriend'. For some reason it made her feel sad to think that he was already spoken for, despite the fact that she was too. 'Look,' he went on, 'why don't you tell me what you're looking for and then I'll tell you honestly whether I can do it. You mentioned that you were trying to find someone?'

'Yes.' Holly's throat suddenly felt dry as dust. 'I ... I want you to find out who I am.'

Their eyes met, and a tiny shiver of pleasure ran tingling down Holly's spine. Ooh, she thought, he *is* cute.

'You know, I think I'd enjoy that,' said Phil, returning her gaze with a twinkle-eyed smile. 'I think I'd enjoy that very much.'

An hour later the two women emerged from the office, and onto the High Street.

Nesta was in full flow before the door had even closed behind them. 'You were flirting with him!'

'I was not!' insisted Holly, feeling her reddening cheeks betray her.

'Yes you were, you were flirting. And you and Murdo are prac-tically engaged!'

Holly's heart, which had felt as light as a butterfly while she was talking to Phil Connell, abruptly sank back to ground level. 'I'm *not* engaged to Murdo – and in any case, I wasn't flirting with Phil.'

Nesta gave her the eyes-narrowed, can't-fool-me look that never failed to take the wind out of Holly's sails. 'Oh come on, Hol, it's going to take the poor guy the rest of the afternoon to mop all the drool off his office floor.'

As the two of them walked back in the direction of civilisation, Holly couldn't help wondering if Nesta was right. Was I really that obvious? she asked herself, embarrassed at the very thought of it. Because if Nesta had noticed, then he must have noticed too. What if he thinks I'm some kind of loony stalker woman? she thought. And should I really be having these carnal thoughts about some guy I've only just met? Shouldn't I be having them about Murdo?

A few moments later, Nesta cut into her thoughts with: 'I was wondering – have you told Murdo yet?'

'Told him what?'

'That you've decided to try and track down your birth mother.'

'No, not yet. Do you think he'll be interested?'

'Oh, I should think so,' mused Nesta, 'especially if he thinks you're having impure thoughts about the private investigator.'

Holly's jaw dropped. 'You'd never tell him—'

'Of course I wouldn't, stupid!' Nesta punched her on the shoul-der. 'Honestly, how many years have I been your best friend in the whole world? Thirty this year. And how many times have I snitched on you? Not once. No,' she said, suddenly subdued, 'I'm just a bit worried about you, that's all. Are you sure you and Murdo are OK?'

'We're absolutely fine!' blustered Holly. 'Whatever makes you think we're not?'

'Oh, I don't know ... I expect I'm imagining it.' Nesta brightened. 'Phil Connell *is* a hunk, by the way. In case you were wondering, I wouldn't kick him out of bed, either.'

Holly laughed. 'I saw him first.'

'Did I do the right thing, Dad?'

Harry Bennett looked up and gave his eldest daughter a reassuring smile. 'Yes, love, you did exactly the right thing.'

'You're sure you don't mind me inviting him round here to have a chat with you and look at the things you found me with?'

'Mind? Why on earth would I mind? I told you before, I'm behind you on this, one hundred per cent. Now sit down, love, before you wear a hole in the carpet.'

It was almost seven o'clock, and Holly could barely remember ever being so nervous. Not, in fact, since the day she'd had her interview at Payne, Rackstraw and Bynt and managed to lock herself in the loo with only five minutes to spare. If Murdo hadn't been there to soothe her embarrassment when the caretaker prised her out, banishing her nerves with good humour and a quick shot of caffeine, things might have turned out rather differently, she mused.

But tonight isn't about Murdo, Holly reminded herself. This is about me. In fact, nothing in my entire life has been so intensely about me, not since the *Courant* first snapped me in my tartan blanket. She went and perched on the arm of the family's well-loved sofa, one eye on Great-granddad Bennett's old wooden-cased mantel clock and the other on her dad, who, perfectly untouched by the drama of the occasion, was dismantling a carburettor on the hearthrug.

'Dad.'

'Hm?'

'Do you have to do that now? He'll be here in a minute.'

Harry pushed his spectacles up his nose with a grimy finger. 'I promised Graham down the road I'd have this sorted out by tomorrow, sweetheart.'

Holly let out a groan of exasperation. 'Do you have to do favours for the whole of Cheltenham?'

Harry laughed softly, and wiped his greasy hands on his old blue overalls. 'Don't worry, sweetheart,' he said. 'I'm sure this evening will go just fine.'

She didn't even have time to lie and say she wasn't worried anyway, because two seconds later the front door knocker clattered against sturdy Victorian pine, the sound echoing through the whole house. Oh God that'll be him, she thought, leaping to her feet. Do I look all right?

Then she reminded herself that this was a business meeting, not a date. Behaving like an overexcitable sixteen-year-old wasn't going to help matters one bit.

Nevertheless she half walked, half ran to the front door and opened it. Phil Connell was standing in the porch, sheltering from the April drizzle. 'Phil, hi. Come on in. Let me take your coat.'

'Hi, Holly. Thanks for asking me round.'

He wiped his feet politely on the doormat and followed her down the hall and into the front room, where Harry was still sitting on the hearthrug, still placidly disassembling bits of greasy metal. Holly cringed at the sight, but Phil didn't seem in the least fazed.

'Mr Bennett? I'm Phil Connell, very pleased to meet you.'

Holly despaired of her dad as he wiped a hand on his overalls and shook on it. But Phil seemed positively interested in the greasy mess on the hearthrug. 'Carburettor?'

'From a Ducati 1100.'

'Nice bike. I had a 500 once, then a Norton Commander, but a car's more use in my line of work. These days, the closest I get to messing about with engines is playing with my model train set.'

Harry's eyes lit up. 'Train set?'

Holly groaned. Now Phil had mentioned train sets, she'd never get Harry off his favourite subject.

'Just a modest one. Of course, I'd like to add to it in time . . .'

Harry was on his feet. 'I've got a layout in the spare room. Hornby 00 gauge. Would you like to see?'

'Dad!' protested Holly as the evening threatened to descend into farce. 'Mr Connell's not here to talk about train sets!'

The two men looked at each other and shrugged.

'Sorry,' said Phil. 'I started it. Should we get down to business then?'

Holly looked expectantly at her father, who cleared his throat. 'I suppose you'll want to hear what happened that night, then,' he said. And he began to tell Holly's story.

'So you see, that's all we know,' said Holly ruefully as her father's tale came to an end. 'I'm a complete mystery.'

Phil scratched his chin. 'Didn't you say something about a box of things that were left with you?' he asked.

'There isn't much,' replied Harry, getting to his feet and heading for the cupboard under the stairs. 'Nothing to give you much of a clue.'

He returned a couple of minutes later with the small cardboard box Holly knew so well. 'That's all there is,' he said, placing it on the coffee table. 'Just the tartan rug and some kind of religious necklace. There was a carrycot too, but the hospital managed to lose that.'

'At first, the police reckoned my mum must have been Scottish, or maybe Irish,' explained Holly as Phil fingered the soft blue tartan blanket. 'But I suppose loads of people have tartan travel rugs, don't they?'

A slow smile spread across Phil Connell's face. 'Not rugs like this one,' he replied. 'This isn't Scottish tartan, it's Manx.'

Harry and Holly looked at each other in mutual incomprehension. 'What's Manx?' asked Holly.

'It means from the Isle of Man. My mum was born there.' Phil laughed. 'In fact my granny still lives there. That's how come I recognised the tartan.' He picked out the colours with his fingertips. 'Blue for the sea, gold for the gorse, purple for the heather—'

'Didn't we go to the Isle of Man for a holiday once?' Holly asked her father.

'No, that was the Isle of Wight. The Isle of Man is where they hold the TT Races. And they have cats with no tails.'

'So where is that ... exactly?' wondered Holly, appalled by her own lack of geographical knowledge.

'In the Irish Sea, between Cumbria and Ireland,' Phil replied promptly. He stroked the blanket. 'You know, this could be a really important clue, Holly. I think when your mother wrapped you up in this blanket, she wanted people to know where she – and you – came from.'

'So my mother was Manx?'

'And proud of it. I'd stake money on that.'

'And what about the necklace?' Eagerly, Holly unwrapped the delicate silver chain from the tissue paper it had lain in for the last thirty years. 'It's got a religious picture on it, see? And a date on the other side.'

Phil turned it over in his hand. 'I've never seen anything like this before,' he confessed, 'but then again I am a lapsed agnostic. Looks Roman Catholic to me. I'll tell you one thing though,' he went on, 'that date can't realistically be your mother's birth date. She'd have been impossibly young when she gave birth to you.'

'So what else could it be?'

Phil shook his head. 'Dunno yet,' he admitted. Then a mischievous smile lit up his face. 'But if you'll let me, I'm willing to have a bloody good go at finding out.'

'I . . . I'd really like you to,' said Holly, hesitantly. How could she put this without sounding like a cheapskate? 'But my, um, budget isn't that big.'

'What Holly's trying to say,' butted in her father, 'is that before she goes any further, she needs to have some idea of how much this is all going to cost her.'

'OK.' Phil nodded. 'Well, this is my official daily rate.' He handed leaflets to Harry and Holly. 'But—'

Holly took a peek and nearly died. 'Oh my! There's no way I can afford this, even after I've sold the car.'

'That's OK,' Phil reassured her, 'you won't have to. That rate is for business customers, really boring cases and rich people who can afford it. But your case really interests me, and when I'm interested in a case I've been known to . . . well . . . work it for nothing.'

'Nothing!' Harry's eyebrows shot skywards. 'Where's the catch?'

Phil laughed. 'The catch is that I've only ever worked one case for nothing, and that involved a little girl with cancer whose parents had gone bankrupt paying for her treatment. But I do often work at a discount. And in your case—' he looked across the room so that his eyes met Holly's and she was certain she saw his cheeks flush '—I'm sure we can come to some, er, arrangement.'

Seven

'You did what?' Phone cradled between ear and chin, Murdo choked on his lunchtime sandwich; he could hardly believe what he was hearing.

'I said I'd help Phil clear up the mess he's got his paperwork into, in return for a substantial discount.' Holly listened in dismay to the sound of frantic coughing on the other end of the line. 'Are you all right?'

'I am,' replied Murdo, dislodging the last of the crumbs from his throat. 'It's you I'm worried about. You don't know anything about this man. He might be—'

'An escaped axe murderer, yes, I know,' cut in Holly wearily. 'I've already had that from Nesta, thank you – oh, and Grace too. But I reckon he's a nice guy, and surely my opinion counts for something. Besides, I'm only going to be doing a bit of keyboard-ing, filing and whatever, and in the end it's going to save me an awful lot of money.'

'Hmm.' Murdo sighed. 'I wish I was there.'

Holly's hackles rose. 'Why – so you could do your 'big brother' routine and check him out for me? I'm quite capable of running my own life, you know.'

'I know. And that's not what I meant at all. I just wish I was there so I could be with you. Period.'

'Oh.' Holly felt like an idiot. 'Sorry.'

'I miss you and that's all there is to it. Is that hopelessly unmanly of me?'

'No, of course it's not.' She knew what he was waiting for her to say, and she said it because it would make him happy. 'I miss you too.'

Was it true? Yes – and no. She did crave the warmth of arms around her, the companionship, the sex. When she was with Murdo it was fun. But when she wasn't ... well, she had to admit to herself that there were whole days when she didn't think of him. She felt sure that Murdo thought a lot more about her than she did about him. Was that the way things ought to be? Or had Mum been right when she said that there were no rules, that every love affair was unique?

Holly tuned her mind back in to the phone conversation. In the background, she could hear Leonie's distinctive hyena laughter, interspersed with snatches of conversation. 'Sounds like you're having a party down there,' she observed.

'Oh, just a minor celebration. Alex won an award for that awful ad campaign he dreamed up for corned beef. Do you remember Alex's dancing cow?'

'No, I think Alex was after my time.'

'Then you'd better hurry back here before there's no one left that you know! Incidentally,' Murdo added, 'I might just be down your way next week, with another commission for you from the great Mr Bynt himself.'

Despite herself, a sniff of a new assignment always made Holly's toes tingle. 'Another difficult one?'

'Of course it is. He's not going to waste easy jobs on you when he knows you can tackle the impossible ones, is he? He wants you to give us a hand launching a sensitive new product. A shampoo.'

'What's sensitive about shampoo?'

'It's for head lice.'

'So he's coming up next Wednesday to brief me and he'll probably stay overnight,' explained Holly as she and Nesta drank skinny lattes in the café belonging to Holly's favourite bookshop, Crime Inc.

It was a dream of a shop for anyone interested in crime: fiction upstairs, non-fiction on the ground floor, with a separate section for second-hand books and DVDs. Aficionados could buy anything from a first-edition Ellery Queen whodunit to a twelve-inch figure of Hercule Poirot and the latest series of *CSI: Miami*. Holly had read just about everything in the shop, but liked coming anyway, in the hope of adding to her collection. Not that she had room for anything else; the bookshelves in her bedroom were already bowing in the middle, and the overspill had started colonising one corner of Murdo's otherwise minimalist apartment.

Nesta sighed. 'I wish I had someone who loved me as much as Murdo loves you. Driving all that way just to be with you, and staying faithful even with all those temptations in London.'

That instantly made Holly feel guilty for not appreciating him more, and suspicious of the ever-predatory Leonie. 'He's a good man,' she agreed. 'And I'm very lucky.'

'Lucky!' Nesta shook her head in amusement. 'Kiddo, if you ask me that man is one in a billion.'

'Yes,' said Holly faintly.

'Is everything OK?' demanded Nesta, who never missed a thing. She leaned across the table conspiratorially. 'Have you and Murdo had a row or something?'

Holly shook her head. 'No row; we're fine. I suppose I'm just wondering ...'

'Go on,' urged Nesta.

'Well ... when you've been with someone for quite a long time, the way I've been with Murdo, does the, you know ... excitement always wear off? And is it supposed to be different if you meet The One?'

'Oh.' Startled, Nesta sat up straight. 'Don't ask me; I've never been with anybody longer than three weeks, remember.' She lowered her voice. 'Is it like that with you and Murdo then?'

'A bit,' confessed Holly. 'Sometimes. But it's only me, not Murdo. And I do love him. It's just ... I think there must be something wrong with me,' she said sadly. 'I've got the perfect boyfriend, and instead of being happy about what's right, all I can seem to do is fret about what isn't.'

'Maybe there's nothing wrong anyway,' ventured Nesta. 'Maybe if you stop worrying about it, everything will be fine. You always were the kind of person who worries about nothing.'

'I suppose.'

'You've told Murdo you're trying to find your birth mother, right?' Holly nodded. 'Have you explained why?' Holly's face provided the answer to that question. 'Oh Holly! If you're desperate to have a baby, don't you think Murdo has a right to know?'

'I'm not desperate.' Holly drew a heart in the foam on her coffee. 'And I'm a coward.'

'I don't understand.'

'I'm frightened that if I tell him, he'll think it's the green light for the two of us to move in together, get married and start a family.'

Nesta was confused. 'I thought that was what you wanted: a family of your own.'

'It is. I'm just not sure if this is the right time or place.' She raised her cup to her lips. 'Anyhow, I'm not going to have much time to be worried, am I? I've got to deliver the post every morning, go round to Phil Connell's office every afternoon and help him out, babysit for my sisters' kids and somehow fit in this lovely job Murdo's bringing me.'

Nesta giggled. 'Most boyfriends bring their girlfriends flowers. I bet there aren't many who turn up with a bottle of nit shampoo.'

The following afternoon found Holly at the offices of Bloodhound Investigations. If she half closed her eyes and tried really hard, she could nearly imagine that she was a streetwise private eye in her downtown Manhattan office, not a postwoman moonlighting amid teetering piles of dusty invoices. It was almost romantic.

Then Dweezil lumbered out of his litter tray, leaving behind him a foul stench and a trail of cat litter.

'Is the office the best place for that?' Holly asked tactfully, trying to hold her breath and talk at the same time.

'What?' Phil glanced over the top of his PC monitor, clearly immune to the smell. 'Oh – the litter tray. Yes, I'm afraid so. I tried moving it out onto the landing, but he kept using the office carpet as a loo. I usually banish him to the great outdoors whenever I have clients coming.'

'But not when I came,' Holly recalled.

'Ah, that was because he was asleep. Even Dweezil can't sleep and poo at the same time. If it's a real emergency, like the landlord coming round, I shove him out of the window.'

'The window!' Holly had dreadful visions of Dweezil plummeting twenty feet to the pavement below.

'The toilet window,' Phil explained. 'There's a flat roof outside. The girls from the office across the way use it for sunbathing when it's hot.' He cast a look at the neat little piles of paper which were forming around Holly as she knelt on the floor. 'How are you getting on with those invoices?'

Holly suppressed the urge to scream at the level of sheer chaos Phil had managed to achieve while his partner was away. 'They're a bit muddled,' she remarked. And that's the understatement of the year, she mused. 'And I can't seem to find January at all.'

'January, January.' Phil wandered around the office, looking in desk drawers, filing cabinets, his briefcase, under the cat's bed and finally in a shoebox. 'There you go.' He handed the box to Holly with a cheerful grin. 'I knew I had an overflow system somewhere.'

'You were right when you said you're not good at paperwork,' observed Holly. 'You're downright terrible at it.' He's a disaster, she thought, but somehow that just made her like him even more.

Phil's schoolboy grin faded. 'I know, I'm totally crap at it. But I am good at my job as a detective,' he emphasised. 'I'm just not a very good form-filler. That was – is – Sita's job.'

Holly couldn't resist the urge to know more. 'Your partner seems to have been away for quite a while,' she said. 'She's on some kind of long-term assignment, you said?'

'That's right. Very long term.' Holly watched the muscles of his throat contract as he swallowed hard. 'I'm afraid I've no idea when she'll be back.'

'Is she often away then?'

'Yes, you could say that, but ... Hey, can I get you another coffee? And maybe some biscuits? I'm pretty sure there are some chocolate ones in a tin in the kitchen.'

Holly watched him disappear into the kitchen, even more intrigued than ever. He's lying about his business partner, she thought, I just know he is. But why? And what exactly is going on?

It crossed her mind for a few seconds that Murdo and her sister might be right, that Phil Connell might be some kind of crook who liked to lure innocent young postwomen into his lair and then ... what? No matter how hard she tried, Holly couldn't imagine Phil doing anything worse than filling in his VAT form wrong. And she had a hunch that cats like Dweezil didn't hang around unless they were treated well. The furry igloo bed, matching food and water bowls and array of cat toys all pointed to the fact that Mr Connell was in fact a great big softy.

As she and Phil munched on chocolate biscuits and Dweezil chewed contentedly on a large brown envelope marked 'HM Revenue & Customs', Holly wondered what it was that Phil Connell wasn't telling.

Grace was in good form.

As she, Jess and Holly enjoyed one of their rare girlie afternoon teas around the big round family kitchen table, and the babies took a nap in the next room, Grace lectured her captive audience on the merits of networking.

'So you see,' she went on animatedly between bites of Holly's home-made cherry scones, 'the whole thing was down to Steve "working" the party after the fashion show. If he hadn't been brave enough to start up conversations with all those influential people, he'd never have met Sir Chesney Trentham. And if he hadn't met him, he'd never have found out that Sir Chesney was looking for someone to install a computer network at Trentham Hall.' She swallowed the last morsel of scone and licked the butter wickedly off her fingertips. 'And as you know, when it comes to IT systems there's nobody can touch my Steve. Give me another of those scones, I'm celebrating.'

It was good to see Grace so bubbly, thought Holly. After all the misunderstandings and rancour of the past few weeks, there had been times when she'd wondered if Grace's old self would ever shine back through. But now here she was again, singing Steve's praises, telling the world that Adam was the next Albert Einstein, and trying to drag her sisters back into line.

'So, have you and Kev sorted yourselves out yet?' Grace demanded, focusing her gimlet gaze on Jess.

She looked and sounded, thought Holly, like an interfering head-mistress. And she was pretty sure that was the last thing Jess needed right now. 'Grace—', Holly began, her eyes miming 'shut up', but

Grace paid no attention to her elder sister. Then again she rarely did, thought Holly ruefully, recalling the day, twenty years ago, when little Grace had pranced home from school, proudly declaring: 'Mrs Jenkins says that when I grow up, I'm going to be a proper little madam.'

'Well? Have you sorted yourselves out or not?' repeated Grace, rather tetchily this time.

Jess's bruised and battered soul had had enough of everything and everyone. 'If we had,' she spat, 'don't you think I'd have found something better to do than sit here all afternoon listening to you and eating fucking scones?'

After a long and expressive pause, Holly said gently: 'So nothing's changed the way Kev feels about the baby then?'

Jess snorted, more in despair than anger; at least that was how it seemed to Holly. 'I was so sure he cared about us,' she said, 'but I was wrong. All he cares about is making it in the music business. And that's about as likely as ... as me winning a multimillion-pound contract modelling bikinis.'

'You used to believe in Kev,' Holly reminded her.

'She used to hang around in bus shelters and drink cheap cider,' retorted Grace, 'but she grew out of that, too. Thank God.'

'That's a bit mean,' protested Holly.

Jess wiped her eyes on the sleeve of her Slipknot sweatshirt and waved away Holly's well-meaning intervention. 'No, Grace is right,' she said gloomily, as if the terrifying fact of Grace being right was a prelude to Armageddon. 'I think I've been growing out of Kev ever since I got pregnant with Aimee. Blokes don't grow up the same way women do. They can go through life pretending they're still just lads with no responsibilities. But we women have to grow up, don't we, because we're the ones who get landed with the kids?'

'Not all men are immature,' cautioned Holly, automatically

thinking of Murdo. Some men can be a bit too mature, she thought, though she knew deep down she ought to be grateful that Murdo wanted to take care of her, that he would never let her down the way Kev was letting down Jess. After all, she reminded herself, if I want a baby I'm going to be glad of that kind of security. She very nearly convinced herself.

'That's very true,' Grace agreed, cutting another scone into the neatest of quarters. 'If only you'd kept your legs together, Jess, finished college and waited till you found yourself a nice, responsible man like Steve or Murdo—'

'Shut up, will you?' pleaded Jess, raking a hand through her lank, two-tone hair. 'You're not my mother – so will the two of you stop punishing me and just leave me alone? I don't need you to tell me how stupid, feckless and generally crap I am, and I definitely don't need you drivelling on about it every five minutes.' Her head hung slackly between her skinny shoulders as she repeated in a sad whisper, 'You're not my mother.'

Her heart aching in sympathy, Holly laid a hand on her sister's shoulder. 'I'm so sorry, sis. I miss Mum too; I think about her every day. If I wasn't certain that she was still with us, I think I'd have gone crazy by now.'

She looked across the round pine table at her other sister, willing her to say something supportive. But Grace was staring back at her with an expression verging on cynicism. Oh God, Grace still doesn't believe me, thought Holly, heart in mouth. Because I'm trying to trace my roots, she doesn't think I miss Mum at all. The thought slapped her in the face, almost made her want to cry, but anger took over before the tears reached her eyes. She knew it would be better not to say anything, but she couldn't stop herself blurting out defiantly: 'She was my mum too, you know! She was just as much my mum as she was yours, and I'll never, ever forget her.'

101

'I never said—' began Grace, instantly on the defensive.

'You didn't need to,' replied Holly.

An uncomfortable moment passed, measured out by the ticking of the mantel clock Harry's grandfather had been given to mark fifty years counting invoices at the brickworks. Holly's heart was racing so fast that she could hardly breathe. Why did I start this? she agonised.

It was Jess who pointed out the ludicrousness of the situation. 'Why the hell are we arguing?' she asked. 'We all miss her – it's not a competition, you know.'

Grace let out a long breath. 'I'm sorry. It's just—'

Holly finished the sentence for her: 'It would have been her birthday next week. I think we're all a bit on edge.'

The air at least partially cleared, Holly dragged out a dusty bottle of cooking brandy from the cupboard under the sink, and they drank a toast to celebrate Maureen's birthday.

'Isn't it your Murdo's birthday next month?' enquired Jess. 'What are you buying him?'

Holly laughed. 'A bottle of nit shampoo, seeing as he likes it so much.'

'He certainly invents some wacky excuses to come up and see you,' observed Grace. 'Is he really driving up to Cheltenham to brief you about head lice?'

''Fraid so. The great Mr Bynt has decided I'm the perfect girl for the job. Do you think I should be flattered or offended?'

'Well, he obviously likes you,' replied Grace. 'I reckon he's planning to promote you both when you get married.'

'Me, marry Mr Bynt? Dream on.'

'You and Murdo, stupid!'

Holly shrugged. 'Who says we're getting married? He hasn't asked me.'

Jess waded in: 'So encourage him!'

'I'm sure he's only waiting for you to give him a sign,' agreed Grace. 'Drop a few heavy hints, and he'll be on one knee faster than you can say, "confetti."'

Maybe that's what I'm afraid of, thought Holly. She was about to say something non-committal when there was an enormous crash from the hallway, followed by a strangled: 'Ow – bloody hell!'

Holly was on her feet in seconds. 'Dad?'

By the time the three sisters reached him, Harry and his precious cargo were sprawled across the bottom of the stairs, amid the ruins of the Queen Anne-style telephone table.

'Dad, are you OK?' Grace asked, deftly checking him over for signs of broken bones.

'I'm fine.' He winced – but manfully – as he pulled a long splinter out of the seat of his overalls. 'I tripped over the telephone wire, and this ruddy orang-utan weighs a ton.'

Somebody had to ask the obvious question. 'Dad,' said Holly slowly, 'what are you doing with a stuffed orang-utan? And why has it only got one leg?'

'It's OK,' Harry assured her, getting gingerly to his feet. 'The other one's in the van. Good, isn't it? The Bristol Old Vic lent it to me for nothing as long as I promised to renovate it for them.'

'I bet they did!' Holly prodded its mangy ginger fur. It was a very ex-orang-utan. And whatever it was stuffed with seemed to have shifted somewhat, making it bulge in some places and sag in others. 'But what's it for?'

Grace's face lit up. 'I know, it's for *Tarzan and Jane – the Musical*, isn't it? Dad, you're a genius! It'll look fantastic on stage. Oh, by the way,' she added, 'I've got some great news. Remember I told you I had to audition for the part of Jane?' Her sisters nodded.

'I thought you didn't get it,' said Holly, well remembering the sobs over the phone.

'I didn't. But the first-choice girl caught glandular fever, so I got it instead! Isn't that great?'

'Not for the girl with glandular fever,' commented Jess. Harry was too busy examining his prized orang-utan to notice. Jess looked at her sister quizzically. 'Just let me get this straight – you're actually going to be singing? In front of people?'

'Of course I am.' Grace didn't get it.

'Er, Grace . . .' began Holly, not quite sure how to put it tactfully.

Jess solved the problem for her. 'Don't be daft. You can't sing! You can't carry a tune in a bloody bucket, you said so yourself. Is the musical director deaf, or are you sleeping with him, or what?'

'Jess! How can you even think . . . !' Grace looked absolutely mortified. She took a calming breath. 'Yes, I agree, my voice may not be quite up to it at the moment, but Claudio says—'

'Who's Claudio?' asked Holly.

'My vocal coach. He's convinced I'll be wonderful by the time we put the show on.'

'He must fancy you,' concluded Jess.

'I very much doubt it,' retorted Grace. 'He has a live-in boyfriend called Antoine. Anyhow, we're working on my bottom at the moment,' she confided. 'It's a little bit wobbly.'

'Your bottom?' Holly tried so hard not to laugh that the tears were running down her cheeks.

'That's right, my bottom notes,' Grace went on brightly, completely oblivious to the hilarity she had generated. 'And you'll all be able to check me out on the night. I've put you down for two pairs of tickets each. And that includes you, Daddy.'

'Two!' exclaimed Harry, aghast.

'Yes, Daddy.' Grace smiled sweetly. 'After all, it is for charity.'

Eight

Holly straightened her bedroom curtains, fighting the urge to look out at the Bentley in case its wheels had been nicked. Whenever Murdo came up to Cheltenham for the weekend and insisted on parking outside the Bennett family's humble semi, she joked that this time he'd end up going back to London on the bus. But Murdo – and his car – seemed to enjoy a charmed life. Well, up to now, anyway.

A dark, well-groomed head appeared round the door. 'Is madam ready?'

'Madam is.'

'Then let's go. You look lovely, by the way,' Murdo added as his long legs made short work of the Bennetts' stairs. 'Green suits you; it brings out the red in your hair. Very Celtic.'

'But I'm not—', she began, then broke off, wondering if being Manx counted as being Celtic. She had an inkling that it did, what with the tartan and all that. She'd have to go online and check. 'Thanks,' she said instead. 'You look great too – that Armani suit was a really good buy.'

'Ah well, that's all down to you,' Murdo said over his shoulder as they walked out to the car. 'What would I do without my own personal fashion advisor?'

Murdo programmed the satnav and they set off. They were

driving out to Berkeley Castle that evening, for a traverse production of Marlowe's *Edward II* in the great hall – a highly appropriate choice of play, since Edward II had actually met a grisly end in that very castle. Appropriate for the castle, perhaps, but not for Holly, whose media studies degree had always felt woefully inadequate beside Murdo's Cambridge double first. She'd much rather have gone to see the new Batman film, which was playing tonight at the Brewery multiplex in Cheltenham, or even the cute new animation about talking dinosaurs, but – even after three years of going out with Murdo – she'd rather have died than admit it.

It wasn't that Murdo was a culture snob; just that he genuinely didn't understand people who preferred *Midsomer Murders* and a box of Maltesers to a seminar on Ibsen. And his enthusiasm did sometimes win Holly over. If it wasn't for Murdo, she'd never have discovered Richard Strauss, Jack Kerouac, the Pre-Raphaelites or (perhaps more surprisingly) some of the more obscure Icelandic death-metal bands. She owed Murdo a lot.

But she still couldn't stand Marlowe. Maybe it was in her genes.

'Well, it's official: I've hired Phil Connell to help me try to find my birth mother,' she announced, shading her eyes as they drove along the edge of the Severn estuary and the setting sun illuminated the flocks of birds wading on the muddy banks. 'Just fancy. Me, hiring a real-life private investigator ...'

'I knew you'd go through with it,' said Murdo with a nod. 'You're the kind of person who has to know all the answers. No wonder you can always guess the murderer in those crime novels of yours.' The indulgent way he said 'crime novels' made them sound like something a six-year-old might read under the bedcovers. 'For what it's worth, I think you're doing the right thing.'

She turned to look at him. 'You do?'

'I've never told you this before, darling, because it's something of a family skeleton, but my grandmother on my mother's side was born illegitimate.'

Holly's jaw hit the deck. 'The Welsh one with the posh accent? She never was!'

'Oh yes. Her mother was the live-in maid for a barrister and his wife, and the eldest son got a little too friendly. My gran was the result. The barrister gave her mother a few quid and threw her and the baby out. Well, Gran grew up and married well and had a happy life, as you know, but it always haunted her that she never met her father – even if all she'd have ended up doing was punching his lights out.'

'I can imagine.' Holly gazed out at the river waters, tinged pink and orange by the setting sun. 'But, personally, I've no interest in finding my genetic father.'

'It takes two to make a life,' pointed out Murdo, echoing what Nesta had said.

'Maybe so. But a man who treats a woman so badly that she feels driven to give her child away isn't worth knowing. Not in my book anyway.' She sat back in her seat, tension making a slight headache throb in her temples.

'So what's driving you?' asked Murdo.

'Sorry?'

'What's driving you to want to find your mother? Why now?'

A stupid surge of panic gripped Holly. Do I tell him? she asked herself. Do I tell him how much I want to have a baby, and that that's why I want to find out who I am? What if it gives him ideas and he starts putting pressure on me? I know we can't go on like this forever, neither one thing nor the other, she thought, but I'm terrified to take the next step. Then again, perhaps he is too.

'It was Mum dying,' she answered. That was at least partly true. 'I'm not trying to find a replacement for her,' she added hastily.

'Nothing could ever replace Mum; she was my anchor and my inspiration.'

Murdo reached out and squeezed her hand. 'I know she was. She was a very special woman. I could see that, and I only knew her a short while.'

'The thing is . . .' Holly began. Her heart thumped a little faster as she took the plunge. 'I'm not getting any younger, and one day – you know, in years to come or whatever – I might want a family of my own. And when I do, it would be nice to know exactly where I came from, who I am. In fact I . . . I don't think I can move on much further with my life until I've at least tried to find out.'

For a few moments Murdo said nothing. Then he signalled left, and brought the car to an abrupt halt by the roadside. 'You weren't that bothered about the Marlowe, were you? Only I think we need to talk.'

Holly gaped at him like a stranded haddock. This wasn't like Murdo at all. He never did anything on the spur of the moment. 'Talk?' she echoed, terrified of what he was going to say next.

'I want to help,' he explained. 'Private investigators don't come cheap, and I know you don't have a stack of dosh at the moment, so why don't you let me pay?'

Of course. It was the obvious solution, staring Holly square in the face – so how come it had never occurred to her? It was a seductively attractive solution, too: one that would enable her to help Jess and Kev without having to sell Mavis, her beloved Mazda. All she had to do was say yes to Murdo, and everything would be made easy for her – just as things could be made easy for her at Payne, Rackstraw and Bynt if she'd only see sense, move back to London and let Murdo work his wondrous charm on Mr Bynt.

'It's really sweet of you to offer, darling—' Holly began.

Murdo cut in before she had a chance to say anything more. 'But you're turning me down flat? Well, there's a surprise.' He turned his face away from her.

'Please, Murdo, don't take it like that.' She touched his cheek. 'Look at me. Please.' Reluctantly, he turned back to face her. 'You know how I feel about being independent, about taking care of myself.'

'And you know how much I want to take care of you. Is that so much to ask?'

'But you can. You do, in dozens of different ways. This is just one thing I want to do for myself, my way.'

Murdo sighed. A couple of cars droned past on the road. 'It seems to me you do pretty much everything your way,' he observed tartly. 'Are you ever going to settle down and be … I don't know … normal?'

'I don't know,' admitted Holly as the word 'normal' resounded horribly inside her skull. She thought of the appalling Leonie, back in the London office, with her fake smiles and her designer handbags. 'Is that how you really want me to be?'

'No, damn you!' Then the twinkle came back into his dark, espresso-brown eyes. 'I want you to be exactly the way you are – sexy, gorgeous and irritating as hell; but if you could just make a wee bit of room for me in your crazy world now and again …'

'There's always room for you in my world,' she heard herself say.

They kissed, and she rested her head on Murdo's chest as he stroked her hair. It felt good. 'I was thinking,' he said softly, 'that maybe your world and my world could get together. Could you bear to come back to London and be crazy there instead? Could you bear to move in with me?'

'It was a real shock,' admitted Holly as she and Nesta wheeled their Post Office-issue bikes out of the sheds behind the sorting office and into the morning drizzle. 'I had no idea Murdo was going to ask me to move in with him.'

'Oh, come on, it was bound to happen sooner or later,' Nesta pointed out. 'I mean, God knows I'm no expert on relationships but even I know that if a guy and a girl have been going out for three years it's pretty bloody serious. Either that or ...'

'Or what?'

'The relationship's on its last legs, but neither of them can summon the energy to split up.'

'Gee thanks!' Holly felt Nesta's eyes burning into the side of her face. 'So what are you now, some kind of pop psychologist or something?'

'No, just someone with a lot of time on her hands to think.' Nesta moved her gaze away from Holly, and it was as if someone had turned off a blowtorch. 'Anyway, for the past couple of years Murdo's done a hell of a lot of driving up and down the A40 just to see you, and he must be getting pretty tired of it.'

'I guess he must.' Thanks again, Nesta, thought Holly. Now I feel really guilty as well as confused.

'So maybe now he thinks it's your turn to come to him – and move the relationship on to the next level.'

'That's almost exactly what Murdo said.' Holly pulled up her fluorescent hood against the rain. 'Have you been listening at keyholes again?'

Nesta laughed, but not unkindly. 'So – what are you going to do? Hand in your notice and move in with him? You'd be crazy not to.'

'I know.'

But then again I am crazy, thought Holly; Murdo told me so. In her head, she totted up all the plus points Grace was bound to raise in favour of Murdo and his plan: loads of money, lovely apartment, excellent prospects, tolerably good-looking if you liked that sort of thing, fond of children and kind to old ladies ... The list was endless. And the only point that Holly could raise in opposition was that 'somehow it doesn't feel quite right'. Was that any kind of valid reason for not seizing the future with both hands – a future which, in any case, everybody else seemed to have mapped out for her already?

The two bicycles reached the edge of the kerb, and nudged their front wheels into the trickle of early-morning commuter traffic. By now, the drizzle had turned into a steady downpour.

'Just for the record, are you in love with Murdo?' asked Nesta as she swung her leg over the crossbar of a bike built for someone twice her size.

Holly squirmed like a moth on a bug-collector's pin, deeply uncomfortable with her friend's unexpected interrogation. 'I ... sort of ...' She swallowed hard, and then said quietly: 'No.'

'You're sure about that?'

'No,' she admitted haplessly. 'I'm not sure at all. One day I'm sure I love him, the next ...'

'You're hopeless. Right, how do you feel if you imagine him having sex with someone else?'

'I don't know ...' She tried to picture Leonie spreadeagled on silk sheets with Murdo on top of her. 'Jealous.'

'Aha! Then perhaps you are in love with him.'

'Look, you're not being any help at all.' Holly glanced over her shoulder and was mortified to see that Julian and Welsh Dave were behind them, listening in with great interest. 'Oh God, can't we talk about this somewhere a bit less ... public?'

Holly prepared to leave, but Nesta blocked her path onto the road. 'Just answer the question – it's for your own good. Are you in love with Murdo?'

All at once the truth welled up inside Holly: warm, and just a little sad. 'I love Murdo very much, and I can't imagine life without him,' she said slowly, 'but I don't think I'm in love with him. I really don't.'

111

'Well, there's your answer then,' declared Nesta, and pedalled off furiously into the driving rain.

After she finished her round, and before her afternoon stint at Bloodhound Investigations, Holly had promised to keep an eye on Adam while Grace had her hair done.

Grace might have joined the affluent set, but she still had an eye for a bargain – and one of those bargains was a middle-aged mobile hairdresser called Diane, who had worked in the best salon in town until she left to have a family. Every six weeks she visited to spruce up Grace's colour and give her a trim. It was a perfect arrangement, and a great opportunity, as Grace said, for Holly to come round and 'spend some quality time with her nephew'.

What this actually meant was that Holly got to do some unpaid babysitting, while Grace didn't have to worry about Adam sticking heated rollers up his nose or trying to drink the peroxide. Holly didn't mind being taken advantage of. She loved it. What could be more fun than to step into Grace's luxurious bedroom and be greeted by one of Adam's slobbery kisses, or by excited cries of 'Owwy! Owwy!' – which was Adam's best attempt so far at his auntie's name?

However, keeping Adam and the hairdressing equipment apart was not as easy as it sounded.

'Oh no you don't – come here, young man!' Laughing, Holly lunged after Adam. Yet again he was half crawling, half toddling towards Diane's fascinating bag of tricks. 'Look, plastic moo-cow!' She seized it from his toy box in desperation. 'It's much more interesting than electrocuting yourself on those straighteners.'

Adam was unimpressed, and grizzled as Holly scooped him up in her arms, inches from his target. Diane and Grace fell about laughing.

'Never mind, it's all good practice for when you've got kids of your own,' declared Grace. Then: 'What am I saying? Murdo's family are loaded. You'll have a different nanny for each day of the week, and all you'll have to do is lie on the bed eating chocolates all day and getting disgustingly fat.'

'I hope not!' replied Holly wholeheartedly. She hadn't mentioned what Murdo had suggested, and she didn't intend to if she could possibly avoid it. If Grace got a sniff of Holly and Murdo moving in together, she'd have organised the entire wedding (plus reception for two hundred and fifty and an evening disco with nibbles) by teatime. 'When I have kids, I want to look after them myself.'

Diane chuckled. 'Listen, love, everybody says that before they get married,' she said. 'But believe me, once you've actually got them you'd kill to have somebody else take the little buggers off your hands for an hour or two, isn't that true, Grace?'

'You're so right. Personally, I don't know what I'd do without my day nursery,' agreed Grace. 'Adam gets quality pre-school care, and I have a chance to develop my career. I'm determined to nail a sister's post before I'm thirty.'

'You've changed a lot,' remarked Holly, now sitting cross-legged on the lush bedroom carpet with Adam on her lap. 'When you qualified, you used to say all you wanted to do was nurse sick kids and you couldn't care less about promotion.'

Grace looked down at her nicely manicured fingernails. 'Yes, well, things change, don't they? As I recall, you used to say all you wanted to do was be a big-shot advertising executive in London. And look at you now.'

Touché, thought Holly.

Diane snipped away, humming James Blunt songs to herself and chatting with Grace about holidays, celebrity diets and children. Holly played with Adam, delighting to be sharing his childish curiosity in the world around him; a world in which everything was new and exciting and there were no barriers or difficult choices to be made. A world where love was love, and that was all there was to it.

She glanced at the clock radio on Steve's side of the bed. 'I'll have to go in half an hour,' she said. 'I promised I'd do an hour at the agency before I go to the poetry slam with Nesta.'

Diane lifted her head from her work. 'Agency? Temping, is it?'

Grace laughed. 'Not exactly. Private investigation. The agency's supposed to be helping Holly find her birth mother, but if you ask me there's something not quite right about it. I told her to get three quotes, didn't I, Hol?' She peered out at her sister through her soon-to-be-trimmed fringe. 'And my idiot sister here has sold her soul to the guy who runs it, sorting out their paperwork in exchange for a cut-price deal.'

'That's a bit ... unusual, isn't it?' ventured Diane.

Grace snorted. 'Shady is what I call it.'

'Oh you do, do you?' Holly could have strangled her sister. 'Well, what I call it is kind and helpful. If it wasn't for Phil, I'd never be able to afford to use the agency at all. Any agency.'

'Oh, Phil, is it now? It was Mr Connell last week,' commented Grace, now in full sister-tormenting mode. She cocked her head on one side and almost had her ear sliced off. 'I think she fancies him,' she confided to Diane.

'Could be,' giggled the hairdresser. Adam caught the general hilarity of the moment, and giggled along too. 'Look, she's blushing!'

Holly cursed her lifelong ability to turn beetroot red at the drop of a hat. 'Oh shut up. Anybody'd think you were a pair of five-year-olds! Wouldn't they, Adam?'

Diane was now showing Grace the back of her hair in a mirror. 'What I want to know – oh yes, that's lovely, very nice caramel highlights – what I want to know is, if this bloke is such a hot-shot investigator, how come he left the police? And what about this mysterious partner who's never there and never even phones in? Just a touch of hairspray please, not too much, that's gorgeous, thanks. Well, Hol, what's the answer? You're supposed to fancy yourself as a detective – not fancy the detective.'

Holly got to her feet and hauled the happily gurgling Adam onto her hip. 'The answer is you're too suspicious by half. And I'm off to put the kettle on.'

But in the silence of her thoughts, Holly couldn't help conceding that her sister had a point.

'I never thought for a minute you'd be interested,' said Holly, stepping aside so that Phil could lock the agency's outer door. 'Nesta's poetry slams are, well, an acquired taste.'

'How can I acquire a taste if I don't try it?' was Phil's reasoned response. 'I'm game, just as long as I don't have to wear frilly shirts and velvet trousers. My cousin Emily's first boyfriend thought he was a poet,' he added. 'He used to mope around looking like Lord Byron crossed with a transvestite.'

There wasn't much danger of Phil taking after Emily's ex, mused Holly. In his line of work, the last thing you needed on covert surveillance jobs was a taste for flashy attire, and it was pretty obvious that Phil dressed for invisibility. He couldn't have been more different from Murdo and his wardrobe full of designer suits. But even Phil's unironed beige shirts couldn't detract from his cuteness, or dim the bright-eyed, boyish smile that turned Holly's legs to jelly. He could have worn dungarees and wellingtons and she would still have fancied him like mad.

They chatted and laughed as they walked through the streets of Cheltenham to the Happy Rambler pub, where every Tuesday the function room upstairs was given over to a fast and furious knockout poetry competition. Entrants performed their own poems, and marks were awarded for content, presentation and audience response.

'Sounds like a nice relaxing way to spend an evening,' commented Phil as they neared the pub.

'I, er, don't think Nesta would agree with you!' laughed Holly. 'She's been trying to win this damn thing for months, but the best she's ever come is second. It's driving her nuts.' She pushed open the door of the public bar. 'After you, and watch your wallet.'

Phil and Holly had to squeeze themselves through an almost solid wall of people to get anywhere near the bar. 'Blimey, is it always this crowded?' asked Phil as he paid for the drinks.

'You should see it on finals nights; it's much worse than this. Oh look – there's Nesta.'

The Happy Rambler was possibly the ugliest – and smallest – pub Holly had ever been in. It had begun life as the back room of a Victorian abattoir, graduated to a butcher's shop and finally been converted to licensed premises in the early part of the twentieth century. Some said that on foggy autumn nights, the snug was haunted by the ghost of a headless slaughterman who'd perished in a horrible accident. Others said that this was a tale invented by the previous landlord to boost takings and lure in credulous ghost hunters and historians. Either way, some of the dirt ingrained in the bare wooden floorboards was definitely Victorian, if not prehistoric.

Nesta was much too nervous to be bothered about ghosts. 'If it wasn't for him, I'm sure I could win this,' she told Holly and Phil, darting glances across the bar at a man in a floppy felt hat and gaiters.

'Who's he?' asked Phil.

'His stage name's Weasel,' explained Holly. 'He does stuff in broad Gloucestershire dialect – the audience love him.'

'Yeah,' said Nesta. 'I don't know why I bother really. He's won it before we start.'

'Your stuff's local too,' Holly reminded her.

116

'We're all local. But his is funny.'

'And yours isn't?' enquired Phil.

'Mine's downright miserable, actually.'

'You can do funny,' insisted Holly. 'You do funny verses all the time. So why don't you—?'

'Yes, I write funny verses all the time for birthday cards – and I'm bloody sick of it! I want to do my real poetry now. If I want to perform a poem about a dead partridge, I will.'

Holly and Phil gave each other a look that said 'doomed'.

'Oh look,' said Holly. 'Weasel's coming over to say hello.'

Nesta scowled. 'Well, Weasel can kiss my—'

'It's you,' a voice barked above the general pre-slam chatter. 'It is you, you bastard.'

Phil took a step back. 'I'm sorry, do I know you?'

'Oh you know me all right. And you knew my brother too. Remember Brian Derrington, do you? Or has he slipped your mind?'

The broad brim of Weasel's felt hat had shaded his face up to now, but now he was only feet away from Phil, his features were clear enough to recognise. Phil paled, and murmured a quiet, 'Oh shit.'

'What's the matter?' demanded Holly.

Weasel took off his hat. 'Remember me now, Mr Connell? Last time you saw me was in that coroner's court. I've been hoping I might get to have a private word with you one day.'

Slowly he cracked his knuckles, one by one.

By now, the pub had fallen almost silent, as everyone's attention focused on Weasel and the young investigator, who somehow managed to stand his ground.

Phil turned to Holly and Nesta, his face paper white. 'I'm sorry, but I think you two should both leave. This might turn nasty.'

Holly looked from Phil to the tall man in the gaiters. 'Why? I don't understand. What's this all about? Why can't you come too?'

'There's something I have to sort out first,' replied Phil.

'Come on.' Nesta grabbed Holly by the arm and shoved her towards the door. A gap opened up in the wall of bodies to let them through.

As the bar door swung shut behind them, Holly had the feeling that something very bad was about to happen. Reaching into her bag for her mobile, she dialled 999.

Phil finally emerged from the accident and emergency department around midnight, nursing not much more than a black eye and a couple of broken bones in his right hand.

A police constable was waiting for him outside. 'Are you ready to make a statement now, sir?' he asked. 'And press charges?'

Phil thought for a moment, then shook his head. 'I fell down the stairs,' he said, then limped off into the night.

Holly was already waiting in the cafe the following morning when Phil walked in, painfully slowly. His left eye was swollen shut and looked like a purple egg, and as he took his jacket off Holly noticed bruises on his arms.

He followed her horrified gaze. 'Believe it or not I got off lightly, thanks to you calling the cops.' Grimacing, he lowered himself slowly onto his chair and ordered a black coffee. 'I guess you'll be expecting some kind of explanation.'

Holly dropped sugar lumps into her tea. 'I think it's time you did some talking, yes.' She stirred her tea, not taking her eyes off Phil's face. 'You could start by telling me what last night was all about.'

Phil rubbed his good eye wearily. 'That man – Weasel. His real name is John Derrington, and he had a brother called Brian. I killed Brian Derrington.'

'You killed him?' Holly's head couldn't quite take it in. Oh God, she thought, Grace is right, he *is* an axe murderer. 'But, why?'

'Because he was holding a woman hostage and threatening to kill her and her baby, and I happened to be a firearms expert at the time. It was a burglary that went wrong.' Phil drank half his coffee in a single gulp. 'He put a gun to the baby's head.'

'No!'

Phil looked down. 'I'll never forget the look of terror on that woman's face. Someone had to shoot him and it turned out to be me. I can't tell you how much I wish it had been someone else, and I don't mean that just because I got a good beating last night.'

There was a long silence. 'But at least ... he deserved it,' ventured Holly.

'That makes no difference. Take a life, and it haunts you forever.'

'Is that why you left the police?' asked Holly.

'More or less. There was an inquest and I was acquitted of all blame, but the Derringtons aren't the kind of family to forgive and forget. They tried to take out a civil case against me, and after a while I started believing what they were saying about me. It became impossible for me to do my job.'

'I can understand that,' said Holly. 'I can't imagine coping with that kind of stress.'

'In the end, it became impossible to function as a human being.' Phil was visibly struggling to get the words out. 'I ... I spent a couple of weeks on a psychiatric ward, trying to get rid of the depression.' He shrugged. 'The doctors tell you you're not weak, but that's all that goes round your head: the fact that you're a worse person because you've given in.'

'That's rubbish,' declared Holly. 'My aunt suffers from bipolar disorder, and she's one of the strongest people I know. And the way you stood up to Weasel last night – nobody could say that was weak.'

119

Holly could imagine what Grace would be saying if she were sitting in Holly's place: 'Killer! Lunatic! Mentally unstable! Don't touch him with a bargepole!' She smiled to herself.

'What's the joke?' asked Phil. 'I could do with a good laugh.'

'Oh, I was just thinking about my sister: Grace, the middle one. When Auntie Jane went into hospital the first time, Grace told everybody that she was having her tonsils out.'

'Yeah,' sighed Phil. 'Actually, that's kind of how I feel about it myself. I generally keep it to myself; in fact I can't quite think why I've just told you about it. Now you'll probably go off and find yourself a private investigator who's still got all his marbles intact.'

'Oh, I think your marbles are just fine.'

They sat and looked at each other. It was just for a few seconds, but to Holly it felt as though some kind of primal energy was being exchanged between them; as if there was something very strong and very basic that they both shared; as if they had been friends for ever.

A question had been burning on Holly's lips for a long, long time. 'So when did you hook up with Sita?' she asked, trying to sound as if the question was casual, disinterested.

'After I'd been working as a freelance investigator for a while – not very successfully, I might add. As you may have noticed, I'm not very good with the administrative side of the business.'

'Oh, I've seen worse,' Holly lied.

'Anyway, when I met her at a PIs' convention I was knocked right off my feet – she was like nobody I'd ever met before: this dynamic, beautiful, incredibly intelligent woman who, by some miracle, seemed to like me too. We moved in together within a month, and a few weeks later we formed Bloodhound Investigations as a partnership.'

There was a faraway look in Phil's eyes, and Holly guessed that it was Sita he saw, Sita who was filling his thoughts. And a deep ache seemed to crush Holly's heart as an iron fist of jealousy squeezed all the life out of it. Hands off, said a stern voice in her head. Don't even think about him; he belongs to Sita and the chances are he always will.

'So Sita's the organisational genius then?' Holly did her best to sound bright and breezy. 'When's she coming back?'

There was an infinitesimal pause before Phil answered: 'Never.'

Something between a thrill and a chill ran on tiptoe down Holly's spine. 'Never? How do you mean?'

'Never, as in never.' Phil threw down the last of his coffee and ordered another double espresso. 'Last November she walked out on me at five minutes' notice, for someone with more money and better pecs.'

Holly tried to ignore the fact that her heart was beating faster. 'Oh my God, I'm so sorry,' she said, trying to be genuinely sorry, forcing herself not to be glad but failing miserably. 'So where is she now?'

'Japan.' Phil's mouth distorted into a sneer as he said the word. 'Over there, they have agencies where you pay for someone to seduce your husband or your wife so you can get a divorce. Apparently there's plenty of work out there and the money's great if you're good at it. And believe me, she's good at it.' There was an infinity of pain on his face, and Holly sensed that he was far away now, unreachable. 'She sure as hell seduced me.'

The following day was Holly's day off, and she'd planned to get the bus over to Oxford and meet up with an old school friend.

When the doorbell rang at seven-thirty in the morning, she thought it must be the mail, and smiled to herself at the thought that some other poor bastard was having to trudge through the rain at this unholy hour.

She certainly didn't expect to open the door and find her sister on the doorstep, shivering with cold and with tears pouring down her cheeks.

'Jess! What on earth has happened? Come inside and tell me all about it.'

From halfway down the stairs, with his electric shaver in his hand, Harry asked: 'Who is it?'

'It's Jess, Dad. She looks really upset.' Holly turned back to her sister and slid an arm around her shoulders. 'Hey, don't cry.' She rummaged in her dressing gown pocket and pulled out a crumpled tissue. 'Blow. Now, what's happened?'

'I-it's me and Kev,' gasped Jess between sobs. 'I've told him I want a divorce.'

Nine

In Phil Connell's world, Saturdays had always been dedicated to football – first as a muddy child and now as a muddy adult. Over the years he had not got any better at the game; his crosses were still not so much deadly accurate as just deadly: he had once knocked a spectator's false teeth out with a misjudged shot across goal and would probably never live it down. But when it came to sheer dedication, nobody could match him. Even on a freezing Saturday in January, when even polar bears would think twice about running around in shorts and a T-shirt, you would find Phil doing warm-up exercises on the touchline half an hour before everyone else. With April almost over, and the football season with it, he looked forward to a summer of cricket and croquet with utter gloom.

Football wasn't just a hobby with Phil; it was a religion.

For Father Michael McGee, on the other hand, religion was a profession. Father Michael, who wore the number nine shirt for St Olaf's, had been a member of Bath Road Academicals for a couple of years now, ever since he'd got drunk and confessed to Phil that he'd once played centre forward for his seminary. He and Phil went back a long way, to the days when Father Michael had first arrived in Cheltenham, and even though the private investigator was a lapsed agnostic who hadn't seen the inside of a church for twenty years, whenever he had troubles it was always Father Michael he told them to. Lately, he'd done plenty of listening.

They were taking off their boots in the toilet block that served as a changing room when Phil asked: 'Mike, can I ask you a question?'

The burly giant of a priest banged his boots against the wall to dislodge the clods of earth. 'If it's metaphysical, can it wait until we're down the pub?'

'It's not metaphysical – and this time it's not about Sita, either,' he added, before Michael could get the question out. He fished in his pocket. 'Have you ever seen one of these before?'

The priest stood back to let a couple of the other players get past. 'Bye, Lee, bye, Steve. Buy you both a drink later.' He watched Phil unwrap the small tissue-paper packet with interest – an interest that wilted when he saw what it contained. 'Of course I've seen one before – I've seen hundreds of the things.' He looked at Phil quizzically. 'But why have you got one? You're no Catholic, and you're certainly not a girl!'

Somebody laughed and made a rude comment. Phil threw a sponge at his head.

'What is it then?' he asked.

'It's a confirmation necklace. Lots of proud parents give them to their daughters when they're confirmed as members of the Church.'

'Ah, confirmation.' Phil nodded. 'I thought it might be First Communion, only the dates didn't fit.'

Father Michael scratched his chin. 'This would be something to do with a case, I take it?'

'It would. I'm helping someone try to track down the mother who abandoned her as a baby.'

'Really. And does this person want to be "tracked down"?' the priest wondered.

'How could I possibly know that?' demanded Phil.

'Exactly.'

*

She's so brave, thought Holly as she watched Jess rocking Aimee to sleep in her arms. If it was me, could I be brave too?

They were sitting on the sticky sofa in Jess's poky living room, framed by clothes racks festooned with damp washing.

'So what exactly happened?' asked Holly gently.

'We were getting on better, so we decided to go out for a meal last night and afterwards Kev came back here to stay the night. But when it came to it ... I ... I just couldn't have sex with him, Hol. Not with the man who wanted to kill our baby. Who still wants to.' Jess dabbed at her red nose. 'And then we had a terrible row, and I said a lot of things I'd been wanting to say for a long time, and he said I was punishing him when he hadn't done anything wrong. How could he say that, Hol? How could he say he hasn't done anything wrong?'

Holly carefully avoided apportioning blame, sensing that it would only make things worse in the end. 'And that's when you told him you wanted a divorce?' she asked.

Jess nodded. 'This morning. And that's the only thing I got right,' she declared. 'The way I feel today, it's all over between us, end of story. I'm sorry, I shouldn't have come running round to the house like that. It was stupid and childish.'

'Don't worry about it,' said Holly, giving her sister a hug. 'You did exactly the right thing. We're sisters, remember? We take care of each other.'

Aimee was fast asleep by now, and Jess got up and tiptoed across the room to lay her down in her cot. 'I know it's not healthy, her sleeping with all this damp washing around her,' she lamented. 'And look at the mould growing on the wall over there. This place is a hole.' She sighed. 'I guess things aren't going to get any easier without Kev around, but it's not as if he ever brought in any money, is it? Loser,' she declared bitterly.

Jess was certainly right about the flat. The whole place was

125

damp, and it was no place to bring up a little one. No place for Jess either, come to that; Holly looked at her painfully thin, almost diaphanous frame and knew that – however brave a face she might put on it – her sister was suffering too. I shouldn't have closed my eyes and let things get to this stage, thought Holly with a sharp stab of guilt.

'Maybe this will help.' Holly unzipped her handbag and took out the roll of banknotes she'd withdrawn from the bank a few days before and then dithered about handing over. 'It's not all of the money. I thought I should put some into a trust fund for Aimee; I hope you don't mind. But it should be enough to get you into a decent flat and pay your rent for a good long time to come.'

She held it out, but Jess just stared at it.

'What's wrong?' asked Holly, panic-stricken. 'What did I do?'

A single tear trickled down Jess's face. 'Nothing. I'm just think-ing about Mum,' she said, sniffing back the tears. 'Me and Kev wasted all that money she left me. If I'd just had the sense to see what was coming ...'

'It's OK to miss her, you know.' Holly lay the money down on the coffee table and sat down beside her sister. 'I miss her all the time. And God knows, I've made enough mistakes to fill an ency-clopaedia. Why don't you think of this as ... as another chance to get it right? A new beginning – for Aimee's sake.'

'I've never seen this much money all in one place.' Jess reached out and ran a finger wonderingly over a fifty-pound note. 'Why are you doing this?' she demanded. 'You could have used this money to look for your birth mother, and kept your car as well. You loved that car.'

'Yeah.' Holly smiled. 'But I love you more.'

Holly and Phil were sitting drinking huge mugs of tea in the Bloodhound Investigations office, which was starting to look marginally less as if a bomb had hit it, although the litter tray under the desk and the furry cat igloo possibly detracted a little from the air of all-round professionalism. As for Dweezil, he seemed happy to have found a new lap to sit on and a new pair of black trousers to cover with white fluff.

The silver necklace lay spread out on the desk.

'So now we know how old my mother was when she abandoned me?' Holly turned over the necklace and looked at the engraved date.

'More or less. Apparently she would have been around fourteen when she was confirmed, so that would make her sixteen or seventeen when she left you at the hospital.'

'Lots of kids are having babies at sixteen nowadays,' commented Holly. 'Nobody bats an eyelid. But it can't have been like that thirty years ago. It must have been hard for her.' She thought of Jess and Kev. 'And if she didn't have any support from the father ...'

'You sound almost as if you're trying to convince yourself of something,' remarked Phil.

'I think I probably am. No matter how I look at it, I can't imagine him as anything but a bastard.' Holly pushed the necklace away. 'Well, at least we've made one small step towards finding my mother.'

'Are you still absolutely sure you want to?' asked Phil.

Holly looked at him in surprise. 'Why wouldn't I be?'

'Sometimes these things seem like a good idea to start off with, and then ... well, circumstances can change,' he finished lamely. 'Occasionally, clients can find people and then wish they hadn't.'

'You've experienced that then, have you?'

'Not personally, no,' he admitted. 'But I've known it happen.'

'You sound just like Nesta.' Holly looked him straight in the eye.

127

'Are you having second thoughts about this case, Phil, because if you are—'

'No!' His smoky green eyes gazed deep into hers with heartfelt sincerity. 'If I'm sure about one thing, this is it.'

For just a few moments, Holly was convinced that she was seeing straight into Phil Connell's heart; then the feeling was gone and he looked away. Oh dear, a Mills and Boon moment, thought Holly. I was just seeing what I wanted to see, nothing more. Most likely he only tolerates me because I'm his temporary meal ticket. The thought saddened her.

Or maybe I was right and he likes me as much as I like him, she countered, her pulse quickening. In which case there's a very big potential problem, and I should really be spending as little time as possible in his company.

But that's just paranoia, she told herself. There's nothing here but a budding friendship, and where's the harm in that?

'So what happens next?' she asked.

'I'll have a word with my old colleagues back at the police station, see if I can dig anything up,' Phil replied. 'But in all honesty I think the next step is for me to go the Isle of Man. It's pretty clear that's where the trail is leading.'

Holly prickled with instant annoyance. 'What do you mean, *you're* going? If anybody's going to the Isle of Man, I'm coming too!'

Phil looked flummoxed. 'But I'm the trained private investigator,' he reasoned. 'It makes sense for me to go over there on my own, and get the job done as quickly as possible, so that I can save you money.'

'But I can help you,' countered Holly. 'And it is my mother we're looking for.'

Phil protested, but she could tell that his resistance was weakening. 'If we're going to keep costs down, I'll have to rough it at my grandma's cottage,' he warned her. 'There won't be any luxury hotels.'

128

'Good. I can stay there too. If your grandma doesn't mind,' she added as an afterthought.

'Well, I'm sure she wouldn't mind,' admitted Phil, 'but the house is incredibly tiny.'

'Does it have a floor?' enquired Holly.

'Er, yes ...'

'Then we're sorted. I'll bring a sleeping bag.'

It wasn't until she got home that night that Holly realised the full compass of what she'd done. She had just agreed to travel all the way to somewhere she'd barely heard of and certainly couldn't locate on a map, with someone who, while he might score ten on the cute-o-meter, was basically a total stranger.

I could still get out of it, she told herself as she stood in front of the bathroom mirror, trying to decide if she was getting a zit on her nose. I could still get out of it easily if I wanted to. All I'd have to say is 'Sorry, I've changed my mind,' or 'Bad news, I can't get the time off work.' Yes, she thought, that would do it, but I'd have to do it soon because otherwise Phil will have made all the arrangements and I'll have paid for the travel tickets and ... and, oh God, suddenly I feel terrified. Everything's spiralling out of control and it's all my fault!

Yet there was nothing to be afraid of really, was there? It wasn't as if there was anything between her and Phil. He was still hung up on this Sita woman, and she was practically Mrs Murdo, at least in the eyes of everybody else. This was a purely business trip, and she was sure that Murdo would see it that way too.

Once she'd plucked up the courage to tell him.

Ten

It was a Friday morning in early May, unusually warm and bright – the kind of day that brings out T-shirts, bare legs and early butterflies. The tall, dark-haired young man attracted the odd glance as he parked his gleaming Bentley across the street from Bloodhound Investigations.

'He's obviously not from round here,' commented the owner of the pawnbroker's on the corner. 'Do you think we should tell him?'

'Nah.' His assistant went back to polishing a tray of second-hand wedding rings. 'Live and learn, that's what I say.'

Holly's days off might vary from one week to the next, but whatever the day, you'd probably find her spending most of it in Phil's office. Most of the major sorting out had been done, but there were still little jobs that provided valid excuses for being there. It was odd really. On the one hand she was still dreading the upcoming trip; on the other, she was so excited that she couldn't stop talking about it. And the only person she hadn't bored to death yet was Phil.

Holly was sitting at Sita's old desk, idly jotting down ideas for a Bloodhound Investigations advertising campaign that would probably never see the light of day. Phil was typing at top speed, two-finger style, trying to finish off a report for one of his clients.

'Oh yes, I meant to tell you,' said Holly, looking up from her notebook, 'Nesta's not too pleased with me taking leave in June, 'cause we're going to be really short-staffed. She says can't we go to the Isle of Man at the end of May instead?'

Phil looked at her, realised she was serious and burst out laughing. 'Yeah, sure we can. If you fancy swimming the Irish Sea and camping on the beach.'

'Sorry?'

'It's TT fortnight,' he reminded her. 'All the flights and sailings are booked up a year in advance, and my gran earns a fortune from renting out her garden to hairy bikers with tents.'

'Ah. So not the end of May then.'

'Not the first week of June either. I'm afraid we'll have to stick to the dates we agreed. In any case,' he added, 'I booked our tickets yesterday.'

For a moment, Holly felt quite dizzy. Then a feeling of relief swept over her. So that's that, she thought, it's all settled, and I can finally stop worrying about it. All the same, when she looked down at the pencil she was holding, it was shaking ever so slightly.

'So, I take it we're flying from Gloucester Airport then?' she asked. It was the obvious choice – the airport was only ten minutes' drive away and the flight took less than an hour.

'Nope. Far too expensive.' Phil's two digits danced lightly across the computer keyboard. 'We're sailing from Heysham. I got a really good deal off the internet.'

'Sailing? But ...' Holly's brow furrowed. 'Where the hell is Heysham?'

'Up north, near Lancaster. Sailing time to Douglas is about four hours, give or take.'

'What!' Holly had once spent ten minutes in a rowing boat on the lake in Pittville Park. That had been enough to put her off all things maritime for life. 'That's just plain stupid. Surely the plane can't be that expensive ...'

Phil waved away her objections. 'It'll only take us a few hours to drive up there. And anyway, Dweezil hates flying.'

Holly's jaw dropped faster than a runaway lift. 'Hold on a minute. Did you just say *Dweezil*'s coming with us?' At the sound of his name, the cat looked up, yawned and went back to sleep. 'I sincerely hope that's a joke.'

Phil looked deeply wounded. 'I can't leave him here. He comes everywhere with me. He'd pine.'

'He'd what!' Holly's anger flared. 'Are you telling me I have to drive all the way up to God knows where in your crappy van, and then spend four hours chucking my guts up over the side of some old rust bucket, just because your *cat* wants to come too?'

The investigator looked at his client in stunned silence. 'I didn't think you'd mind,' he said finally. 'You and Dweezil get on so well.'

'Phil, he peed on my best shoes.'

'That's only because he loves you,' Phil assured her without a trace of a snigger. 'Look, he'll be in his box all the way there, and then Grandma Christian will look after him. You'll hardly notice he's there. Oh, and, um,' he added, looking up at her with eyes that said 'kicked spaniel', 'I've paid for the tickets and there's no refund.'

Holly let out a long groan. 'You mean *I've* paid for the tickets,' she corrected him. Oh terrific, she said to herself, I'm going to make up a threesome with Inspector Clouseau and the Cat of the Baskervilles.

Just as she was about to say something sarcastic, someone buzzed the intercom downstairs.

'Are you expecting a client?' asked Holly.

'No, nobody till tomorrow morning.' Puzzled, Phil pressed the button to answer. 'Bloodhound Investigations. Can I help you?'

'Murdo McKay,' replied a dark Scottish burr. 'I've come for my girlfriend.'

*

132

'I had a feeling I'd find you here.'

Holly couldn't help but state the obvious. 'Murdo! This is a surprise.'

'It's meant to be,' replied Murdo. 'I'm here to whisk you away on that romantic weekend in Venice you've always wanted. Assuming I can tear you away from your new friend here.' All the time he was speaking, Murdo's eyes were on Phil. And it was pretty obvious from the expression in them that it was far from love at first sight. 'I suppose you must be Phil Connell.'

'That's right.' Phil wiped a trace of cat food from his hand and proffered it, but Murdo wasn't in a shaking-hands frame of mind. 'Pleased to meet you.'

He didn't look it. Neither of them did. But at least Phil didn't look as though he wanted to rip Murdo's head from his shoulders and drop-kick it out of the window. This is not a good start, thought Holly, and for some silly, unaccountable reason, she found herself desperately wanting Murdo and Phil to like each other.

'Phil's the investigator who's helping me to find my birth mother,' gabbled Holly for want of anything less obvious to say. 'I've been doing some work for him in my spare time, haven't I, Phil?'

'Rather a lot of work, I'd say,' commented Murdo dryly.

'Why don't you sit down and I'll make us all some coffee?' There was a faint note of desperation in Phil's voice. 'Or tea if you prefer?'

'No thank you, we're not staying, are we, Holly? Come on. I've packed a weekend bag for you and the car's waiting outside.'

Murdo's eyes were boring into Holly's now, almost daring her to defy him. I don't like this, she thought with a shiver. I don't like this at all. I don't like being pushed around like somebody's possession, and I'm not going to stand for it.

'Well, actually, I was just in the middle of—', she began in protest, then she caught Phil's eye. He was slowly shaking his head and mouthing 'Go.' Was it because he wanted to save her any more hassle, or because he was terrified of Murdo? Was that more than simple friendship she glimpsed in his eyes? It was so hard to tell.

She hesitated. 'I . . . oh, all right then. Just wait a minute while I get my jacket.'

Murdo held the door open for her and she stepped out onto the landing, with a last look at Phil as she left.

'It's going to be a wonderful weekend,' Murdo promised her as they walked down the stairs to the front door. 'I promise you, I have found us the best hotel in the whole of Venice.' He drew her to him and they kissed. Maybe he's right, thought Holly, and this really is going to be wonderful.

It wasn't until they stepped through the door and out onto the street that they realised anything was wrong. Not, in fact, until they saw the Bentley, still parked beside the opposite kerb, but now resting on four neat piles of bricks where there used to be wheels.

Murdo swore colourfully. Holly ventured: 'Perhaps I should get Phil to come down and help?'

But Murdo merely glared, got out his mobile and rang the nearest garage.

The following night, Holly lay swathed in the finest Egyptian cotton sheets, gazing up at an exquisitely moulded ceiling. A gentle night breeze blew in through the half-closed shutters, carrying with it the sound of lapping water.

Murdo had been right: this really was the finest hotel in Venice, and in any other circumstances Holly would have been deliriously happy. But something wasn't right. And it had nothing to do with what had happened to Murdo's Bentley, or the fact that they'd missed their flight and had to wait three hours for the next one.

Holly rolled onto her right side and moulded her naked body

against Murdo's back as he slept. She knew every inch of his body almost as well as she knew her own, and it comforted her to lie skin on skin, drinking in his warmth, matching him breath for breath, until there seemed no room left for any gap between them. Only there was a gap, wasn't there? An unbridgeable gap between Murdo's dreams and the harsh realities of love. It's no use, she said to herself sadly, you deserve something so much better than me.

She lay there, wondering if Phil had anything to do with this epiphany and, if so, whether her interest in him really was completely pointless. Trust me, she thought. Trust me to pine after a man whose only interest is in a woman who left him for a Japanese pimp.

For a moment, she hesitated, then she reached out and stroked Murdo's cheek. 'Wake up! I need to tell you something.'

Murdo grunted, but did not wake. Holly seized him by the shoulders and shook him. 'Wake up!'

This time, Murdo rolled onto his back with a long, loud groan. 'Oh God. What time is it?'

'Just after two.'

'Jesus.' Murdo opened an eye. 'This had better be something serious,' he warned.

'It is.' Holly's stomach churned with apprehension, her skin clammy and her hands shaking. 'I ... I need to talk to you.'

Murdo dragged himself into a half-sitting position and wedged a lace-edged pillow behind his head. 'You're pregnant,' he declared, a note of excitement in his voice. 'I knew you were – the mood swings, the irritability, the—'

'I'm not pregnant, Murdo.' Drawing away from his embrace, she saw the light of expectation go out in his eyes, and felt inexplicably guilty. I'm supposed to make all of your dreams come true, she thought, and look what a mess I've made of it all. 'It's just that I've needed to talk to you for a while now, only I'm a coward and every

135

time I see your face I want to make you smile, because—' she hesitated '—because I love you.'

'And I love you, too. Is that so bad?' Murdo asked, clasping her hand before she had time to snatch it away. 'Holly, why won't you let me touch you?'

She swallowed tears that were trickling down the back of her nose. 'Because I want you to listen. If I let you touch me, we'll kiss and then we'll end up making love and I won't get round to saying what I need to say.' Her eyes pleaded with him to understand as she said, slowly and deliberately, 'I think we need a break from each other.'

'I ... What?'

'A break.' The words were like individual stabs of pain. 'A trial separation.'

'Oh.'

It was a moment frozen in time. In the pale-yellow glimmer from the bedside lamp, Murdo's face seemed chiselled from stone, its jaundiced skin paper thin and semi-transparent, like vellum. He said nothing.

'Murdo?' asked Holly.

Murdo's eyes screwed tight shut, and she saw his hands clench into fists as though he was fighting some invisible enemy within. When he opened his eyes again, they seemed little more than dark shadows in an empty face. 'You don't mean it.'

'I'm sorry, Murdo, but I do. The way things are at the moment, I think there's a ... a gap between who I am and who you want me to be, and I just can't live up to your expectations. Maybe if we spend some time apart, we can learn to appreciate each other for what we really are.'

'That sounds like crap off some agony-aunt page.'

'It might sound like that, but it's the truth.'

He thought for a moment. 'Marry me, Holly. Marry me now. I

136

should have asked you a long time ago but maybe I'm a coward too.'

Holly hung her head. 'I can't, Murdo,' she whispered. 'I just can't.'

'Because you don't love me?' His voice was harsh and probing.

'Because I'm afraid I may not love you ... the right way.'

Murdo laughed bitterly. 'For God's sake don't tell me you love me like a brother. If you're dumping me, at least do me the dignity of hating me.'

Tears flooded Holly's eyes. 'Oh, Murdo, I could never hate you. Not if my whole life depended on it. Maybe I just need a bit of time apart so I have room to grow up.'

Murdo stroked the hair back from Holly's forehead. It felt so good, so tender that she half wanted to cling to him, tell him that everything she had just told him was an aberration, that of course she would marry him if that was what he wanted her to do.

'It's him, isn't it?' he said in a hoarse whisper.

Holly drew back and looked at him. 'I don't understand.'

'Please, Holly, don't play games with me,' Murdo begged. 'It's that loser of a private investigator, isn't it? I saw the way you were looking at each other.'

'No, no, you've got it all wrong,' Holly insisted. 'We work together, that's all.'

'Come off it! I know you spend every spare moment with him in that pigsty of an office. And I know the two of you are off on a little "business trip" in a couple of weeks' time. How very cosy.'

'He's trying to trace my birth mother, for Christ's sake!' snapped Holly. 'She could be living on that island. Of course I'm going with him!'

'Admit it, Holly. You're having an affair with him.'

'Don't be so childish!'

'You dump me, then expect me to believe that you're still in love with me, and I'm the one who's supposed to be childish?'

'Please, Murdo. Just give me some time on my own to work things out.'

Murdo laughed humourlessly. 'Frankly, I don't seem to have much choice, do I?'

'I'm so sorry. I really, really am.' A cool night breeze wafted in through the open window, drying the sweat on Holly's forehead. Head in hands she felt dizzy, and sick, and guilty, and confused, and in pain. 'I didn't mean to hurt you,' she said earnestly. 'All I wanted to do was be honest.'

The anger had melted from Murdo's face, leaving only sadness. 'I know,' he said wearily. 'And all I've ever wanted to do is make you happy. Pity I'm not better at it. Get some sleep,' he added, picking up his pillow and a bedspread. 'I guess I'm taking the sofa tonight.'

Phil might have been out of the police force for several years, but the duty desk sergeant recognised him the moment he walked through the door.

'Blimey, if it isn't DC Connell.' He spoke with malicious enjoyment. It was a pity the station was empty and he didn't have an audience. 'I haven't seen you since they nearly banged you up for – what was it now? oh yes, manslaughter.'

'Fuck off, Bates.' Phil refused to be goaded by his old arch-enemy. 'I've come to see Reg.'

'He's out.'

'That's OK. I'll wait.' Phil sat down on one of the grey plastic chairs usually occupied by suspects and grieving widows.

'You still working with that good-looking bird then?'

'No.'

'Couldn't give her what she needed, eh?' Bates chuckled dirtily.

'Gone off with a real man, has she?'

Phil looked Bates coldly in the eye. 'Actually she's gone to Japan to be a high-class prostitute,' he replied. 'Any more questions?'

That shut him up for a moment or two, but Sergeant Bates' curiosity eventually got the better of him. 'What do you want with Reg anyway?'

'Nothing. He's just doing me a favour.' The station's double doors swung open, and a grey-haired constable appeared, super-market carrier bag in hand. 'And here he is now. Hi, Reg.'

'Sorry I'm late.' Constable Reg Grundy wiped sweat from his brow. 'The missus wanted me to get some potatoes for dinner tonight.' He went behind the desk and signed out a bunch of keys. 'Come on then. Let's go and find what you're after before the station gets busy. There's always a rush of shoplifters on a Thursday afternoon.'

There was a maze of storage rooms underneath the police station, and Reg was in charge of them all: a nice easy job before retirement. And unlike Bates, Reg Grundy was a genuine kind of guy who deserved it.

'Should be in here,' announced Reg, unlocking a door. It swung open to reveal what seemed to be mile upon mile of shelves, groaning under the weight of plain brown filing boxes filled with decades' worth of evidence. The whole room smelled of ripening mildew.

Reg checked the note in his hand as he walked along the rows. 'Row Q, box forty. Yep, that's the one, right up there on the top shelf.'

Phil stretched on tiptoe to reach it down. All it said on the side was 'Baby Holly' in black marker pen, the case number and the date when she was found.

'We really shouldn't be doing this, you know,' Reg reminded him nervously as Phil broke the seal on the box. 'Tampering with evidence. If it wasn't such an old case that nobody was interested in ...'

'I know, Reg, and I'm grateful for your help. And just think how grateful my client will be if this helps her to find her mother.'

Phil took the lid off the box and looked inside. 'Oh crap,' he muttered. It was empty.

In the staff canteen at the sorting office, the atmosphere was far from buoyant.

'Are you sure about this?' demanded Julian as he, Holly, Nesta and three of their colleagues sat around one of the tables at morning break time.

'As sure as I can be.' Nesta stirred sugar into a cup of very black coffee. 'I only got a chance to skim the memo before Colin realised he'd left it in the photocopier, but it definitely mentioned redundancies.'

'Brilliant,' groaned Alexander, who'd only been working at the depot for six months. 'Well, if it's first in first out I'm stuffed.' He got up, drained the dregs from his cup and wiped his mouth on his sleeve. 'See you down the Jobcentre, folks.'

As the group broke up, Nesta and Holly remained in their seats. 'If you're right,' said Holly, 'Alexander's not the only one who might be stuffed. I've only been here almost two years. That's nothing when there are people who've been here for twenty.' Then Holly had another thought. 'And what about you? This place is your life.'

Nesta shrugged. 'I'll just have to find somebody who wants to employ a not-very-good poet with a sideline in personalised greetings cards, won't I?' Either that or work in my cousin's chip shop in Rhyl.'

'Oh God, I hope it doesn't come to that,' sympathised Holly. She groaned. 'And I'll have to tie up all my belongings in a red spotted handkerchief, tie it to a pole and hit the road.'

'In which case I guess you'll be going back to London after all,' said Nesta, watching her friend's expression closely.

'Oh hell.' Elbows resting on the table top, Holly's head sank into her hands. 'I honestly don't know what I'm going to do, Nesta. Grace thinks I'm doing a pretty good job of ruining my life, and perhaps she's right.'

Nesta grimaced. 'I don't think I can remember a single time when your sister was right,' she snorted. 'And do you really want to take advice from somebody who cares about nothing but cash?'

'No,' Holly admitted wanly. 'I'd rather take advice from you.'

'But I'm not going to tell you what to do. You have to figure this one out for yourself.' Nesta sat back in her chair. 'What exactly happened in Venice anyway? You didn't really tell me the gory details; you just cried on my shoulder.'

There was a horrible ache in Holly's chest as she relived the disastrous 'dream' weekend with Murdo, from the missed flight to Venice to the excruciating politeness of the journey home. 'I told him I wasn't sure about my feelings for him,' she concluded, 'and that I thought we should take a break from each other for a while.'

'In other words, you dumped him.'

'Well . . .' The word sounded so harsh, so emotionless. But Nesta was right. She was always right. 'Yes,' admitted Holly. 'Sort of.'

'So did you or didn't you?'

'I did. But I said it might not be permanent.' She found herself looking beseechingly at Nesta, almost like a dog looking to its mistress for approval, afraid that she'd done the wrong thing and would be punished for it. 'Just till we'd worked things out.'

Nesta sighed. 'So you tore his heart out of his chest, and then handed him a teensy Elastoplast of hope?'

Holly winced. Sometimes her best friend was given to lurid turns of phrase, and the way she was feeling at the moment, it didn't help

141

at all. 'Stop it, Nesta. I meant what I said. There's a chance we could work things out, isn't there?'

'If you believe that, you're still living in cloud cuckoo land,' replied Nesta. 'You and Murdo have been drifting apart ever since you came back to Cheltenham, and can you honestly say you're certain that you two were right for each other in the first place?'

Like antiseptic on a fresh wound, that stung. 'No, I can't,' conceded Holly. 'But is anybody ever really certain?'

Nesta thought for a moment. 'My mum was certain about my dad,' she said. 'She knew the moment she first saw him that they were meant for each other. They both did.'

This was all too much for Holly. 'Well, that's all very lovely and romantic, I'm sure,' she snapped, 'but some of us are living in the real world, where feelings are a bit more mixed up!'

'I understand that,' said Nesta. 'And some of us are so terrified of saying "yes" to Mister Wrong that we say "no" to Mister Right. God knows, I've done that myself and I'll never forgive myself for it. And then there's you.'

Puzzled, Holly asked: 'What are you on about, Nesta?'

'I'm on about you. You and your feelings for Phil Connell.'

Holly felt as if someone had just shone an interrogation lamp right into her face. 'I ... um ...' she stammered.

'And don't pretend you don't have any feelings,' Nesta added. 'You've been going on about how kind and nice and cute he is for weeks. Don't you think it's time you admitted to yourself that he's the real reason you broke up with Murdo?'

After Nesta's interrogation, nothing felt quite the same to Holly. She found herself examining everything she did, questioning her every thought and action in case it concealed something she didn't want to acknowledge. And the more she did it, the more confused she became.

She knew that Nesta's words had only hit home because they were – at least in part – true. Yes, OK, she told herself with a quickening pulse, I do feel attracted to Phil; there, I've said it. I fancy a man with a smelly cat and no money. But in itself that doesn't mean a thing, does it? I could be attracted to Daniel Craig or the Secretary-General of the United bloody Nations, but that doesn't mean they'd have the slightest interest in me. And in the case of Phil Connell, she thought ruefully, he doesn't.

Still, at least while they were working together she had an excuse to spend time with him. Which was why she was sitting talking to him in his stuffy office on a fine June day, instead of lazing in Imperial Gardens with a chilled beer.

'I managed to persuade Reg to take me down to the storerooms where the evidence is kept,' Phil went on, 'and we found the file box relating to your case. Unfortunately . . .'

'What?' demanded Holly with bated breath.

'It was empty.'

'What – completely empty?' Holly's hopes abruptly deflated. She'd been so sure that the box would contain all kinds of useful information. 'Do you think somebody stole the evidence?'

Phil laughed. 'This isn't an episode of *CSI*, you know,' he chuckled. 'No, I just think there wasn't any evidence to begin with. And actually,' he admitted, 'the box wasn't one hundred per cent empty. While Reg was looking the other way, I nicked this.'

With a flourish, he produced a long white envelope, addressed to the chief inspector at the station.

'What's in it?' Holly's hopes flickered back to life.

'Nothing,' confessed Phil. 'Apparently it had money in it originally. A lot of people donated money for Christmas presents when they heard about you being found on the hospital steps – everybody loves a Christmas baby story. But this donation arrived by post, with no sign of where it had come from. Even the postmark's too

143

blurred to read,' he lamented, squinting at it under the beam from the desk lamp but getting nowhere. 'Apparently they spent the money on a nice new cot for you and presents for the kids in the hospital. Happy endings all round.'

'Wait a minute – you went to all the trouble of stealing an empty envelope?'

'Yep. Just call me Raffles the wonder thief.'

Holly started laughing and then Phil joined in. And they kept on laughing until the tears were rolling down Holly's face and Dweezil took refuge behind a filing cabinet.

'I guess we'll take it with us anyway.' Phil slid the envelope back into Holly's case file. 'Never know when you'll need an empty envelope.' He pulled out a sheet of paper. 'Ta-da! Here's the itinerary for our trip. We're driving up to Lancaster on Monday, and I've booked you a B & B for that night. Then we—'

Holly held up her hand. 'Hold on. You've booked me into a B & B? Where are you staying?'

Phil looked sheepish. 'Oh, me and Dweezil will sleep in the van. Can't imagine any self-respecting hotelier taking Dweezil on, can you? I tried smuggling him in once and he ate the corner off the duvet. I had to say I did it.'

'Can't you just leave him in the van and book yourself a room?' reasoned Holly.

'Oh no, I wouldn't do that to Dweezil. Would I, mate?' Phil rubbed Dweezil's piebald head and the office was instantly filled with a gigantic, low rumbling sound like the beginnings of an avalanche.

'But – why?' Holly still couldn't quite understand. 'I mean, I know you love him dearly, but is a stinky cat really worth giving up a decent night's sleep for? I thought you said he was just a stray who wandered in one day and turned into the office cat.'

'Ah, and so he was.' Phil chucked Dweezil under the chin affectionately. 'The thing is, over the last year or so not many people have stayed true to me. Not even "close" friends. But Dweezil has. He's never let me down and even when I was at my lowest ebb he never once walked away or refused to listen. He just curled up on my lap and purred, as if he wanted to let me know that things were going to be OK.' Phil smiled. 'Maybe I'm anthropomorphising a bit too much and really he's only with me for the catnip mice, but I like to think he understands.'

'Perhaps he does.' Holly extended a hand and Dweezil ran his rough tongue over the skin. 'But I'm still not looking forward to sharing the van with him and his bad breath.'

Early on Monday morning, a small crowd gathered outside the Bennett residence. Much to Holly's surprise, the whole clan had turned out in force to see her and Phil off on their epic voyage: Harry, Grace and Steve with Adam dozing in his pushchair, and Jess with Aimee in a baby sling. Only Kev was missing, possibly because Jess had made it clear that if he came anywhere near her she would slice his head off and shove it down his throat.

Nesta couldn't be there because of work, but the previous evening she'd given Holly a teddy bear, 'to cuddle if you get the urge to cuddle anything else'. It was now peeping sternly out of the zip-up pocket on the front of her suitcase, as though Nesta's wagging finger of reproach had taken on a furry life of its own.

Harry gave his eldest daughter a bone-crunching hug. 'Hurry back, love. We're all going to miss you.'

'Dad, I'll be back before you know it,' laughed Holly. 'It's only for a week or two, just until we turn something up – or the money runs out.'

'We might not find anything, Mr Bennett,' Phil reminded him.

'You'd better,' warned Grace. 'After all this money my sister's paying you.' Everybody looked down at the toes of their shoes, but

145

Grace didn't know the meaning of the word embarrassment. 'And if she catches MRSA from that thing,' she added, glaring at Dweezil in his cat box, 'I'll ... I'll make sure you never work a case in this town again.'

Jess patted her sister on the shoulder. 'I think you've been watching too many gangster movies, sis. I'm sure Holly's going to be fine.'

Grace turned to her husband, who was as usual looming silently over the proceedings. Steve couldn't help looming: he was enormous. And years of playing rugby every weekend had given him a face that looked as though it had been in collision with a double-decker bus – and won. People who didn't know him found it hard to believe that his favourite hobby was stamp collecting.

'Steve,' Grace prompted, 'didn't you want a quiet word with Mr Connell before they leave?'

Steve drew Phil to one side, out of earshot of the others. Intrigued, Holly strained to hear what they were saying, but it was no use, they were just too far away.

'Is there something wrong?' asked Phil, looking up at Steve with surprise and just a hint of apprehension.

'Not at all,' replied Steve. 'And I trust there won't be.'

'I don't quite understand ...'

Steve smiled pleasantly. 'Just a bit of friendly advice, Phil. You know, man to man. My wife's very fond of her sister, and so am I. So here's hoping you have a really successful trip. But just you take good care of Holly, understood? Because if any harm comes to her you'll have both of us to reckon with. '

Holly was more intrigued than ever. She knew that whatever Steve had said to Phil had shaken him up, but whatever it was, he wasn't talking about it. She probed gently as they sped up the motorway in Phil's van.

'So you and Steve had a chat then, did you?'

'Sort of.' Phil hummed softly to himself as he deftly switched lanes and left a string of slow-moving lorries behind.

'He's a big lad, isn't he? Grace told me that when he's in rugby training, he eats three whole chickens a day.'

Phil's eyebrows arched. 'Are you sure you don't mean three whole private investigators?'

Holly frowned. 'Is something wrong? Did Steve want to give you some advice then or what?'

Phil's humming took on a slightly strangulated quality. 'You could say. Tell you what, shall we stop at the next services and get a bite to eat? I'm starving.'

As they drove north through the English countryside, the games got progressively sillier.

'I spy with my little eye, something beginning with c.'

'Cow,' said Holly immediately.

'How did you guess?' demanded Phil.

'It was cow last time, remember?'

'Ah, but this is a different cow. A brown one.'

'How can you tell?' protested Holly. 'It's nearly dark!'

'Didn't I tell you? I have X-ray vision.'

Holly giggled. 'You're mad, do you know that?' She sniffed. 'And this cat's halitosis is worse than ever. Did you really have to let him out of his box?'

Phil glanced across at Dweezil, who had parked himself comfortably on Holly's lap and was sleeping with one eye half open. 'He hates it in that box. Just look how much happier he is now he's got you to sit on. Anyway,' he said as they turned off the motorway, we're nearly at Lancaster so you'd better watch out for your B & B.'

147

The B & B turned out to be a very nice detached house built of the pale local stone, a few miles out of Lancaster and looking out over the hills of the Lake District. There was plenty of hard standing outside, and Phil parked the van just a stone's throw from the front door.

'You go inside and get a good night's sleep,' advised Phil. 'You've got to be up bright and early tomorrow for the boat.'

'But what about you? How will you sleep?'

'Dweezil and I will be fine. I've got a sleeping bag and I'll make up a bed in the back of the van.'

Although it was June, the night air had just a hint of chill about it, and rain was sprinkling lightly as Holly took her overnight bag out of the van. She meant to go straight into the house, but an awful feeling of guilt made her turn back.

The van doors were open and Phil was unrolling a sleeping bag. Dweezil was idly stalking a moth attracted by the light from the B & B's windows.

'Phil.'

He turned and looked at her. 'Yes?'

'Won't you be cold out here?'

He smiled. 'I told you, we'll be fine. Won't we, mate? We always are.' Phil shook cat biscuits into a bowl and offered it to Dweezil.

'I could stay with you in the van,' she suggested, realising as soon as she said it that it was stupid. But she wanted to feel a part of the team, not Lady Muck, feasting in the big house while everybody else roughed it. And part of her wanted very much to be with Phil.

'I don't think you'd like it much,' said Phil. Their eyes met. 'Go on,' he said. 'You can smuggle me out a bacon buttie in the morning. 'Night, Holly.'

''Night.'

*

Standing on the deck of the *Ben-my-Chree*, the wind buffeting her face and turning her hair into a tangled skein, Holly gazed down into the blue-green waters of the Irish Sea. The churning waters seemed to form faces – some familiar, others which she knew were mere phantoms created by her mind as she wondered what her mother might look like.

Excitement quickened in her heart. Each moment was carrying her closer to the place where all her questions might – or might not – be answered, the place, perhaps, of her birth. Now there was no going back. She searched her heart for feelings of regret, but there were none. Even if nothing came of this quest, she was glad that she had set out to find her birth mother. Already she had learned a lot about herself.

And then there was Phil Connell. If she hadn't stuck that pin in the list of private investigators, she would never have met him. Holly knew that her sisters were wary of him, but instinct told her that they were wrong. And if she couldn't trust her instinct any more, what could she trust? If she had listened to her instinct before, she would have separated from Murdo a long time ago and saved a lot of heartache on both sides.

Murdo was still there in her heart. You couldn't love someone for so long and just wipe him from your life. Sometimes she heard a voice or saw a face in a crowd and thought it was him, and then it hurt, knowing what she had done to him. And she wondered if she should have stayed with him, not for her sake but for his, because even the wrong kind of love was still love, and the last thing she had wanted to do was to break his heart.

Footsteps echoed on the deck and then Phil was standing next to her, arms on the ship's rail, brown hair blowing back from his face. Something in her heart danced a little jig of happiness.

'Where's Dweezil?'

'I left him in the cabin. I couldn't stand any more looks of

149

reproach. I mean, is it my fault if the rules say he has to stay in his cat box?'

'How much longer till we reach Douglas?' asked Holly.

'About an hour. Can you see the island yet?'

Holly shook her head. 'It's too misty; I can't see a thing.'

'Actually there's a legend,' said Phil, 'that this ancient wizard called Mannanan casts a cloak of mist around the island to hide it if he doesn't want someone to find it. I've noticed he always does it whenever a member of the Royal Family visits, so I'm guessing he's a republican.'

'Don't you think he wants us to visit the island then?' asked Holly.

'Of course he does. It'll clear in a minute, you'll see.' As Phil gazed into the swirling mist, the wind raked his hair back from his face, emphasising the determined set of his jawline. 'And in any case, we're visiting whether he likes it or not.'

Holly shivered slightly, and huddled into her jacket. 'Well, just as long as he doesn't try to stop us finding out what we need to know. If it's there, that is.' Holly turned back to the misty horizon, and suddenly her heart skipped a beat. 'Oh my ... Look, Phil!' She grabbed his arm. 'There it is!'

As if someone had parted a curtain, the island appeared in all its glory through the clearing mist: an undulating terrine of grey and green and brown against the pale sky.

'Told you so,' said Phil, beaming broadly as if he'd engineered the meteorological party trick himself.

I mustn't get too excited, Holly commanded herself. I really mustn't. But all she could think was: I'm coming home! I'm finally coming home.

'Does everybody drive this slowly?' enquired Holly, as the van idled along the road to Peel behind a long queue of cars and a tractor.

'Not everybody,' admitted Phil. 'Most do, but a few drive like maniacs. You should be here on Mad Sunday.'

'What's Mad Sunday?'

'The Sunday between TT Practice Week and TT Race week. Anyone is allowed to ride their bike along the TT mountain circuit, and there's no speed limit on a lot of the roads, either.'

'My God! Are these people insane?'

Phil chuckled. 'No. Just Manx.'

The road across the island ran through rolling hills and lush pastures that reminded Holly of Ireland and Scotland and the Lake District, all jumbled up together, yet somehow indefinably different. From time to time, as they came round a bend, they found themselves gazing down at a panorama of neat fields, spread out under a vast dome of misty-blue sky, arching over it all like a cathedral of air.

The scenery was enough to occupy Holly to begin with, but as they got nearer and nearer to Peel, nerves began to flutter in her stomach.

'Are you sure your grandma won't mind me staying too?'

'Positive.'

'Absolutely positive?'

Phil flashed Holly a 'don't be silly' look. 'I told her all about you,' he insisted, 'and she's really looking forward to meeting you.'

All this did was worry Holly even more. 'What exactly did you tell her about me?' she demanded.

The expression on Phil's face didn't change, but Holly was almost sure that his ears turned a deeper shade of pink. 'I just said you were very nice and that she'd like you,' he replied, directing his attentions firmly at the road ahead. 'Grandma Christian's really sociable,' he added, just as Holly was beginning to feel flattered. 'She likes everyone.'

'Hm,' said Holly. 'So I could be a rampaging yeti and she'd still like me?'

'Oh, I should think so. As long as you were a nice yeti.'

A few minutes later, as the countryside began to give way to houses and gardens, Phil gave her a nudge. 'Stop day-dreaming, Holly, we're nearly there.'

Peel, the 'Sunset City', clung to the western shores of the island, and was famous for its kippers, Vikings and sunsets, not necessarily in that order. Although it was the tiniest city Holly had ever seen, it still managed a castle and two cathedrals, not to mention the most gloriously soft beach of caramel-coloured sand that just begged her to wriggle her toes into it. And it had such narrow, winding streets and quaint red sandstone cottages that Holly could almost hear the smugglers bringing home their barrels of brandy and tobacco, to hide in the cellars until the excisemen had come and gone.

Phil squeezed the van round a corner that only a native could negotiate, eased it up a blind alley not far from the seafront, and brought it to a standstill beside a sign that read: *No Parking*.

'Here we are,' he declared. 'Home.' As if in agreement, Dweezil meowed loudly and produced a tremendous fart. 'Everybody out.'

'Hang on a minute.' Holly grabbed Phil's sleeve as he removed the ignition key and made to get out. 'We can't leave the van here.'

'Why not?'

'It says NO PARKING – look! You'll get a ticket.'

Phil shook his head pityingly and laughed. 'It's obvious you've not been here before,' he commented. 'Come on. I bet Grandma C's got the kettle on already.'

Still baffled, Holly eased her aching limbs out of the van. Several hundred miles in a small delivery van had done nothing for her back, and her legs felt as though they'd been folded up and squashed into a suitcase for a week. Even if she was on a road trip with a lunatic PI and a smelly cat, it felt unbelievably good to be standing upright again and breathing in the brisk, salty air.

She followed Phil to a blue door flanked by hanging baskets filled with trailing clouds of blue lobelia and white alyssum. A nameplate read: THIE VEG.

'Grandma likes jokes,' explained Phil. '"Thie Veg" is Manx for "little house".'

'OK.' Holly scratched her ear. 'But where does the joke come in?'

'It's also Manx for "Toilet".'

Holly stared in disbelief. 'So you're telling me that your grandma lives in a house called "Toilet"?'

'I told you she was different.' Phil hammered on the door knocker – a tailless brass cat – and stepped back. A lace curtain twitched at the front window, and seconds later the door opened.

'Philip! Come in! Come in and give your old grandma a big hug.'

Holly had pictured Grandma Christian as a little grey-haired figure with an apron and permanently floury hands. But Phil's grandma was taller than Holly, and built as solidly as a barn door. Her long dark hair, streaked with reddish highlights, was tied in a loose pigtail, and she wore a crystal pendant with her red cheese-cloth smock and loose trousers. If Glastonbury had bouncers, thought Holly, Grandma C would be one.

'You're looking very thin, Philip,' she admonished her grandson, tweaking his cheek. 'I can see I'll have to feed you up. Not Dweezil though.' She peered into his travelling box. 'I'm sure he's as greedy as ever.' She turned her attentions to Holly. 'Now then, this must be the ... friend you've been telling me so much about.'

'Grandma, this is Holly Bennett, m-my client,' stammered Phil. 'Holly, this is Grandma Christian.'

Grandma C gave Holly a kiss on either cheek and squeezed her hand so hard that all the feeling went from her fingers. 'It's so nice to finally meet you.' She beamed. 'Come in, come in.' As they trooped inside, she half turned and added, 'Please call me Eileen. All my friends and clients do.'

153

'Grandma's a reiki therapist at the alternative medicine centre in town,' Phil explained. 'And she's very good at it too. If your chi's out of alignment, she'll straighten you out in two seconds.'

'I thought you didn't believe in alternative medicine,' objected Holly, recalling a conversation they'd had over beer and crisps.

'I don't,' he agreed with a smile, 'except when Grandma's doing it.'

Eileen swatted her grandson affectionately about the ears, and led her two guests inside.

It certainly is a tiny house, thought Holly. Like a doll's house – or the one Alice got stuck in, in *Alice in Wonderland*. For one thing, there was no hallway; the front door opened directly onto a ridiculously steep staircase. Eileen strode straight upstairs with their bags, past a long row of *Kama Sutra*-style erotic prints.

'I'm so sorry,' she told them as they reached the landing. Holly wondered if she was about to apologise for her taste in art, but she went on: 'You remember I had woodworm in the loft last autumn?'

Phil nodded.

'Well, last week the ceiling in the guest bedroom fell in, so I'm afraid I've had to put you two in my room. There's a nice double bed in there, don't worry,' she added with a wink. Then she picked up Holly's suitcase. 'Let's get you settled in. I'll take the sofa bed downstairs; it's very comfy.'

She vanished into the bedroom with the suitcase, and a dreadful realisation crept over Holly. She looked at Phil, and found him looking back at her with equal apprehension. 'Phil,' she hissed, 'what the hell did you tell your grandmother about you and me?'

'Nothing!' he protested, hands up in self-defence. He rubbed his stubbly chin. 'Well, nothing much. Maybe that was the problem ...'

Holly looked at him and rolled her eyes heavenwards. 'Dear

God, if all men are as daft as you it's a wonder the human race ever got started.'

'I know,' said Phil sheepishly. He nodded towards his grand-mother's bedroom and the sounds of happy humming. 'Do you want me to tell her?'

'No,' sighed Holly. 'I'll sort it out.'

She edged open the bedroom door. Eileen was smoothing out a beautiful handmade patchwork bedspread. Holly cleared her throat, and Eileen turned to look at her, smiling.

'I'm ever so sorry, Eileen,' began Holly sheepishly, 'but I think your grandson may have given you the wrong impression.'

'Really, dear? What about?'

'Well ... Phil and I can't share a room – you see, we aren't actu-ally a couple. We're not even going out together or anything.' She threw Phil a meaningful glare. 'Are we, Phil?'

'N-no!' he agreed. 'I thought I'd told you, Grandma: Holly's my client.' The tips of his ears went pink. 'Holly, if this is my fault, I do apologise. I'll—'

'No, don't do anything,' said Holly, regaining possession of her suitcase. 'You've done enough already. I'll just go and find myself a B & B. I'm sure Eileen can recommend somewhere not too expensive.'

'No, no, no.' Eileen laid a hand on her arm. 'Please, dear, don't do that. There's absolutely no need. You and Philip can sleep downstairs in the living room.'

'We ... can?'

'Yes, of course!' Eileen's face radiated her happiness at finding a solution. 'It'll all be perfectly nice and decent. There's a nice sofa bed for you, Holly, and I've got a perfectly good inflatable mattress that Philip can use. I got it last Christmas from a catalogue, and I haven't had a chance to use it yet.' She giggled like a schoolgirl. 'I can even put my Chinese screen across the room to preserve your modesty.'

'Well ...' said Holly, still slightly uncertain about spending her nights in the same room as Phil, with or without a modesty screen. 'I really don't know if—'

'It's OK,' cut in Phil. 'I can see you're not happy. I'll go and sleep at Jimmy Qualtrough's round the corner. I'm sure he'll let me have the use of his sofa.'

'No, don't go,' Holly blurted out, much to her own surprise. 'I really don't mind if you stay.'

Phil blinked in amazement. 'Really?'

'Really. I'm sure we'll be fine downstairs, won't we, Phil? As long as there's a screen, of course.'

'Er ... yes. Of course.' Phil looked thunderstruck. 'Whatever you prefer.'

'Wonderful,' said Eileen, beaming. She swooped on Holly's suitcase and started back downstairs. 'It'll be perfect. And of course, you'll have Dweezil to keep you company.'

Bugger, thought Holly. I hadn't thought of that.

'Now,' declared Eileen, 'shall I go and put the kettle on?'

Later that evening, when Phil was out visiting his mate Jimmy Qualtrough and Eileen was in the kitchen baking a batch of bread, Holly unzipped her suitcase and rummaged around for her toilet bag and the crime novel she'd packed for moments of boredom – not that it looked like there'd be many of those.

As she slid her hand underneath a pile of neatly folded knickers, it came into contact with something small, soft and furry. It was the little teddy bear Nesta had given her to keep her on the straight and narrow. She sat it on her knee and in her mind's eye she saw her best friend, warning her not to go and do something stupid: 'Hey, Holly, cuddle this if you get the urge to cuddle anything else.'

'Sorry, mate,' she said, patting the little bear on the head and then shoving him deep down under the pile of pants. 'But this time I'm flying solo.'

Then she zipped up the suitcase, sat back down on the sofa bed and waited for bedtime.

Eleven

Early the next morning, Holly eased herself into full, painful wakefulness on the 'really comfy' sofa bed. Easing aside the Chinese screen, she glanced across the room at Phil, snoring away on his Argos inflatable mattress with a cat on his head, and felt a pang of envy. After a night spent trying to contort her body round the hard metal bits, even that had to be an improvement.

The room was quite light. Sunlight was creeping in through the gaps in the curtains, which boded well for a decent sort of day. So much for Phil and his warnings that 'it rains a lot over here, so make sure you bring your waterproofs'. He seemed to be a pessimist about most things, reflected Holly; maybe his experiences with Sita had made him like that, maybe it was the bad things he saw in his line of work, or perhaps he'd always been that way. But surely pessimism wasn't the best frame of mind for a private investigator, was it? Well, she thought, I'll just have to be the optimistic one on the team, make sure things keep moving along.

But right now, what I need is a nice cup of Manx tea.

Sliding her feet into her slippers, she creaked her body upright with a twinge of pain. Just as she was about to head for the kitchen, she saw it, or rather glimpsed it: a flash of movement, out of the corner of one eye. Whatever it was, it seemed to be in the fireplace.

Turning round, she was just in time to see a naked pink tail curl around the edge of the fire grate and disappear.

'Aaah!' She nearly jumped out of her goose-pimply skin. 'Phil!' She bent over the mattress, shaking his inert body for all she was worth. 'Phil, wake up – it's a rat! A ra—!'

The word died abruptly as Phil shot upright and his large hand clamped over Holly's mouth. 'Shhh!' he hissed urgently as he loosened his grip. 'Whatever you do, don't you ever, ever say that word again.'

She stared at him in bafflement. 'What – you mean "rat"?'

The hand clamped over her mouth again. 'I told you not to say it! Listen to me Holly, nobody over here mentions R-A-T-S. Not ever. If you have to mention them, say "big fellas" or "long-tails".' Embarrassed, his ears pink once more, he released her. 'Er ... I'm sorry.'

'Hm. It's OK. I guess. As long as you don't do it again.'

'I won't,' he promised. 'Just promise me you won't ever say that word again.'

'But – why?'

Phil sighed. 'Because the older people on the island really have a thing about them. I'm not sure why. In the olden days, the government used to pay a bounty on the tails – 3d for male ones and 6d for female.'

Holly was incredulous. 'How on earth do you tell if a tail is female?' she whispered.

'Beats me. I think they decided that every sixth one was female, or something like that. But believe me, the sight of a Rentokil van outside your house is social suicide around here. So please don't wake Grandma up, or she'll be running round the room with a shovel, trying to beat the bloody thing to death.'

Trying not to think about squashed rats on the hearthrug, Holly lowered herself onto the blow-up mattress. 'I've got an awful lot to learn about this place,' she remarked as she sat down next to Phil.

'So have I. And I've been coming over here since I was zero years old. Now,' Phil went on, 'what's our plan of action for today?'

'That's what I'm paying you to tell me,' Holly pointed out.

'Good point.' Phil scratched his tousled head. 'Well, I suggest we have a word with Canon Michael O'Keefe.'

'Who is—?'

'The priest in charge of the Roman Catholic parishes around Douglas. Grandma sniffed him out for me before we came over. He should have an idea how and when confirmations are carried out, and where the records are kept. I'm just hoping they're all kept in one place,' he added.

'You mean ... there's more than one Catholic church on the island?' Holly was genuinely stunned. On the map, the Isle of Man had seemed like such a tiny, boring blob where nothing ever happened, but now they were here it wasn't like that at all.

'More than one?' Phil laughed. 'At the last count I made it eight.'

There weren't many people who slipped under Eileen Christian's radar. Then again, the island was that kind of place: a place where everybody knew everybody else's business. A place you either loved or hated, Holly guessed. She'd thought she would find the place horribly oppressive, or irritatingly slow, but already she sensed that she was starting to adjust – just as she'd adjusted when she left London and came back to Cheltenham. Maybe it's something in the air, pondered Holly as she watched two drivers stop in the middle of the street, wind down their windows and strike up a conversation.

The following lunchtime they drove into Douglas, the island's capital; not the prettiest of seaside towns, perhaps, but redeemed by a deep bay that scooped between two grassy headlands, and by a stubborn quaintness that seeped through even between the swanky new apartments and the offshore banks. Even here, at the hub of the Isle of Man's offshore finance industry, life went on at a civilised pace.

Holly and Phil met the Reverend Canon Michael O'Keefe at a little restaurant near the Manx Museum, which enjoyed spectacular views across Douglas Bay. Although he was off duty and not wearing a clerical collar, the canon wasn't difficult to spot. He was easily the biggest man Holly had ever seen; he even made Grace's Steve look small. And it wasn't just the fact that he was solidly built. As he stood up to greet them, a napkin tucked into the neck of his pullover, he towered so high that Holly feared he might scrape his head on the ceiling.

He extended a hand as big as a tea plate. 'Hello there! You must be Miss Bennett and Mr Connell. Forgive my starting first; I'm afraid good food is a weakness of mine.'

The canon drew out a chair for Holly and she tucked her legs under the table, resisting the urge to take a peep underneath to see how it managed to accommodate his several yards of leg.

'So, how can I help you?' he asked, his shock of pale-red hair bobbing about as he chewed on a juicy slab of the local lamb.

'Well ... Father,' Holly began uncertainly, never having addressed a Roman Catholic priest before, 'thirty years ago, when I was a baby, I was abandoned and later adopted.' She toyed with a bowl of soup and tried not to marvel at the canon's gargantuan appetite. It was hard not to stare; it was like watching a cement mixer on full power. 'And now I'm looking for my birth mother.'

'I see.' The canon's knife and fork paused in mid-air. 'And your mother was Manx?'

'We think so,' said Phil, reaching into his pocket and carefully taking out the plastic bag containing the silver necklace, 'though we can't be certain. Holly was wrapped up in a Manx tartan blanket, and this was also with her.'

He handed over the necklace. The canon nodded. 'A confirmation necklace, I see. And that would give you some idea of the woman's age.' He handed it back. 'So what you're looking to do is consult the confirmation records over here?'

'That's what we'd like to do, yes.' Holly's heart skipped a beat. 'Is there a problem about that?'

'We were wondering if there's some kind of central record of confirmations,' cut in Phil. 'It would make life much easier.'

The canon smiled and nodded. 'It certainly would. Unfortunately it's not quite as simple as that.'

Phil sighed and sat back in his chair. 'How did I know you were going to say that? So what exactly is the problem, Father O'Keefe?'

Canon O'Keefe took a brief breather from his meal to chase it down with a glass of wine. 'Let me explain. There are around seventy thousand people on this island, about ten thousand of them Roman Catholics. These worshippers are divided up into parishes. I look after the parishes in and around Douglas, for example. Now, every so often the bishop will come over from the mainland to confirm a group of young Catholics – aged around eleven or twelve for the most part – but this is done on an individual parish basis.'

'So it's not like everyone on the island gets confirmed in the same place, at the same time?'

'Precisely. Consequently, in any one year there may be confirmations in one parish and not another.'

'But isn't that a good thing?' cut in Holly. 'We have a date on my mother's necklace. If only one parish had confirmations on that date, wouldn't that cut down the numbers of people a lot?'

Phil snapped his fingers. 'Good thinking. So all we have to do is find out which parish it was, and we've narrowed things down considerably.'

'Indeed,' agreed the canon. 'But unfortunately, in order to do so, you will probably have to contact all the parishes on the island. You see, there is no central archive. The records are held in the parishes. I'm sorry if that wasn't what you wanted to hear,' he added with a look at their glum faces, 'but I'm sure you'll be able to do a lot by phone.'

'Father,' said Holly.

'Yes?'

'You know you said there are about ten thousand Catholics on the island?'

The priest nodded.

'Well ... about how many of them get confirmed in a parish at any one time?'

She held her breath, certain that the number was going to be astronomical. Then again, she'd never been much good at arithmetic.

'I'd say I have around sixty or seventy confirmations in my area each year,' replied Father O'Keefe.

Holly breathed a huge sigh of relief. 'So if only sixty or seventy other girls were confirmed at the same time as my birth mother ... Phil, that's not too bad at all. It's a manageable number, at least.'

Phil raised an eyebrow. 'I bet that's not what you'll say if you have to visit every single one of them,' he remarked.

It was Saturday night in the Christian household.

'You know, I really can't abide *Strictly Come Dancing*,' complained Eileen, pointing the remote control at the TV set and extinguishing Bruce Forsyth in mid-flow. 'Why can't they have more programmes about sex?'

Holly choked on a Quality Street. 'Pardon?'

'Sex, dear,' Eileen repeated. 'Everybody should have more of it. It's the finest therapy in the world. Charles and I did it every single night of our marriage, for thirty-two years, and he was the

163

fittest man you've ever seen. Until he dropped dead of a heart attack one day when we were right in the middle of it,' she added thoughtfully.

'It's not the worst way to go, Gran,' commented Phil, patting his grandma affectionately on the shoulder. 'Hope you two don't mind, but I'm just popping down the pub for a swift half with Jimmy. See you both in a bit.'

The front door clicked shut behind him, leaving Holly and Eileen in an awkward silence at opposite ends of the settee, with Dweezil wedged between the seat cushions in the middle, like a little furry Buddha. Holly could feel her face burning scarlet from her neck to the tip of her nose.

'Um ... Chocolate?' In desperation, she grabbed the tin and thrust it at Eileen. 'There are still some nice hard ones left.' Scarlet turned to crimson as she realised her double-entendre. 'I mean—'

'Charles was a wonderful man,' said Eileen with a sigh, wistfully twirling a toffee out of its wrapper. 'I do miss him.'

'Of course you do,' said Holly, feeling on slightly safer ground.

'He had the biggest—'

Holly screwed up her face in anticipatory dread.

'—heart of any man I ever knew.' Eileen looked at Holly in concern. 'Are you in pain, dear? There's some Alkaseltzer in the kitchen cupboard.'

'I'm fine. Really I am.' Holly made an effort not to be a silly little wuss. She was nearly thirty years old, for goodness' sake!

'Is my talking about Charles making you think about your birth mother? Phil told me how much it means to you to find her.'

'Well ... yes. But the feelings I have are kind of complicated.' Holly scrunched up a toffee wrapper, waved it alluringly in front of Dweezil's face and then threw it for him to chase. He looked at her as if she was totally insane, and went back to sleep. 'It's hard for me to know quite what I feel about my birth mother. Sometimes

I think I hate her, just for existing. I was very close to my adoptive mother, you see. And then she died of motor neuron disease.'

'I'm so very sorry. Philip didn't tell me the exact circumstances.' There was another short, uncomfortable silence. 'You won't believe me, but he used to be the most confident man I've ever known. How else would he have made it to detective constable and police firearms expert?'

'I did wonder,' admitted Holly. 'He seems so ... shy. No, not shy exactly, reserved. As if there's a part of him that's closed off to outsiders.'

Eileen scowled. 'It was that woman who did it to him.'

'Sita, you mean?'

The very mention of the name made Eileen's whole body tense. 'You know what she did? She went all out to make him fall in love with her, and then, when she knew she had him in the palm of her hand, she shredded his heart into tiny little pieces and stamped on them. The moment I first met her I knew there was something cold and twisted about her; but Philip was besotted, so I tried to make her welcome. You can't tell people who to love, can you?'

'No,' agreed Holly, thinking about Murdo. 'But why would Sita want to do that to Phil?'

'I tried to figure that out for a long time, but in the end I realised it was just because she could. I think all she ever wanted to do was hurt him, because hurting people was the only thing that gave her any kind of pleasure. Sad, isn't it?'

'Frightening,' replied Holly with a shudder. 'I hope I never meet her.'

'Oh, I shouldn't think you will,' said Eileen, taking another chocolate from the tin. 'I'm sure the life of a high-class prostitute suits her down to the ground.'

Holly hadn't expected that. 'I knew she was in Japan now,' she said, 'but ... she's a prostitute?'

'As good as. She's paid to lure businessmen into affairs, so the agency she works for can get incriminating pictures and tapes, that sort of thing. Disgusting, isn't it? And I should imagine she's very good at it too. But that's enough about Sita,' she said, wiping chocolate-smeared fingers on a tissue as though she was wiping Sita away too. 'It's so nice to see Philip with a lovely girl like you.'

'We're not actually together,' emphasised Holly, her words sounding peculiarly prim. 'I did explain.'

Eileen patted her on the knee. 'Yes, dear, but that's just words, isn't it? The fact is, you make him happy. For once in his life, he's not gone for the wrong sort of girl. I haven't seen him smile so much since before you-know-who.'

'But I'm just a—' squirmed Holly.

'But nothing,' Eileen declared firmly. 'You're good for him, and I don't think he's so bad for you either. Now, come and help me make some tea, and you can tell me how you're getting on with your search.'

In the small, low-ceilinged kitchen, Eileen busied herself with the tea caddy and mugs decorated with a Manx fuchsia pattern. The whole house was like a hymn to patriotism, thought Holly, with its three-legged door knocker, its Archibald Knox Liberty vases and the framed Manx national flag displayed on the wall opposite the cooker. It must be good to feel such a sense of belonging, she reflected wistfully, wondering if she ever would.

'So how far have you got with your search then?' asked Eileen, arranging home-made fruit *bonnag* on a hand-painted plate. 'Philip told me you've been doing an awful lot of phoning round.'

'More than you can possibly imagine!' Holly carried the tea tray back into the sitting room. 'It feels as if we've rung every parish ten times, what with trying to track records down and then having to ask permission for this, that and the other. They don't let you see

166

the register entries yourself,' she explained. 'You have to ask for exactly the information you want. But I think we may be on to something at last.'

Eileen registered interest. 'What exactly?'

'Well, so far we've only found one parish that had confirmations on the date engraved on the necklace, and that's Port Erin. Only sixty-eight people were confirmed that day, and forty-five of those were girls.'

'Progress,' agreed Eileen. 'So, do you think your mother was one of those forty-five girls?'

Holly's stomach was turning backflips. She hardly dared put her hopes into words, in case the very act of expressing them made them vanish in a puff of smoke. 'Perhaps,' was the best she could manage. 'Do you know many people from Port Erin?' she ventured.

'Oh, dozens. Probably hundreds. I may not be best friends with all of them, but when you've lived in a place almost all your life you tend to know just about everyone to some degree – especially on an island that only measures around thirty-two miles by fifteen.'

Holly's pulse quickened. 'So, do you remember any young girls from Port Erin leaving the island about thirty years ago? Sixteen-year-old girls?'

Eileen laughed. 'I'm sorry, I'm not laughing at you; it's just ... well, back then just about every sixteen-year-old girl wanted to leave the island – including me. There was so little work over here. And before you ask,' she added, 'no, I didn't abandon any babies in Cheltenham. But I did get a job in Manchester. I had a great time for about five years,' she reminisced, 'until I started getting home-sick. That's when I came back home, met Charles and settled down.'

Holly thought about the list of forty-five names Phil had been promised by the priest in charge at Port Erin. 'Might you recognise some names from thirty years ago, do you think?'

'My memory's not what it was when I was sixteen,' lamented Eileen. 'But, hey, I can only try. Show me the final list when you have it.' She yawned. 'I've got a lot of clients tomorrow; I think I might go up. Night, Holly.'

'Night, Eileen.'

'Oh, by the way—' Eileen spun round as she reached the door '—I forgot to mention it – Cedric has promised to bring his terrier round to sort out the rat problem.'

Holly stared at her. 'Did you just say "rat"?'

'Yes: they got in through that hole in the cellar again. But don't tell Phil – he's scared stiff of them.' Eileen looked at Holly's bemused expression and twigged. 'Don't listen to everything Phil says, dear,' she advised wearily. 'He means well, but I'm convinced he thinks I'm still living in the Middle Ages. A rat's a rat, Holly, and when it comes to getting rid of them, Cedric's terrier beats a shovel any day of the week.'

Phil drove over to Port Erin to pick up the list a couple of evenings later. By the time he got back to Peel, it was late and he found Holly and Eileen side by side on the settee, fast asleep, with the television on.

Holly awoke with a start, to the squeaky sound of Phil pumping up the inflatable mattress. In her dream, she'd been pursued by giant rats in Post Office uniforms, squeaking at her to hurry up or she'd be late for her round. They all looked just like Grace.

She rubbed her eyes and looked around her. 'Where's Grandma C?'

'I packed her off to bed ten minutes ago. You're very entertaining when you snore, by the way.'

'I do not snore!'

Phil slipped a hand into his shirt pocket. 'Got it all on my mobile. How much will you pay me not to email it to all your friends?' he enquired teasingly.

'Phil, blackmail only works if you're blackmailing somebody who's got money,' Holly pointed out. 'So you're onto a non-starter with me.'

'Damn.' Phil finished pumping up the inflatable mattress, and detached the foot pump. 'I knew I'd forgotten something.' He winced as he stood upright. 'Lordy, that thing's a killer. D'you want me to help you set up the sofa bed?'

It must have been the look on Holly's face that did it, but the next thing Phil said was: 'Something tells me the sofa bed's a big no-no.'

'Only if you're not into S & M.'

'Ah. Well, we can swap beds for tonight, if you want.'

'That's very gallant of you,' said Holly suspiciously. 'So what's wrong with the Argos special?'

'Nothing!'

'So it won't explode if I lie down on it then?'

'I'm not even going to answer that.'

Holly kicked off her slipper and prodded it with her toe. It seemed pleasantly firm to the touch, and free from wires, springs and lumpy bits. 'You've got a deal.'

She could hardly bear to look as Phil pulled out the sofa bed and tried a preparatory bounce.

'Jeez! What's this stuffed with – barbed wire? How on earth did you manage to sleep on it?'

Conscience got the better of Holly. 'Tell you what,' she said with a sigh, 'why don't we just share the mattress? Then nobody gets lacerated buttocks.'

If Phil's eyebrows had shot any higher, they would have reappeared on the back of his neck. 'Share? You and me?'

'And Dweezil, of course.' She and the cat shared a moment of malevolent communion. He hates me, she thought, but in a nice way. 'Look, I'm not coming on to you, if that's what you think.' Phil looked as startled as if the local vicar had just mooned at him. 'I'm just proposing a perfectly practical arrangement.' She picked up two pillows and threw them at him. 'Lay these down the middle of the mattress, and keep to your own side.' She pushed out of her mind a treacherous hope that he might not. 'OK?'

'Er ... sure. OK.'

'So I'll see you in the morning, all right? Oh, and Phil ...'

'What?'

'No nicking the duvet.'

Phil lay in the darkness, listening to Holly breathing and the distant swish of the sea as it crept up the beach.

He wondered if she was awake too, but something was stopping him reaching out to her, and it wasn't the big fat pillow wedged between the two of them, nor the even fatter Dweezil, who was crushing the life out of Phil's legs.

Nor was it the memory of Steve's 'bit of friendly advice' as he and Holly set off on their quest. Admittedly Phil had no great desire to get on the wrong side of someone as enormous as Steve, but he'd have braved even that misfortune for a chance to take Holly in his arms.

No, the thing that was holding him back was his own stupid sense of honour. Maybe he was wrong, but no matter how often Holly insinuated that she and Murdo had split up, Phil was still convinced that he could sense an unbroken bond between the two of them.

And if there was one thing he simply wouldn't do, it was hit on another man's girlfriend.

Although he didn't want to admit it to himself, Phil was dreading the end of this assignment, because he knew deep down inside that there was something really special about Holly Bennett.

Twelve

While Cedric from round the corner's terrier, Wishbone, was busy in the cellar sorting out Thie Veg's rat problem, Holly sat upstairs in the living room, chatting to Nesta on her mobile.

'How's it going at the sorting office?' she asked.

'Mostly the same as usual. I wrote a really smutty verse for Julian's twenty-first birthday card and all the guys signed it. I forged your signature, by the way.'

'Very enterprising. Any more news on the job cuts?'

'It's official: three to go, but we don't know who. Bloody management. By the way, Colin got arrested last week!!!'

'What?!'

Holly almost fell off her chair. Colin, the acting depot manager, was not the most popular of people down at the sorting office, partly because he looked and moved like a human slug, and partly because he was in cahoots with senior management. If anything bad happened to union members, you could be sure that Colin was totally in favour of it.

'He got caught passing a stolen credit card in Seuss & Goldman. When the police arrived, they found he had a whole wallet full of them!'

'So Colin's been stealing from the mail?'

'Sure looks like it.'

Wonders will never cease, thought Holly. 'You're not planning any bank jobs, are you?'

'Can't afford the getaway car. So how about you?' probed Nesta. 'Any exciting news?'

'Well ... maybe.'

'Stop teasing and spit it out.'

Holly's gaze wandered to the pages she'd just printed off. Her fingers trembled as she fumbled the words she could hardly believe herself. 'We think we've finally got a list of possible names.'

'No! Really? Lots, or just one or two?'

'Seventy-three.' Holly groaned inwardly. 'It could have been a lot worse,' she added, as much to convince herself as Nesta. 'Actually we thought there were only forty-five but then some more turned up from another parish.'

Time passed silently for a few seconds. Nesta didn't usually have to think about what to say next, but then this wasn't a usual topic of conversation. Finally she volunteered the cheerful observation: 'One or two of them are probably dead. So that's a start.'

'Yes, but what if one of the ones who's dead was my mother?'

Another thoughtful pause. 'Well, at least you'll know. And it's not as if you knew her very well, is it?'

Holly almost answered that this was the whole point, that she longed to know her birth mother, and almost asked Nesta how she'd feel if she'd never had that chance. But Nesta had a mother – a mother she seldom if ever got on with. In fact, Nesta's mother was the reason why Nesta had left home as soon as she hit sixteen. This was one of those rare things that Nesta wouldn't – and couldn't – understand.

'Phil's at the Registry in Douglas,' Holly explained, 'checking out marriage and death certificates, divorces and so forth.'

'Ah yes. The gorgeous Phil,' giggled Nesta.

'Your words, not mine!'

173

'Oh come on, you know you really fancy him. You told me so. But have you told him yet?'

'Of course not!'

'Do you think he's worked it out for himself?'

Good question, thought Holly. She'd made sure Phil knew that she and Murdo weren't together any more, at least temporarily, but there'd been a complete absence of reaction from Phil. She couldn't bring herself to admit to Nesta that they'd even shared a bed for the last three nights and still nothing had happened!

'I don't think he's interested in me,' she lamented.

'Don't talk rubbish. If the man has a pulse, he fancies you.' Pause. 'Is he gay?'

'I severely doubt it. But Grandma C says Sita well and truly broke his heart, and he's barely looked at a girl ever since.'

'Great. Damaged goods. Well, you'll just have to don a bikini and belly dance your way into his heart or take up stamp-collecting or whatever his thing is. Turn on the seductive charms.'

'I don't think I have any.'

'All right then. Give up.'

Hmm, give up, thought Holly. The prospect had its appeal. And yet the more she thought about it, the less she wanted to do it. But what if she just wasn't Phil's type?

'You still there?' asked Nesta, unheeded.

She has a point, thought Holly. If I'm not Phil's type at the moment, then maybe I can make myself his type. Once I find out what his type is …

It was late, and Holly was about to lie down on her side of the inflatable mattress when her mobile rang.

Phil groaned and stuck his head under the pillow. 'Switch it off.'

She almost did exactly that, but then she noticed that the caller's number had a Cheltenham code. 'Holly Bennett,' she answered.

Someone was breathing heavily at the other end of the line. Oh God, Holly thought, it's one of those perverts who scare the hell out of single women. She opened her mouth to give him a piece of her mind, then a voice that sounded very far away said: 'Holly? It's Kev. You've got to help me.'

The sound of her sister's estranged husband's voice jolted Holly out of the small world of her own concerns, bringing her back abruptly to the fact that while she was playing at detectives, Jess and Kev's domestic drama was teetering on the brink of becoming a tragedy.

Cupping her hand around the phone, she tiptoed out of the living room and into the kitchen. 'Kev, what's up?'

'It's Jess. Holly, you have to talk to her; she's refusing to let me see Aimee!'

Holly sank onto a wooden chair. In the gloom, relieved only by a tiny glimmer of moonlight, the tick-tock of the kitchen clock sounded like a countdown to disaster. 'Surely Jess wouldn't do that. You're Aimee's father ...'

'Oh wouldn't she? I went round this afternoon and she'd changed all the locks. She told me to get out of her life and Aimee's, and said if I didn't she'd get the police on to me and say I'd been threatening her. Please, Holly, you're the only one she'll listen to.'

'OK, OK, calm down, Kev. I can hardly hear what you're saying. Give me a minute to think.'

Holly's brain spun. Jess had always been a bit impulsive, but there'd never been any hint that she might do something like this. Holly could remember a time, not so long ago, when she and Kev had been closer than Siamese twins: inseparably in love, and besotted with their little daughter. Had it really come to this?

'Right,' she said. 'Have you tried getting Grace to speak to her?'

Kev's snort of derision crackled in her ear. 'Who do you think has been putting her up to this?'

'Oh, I'm sure she wouldn't—'

'Come on, Holly, Grace has always hated me, you know that. She's got no time for me or my music. She thinks I'm nothing but an idle waster.'

Holly struggled to contradict him. 'But surely—'

'I know what I'm talking about, Holly. You know what Grace calls me? "The government artist" – because I draw dole.'

Holly knew that what Kev was saying was largely true, yet she didn't want to make him feel even worse by agreeing with him. She took a moment out to think. 'OK, what about Dad?' she asked. 'Have you spoken to him?'

'Your dad's a decent guy,' conceded Kev. 'But you know what he's like, he never takes sides. When it comes to his family, he doesn't want to hurt anyone so he ends up saying nothing. You have to help me, Holly.' His voice cracked with emotion. 'There's nobody else.'

As Kev spoke, Aimee's face kept coming into Holly's mind: the face of a happy, trusting little girl mastering the words 'Mummy' and 'Daddy', with no understanding of what might happen if Mummy and Daddy decided they didn't want to be together any more. Holly understood how Kev felt, and sympathised with Jess's attitude, but her heart was breaking for her little niece. If there was anything she could do to help, she knew that she must do it.

'I'll talk to her,' she promised, 'but it may not do any good. There's not much I can do from hundreds of miles away.' She paused. 'Have you thought about apologising to Jess and asking if you can come back home?'

There was the sound of a sharp, indrawn breath. 'I knew you'd take her side,' said Kev bitterly.

'I'm not taking anybody's side,' protested Holly. 'But sometimes it's best to say you're sorry even if you're not, if it means you can put things right again.'

176

'Only they're not right, are they? Jess got herself pregnant deliberately, I know she did. She knew we couldn't afford another kid, but she decided to have one anyway.'

'Jess says it was an accident.'

'Jess is lying.'

'Does it really matter that much?'

'Of course it matters! If I can't trust her about this, what else can't I trust her about?'

'But if you love her and Aimee,' pleaded Holly, 'couldn't you try to be supportive about the new baby and—?'

Clunk.

It was no use. Kev had rung off, and Holly was left sitting alone in a darkened kitchen with nothing to listen to but the tick of the clock, the swish of the sea and the deafening tumult of her own troubled thoughts.

The post arrived late in Peel, like quite a few other things, but Holly was beginning to get used to the newspapers sometimes not arriving because it was too foggy for the planes to fly, and the toilet wall that had been left unplastered for three months because the plasterer had decreed that there was 'time enough' to get round to doing it.

Apart from her burning need to find her birth mother, Holly had adjusted well to this new, slower pace of life. All she had to do was stand on the porch of Thie Veg in the early morning and take in a long, deep breath of salty-tasting sea air, and she could feel all the knots of tension in her body instantly melt away. Like so many others before her, Holly Bennett was falling in love with the island.

'Something for you today, dear,' announced Eileen, extracting a single item from the bundle of mail.

Holly thanked her and took it. She and Phil were still sitting at the breakfast table in the kitchen, going through all the information Phil had gleaned from the registry in Douglas. It was a long and largely thankless task, and Holly was glad of the diversion.

Phil looked up from his piles of paper. 'Anything interesting?'

She examined the envelope: a Cheltenham postmark and her father's unmistakably painstaking handwriting. He always said that if a postman couldn't write legibly, then what hope was there for the general public?

'Something from Dad. I hope nothing else is wrong back home ...'

Holly tore open the envelope and slid out the contents. First she frowned, then she giggled. 'Look!' She held it up. 'Dad's sent me a postcard of Cheltenham Croquet Club! And a really terrible one of the Montpellier roundabout!'

Phil rubbed his nose. 'Er ... why?'

Holly read out loud: 'Dear Holly, thought I would send you these to make you homesick, in case you are settling in too well over there. We are all missing you, especially me as I can't remember how to work the washing machine. Hurry home or you'll miss *Tarzan* – and how often do you get a chance to see your sister wrestling a wooden crocodile?' The laughter in Holly's heart faded away. 'Jess seems sad and tense. Went round to see her and Aimee, but couldn't get Jess to talk about Kev. Have you and Murdo made up yet? Wanted to know if I should send him a birthday card. Love, Dad.' She sighed. 'Oh great.'

'Ah,' said Phil. 'Delicate subject?'

'Just a little. Dad's always been fond of Murdo. When I told him we were splitting up he was convinced it was just a temporary blip.'

'And is it?' Phil suddenly realised what he'd said. 'Sorry, that's none of my business.'

They looked at each other in idiotic silence for a few moments, each clearly searching for the right words. Something inside Holly's head urged her: Go on, say it. If you don't say it now, you never will.

'It could be your business,' she said slowly. 'I mean ... I could. If you wanted me to be.'

Phil's Adam's apple bobbed up his throat as he swallowed hard. Oh God, thought Holly, I've made a complete exhibition of myself and now I've totally embarrassed him and we won't be able to work together any more. And he warned me that he wasn't over Sita. Plus I'm not even sure I want to be over Murdo! I'm such an idiot.

'I ... um ...' was all Phil managed to get out before Grandma Eileen hove into view again, this time with a plate of buttered toast.

'Fuel for the workers,' she explained. 'So, how far have you got with it?'

'S-sorry?' Startled, Phil looked away, breaking the link between him and Holly.

'The list,' Eileen prompted, sitting down between them at the table. 'How far have you got?'

Holly noticed that Phil's fingers were trembling slightly as he leafed through the papers. 'Thirty-seven,' he said, clearing his throat. 'That's how many names we've got it down to so far.'

'And now we're stuck,' said Holly. 'Unless you can help, that is.'

'Me?'

Phil slid a list of thirty-seven names under his grandmother's nose. 'Do you recognise any of these?' he asked.

Eileen fumbled in her apron pocket for her reading glasses, wedged them on her nose and peered down at the list.

'Mary Andrews? She was at school with your mother. Her dad ran that pub on Station Road. Don't remember her ever leaving the island.' She ran her finger down the list, picking out a couple of other names: one who'd emigrated to Australia with her family, and one who'd worked in the wool shop in Douglas. Neither of

179

them had spent any suspicious periods of time away from the island, or at least, not as far as Eileen knew.

Phil was about to thank her for her help and give up when she turned over the paper and let out a little gasp of surprise. 'Well! There's a turn up for the book.'

Holly peered over Eileen's shoulder. 'What is it?'

Phil's grandmother pointed at a name. 'Christine Kennaugh. If it's the same one, she's my assistant at the complementary therapies centre! And before you ask,' she went on, raising a hand in defence, 'I have no idea what she was doing when she was sixteen. For that, I'm afraid, you'll have to ask her yourselves.'

Christine Kennaugh might be a reiki practitioner, but there was nothing ethereal about her. She looked like what she was: a sturdy farmer's wife who'd borne five children and gone back out to work once the last of them had flown the nest.

'I didn't have to work,' she explained, 'not financially, but I needed to. Can you imagine how lonely it is, with just two people rattling around in a big empty farmhouse that was meant for hordes of children?' Holly agreed that it must be. 'So I decided to get off my backside and learn something new.'

'So reiki's not what you trained for when you left school?' enquired Phil, forging himself a roundabout route to the heart of the matter.

'You're kidding!' Christine wiped away a tear of mirth. 'As a matter of fact I wanted to be an actress, but Mum knew that was just pie in the sky and she sent me on a shorthand-typing course. I worked in London for a while, temping while I tried to get into acting; then I saw sense and came back home. A couple of years later, I got together with my husband.'

'How old were you when you moved to London?' asked Holly.

'Ooh, let me think.' Christine smoothed a fresh runner over

180

Eileen's examination couch. 'I'd be about eighteen when I left here. Why do you want to know?'

Holly hesitated. She glanced at Phil, and he nodded encouragement. 'I'm looking for someone,' she admitted. 'My ... er ... biological mother. And I thought for a minute that it might be you.'

'Gracious.' Christine sat down heavily on a carved Indian stool. 'Whatever made you think that?'

'The fact that you left the island for a while. I was abandoned in Cheltenham as a baby, and we're pretty sure that my mother was a Manx girl, about your age.'

'There are an awful lot of Manxwomen about my age!' laughed Christine.

'So we've discovered,' said Holly ruefully. 'Ah well, at least we can cross one more name off the list.'

'Speaking of lists ...' Phil magicked the sheet of paper from somewhere and held it under Christine's nose. 'The lady we're looking for could be here; most of these are maiden names, by the way. Do you recall any of them?'

'Yes, of course,' replied Christine, scanning the list of names. 'I remember most of them from church when I was a kid.'

'Can you tell us anything about any of them?'

Christine gave a wry smile. 'Where do you want me to start? Take Sarah Jones: lovely girl, bit of a weakness for older men. Mary Reilly – joined the WRNS straight out of school; last I heard, she was living in Dubai with a millionaire. Then there's Denise Kinrade – a right tearaway at school, she was, but she pulled up her socks and now she's an MHK.'

'That's the Manx equivalent of an MP,' Phil explained for Holly's benefit. 'Can you tell us if any of them left the island when they were about sixteen?'

'Temporarily or for good?'

'Either.'

'What – all of them?' Christine frowned. 'I hope you two aren't in a hurry,' she remarked, 'because this is going to take some time.'

Holly kicked a stone and watched it roll away down the grassy slope of the castle mound. 'It might have been easier,' she observed, 'if we'd just asked Christine Kennaugh which girls *didn't* leave the island when they were sixteen.'

She and Phil were standing amid the ruins of Peel Castle, gazing down at the tiny city where Vikings had once rampaged and smugglers crept through its darkened, winding streets.

'She did give us some leads,' Phil pointed out.

'Yes – too many! Now it feels as if any one of those names on the list could be the one. How on earth are we going to get any further with this? Are we going to have to track down everyone and talk to them individually? And even if we do, what if they don't tell the truth? It's impossible!'

Holly could feel her heart pounding against her breastbone. She was profoundly grateful when Phil laid a hand on her shoulder and said quietly: 'Calm down, we'll figure it out.'

'You really think so?'

'What's that really cheesy saying – "The impossible we do at once; miracles take a little longer"?'

In the distance, seagulls swooped and soared in the wake of a trawler, as it cut an arrow-straight furrow through the sparkling sea. Even though we seem to have hit the buffers, thought Holly, there are a lot worse places to be. A little piece of her heart tugged her in the direction of Cheltenham, where Jess and Kev's differences had still to be resolved. But even if I was there, she thought to herself, could I really make much of a difference? Am I flattering myself, thinking that anything I say or do is relevant?

All the same, Holly told herself, I promised Kev that I would call Jess and I must. Maybe she'll listen; maybe all she needs is a bit of big-sisterly chat. And maybe I'm the man in the moon, she thought with a wry smile.

'Penny for 'em,' said Phil.

'What!' Holly nearly jumped out of her skin.

'Hey, it's OK. I was just wondering what you were so deep in thought about. I know, I know,' he went on before Holly had a chance to answer, 'you want me to bugger off and let you have a proper think. It's OK, I get moments like that too.'

'You do?'

'All the time.'

She looked into his soft grey-green eyes and almost forgot her resolution not to embarrass herself again. It would be oh so easy to pour out her heart to him, but he had yet to confide anything to her, and Holly had no desire to embarrass him either. Increasingly, she was coming to the conclusion that she'd been right in the first place and he wasn't interested in her – or in any other woman, for that matter. Because no woman could ever match Sita, or replace what she had taken from him.

They stood looking awkwardly at each other, Holly endeavouring to hold down her flapping cardigan as it tried to take off in the chilly evening breeze.

'You're cold,' said Phil.

'I'm fine, really.'

'Do you want my jacket?'

'No, honestly, I'm fine.'

'I haven't done something I shouldn't, have I?'

Holly laughed. 'No. No, of course you haven't. I'm just having one of those, you know, pensive moments.'

'I'll walk back home and leave you to it then, shall I?'

Holly answered with a nod and a polite smile, and Phil turned and walked away, down the grassy slope.

*

As Phil walked away from Holly, he had to force himself not to stop in his tracks, turn around and gaze at her, spellbound.

Tongue-tied as he was, he had no way of explaining the incredible way it made him feel just looking at her. In all the barren, empty months since Sita had left, he had never once felt the urge to look – *really* look – at another woman. But then Holly had exploded into his life, and since that day her image had conquered not only his dreams, but his every waking moment. He felt as if she had brought him back from the dead.

You've got it bad, Connell, he told himself as he carried on along the seafront, hands thrust deep in his trouser pockets. One step further and you'll be way out of your depth – you do realise that, don't you?

Dare you take the risk?

Jess answered the phone with the thin, high wail of a baby in the background. 'Yes, Aimee, it's OK. Mummy'll be there in a minute.'

'Jess, it's me; Holly. Is this a bad time? Should I call back later?'

'No, you're OK. Hang on a minute while I sort out Aimee.' Softly murmured words reached Holly in muffled bursts, then Jess returned. 'It's all right, she's just teething. So, what can I do for you?'

Jess's breezy, almost brittle tone took Holly aback. It was hard to tell if it reflected Jess as she really was, or if it was an act that Jess was putting on for Holly's benefit. Why couldn't people just behave the way they really were? wondered Holly. Then she thought of how she was behaving with Phil and Murdo, and realised how hypocritical that sounded.

'I was wondering how you were, so I thought I'd give you a call.'

'I'm fine. Well, nearly fine. As fine as someone can be when they're trying to cope on their own with a teething baby and a boiler that keeps breaking down.'

'Won't the landlord fix it?'

184

'The landlord wouldn't get out of bed if the bloody house exploded.'

'Well, you've got a bit of money now,' Holly reminded her, trying to sound as encouraging as possible. 'Should be enough for the deposit on a better flat.'

Jess let out a tetchy explosion of breath. 'Did you just call to boss me around? Only Grace does it better, and she's only down the road.'

This isn't going quite as well as I'd expected, thought Holly. As a kid Jess had always been an awkward character, but she'd been so much calmer, so much ... well ... nicer since she'd settled down and had Aimee. But now Kev wasn't around, it was pretty obvious that the stress was starting to tell. Anger and chaos had overwhelmed Jess all over again, just like they had when she was a wild thirteen-year-old and Mum and Dad had despaired of ever getting through to her. But on the other hand there was Grace, Holly mused. Haughty, harsh, rude Grace – who almost overnight seemed to have become calmer, more accepting, more ... human.

Why don't I understand my sisters any more? she wondered sadly. And why don't they understand me?

'I just thought I'd phone you and see how you were,' said Holly, making an effort to sound upbeat. 'That's OK, isn't it?'

Jess grunted something inaudible. 'Have you found this substitute mother of yours yet then?' she demanded.

Put like that, it made Holly wince. 'No, I haven't traced my birth mother,' she replied pointedly. 'Not yet.'

'Bummer. So are you shagging that Phil bloke? Seems like a waste to go all that way and not get anything out of it.'

Really, thought Holly, it's enough to take your breath away. 'No,' she replied, 'I'm not. And I didn't phone up just to give you the details of my non-existent sex life!' Just in time, Holly reminded herself that losing her temper right now would be a very bad idea.

185

She was supposed to be the peacemaker, after all. 'Look,' she said, somewhat more calmly, 'I'm calling because—'

'Because Kev asked you to?' enquired Jess.

'Yes, all right,' Holly replied with a sigh, 'because Kev asked me to. But that doesn't mean I wouldn't have rung you anyway.'

'Hm,' was Jess's sceptical reply.

'Kev is desperate,' pleaded Holly. 'You can't stop him seeing his own daughter, for pity's sake!'

'Oh yes I can. He's not fit to be a father. He wanted to kill our baby, or have you forgotten that?'

'Of course I've not forgotten, but—'

'Has he told you he's sorry about trying to make me have an abortion?'

'Well, not exactly, but he seems—'

'Then he can get stuffed,' declared Jess. 'You can tell him if he comes back to me on bended knee and apologises, then maybe I'll consider it. Otherwise, he can keep on handing over half his benefit cheque, and I'll see him in court.'

Jess's cold anger shocked Holly. This isn't my sister, she thought. She's stubborn and she can be irritating, but Jess would never do this. Not normally. 'Jess, I'm really worried about you,' she said.

'I told you,' Jess snapped, 'I'm fine.'

'But what about Aimee? Is she fine, without a daddy?' She hesitated for a moment, before adding: 'Mum would never have let this happen to us, and you know it.'

'Don't you bring Mum into this! You're the one who's trying to find a replacement for her!'

'You and I both know that's not true,' Holly replied quietly. 'All I want is to know where I came from, so that if I ever have children they'll know too. And if I do,' she added, 'I'll make sure they know their dad.'

Unfortunately this turned out to have been exactly the wrong thing to say. Jess blew up like a miniature volcano, practically setting the phone line alight. 'Don't you dare say that to me!' she snarled. 'Don't you dare! I know what's right for my baby, and you know jack shit! Why don't you fuck off back to London and marry that creep Murdo? You two are made for each other.'

And then Jess rang off.

Holly sat alone on the seafront at midnight, watching the lazy tide creep up the beach like black oil. She closed her eyes and let the breeze caress her face, soothing away the hurts of the day.

She'd slipped out of the house when Phil and his grandma were asleep, not bothering to lock the front door because nobody round here did, and walked the fifty yards or so down to the promenade. She had to think, and for that she needed to be alone with the darkness and the sea.

I should be doing something to help Jess, she told herself. And Kev. Poor Kev. Maybe he'd done wrong, but she firmly believed he didn't deserve to be excluded from his daughter's life. Come to that, maybe there was still hope for him and Jess as a couple. If only Holly could find the key.

She recalled them only a year ago, arm in arm and giggling like a pair of idiots, so in love and so excited to be expecting their first baby. What had gone wrong? she wondered. Straight away, she answered her own question: what went wrong is what always goes wrong. Love doesn't last like it did in the old days, in Mum and Dad's day. Nowadays, people are madly in love for fifteen minutes, get bored, and move on to the next partner, forever looking for perfection, for something that doesn't exist. Nobody sticks with anything – or anyone – any more.

Me included, she thought; and her thoughts went out to Murdo, hundreds of miles away and still hoping they'd get back together. Now Holly knew that they never would. Perhaps she always had.

Either way, she had to find some way of telling him that wouldn't hurt him. Why did people always have to get hurt?

There were tears in her eyes but she wiped them away with the back of her hand. This isn't about me, she thought. I'm supposed to be thinking of a way to help Jess and Kev. What kind of family is it for Aimee without a father?

She thought and thought but the only image that would come to her was the image of a box containing a Manx tartan rug and a silver necklace. At least I have something of my mother's, she told herself. I know nothing at all about my father.

Hands in pockets, she stood up and walked slowly along the promenade, the dark silhouette of the castle looming behind her. Was she wrong to decide not to try and track down her father? Was she wrong to make assumptions about the kind of man he was, or had been? No, she decided. I have a father, the best father in the world; there's no room in my heart for any other. And no matter how bad things got, Dad could never be the kind of man who fathered a child and then stood by as the mother abandoned it.

But what if my biological father wasn't like that, what if he didn't even know ... ?

Holly's head sank into her hands. This was all too much to bear. And maybe, when it was all over, she'd end up knowing no more than she did at the beginning.

Thirteen

The next morning, Holly and Phil held a council of war, sitting on the carpet in Grandma Christian's front room.

'So, what do we do next?' pondered Phil. 'The ball's in your court ... Hol.'

A little shiver of silly excitement ran through Holly; that was the first time he'd ever called her by her pet name, the name that only her closest friends used.

'I guess ... we give up and go home.'

Phil looked doubtful. 'Are you sure about that?'

'No,' she admitted, 'but somebody has to make a decision, and this can't go on for ever, can it? For one thing, my money's running out.'

Phil looked across at her. 'Let's not think about the money. The money's not important.' Somehow, she knew he meant it. 'I don't need to earn that much to survive. Let's not give up until you're absolutely sure.'

'It's a long way to come and then go back empty-handed,' agreed Holly. 'But what do we have? Thirty-seven names, any of which might be my birth mother – or maybe none at all. Even if they all lived on the island – which they don't – we couldn't barge into the lives of thirty-seven women, asking questions about illegitimate babies.'

'And then there's always the possibility that they might lie,' agreed Phil. 'I mean, if you hadn't told your husband that you'd had an illegitimate baby before you met him, and then this odd couple turned up and started asking embarrassing questions, what would you do?'

'Send them away with a flea in their ear,' replied Holly. She took a sip from the mug of tea on the coffee table. 'So, we'll rule that out then. What does that leave us with?'

'A rug and a necklace.' Phil extracted them from the case file he'd created. 'Oh – and an envelope. A blank, empty envelope.'

'Great. That's not going to tell us much, is it?'

'I doubt it.' Phil turned it over in his hands, examined every corner, looked inside and finally held it up to the light. 'Hang on a minute though ... Let me get this to the window.'

He scrambled to his feet and half ran over to the cottage's small front window. Holly was not far behind. 'What have you found?'

'Maybe nothing. Or ... maybe ... a watermark! Here, look.'

He handed the envelope to Holly and pointed to the flap. As she held it up to the sunlight, she made out a blurred picture of something that looked like a building, and four words:

EAGLE'S NEST
PORT ERIN

'Oh my God!' she gasped, looking again. 'What do you think it is – a hotel?'

'Bound to be. Mustn't get too excited though.'

'No, of course not.'

They looked at each other, and suddenly they were both grinning like children.

It wasn't much, but it was something.

*

Holly had been expecting Murdo to call, but even so, the sound of his voice came as a shock. She was taking an anxious walk along the beach, while Phil found out about the Eagle's Nest, and the last thing she felt like doing was explaining things to him, especially over the phone.

'How are you?' he asked. 'Sorry I haven't rung before but we've had a ton of work at the office.'

'That's OK, I understand.'

'And last time we spoke, I got the feeling you didn't want to talk to me for a while.'

'Well . . .'

'And of course, if you had wanted to, you could have phoned me.'

'Now I feel like a complete bastard,' she said.

And she did. She might not actually have done anything wrong, but she felt as if she had. And she'd certainly dreamed about it, she thought, as she recalled lying in bed next to Phil and longing for him to reach out and touch her. What if he had? Would she be admitting it to Murdo now? She had a feeling that she wouldn't, and that just made her feel even guiltier.

'Why?' asked Murdo. He sounded surprised. 'You couldn't be a bastard if you tried, not even an incomplete one.'

She tried to laugh, but it came out more like a strangled cough. 'Neither could you. I've always thought you were the kindest, most generous man I've ever met.'

'Now you're making me nervous,' he said.

It was Holly's turn to ask 'Why?'

'Because you're making me sound as if I'm in the past. Am I in the past?' he asked.

'I . . . don't know,' she lied, hating herself for not being honest with him. But she had loved him once, and there was enough of that love still inside her for the thought of hurting him to hurt her too.

191

'That's OK,' he said. 'I don't want to put any pressure on you. I just want you to be happy, and I want to be the man to make you that way. Now,' he went on, changing the subject, 'are you going to tell me how you're getting on with this great quest of yours?'

Holly was overwhelmed with a feeling of guilty relief. If he'd gone on questioning her, she knew that the truth would have come spilling out of her, and that would have been wrong. When she told him, she needed to be with him, not hundreds of miles away on the end of a crackly telephone line.

'To be honest, we thought we were going to have to call it a day and come home, but – You remember that blank envelope I told you about, the one that had the money in it? – Well, Phil held it up to the light and spotted a watermark. We think it belongs to a hotel in Port Erin, so once Phil's figured out exactly where it is, we'll be off to take a look.'

'That's good news.' There was the tiniest of pauses. Then Murdo said: 'So you're getting on well with this Phil, are you?'

'Very,' she replied, with perfect honesty. 'As a colleague.'

'Nothing else?'

'No,' she replied, honestly again, 'nothing else.'

'I'm sorry, I just—'

'Don't apologise. I understand.'

'It's just that I love you, you see.'

'I know.' If Murdo had been there, he would have seen the tears trickling down Holly's cheeks. 'I ... I have to go now. We'll talk when I get back.'

'OK, I'll see you then. Bye.'

'T-take care.'

She barely managed to ring off before the rest of the tears came; tears not just for Murdo, but for her own cowardice.

'Is something wrong, Hol?' asked a familiar voice behind her.

'I'm OK, Phil.' She tried to hide her face from him.

'No you're not, you're crying. What's wrong?'

She took a deep breath. 'That was Murdo on the phone. I was trying to tell him it was all over, but I couldn't.'

'Ah,' said Phil. 'Then maybe it isn't over?'

'Believe me, Phil,' she said, looking him straight in the eye, 'it's been over for a long time, it's just that neither of us could bear to admit it. Don't suppose you have a clean tissue?'

'Sorry. But I do have a very absorbent shoulder.'

She laughed, and sniffed back the tears. 'Thanks, but I think I can manage till we get back.'

'I just came out to find you to tell you the news,' explained Phil. 'You know, about the Eagle's Nest.'

Holly looked at him expectantly. 'Well? Is it a hotel then?'

'It ... *was* a hotel,' Phil replied slowly, 'thirty years ago. Up on the side of Bradda Head. Amazing views.'

Holly's heartbeat quickened. 'Was? You mean it's not any more? Has it been turned into a conference centre or something?'

'Er ... not exactly.' Phil had the look of a man searching for the right words, all of them bad. 'Eighteen years ago it went out of business, and was sold to a property development company. Then the property development company went bust.

'And twelve years ago, the whole place was demolished. There's nothing left on Bradda Head now but hikers and sheep.'

Fourteen

'Let me do a bit of digging,' Phil pleaded. 'Let me try and find out something – anything.'

'I don't know.' Holly rubbed her aching head and sank into Eileen's sofa. 'Maybe it's just time to call a halt and leave.'

'Just a couple more days? We can book ourselves and the van onto the boat at short notice, that won't be a problem.'

As usual, Dweezil was sitting between them on the sofa, and he was gazing up at Holly with such big, round eyes that she could have sworn he was echoing Phil's 'just a couple more days'. But then he would. Dweezil loved hunting rats in the cellar and he loved Eileen's home-made chocolate chip cookies, possibly a little too much to judge from the size of his paunch.

She rubbed Dweezil's flat, furry head until he rumbled with pleasure. 'Oh all right then. But I'm not going to let things just run on and on. Nesta says they're desperate for me at the sorting office now Colin's been remanded in custody.'

Phil grinned. 'Do all your friends consort with dangerous criminals?' he enquired.

Holly stuck out her tongue at him. 'Ha ha, very funny. I'd hardly call Colin dangerous.'

'But you told me yourself he head-butted a policeman.'

'No, I didn't say he head-butted a policeman,' Holly corrected him. 'I said he tripped over trying to run away, and accidentally hit his head on a policeman's nose.' She thought for a moment. 'Come to think of it, that does sound pretty damning. But Colin always was a complete klutz.'

'So Nesta's running the show single-handed, while Colin's in chokey?'

'Virtually. I mean, the actual depot manager, Graham, is never in the place. Rumour has it he's having an affair with someone from Parcelforce, but nobody's actually caught them at it yet. Trouble is, his prolonged absences mean even more work for Nesta. She's having trouble keeping up with the orders for personalised poems.'

'And that'll never do,' Phil remarked, hopping briefly into the kitchen and emerging with the biscuit tin. 'Don't tell Grandma,' he urged in hushed tones, 'but I could just murder a couple of her cookies.'

They helped themselves, and Dweezil caught the crumbs in his mouth.

'Anyhow, that's why Nesta needs me,' Holly explained. 'She's got all this on her plate, and she's short-staffed already, and now there's this trouble with Welsh Dave.'

'Who?' asked Phil through a haze of biscuit crumbs.

'This horrible, slimy little toad of a postman who gets his kicks reading people's mail and spreading nasty rumours. He got caught peering through some lady's window while she was taking a shower, and now she's pressing charges. Serves him right; he's getting a taste of his own medicine, now his face is plastered all over the *Cheltenham Courant*. Which is great, except that it means Nesta's got to find someone to cover his round.'

The front door opened and closed in quick succession, and Eileen appeared in the lounge doorway. 'What's the verdict?'

'We're staying,' said Phil.

'Just for a couple of days, mind,' said Holly.

Eileen beamed. 'Glad to hear it.' Her eagle eyes took in the half-empty biscuit barrel. 'Looks like I'll be making some more chocolate chip cookies.'

'Sorry, Grandma.' Phil didn't look it. 'I can't help it if they're irresistible.' His hand waved a little too close to Dweezil, who leaped up with surprising agility and grabbed the entire cookie. Phil shrugged, and helped himself to another one. 'And he can't help it if he's a cat of impeccable taste.'

'I thought we were going to get out there and do some digging,' Holly reminded him through her laughter.

'We will,' Phil promised her. 'Just as soon as I've finished this biscuit.'

As they sat there on Grandma Christian's carpet, covered in crumbs and laughing like teenagers, Phil suddenly realised that this was the happiest he had ever been in his life. No contest.

But almost immediately, his stomach was filled with a horrible leaden feeling. It's all going to come to an end, he reminded himself, and the thought found a doleful echo in his heart. Far, far too soon all of this would be gone – and so would she.

It was almost too much to bear.

There was not much point asking around in Peel, so there was nothing for it but to get in the van and drive down to Port Erin, in the south-west of the island.

It had been drizzling all morning, but as soon as they got within sight of the little town, the clouds parted and a watery sun appeared.

'Good omen,' decided Phil. 'Now, see that big, beautiful head-land coming up in the distance?' Holly nodded. 'That's Bradda Head, where the Eagle's Nest used to be. And that tower on the top is Milner's Tower. It was built by a local lock maker, and legend has it that it's shaped like one of his locks. I've no idea if it's true, mind you. This little island is full of smoke and mirrors.'

'Is that why you love it so much? Because of the sense of mystery?' wondered Holly.

'Maybe – though it infuriates the detective in me.' He rested his hands loosely on the steering wheel as they coasted along the long, straight road. 'But mainly because I just feel I belong.' He snatched a glance at Holly. 'Don't you feel it too, the way it draws you in? They say that once you've been here, the island never leaves you, and you keep on coming back.'

They drove into the little town along Station Road, slicing through a cloud of vapour from the steam railway station on the left, passed the Falcon's Nest Hotel, and parked the van on a road that curved around a truly beautiful bay. Do I belong here? Holly asked herself as she took in the cool blue waters and the towering headland. Do I belong here, or in Cheltenham, or nowhere – and will I ever know?

'Well, this is it,' said Phil, clearly enjoying his role as a tour guide. 'That grey smudge on the horizon is Ireland, by the way. The Mountains of Mourne. Now, to your left, breakwater and the former Marine Biological Station; to your right, Bradda Head; and in the middle—' he indicated the Falcon's Nest Hotel behind them with a wink '—some of the best ale in the Isle of Man.'

'I might have guessed you'd get beer into this somehow,' said Holly, following him inside. 'This had better be research.'

The Falcon's Nest Hotel had been a feature of Port Erin for over a hundred and twenty years. Gladstone had spent his holidays there once, and his portrait glared grimly down at diners in the restaurant. It was enough to put anybody off their dinner. But the hotel itself was warm, bustling and friendly. Holly felt at home the moment she stepped into the bar.

It was well after lunchtime, but there were still quite a few regulars at the bar and at the tables, lingering over half-drunk pints and putting the world to rights.

'Promising,' said Phil. 'Some of these guys look like they were here when Gladstone was a lad. Look at that one with the enormous beard.'

'Shh! He'll hear you.' Holly swallowed down the urge to giggle like a fourteen-year-old. What had got in to her, this last couple of weeks on the island? Her heart seemed to veer between being as heavy as lead and as light as a beach ball, with nothing in between.

Phil bought himself a half of Bushy's Best, because he was driving, and a glass of wine for Holly, and pocketed the change. 'Great beer,' he commented to the young, red-headed barman by way of an ice-breaker. 'I always miss it when I'm off the island. I'm Phil, by the way, and this is Holly.'

The barman answered that he was Henry, and that on the whole he preferred tequila slammers, but you couldn't beat a good Manx ale. 'On holiday, are you?' he asked, polishing up a pint glass.

'Not really,' Holly replied. 'We're looking for someone. I—'

Phil signalled to her to let him do the talking for now. 'We're doing a bit of research into the old Eagle's Nest Hotel. Don't suppose you're old enough to remember it?'

Henry scratched his freckled nose. 'Eagle's Nest? Wasn't that the old place on Bradda they knocked down years ago? Yeah, that's right: some bloke's submitted a planning application for luxury apartments – it was in the *Examiner* a few weeks ago. So what are you researching then?'

'Oh, just the history of the place,' Phil replied, casually turning his glass in his hands. 'And we're especially interested in the seventies. It'd be great to have a chat with someone who used to work there back then.'

Henry gave his nose another scratch. 'Let's see ... There's old

Juan Collister, but he retired in the sixties. Can't think of anybody else.' He rang the big pub bell, and the whole place instantly fell silent. 'Anybody here used to work at the Eagle's Nest back in the seventies? There's a couple here doing some research.'

'I used to mow the lawns there,' volunteered the man with the enormous white beard.

'Better than nothing,' Phil whispered to Holly. 'That's great,' he said to the bearded man. 'Could we have a chat and I'll buy you another beer?'

'We can, and you can buy me as many beers as you like,' came the reply, 'but I don't know nothing about the hotel.'

'But you said—'

'I only used to mow the lawns, see. I had my own shed and they used to leave my money for me there. Never went inside the place except once when I needed new blades for the mower and the manager had to sign my chitty.'

'Oh,' said Phil, deflated. 'Well, thanks anyway. Anybody else?' he enquired, surveying the room. Heads shook apologetically. 'Anybody know anybody who used to work there?'

'Well, there's my wife's cousin Mick,' ventured a tall man in fisherman's gear. 'He was under-manager there for a while.'

'Brilliant!' Phil's face lit up. 'So is it OK if we talk to him?'

'You can try,' replied the fisherman, 'but you'll need a medium. He's been dead seven years.'

After some general chat with the regulars about Port Erin, Holly and Phil emerged onto the corner of Station Road. The sun had been swallowed up by a flotilla of heavy grey clouds. A brisk breeze was whipping up the skirts of passers-by, and it looked as if it might rain at any moment.

'That wasn't exactly a resounding success,' remarked Holly, turning up the collar of her jacket.

'No, but we did get a free sandwich each as a consolation prize,' Phil pointed out. 'You can't say they weren't friendly. Just not very informative.'

'And our next move is?' enquired Holly.

'We visit every shop, hotel, church, you name it, in Port Erin until we find somebody who can tell us something.'

'I was afraid you might say that.' Port Erin had seemed small when they first arrived, but suddenly it started to look rather big. Holly wished she'd worn more suitable shoes and remembered to bring an umbrella as well as a map.

'This is all about you, remember,' said Phil. 'You're the boss. You can call the whole thing off if that's what you really want.'

'No.' Holly told herself to get a backbone. 'It's not. Come on then, I'll take the library and you can take the arts centre.'

They were about to go their separate ways when Phil's mobile rang. He fished it out of his jacket pocket. 'Grandma? What's up?' He listened for a while, then exclaimed: 'What? You never have! Give me the address then, you clever girl.' He tucked the phone under his chin and searched his pockets in desperation until he found his notebook and pencil. By the time he rang off, his smile was as big as the horizon.

'Well?' demanded Holly.

'That was Grandma.'

'Obviously! And?'

'And she's been asking around her cronies, and one of them has a son who – guess what – was a trainee manager at the Eagle's Nest back in the seventies!'

Holly's heart pounded. 'And will he talk to us?'

Phil squeezed her hand firmly. 'He will, Hol; whether he wants to or not.'

Fifteen

Jim Stephenson's house stood in a cul-de-sac at the top end of Bradda East; an ordinary bungalow in an ordinary setting, were it not for the amazing view it commanded across the bay and along the coast towards the Calf of Man.

The moment he opened the door, Holly felt the power of speech desert her. She was profoundly grateful for Phil's easy professionalism. If he hadn't been there, she'd probably just have stood there for a minute or so, mouth flapping uselessly, then taken flight down the garden path.

'Mr Stephenson? I phoned you a little while ago,' said Phil with a practised smile. 'My grandmother said you might be willing to have a chat with us.'

'You must be Miss Bennett and Mr Connell,' observed Jim. 'I suppose you'd better come in.'

He was an extraordinarily ordinary-looking guy in his mid to late forties, Holly noted; the sort who went totally unnoticed all their lives, until one day they ended up on the local news, after going bonkers and trying to hold up a sub-post office with a can of aerosol air-freshener. Jim Stephenson showed no sign of going bonkers, but she could tell from his body language that he wasn't entirely at ease. Then again, who would be? It couldn't be every day that two complete strangers turned up on your doorstep, wanting to ask questions about things that happened thirty years ago. Maybe there were things from thirty years ago that he'd rather not remember.

He showed them into a front room dominated by an enormous table-top train set. Phil's eyes lit up. 'Incredible – my uncle had a set in the shed when I was a kid, but it wasn't half the size of this one! And mine's just a tiny thing in the corner of my living room.'

'Bit of an enthusiast, are you?' Jim relaxed a little, clearly on familiar ground. 'I've only just finished painting the *Flying Scotsman* and the first-class carriages – what do you think?'

'Awesome.' It was obvious that Phil meant it. 'May I?'

'Go ahead.'

Phil flicked the switch that started the trains running, snaking over bridges and through tunnels. Even Holly was impressed, and she'd suffered her father's model-train infatuation for the past thirty years.

'So what exactly did you want to talk to me about?' asked Jim, perching on the arm of an armchair. 'You're not with the police, are you?'

Holly wondered what Jim had to fear from the local constabulary, but shook her head. 'I'm just a girl trying to find her mother, and Phil here is a private detective who's helping me.'

'We think she may have had a connection with the Eagle's Nest Hotel,' Phil explained, 'and my grandma told us that you used to be a trainee manager there back in the seventies: exactly the time when she might have been around.' He flicked the switch again and the trains all froze. 'We'd really appreciate any help you can give us.'

Jim frowned. 'What's this woman's name?'

'We don't know,' Holly admitted.

'Then how—?'

'We'd better tell him,' said Holly, and went on to explain about the necklace, the tartan rug and the envelope.

'I'm afraid it's all pretty circumstantial,' admitted Phil, 'but it's all we've got.'

'So you're saying you've got a list of women who might be your mother, and you want me to tell you if any of them had links to the Eagle's Nest?' Phil and Holly nodded. 'OK, better show me the list then. Can't promise I'll remember, though; it was a long time ago and I was just a young lad.'

Phil took the list out of his document case and handed it to Jim. Holly offered up a silent prayer as he scanned the columns of names.

'Just that one,' he said, pointing to a name halfway down the second column. 'She came to the hotel quite a few times.'

Holly leaned over and read the name: 'Denise Kinrade.'

'Denise Collister, as she is now,' cut in Jim. 'Done well for herself, one way or another.'

Holly's heart gave a big, melodramatic thump. 'Didn't Eileen say Denise Kinrade was an MH-whatever-it-was now?'

'She's a member of the Manx parliament, yes,' said Phil. 'An MHK.' He focused all his attentions upon Jim. 'Are you sure about this?'

'Cast-iron certain.'

'And you don't recognise any of the other names?'

'One or two,' conceded Jim. 'It's a small island. But none that had any connection with the hotel.' He paused, looking down at his feet. 'If you want to know why I remember Denise so clearly, I had a good reason to: I was madly in love with her.' He laughed. 'Not that she even noticed. She was far too preoccupied with her English sugar daddy.'

All of this information left Holly numb and shaken. Was this woman her mother then? After all the searching and the despair, had they really found her at last? Neither her heart nor her head could quite adapt to the idea that they might actually have succeeded. She felt dizzy and disorientated, as if Jim Stephenson's armchair was slowly swallowing her whole. Phil was standing like a statue, waiting to take his cue from her.

'What ... exactly ... happened?' she heard herself ask. 'With her and this ... sugar daddy?'

'Back then I was the trainee manager,' began Jim, 'which basically meant dogsbody. I had to work hours and hours of unpaid overtime. I was on the front desk one afternoon when this really pretty Manx girl turned up with this older English bloke. I mean, she was no more than fifteen or sixteen and he must have been forty if he was a day. She was giggling and he was all over her; it really turned my stomach. You could even see the dent on his finger where he'd taken his wedding ring off.'

'So she was having an affair with a married man?' Holly wondered why the thought shocked her, even mildly. She'd known all along that something of the sort must be behind her own life story. It was just that hearing it put into words made it all sound so ... grubby.

'A lot of that sort of thing used to go on back then. It probably still does. English businessman works Monday to Friday on the island, so he has a nice little Manx girlfriend over here and goes home to his loving wife at weekends.'

'All very convenient,' agreed Phil. 'For him.'

'Anyhow,' Jim went on, 'they took a room, and I didn't see them again until breakfast time. You can fill in the missing bits yourself. It broke my heart to see that girl being used, but who was I to say anything? And she seemed happy enough at the time. From what I could gather, they both worked in one of the offshore banks in Douglas; she was the office junior.'

'It must have made her feel really important,' mused Holly,

'sleeping with the boss.'

'It went on for a few months, I guess,' Phil continued. 'And then one night I was on duty and suddenly everything was different between them. He had a face like thunder, and her eyes were all red – you could see she'd been crying. Well, I admit I was curious, more than curious, obsessed. I'd got into the habit of taking the pass key and letting myself into the empty room next to theirs, so I could listen to them through the wall. I know it sounds creepy, but you have to understand, I was besotted with the girl.'

Holly nodded, dry-throated. 'Go on.'

'I did the same that night. Only this time, I heard them having a terrible row. She was in floods of tears, screaming that he couldn't make her kill their baby, and he was yelling at her that if she had any sense she'd take the money, get rid of it and then they could forget all about it. She said there was no way she was having an abortion, and that when he saw their baby, he'd change his mind and leave his wife. She said she'd follow him home to England and make him leave. He told her to stop living in dreamland.

'All of this went on for a while longer, then I heard the door of their room bang and footsteps going downstairs. And after that, there was nothing but the sound of her crying.'

'What did you do?' asked Holly.

'What could I do? I wasn't supposed to be there, listening in to private conversations, was I? All I could do was go back to the front desk and pretend I hadn't heard anything.' Jim looked from Holly to Phil, as though hoping for some sign of forgiveness. 'I didn't see him again. She checked out first thing next morning, looking like death. I asked her if she needed any help, and I think she guessed that I knew ... but she said no, and that was the last I saw of her for two, three years.'

'Did she go to England?' asked Holly, her hands trembling. 'Did her lover live in Cheltenham?'

Jim shook his head sadly. 'I'm sorry, I don't know. All I know is that she left the island for a couple of years, and when she came back there was definitely no sign of any baby. Not that anybody but me was expecting to see one,' he added. 'I know how to keep my mouth shut. I haven't told this to anyone in thirty years.'

'So why are you telling us now?' demanded Phil.

'Because I feel guilty, I guess.' Jim let out a long sigh. 'Maybe I could have done something to help her, all those years ago.'

'Could have, but didn't,' said Phil pointedly.

'No. All the same,' Jim pleaded, 'in the long run she hasn't done badly out of life. Couple of years after she came back, she married this rich landowner.' He smiled weakly. 'I'd always kind of hoped she might prefer me, but what's an assistant manager in a crap hotel got to offer a woman like her?'

'Quite,' said Phil.

'Anyway, they got divorced a few years later and she got a pile of money out of it. Then she went into politics, and got herself elected to the House of Keys. She didn't meet Gary Collister and marry him until about ... oh ... around ten years ago, it would be. The kids are still at primary school.'

Holly felt all the blood drain from her face. 'Kids? She's got young children?'

Jim nodded, oblivious to the effect his words were having upon Holly. 'Boy and a girl. Little girl looks a lot like you, come to think of it.'

Suddenly, everything around the edges of Holly's field of vision turned fuzzy and grey, and Jim's voice sounded as if it was coming from the other end of a very long tunnel.

It was only Phil's timely catch that prevented her from crashing to the floor.

Half an hour later, Holly was sitting outside the Cosy Nook café on Port Erin beach, and Phil was plying her with sugary tea and slabs of buttered toast.

'I've never fainted in my life before,' she muttered embarrassedly. 'Look, you don't need to fuss ...'

Phil shrugged. 'What if I like fussing? Drink that tea up,' he ordered, 'or I'm taking you to the doctor's.'

'I'm completely OK, really I am,' insisted Holly. 'It was just a shock, finding out that I've got a half-brother and half-sister I never knew I had. That is, assuming Denise Collister really is my birth mother.'

'We'll never know that for certain, not one hundred per cent,' replied Phil. 'Not unless you're willing to ask her to provide a DNA sample.'

Holly shivered at the prospect. The sun was warm but she felt cold. 'Do you really think Jim Stephenson will keep his mouth shut about all this?' she asked.

Phil pondered for a few moments. 'Something tells me he might. I can't see him spreading rumours that might damage his beloved Denise's reputation – or make himself look bad. Then again, does it matter?'

'What do you mean, does it matter?' asked Holly, alarmed.

'The whole object of all this was to find your birth mother, right?'

'Right,' agreed Holly, cautiously.

'To find her so that you could find out about yourself. Now, the only way you're going to get all your questions answered is to actually talk to the woman and tell her that you think you're her daughter. And once that gets out, the whole island will know in five minutes that young Denise Collister wasn't quite such a good Catholic girl as they thought she was. You have to ask yourself, Hol: is that what you want?'

Holly gazed into the murky depths of her polystyrene tea cup. 'Oh shit,' she murmured.

*

She was still agonising that night, when she and Phil went for a midnight walk on Peel beach. Why did things have to be so difficult? Why hadn't she thought this through properly before she started?

That, she mused, was in danger of becoming her motto.

They walked side by side along the water's edge, hair's breadth-close but not quite touching, their fingertips occasionally brushing against each other. The intermittent contact sent shivers through Holly that had absolutely nothing to do with the head cold she was developing.

'Have you decided what to do?' asked Phil.

She kicked at a pebble, and it splashed away into the moonlit sea. 'Yes.'

'Are you going to talk to her?'

Holly hesitated. 'Kind of.'

'What does that mean?'

She looked at him and smiled for the first time that day. 'Wait and see.'

They walked on a little further, then Phil said: 'Look, the tide's coming in; we've almost run out of beach.'

'And time,' Holly said softly.

Phil's hand sought out hers and for the first time their fingers entwined. 'You're right, it's almost over,' he said.

'Not quite.' It was not so much a statement as a plea.

They stopped, and turned to face each other. 'When it's over,' said Phil slowly, 'will you promise me that you won't just vanish out of my life again? Because if you did, I don't think I could bear it.'

How could she tell him? Tell him how afraid she was that he would vanish from her life and leave her empty and alone? Tell him how alive he had made her feel, and how she was dreading the return to normality? There were words she longed to say, special words, but when she opened her mouth they wouldn't come, because all she could think of was Murdo, and the words she had yet to say to him.

'It's late,' she said, gently detaching her hand from Phil's. 'We should go back now; tomorrow's going to be a busy day.'

Late that night, before Holly slid under the covers next to Phil and Dweezil, everyone back home received a text message from her. It was short and to the point. All it said was:

THINK WE'VE FOUND HER.

Sixteen

Fuchsia Court was aptly named. Although surrounded on three sides by high walls, these were virtually invisible beneath a thick, luscious covering of wild fuchsia, its bell-like blossoms spilling over the brickwork in a crimson and purple waterfall.

'This has to be it,' said Phil, consulting the map. 'Quite some pad, huh?'

'Wow,' was all Holly could manage.

'Is it what you expected?'

'Phil, none of this is what I expected.'

They had driven a couple of miles out of Port Erin, along the rugged coast, until they found a sheltered inlet. It was completely deserted, save for the imposing residence perched high on the cliff top, overlooking the bay.

'OK, I'm ready,' said Holly, getting out of the van.

Phil followed her, pocketing the van's keys. 'Wouldn't it be a better idea just to walk up to the front door?'

'If we do that, we'll have to explain why we're here, and then the whole thing will come out.'

'But ... I thought you said you were going to talk to her anyway,' protested Phil.

'I am. Come on,' urged Holly, 'you're the private investigator, remember. Where's your sense of adventure?'

Only weeks ago, thought Holly to herself, she'd never have entertained the idea of spying on anyone, let alone a member of the Manx parliament with more money than she could shake a whole forest full of sticks at.

Anyone who had happened by at that moment would have seen two people, a man and a woman, sneaking up to the high wall at the end of Fuchsia Court's back garden. The woman clearly hadn't mastered the art of looking inconspicuous, while the man looked as though he wished he was somewhere else entirely.

'Give me a leg-up then,' whispered Holly.

Phil glanced around him uneasily, though there were no spectators in range give or take the odd sheep, and joined his hands together. Holly sprang up, with an agility she hadn't realised she possessed, and got a grip on the fuchsia-covered wall.

Ever so carefully, millimetre by millimetre, she raised her head until she could just see over the top of the wall.

Oh my God! Excitement and terror mingled in Holly and she momentarily swayed, clawing at the foliage to maintain her balance. That's her! It must be. And that must be my half-brother and my half-sister.

The woman was dark-haired and slim. Her eyes were closed, and she was reclining in a garden chair with a book on her lap while the two children played noisily around her, chasing each other in and out of the flowerbeds. Holly hardly dared breathe, convinced that any moment now one of them would look up and say: 'Mummy, who's that funny lady looking at us over the wall?'

But they didn't. And Holly went on watching them, lost in some place outside time and space where only they and she existed, quite oblivious to Phil's increasing struggle to hold her up.

Do I look like her? The question buzzed obsessively around the inside of Holly's head. Her hair's darker than mine, but perhaps it's dyed. She's much slimmer than I am. I wonder what colour her eyes

211

are. Her face is a completely different shape. Am I like her at all? Can this really be the woman who gave birth to me?

She might have gone on gazing at the three of them all day, if Phil had been up to the challenge. But all of a sudden she found herself lurching sideways; she tried to hold on, but there was no strength in the fuchsia tendrils and a moment later she was sprawling on the grass at the foot of the wall, with her skirt up round her bottom.

'You let go of me!' she protested.

'Holly, I've been telling you to get down for the last five minutes. I'm not Arnold Schwarzenegger, you know.'

'Are you saying I'm fat?'

'No! Just ... curvy.'

'Fat.' Holly sighed. 'Not like her.'

'You saw her then?'

Holly nodded. 'I saw her. And the children. I really don't think I look anything like her, Phil. Do you think we could have made a mistake?'

'Realistically? No.' Phil patted grass stalks off his jeans and helped Holly to her feet. 'She's on the list of girls who were confirmed on the date engraved on the necklace; she was pregnant out of wedlock around the time you were born; and she had a link to the Eagle's Nest. She's the only one who fits the bill, Hol.'

Holly nodded. 'I know. Not everyone looks like their parents, do they? Believe it or not, people used to say I looked like Mum – and I was adopted! All the same ...'

'You were hoping for some kind of dramatic resemblance?'

'Yeah. I guess. Still, at least now I know what she looks like. And that's going to make her a whole lot easier to follow.'

Back in Cheltenham, the last few weeks had been an unremitting hell for Kev. It didn't matter how sorry he was; how desperately he regretted trying to persuade Jess to have a termination: as far as she was concerned he could go off and die in a ditch and the world would be all the better for it. And perhaps she was right.

He might have given up and ended it all, if it hadn't been for two things: his kids and his music. He already had a daughter he loved more than the world, but couldn't see because Jess wasn't having any of it, and with a second child on the way, he knew he had to find some way of getting through to her. Maybe he could go to a solicitor and force her to let him see his children, but as far as Kev was concerned that was the last resort. He didn't want to force Jess into anything. He wanted to find a way of persuading her that he was truly sorry for what he'd said, and for walking out on her and Aimee, and that she was wrong about him being a murderer and a failure. Maybe even persuade her to take him back.

Music offered him that chance. OK, so he hadn't been very successful so far in making it as a singer-songwriter. He didn't need Jess's taunts to tell him that. But he wasn't just eager any more; now he was driven. And since he'd found his new song-writing partner, things just seemed to have clicked into place. He wrote the tunes; she supplied snappy lyrics he could never have written in a hundred years.

With the new songs under his belt, he'd already played a couple of successful local gigs and had promises of several more.

He had high hopes of the future as he slipped concert tickets into an envelope and mailed them to Jess.

The envelope plopped softly onto Jess's doormat the following morning. Even before it reached the ground, she had recognised the handwriting.

'Bastard,' she said out loud, though there was no one around to hear or care. Aimee was asleep in her cot, and Jess's only company was the morning DJ from Chelt FM, droning on inanely in the background.

213

She stooped to pick up the envelope, intending to tear it up, then she hesitated. There might be money inside, and however bad things might be between her and Kev, she wasn't too proud to take his cash.

She opened the envelope carefully, and let out a contemptuous hiss. Concert tickets. What the hell use were they to her and Aimee? Why the fuck would Kev imagine she'd want to go and watch him cavorting around like the pathetic fantasist he was?

She'd have gone once though, wouldn't she? Once, when she still believed in the dream future Kev's ambitions had conjured up for them.

Tearing the tickets into tiny pieces, she watched them drift down into the waste bin like confetti for a broken marriage. Then she sat down on the floor and cried her heart out.

Harry Bennett was putting the finishing touches to Tarzan's jungle tree house when Grace found him, in the middle of the stage at the Playhouse Theatre, surrounded by hammers, nails and pots of paint. She smiled to herself as she walked towards him up the centre aisle. You could have dropped a bomb on the theatre, and when you cleared away the rubble, Dad would still be there, hammering away, lost in his own little world.

'Dad,' she called to him from halfway up the aisle, but he was miles away. She was practically on top of him before he heard anything and looked up from his work.

'Grace! You nearly gave your poor old dad a heart attack, creeping up on me like that.'

She tried not to laugh. 'So is this Tarzan's new abode? Very swish, I must say.'

'That's right. One bedroom, no mod cons, and hot and cold running chimps in every room: what more could the king of the jungle want? Learned all your lines, have you?'

214

'Yes, Dad, such as they are.' Grace's air of superiority reasserted itself, albeit temporarily. 'I must say, I could have made a much better job of the script myself. I really can't see the wisdom of getting three junior housemen to write it; their humour is so ... puerile.'

'Yes, dear,' replied Harry, nose already buried in his work again, and clearly not listening.

'I'm really not happy about all the romping around in nothing but a tatty bit of leopard-print fake fur, either.'

'No, dear.'

Grace hauled herself up onto the stage. 'Dad, are you listening to me?'

'Yes, dear.'

'Dad, I'm being serious now! You have to listen to me.' She stood between him and the tree house. 'It's about that text message we all received from Holly. The one that said, "think we've found her".'

Harry looked at his middle daughter in mild surprise. 'What about it? It seemed pretty self-explanatory to me.'

'Well, yes, exactly!' Grace despaired of her father's detachment from the ways of the world. 'And if Holly really has found her birth mother, well, what are we going to do about it?'

Harry's mild surprise changed into astonishment. 'Us?'

'Yes, Dad! Us. We're Holly's family, aren't we? Shouldn't we offer to help, or ... or mediate, or something?'

Harry pushed his old, paint-spattered cap to the back of his head. 'Grace love, do you really think this is any of our business?'

It was Grace's turn to look aghast. 'How could it not be? We're her family. Dad, at the very least we should be around to pick up the pieces when – I mean if – it all goes wrong.'

'Perhaps so,' Harry replied. 'But for the time being I think we should just wait.'

'Wait?'

'Wait. And let things be. Things will work out, they generally do. Now, come on, Grace,' he urged, ignoring his daughter's smart suit and heels. 'Pick up a hammer and help me get this roof on, there's a good girl.'

In two whole days of following Denise Collister around at a safe distance, Holly hadn't found a single opportunity to approach her. Not until now.

The previous night it had rained in torrents, with winds buffeting the island's shores and whipping the waves up into foam-tipped breakers that lashed the rocks and cliffs. Who would have thought that today would be the perfect June day, with oceans of clear blue overhead and a sky full of sunshine to bask in?

Holly and Phil were on the promenade at Port Erin, trying to blend in with the early holidaymakers as they leaned on the rail by St Catherine's Well, overlooking the beach. Holly had almost fainted with tension as Denise Collister and her children walked past on their way to the sands, complete with buckets, spades and beach towels.

Holly stood and watched for a little while, then turned to Phil. 'I'm going to do it.'

Phil's eyes widened. 'You mean – talk to her?'

Holly nodded. 'You're the one who said it: if I don't do it soon, the moment will be lost.'

'And you've really thought this through?'

She pulled a face. 'Of course I've thought it through. You must think I'm really stupid, Phil Connell.'

'Actually, I think you're one of the smartest people I've ever met, but that doesn't mean you're not crazy. Now, get down on that beach and talk to her before you chicken out.'

I think I'm already chickening out, thought Holly as she walked down the ramp onto the sands, her legs trembling so much that she feared they might buckle under her. But I can't, because if I chicken out Phil will see, and I can't let him see that I'm really just a cowardly little girl, can I? Not after he told me I was one of the smartest people he'd ever met . . .

Any lingering pleasure from Phil's compliment vanished as she got closer to where Denise and the children had set up camp on the beach. How do you strike up a conversation with your mother, when she doesn't even realise she's your mother? wondered Holly. And then, a moment later, she was standing right next to her and there was no time left to think.

'Er . . . Hi,' said Holly.

Removing her expensive sunglasses, Denise Collister smiled and looked up at her, shading her eyes with one hand. 'Hi.'

'It's . . . um . . . really beautiful here, isn't it?' Holly ventured.

'It certainly is,' Denise agreed, looking Holly up and down. 'I never get tired of looking at the view.'

'It's my first time,' admitted Holly. 'But I'm sure it won't be the last.'

Denise nodded. 'You're over here on holiday, are you?'

I could tell her right now, thought Holly. Drop the bombshell. But instead, she just answered: 'Yes, I'm staying with a friend in Peel.' She pointed to a sunny spot near to Denise. 'Would you, er, mind if I sat there? It's sheltered, and the sand looks nice and warm.'

'Be my guest. You may get hit on the head with a tennis ball though,' Denise cautioned dryly. 'My kids are playing beach cricket, and they're not very good at it.' She pointed at a boy and a girl, playing near the water's edge. 'That's them over there, the little villains.' She raised her voice and shouted: 'Play nicely, Sean! Stop trying to hit your sister.'

Holly saw love fill Denise's eyes as she talked about her children and, for a moment at least, it hurt more than anything else had ever done. Then a whole cascade of questions filled her head, demanding answers she had waited thirty years to hear. Why did you abandon me? Holly yearned to ask, but the words just wouldn't come. Did you follow your married lover to England and then decide to get rid of me when he rejected you? Did you leave me on the hospital steps because you truly believed that someone else could give me a better life than you ever could? Or wasn't it like that at all?

Did you ever love me, Mother? Did you ever care at all?

'They look like nice kids,' remarked Holly when she finally found her voice.

'They're my pride and joy,' replied Denise. 'You know, I think having them late in life has made me appreciate them even more.'

Holly's throat felt sandpaper dry. She struggled to try to sound friendly yet casual, disinterested. 'So you ... didn't fancy being a young mum then? Lots of women are leaving it later these days.'

Denise didn't seem to notice the tremor in Holly's voice. She was too busy looking uncomfortable. 'Oh, you know how it is,' she said, colouring almost imperceptibly and looking away. 'It's all about meeting the right man at the right time, isn't it?' When she turned to face Holly again, the smile was back in place. 'How about you? Any kids?'

'Not yet.' Then she heard herself blurt out: 'But sometime soon, I hope.'

'Aha.' Denise's eyebrows arched in amusement. 'So you've found Mr Right then?'

Holly's gaze drifted to the promenade, where she could see Phil still leaning on the handrail, ostensibly looking out to sea. 'Maybe ...'

'Only "maybe"?' probed Denise, her curiosity clearly aroused.

Flushed with embarrassment, Holly cursed her big mouth. 'It's just that I ... um ... I know he's my Mr Right but I don't know yet if he knows he is,' she babbled. 'Does any of that make sense?'

'Of course it does.' There was a faraway look in the older woman's eyes. 'Relationships are complicated things, aren't they? I wouldn't be young again, not for anything.'

They sat there for a little while longer, talking about nothing very much. Holly found that, once she'd skirted around the enormous fact that Denise Collister was almost certainly her natural mother, it was really hard to think of anything else to talk to her about. Do we have anything in common at all? she wondered. Anything except our genes?

Eventually the sun moved to a different part of the beach, and it became chilly enough to give Holly an excuse to move on.

'I hope things work out with your Mr Right,' Denise said as Holly got to her feet, brushing sand off her jeans. 'Maybe he'll get down on one knee the minute you get home.'

'Thanks.' Holly laughed. 'You never know.' She picked up her handbag. 'Be seeing you then.'

'Have a good trip back to ...' Denise called out as Holly moved away. 'Oh, where was it you said you came from?'

I didn't, thought Holly. 'Cheltenham,' she called back. And for just a split second she thought she saw something in Denise's eyes, just the suggestion of a flicker of a crazy possibility ... Then it was gone.

'Bye then,' said Denise, and she lay down on her beach towel, pulling her sunglasses firmly down over her eyes.

I could have told her everything, thought Holly. I could have told her that I know all about Cheltenham, and all about her Mr Wrong, and all about ... me. And I could have crashed into her life like a speeding train, wrecking everything in its path: husband, career, happiness, everything. I could have taken my revenge on her for all the times I've wondered who I really am, and why she let me go.

But instead, I'm just walking away, having told her precisely nothing. Am I being sensible and sensitive – or just a coward?

'You didn't tell her, did you?' said Phil as they walked back towards the van. 'I knew you wouldn't.'

'Why?' asked Holly.

'Because you could never be that cruel.'

Eighteen

It was the happiest Kev had been in a long time.

Playing bass guitar in a band and actually getting paid for it was a dream come true – even if the band was accompanying final rehearsals for *Tarzan and Jane – The Musical*. At last he had a chance to show that he was a good musician, and it was all thanks to an unexpected benefactor: Grace. He'd never imagined that Jess's snooty sister, of all people, would get off her high horse and do something to help him, particularly since – as he was all too painfully aware – he was the bad guy in all of this.

'OK, boys and girls, take five and then we'll do another run-through of the scene with the cannibals,' trilled Emma Atkinson, deputy, director and consultant eye surgeon at Cotswold General. It was obvious to the cast, crew and band that she'd seen one too many episodes of *Fame*, but at least Emma knew her upstage from her downstage and her wings from her flies. This was more than you could say for the musical director, Leo, who knew more about chiropody than amateur dramatics, and conducted the band of five instrumentalists as if they were the Boston Symphony Orchestra.

But Kev didn't care. He was just happy that something positive had come back into his life, and he wanted to make sure that Grace knew how grateful he was.

He found her backstage with the elephants. They (three trainee

221

physiotherapists and a consultant rheumatologist) were all lounging around in their grey papier-mâché costumes, enjoying chocolate biscuits and a brew-up, but Grace was sitting cross-legged on the floor, back to the wall and wearing little more than half a metre of fur fabric. That wasn't like Grace. Normally she made a big fuss about covering up between scenes to avoid being ogled; this evening, she didn't seem to care one way or the other.

'Grace.'

He had to say it twice before she became aware of his existence and looked up. 'Oh, it's you.'

'Are you OK?'

'Of course I'm OK,' snapped Grace. 'Why wouldn't I be OK?'

'I've no idea,' Kev admitted, 'but you don't look too happy to me. Is it first-night nerves?'

Grace gave him one of the weary looks she reserved for imbeciles. 'I know the script backwards, all my songs are note-perfect and I could execute all the dance routines in my sleep. Why in God's name would I have first-night nerves? Now, can I do something for you or are you just going to stand there asking stupid questions?'

'I just wanted to say thank you,' replied Kev, hovering somewhat indecisively. 'But if you prefer I could just go away and leave you alone.'

'Oh.' Grace looked startled. 'OK.'

'Is that OK to saying thank you, or OK to going away and leaving you alone?'

Just the faintest trace of a smile twitched the corners of Grace's resolutely glum mouth. 'It'll be OK to strangling you with that jungle creeper if you're not careful,' she replied.

'This means a lot to me,' said Kev. 'You know, playing in the band with the real professionals. That's all down to you putting in a good word for me with Leo.'

Grace shrugged. 'You're a highly competent musician, Kev; I've never doubted that for a moment.'

'What about as a husband and a father?'

'Is this some kind of game?'

'No. No, I really want to know.'

Grace sighed and pushed the hair back from her face. It looked lank and weary and so did she. 'If you really want to know what I think, Kev, I think you were right. You were completely right when you said you and Jess couldn't afford another baby.'

A look of shock froze Kev's features. 'But I—'

'And you know what I really think? I think most ordinary people can never really afford babies. They just come along and you cope somehow. You were right in a way, but wrong because of what you did to Jess. You can't expect a woman who's carrying a baby to think of it in terms of pounds and pence, Kev. She'd rather have to move to some rat-infested garret than get rid of it.'

'I know,' said Kev forlornly. 'I know that now. But what good is that if Jess hates me?'

'She might not hate you for ever.'

'You really think so?'

Grace stared down at the floor. 'I don't know why you care what I think,' she said. 'It doesn't matter what I think. In fact, if I'm realistic nothing matters much any more.'

Kev stared at her. 'What are you saying? What's wrong?'

'Nothing's wrong, Kev. I'm just starting to understand where my real priorities lie.'

Holly was coming out of the bathroom at Thie Veg the following morning, when the door of the out-of-bounds guest room opened and, to Holly's surprise, Eileen emerged carrying a mountain of bedlinen.

This was odd, thought Holly. The door of the guest room had

223

been closed ever since they arrived. Hadn't the ceiling collapsed, causing untold devastation and consigning her, Phil and Dweezil to the Argos inflatable in the downstairs front room? And if that was the case, how come Eileen was now coming out of that very same room carrying what looked like a pile of freshly laundered linen, with not a speck of plaster dust in sight?

Holly's curiosity got the better of her, and she skipped across the landing before Eileen had a chance to close the guest-room door properly behind her.

'Oh, hello, dear,' said Eileen brightly. 'I thought you were still in bed. Shall I make us some tea?'

'That looks ever so heavy,' replied Holly, completely ignoring the question. 'Let me help you with it.'

'There's really no need, dear, I'm quite capable—'

As Holly wrestled the pile of bedlinen from Grandma Christian, she managed to give the door an ever-so-accidental nudge with her elbow, and it flew open, revealing ...

A guest bedroom decorated in complementary shades of pink, with a luxurious-looking double bed, lovely old-fashioned wardrobes – and an absolutely pristine ceiling.

'Ah,' said Eileen, retrieving a pillowcase from the landing carpet. 'I was afraid that might happen.'

Holly was completely speechless for a few seconds, as she drank in the scene and mentally relived a fortnight's worth of nights spent on an inflatable mattress on the floor.

'Eileen,' she said finally, 'what on earth is going on? There's absolutely nothing wrong with that ceiling!'

'No, dear, I'm afraid not,' acknowledged Eileen with more than a tinge of embarrassment. Then she recovered her usual bright smile. 'Shall I make us that nice cup of tea?'

'What do you mean, you "just wanted to give us a little nudge"?'

demanded Holly, as Eileen handed her a cup of Fairy Bridge tea at the kitchen table.

'Exactly as it sounds, dear,' replied Eileen, perfectly matter of fact about it now that she had had time for her feathers to unruffle. 'The moment I saw you, I knew you were good for Philip. I just knew.'

Holly still couldn't quite believe her ears. 'And you lied about the ceiling so that Phil and I would have to share a room? Eileen Christian, I would never have had you down as a devious woman, but now ...'

'I know,' admitted Eileen, 'but needs must, and all that.' She stirred her tea slowly as she spoke. 'You see, Philip has never been very discerning in his choice of girlfriends. To put it bluntly, he's always had a terrible taste in women. And Sita was the absolute worst of the bunch. As soon as we set eyes on each other, we both knew there was going to be trouble.

'Anyway, you know what happened with Sita. She treated him like dirt and then dumped him, and since then he's been a shadow of his former self. Believe it or not, before her – and before that awful shooting – he used to be one of the most self-assured young men you can imagine.'

'This is all very interesting,' cut in Holly, 'but what has this got to do with you lying about the bedroom ceiling?'

'I'm getting to that, dear. You see, Philip had mentioned you several times when he phoned me—'

'He did?'

'Certainly he did – and don't look so surprised about it. You must have known you'd made quite an impact on him. Anyway, as I said, the moment I set eyes on you, I had one of my attunements.'

'Your what?'

'Attunements, dear. Intuitions, if you like. I'm not just a reiki master, you know. I have a touch of psychic power too – nothing very dramatic, but I have an ability to, let's say, tune into people's energies. And I could tell instantly that your two energies were in harmony.'

'Oh,' said Holly, which was as much as she could muster at half past seven on a Monday morning.

'Quick as a flash, I had the thought: I could tell a little white lie, and you two would be, well, nudged a little in the right direction, shall we say.'

Elbows on the table, Holly leaned towards Eileen. 'What if we – what if I – don't want to be nudged?' she demanded.

Eileen gave a little chuckle. 'All I'm doing is giving nature a helping hand, dear. I'm not changing anything in the long run, you know, just speeding things up a little. You're a really nice girl, Holly,' she declared, patting her on the hand, 'and I know you and Philip will take very good care of each other. You were meant to be together.'

Holly swallowed hard. 'Eileen,' she said, slowly but firmly, 'Phil and I are not together.'

Eileen smiled her knowing and inscrutable smile. 'Oh, but I think you are, dear. Now, can I make you a nice bowl of porridge to start the day?'

Phil was rolling up the inflatable mattress for another day, and Holly was in the middle of telling him about his grandmother's subterfuge. To her annoyance, he seemed to find it all amusing.

'It's not funny, Phil!' she protested.

'Oh, I don't know,' he disagreed. 'Perhaps Grandma should set herself up as a psychic dating agency.'

'Well, if she does, she can practise on somebody else,' declared Holly, for some reason desperate to cover up the pleasure she felt at being 'chosen' by Phil's grandma. She knew it was a load of ridiculous old mumbo-jumbo, but even so, it was a nice feeling

226

when someone you liked and respected tried to matchmake you with someone you liked even more.

'Do you fancy doing some sightseeing?' enquired Phil. 'Now that we've kind of wound up the investigation, I could show you some of the sights.'

'Am I still paying for your time?' Holly enquired, tongue in cheek.

'Oh, I think I could manage to spare you a few hours free of charge,' replied Phil with a laugh.

They were arguing about the best place to have lunch when Holly's mobile rang. She rooted about among the discarded bedclothes until she finally found it, inexplicably tangled up in her pyjama trousers.

'Dad? This is a bit early for you to call, isn't it?' A dark premonition gripped her. 'Is everything OK?'

'I'm sorry to bother you, love,' her father replied, his voice heavy with concern, 'I know you've got a lot to think about over there. But it's Jess.'

Holly gripped the phone so hard, her knuckles turned white. 'What's happened to her? Is it the baby?'

'Steady on, love,' urged Harry, 'the worst hasn't happened yet. But she had pains in the night and a bit of bleeding, and they've taken her into the General, just in case.'

'Right, I'm coming home,' declared Holly, her priorities instantly crystal clear.

'There's no need to rush back. It's not like you can do anything right now,' her father pointed out.

'Yes I can,' Holly disagreed. 'I can be with her. Look, I'll sort something out here and get back to you, but I should be home by tomorrow.'

As she rang off, Phil could see from her face that things were bad. 'Your sister's in hospital?'

'I have to go home,' said Holly, breathless with emotion. 'I have to sort out a boat ticket or a plane ticket or something. You'll have to help me, I don't know where to go or anything.'

Phil caught her hands and held them steady. 'Hey, it's OK. I'm coming with you.'

'To the travel agent?'

'No. I'm coming back home. To Cheltenham. We've just about finished here anyway, and if you think Dweezil and I are letting you go back on your own, you've got another think coming.

'Now, sit down and stroke Dweezil while I phone the Steam Packet Company. With a bit of luck we can book ourselves and the van onto the first sailing tomorrow.'

Eighteen

Once more on the deck of the *Ben-my-Chree*, Holly and Phil watched the island shrink until it was no more than a small, dark line on the horizon. I'm going to miss you so much, thought Holly as the salt sea spray mingled with the unshed tears in her eyes. She didn't really understand why she was crying. Perhaps it was the thought that she was losing her birth mother for the second time; or the knowledge that her time on the island had been only a kind of respite, a way of hiding from the inescapable reality that awaited her back home. With Murdo.

Phil squeezed her hand. 'You'll be back,' he said. 'That's what the Manx say. Once the island has your heart, you'll keep on coming back until one day, you never leave.'

'Do you think I did the right thing?' asked Holly. 'Writing that letter and giving it to Denise's parish priest for safe keeping?'

'I'm certain you did. Now, if she ever says she wishes she knew what happened to the daughter she lost, he'll be able to give her the letter and she can get in touch with you.'

'What if she never mentions me?' Holly watched the white foam churning in the ship's wake. 'What if she never gets in touch?'

'You had to take that chance. It was either that, or approach your mother directly, and I don't think either of you would have wanted the fallout from that.'

'No,' she agreed. 'But it's hard. There were so many questions I wanted to ask her, and then when I saw her and her children and her nice life, I knew I couldn't ask any of them.'

'Nobody can predict the future,' Phil pointed out. 'You just have to hope.' His eyes were on her as he spoke. 'It's all any of us can do.'

Three hours later, the *Ben-my-Chree* slid into its berth at the port of Heysham and Holly, Phil and Dweezil made their way to the car deck, ready to disembark. It was as they were driving off the boat that Holly noticed the big, black Bentley parked on the dockside.

'Murdo!' Her hand flew to her mouth in alarm.

Phil peered across at the car. 'Are you absolutely sure?'

'Phil, I'd know that car anywhere. That's Murdo's Bentley.' Holly's heart dropped into her boots. 'Dad must have told him what time the boat arrived, and he's come to drive me home.'

'That's ... nice of him.'

'Yes,' said Holly sadly.

'Guess we'd better go over and say hello then.'

As they were parking the van, the driver's door of the Bentley swung open and Murdo stepped out, his face barely visible behind an enormous bouquet of flowers.

'My God, he really is pleased to see you,' Phil commented, *sotto voce*. 'Those flowers must have cost the best part of a hundred quid.'

'Murdo doesn't worry about money,' sighed Holly. 'He doesn't have to.'

Legs shaking, she stepped onto terra firma, and walked across to where Murdo was standing. Phil followed at a distance, looking uncomfortably unsure whether to hang around for the introductions, or bugger off and leave the lovebirds to it.

'Welcome back, darling,' said Murdo, presenting Holly with the flowers as though she were some visiting operatic diva.

'Thank you, they're gorgeous.'

They stood looking at each other for a few moments, neither of them quite sure what to do next. I'd like to hug him, kiss him even, thought Holly, but I don't want him to think it means more than it actually does. In the end, she was too afraid to do either.

'Good morning, Mr Connell,' said Murdo coldly, looking the private investigator up and down.

'Er ... morning.' Phil acknowledged Murdo's greeting with an uneasy nod.

'I hear you two have enjoyed your time away together,' Murdo went on. 'Perhaps rather too much, or am I just being paranoid?'

Holly stared at him in horror. 'Murdo!'

'Well, am I, Mr Connell?'

'OK, I think this is where I make my excuses and leave,' said Phil calmly. 'I don't want to stick around and cause any trouble for you, Hol. Shall I leave you and Murdo to drive home together?'

'No.' Holly caught his arm as he turned to leave. 'Wait, please. I think I should come back with you and Dweezil, if it's OK with you.'

'Oh,' said Murdo bitterly. 'So it's like that, is it? I turn my back for a moment, and you start playing happy families with my fiancée.'

'I'm not your fiancée, Murdo,' Holly corrected him. 'I never was. And Phil has been the perfect gentleman.'

'Oh, I bet he has.' Murdo's eyes glinted with hostility. 'I bet he knows all the moves, don't you, Phil? Am I right, Holly? Or do you just like a bit of rough?'

If Murdo was hoping to goad Phil into losing his cool, it didn't work. Years of police work had given him a thick skin. But Holly was white-faced and trembling, too shocked and too devastated to cry. And that made Phil an angry man.

'I'm truly sorry if things haven't been going right between you and Holly, Mr Mackay—'

'Yeah, right. Of course you are.'

'—and you're welcome to insult me as much as you like if it makes you feel better,' Phil went on. 'Hell, you can punch me out if you want. But please leave Holly out of it. She doesn't deserve to be treated like this. She's never said a bad word about you, or done anything she should be ashamed of. So please let's leave her out of this.'

Murdo stared at him for a long time. What was going on behind those wounded eyes, wondered Holly. Was he going to attack Phil, vent the full power of his rage and distress upon him? She held her breath, afraid to say anything that might tip the balance into violence.

Then Murdo came back to life. 'Actually I'm driving up to Scotland tonight, to see my mother and father,' he said, avoiding Holly's gaze. 'So I wasn't planning on driving you back to Cheltenham anyway.'

'But—' began Holly, as Murdo walked briskly back to the Bentley, leaving her clutching the bouquet.

'In any case,' he went on, opening the driver's door, 'it's pretty bloody obvious I'm not wanted around here.'

And then, without another word, he got into the car and roared away.

'This is all my fault,' said Holly softly. 'It's all my fault, every last bit of it. If I hadn't been such a coward, I'd have ended it properly months ago and I wouldn't have hurt him like this.'

'This is none of my business,' remarked Phil as they drove down the motorway, 'but punishing yourself like this won't make things any better, will it? For him or for you.'

'You're right,' replied Holly. 'It is none of your business.' And she flattened her face against the cold, rain-soaked window and hated herself for loving Phil instead of Murdo.

'Sorry,' said Phil, gazing resolutely ahead, 'I'll keep my mouth shut.'

Holly sobbed quietly into the glass. 'No, please don't do that,' she begged. 'Please talk to me and make me feel like things are going to be all right again one day.'

'They are going to be all right,' declared Phil. 'Just you wait and see.'

Holly's mobile struck up a ridiculously jolly tune in the depths of her jacket pocket. 'Murdo!' she exclaimed, and delved deep to fish it out before he rang off.

But it wasn't Murdo.

'Dad?' Holly cupped a hand around the phone to try to hear above the engine noise. 'Is everything OK?'

Somehow she knew it wasn't, just from the way he said, 'Hello, love.' And then he said: 'It's about Jess,' and he hardly needed to say any more.

When she put the phone back in her pocket, Holly was sad-faced and red around the eyes. 'It's my sister,' she explained. 'Poor Jess. She's lost the baby.'

It was late afternoon when Phil dropped Holly off at the hospital and then continued through town to the Bloodhound Investigations office.

As he climbed the stairs, he reflected on what hadn't been an easy day, for him or for Holly, and wondered if there would ever be a way for them to be together.

Dweezil, on the other hand, seemed delighted to be home. As soon as the door of his carrying basket was opened, he bounded out onto the landing – or at least, waddled out with more alacrity than usual: all seven and a half kilograms of him. When Phil had unlocked the office door, he immediately made a beeline for the window, heaving his bulk up onto the sill and pawing at the window catch.

'OK, OK.' Phil gathered up the immense pile of post and followed Dweezil at a more sedate speed. 'I'll let you out in a minute.'

Despite his sombre mood, he couldn't help smiling to himself. Dweezil had spent most of the past fortnight asleep, when he could have been out chasing Manx mice all over a gorgeous, verdant island. But now he was home, the black and white monster couldn't wait to clamber out onto his favourite grubby Cheltenham roof and stalk pigeons. Each to his own, he mused.

'Don't know why I bother taking you on holiday,' he commented as he unlocked the toilet window and pushed up the sash.

Dweezil vanished in a cloud of fluff.

Alone once more, Phil sent Holly a text suggesting they get together for coffee soon. Then he wished he hadn't, in case he made her feel under pressure. After all, they'd promised each other that they'd keep things cool until Holly had had a chance to finish things with Murdo. But surely there was no harm in a cup of coffee? Finally, he decided to get out the tea bags and the long-life milk, boil the kettle and settle down to sort through the mail. It was mostly routine stuff: bills, more bills, the (very) occasional cheque, a VAT return and the usual junk mail.

But one envelope caught his eye. In fact it did more than that, it made him freeze in his tracks.

A letter from Japan.

He refused to let his hands shake as he ripped open the official-looking envelope and unfolded the letter. Thank God it's in English, he thought as he scanned the single, typed page.

'Dear Mr Connell
'In accordance with the partnership agreement signed between you and Miss Sita Maria Yossarian ...'

Sita. Phil reeled from the shock.

'... Miss Yossarian hereby gives notice of her intention to dispose of her half of the business ...'

Phil sat down with a thud. She wants me to buy her out, he realised, wondering why he was even slightly surprised. No, let's be honest, he corrected himself, Sita never asks, she demands.

I may be solvent, but only just, thought Phil, thinking bitterly of the thousands he and Sita had spent on fitting out the office. And if I can't scrape up enough money to meet this particular demand, impossible though it is, she's going to reach across from the other side of the globe, sell the business from under my feet and destroy me.

Nineteen

It had been three days, and Holly was almost frantic.

'What am I going to do? You have to help me think of something,' she begged Nesta as the pair of them stood side by side at the depot, sorting the morning's mail. 'I've tried phoning him and leaving voicemails, but Murdo's just not answering his mobile.'

Nesta pushed her glasses back up her nose, and thought for a moment. 'Surely you can contact him through his work?' she reasoned.

'I tried that! I phoned Payne, Rackstraw and Bynt, and they told me he's taken indefinite unpaid leave.'

'Perhaps he felt he needed a holiday,' Nesta ventured, somewhat doubtfully.

'Come on, Nesta, you know what he's like. Work always comes first. I practically had to club him over the head and kidnap him to get him to go on that fortnight in the Greek islands. Indefinite unpaid leave? Something's seriously wrong.'

'Well, it's not that difficult to work out what,' Nesta pointed out. 'He thinks you're having it off with Phil. Which you are.'

'I am *not* having it off with Phil!'

Julian's head popped round the side of Nesta's set of pigeonholes. 'What's that about having it off? Can we all join in?'

'Bugger off, Julian,' snapped Nesta. 'Human beings only need apply.' She turned back to Holly. 'Like I said, he's upset because you're shagging Phil.'

Holly felt like screaming. 'How many times do I have to tell you? I am not shagging, screwing or having it off with Phil Connell.'

'Yet,' said Nesta firmly. 'I mean, come on Hol, admit it: you really want to, don't you? And Murdo senses that. You and he badly need to have that talk that begins "It's not your fault, it's mine."'

Holly's eyes filled with tears of frustration. 'How can I tell him it's over if he won't answer my calls?'

'Perhaps that's the whole idea,' suggested Nesta. 'If you can't tell him it's over, then it isn't.'

Holly flung down the last bundle of unsorted mail, and marched off to the ladies', punching open the door with an agonised rage that skinned her knuckles. Nesta found her bending over a washbasin, splashing her face with cold water and trying not to cry over Murdo, and Phil, and Jess's lost baby, and everything.

'Come on, tiger.' Nesta put an encouraging arm around her best friend's shoulders. 'I know this is a tough time for you, but nothing's ever as bad as you think it is.'

'No, sometimes it's worse,' replied Holly from the echoing depths of the washbasin.

'Hey, that doesn't sound like the Holly I know and love.'

'I'm having an Eeyore moment.'

Nesta sighed, and patted her friend's back. 'Well, make it a brief one, eh? You know how short-staffed we are right now.'

'Huh. Fat lot of sympathy I get round here.' Nesta handed Holly a big bunch of paper towels and she swabbed her face dry. 'What am I going to do? I've tried ringing round all his friends – even that weird couple who live in a converted public toilet on the North

Circular – and nobody's heard a word from him in days. Should I go down to London or what?'

'Didn't he tell you he was on his way to Scotland?'

'Yes, but I think that may have been a lie.'

'So phone his parents and find out.'

'I ... I can't. I'd have to tell them what was happening, and I don't think I could do it.'

'Then, m'dear,' replied Nesta, 'you are stuffed.'

The door of the ladies' washroom opened a few inches, and Julian's face peered in. 'This is none of my business,' he admitted, 'but—'

'But nothing!' exclaimed Nesta. 'He's been eavesdropping. Get out, you dirty little perv.'

'No,' sighed Holly, 'let him say whatever he's got to say. I mean, hey, why not?'

'Well, like I said,' Julian went on, with occasional nervous glances at Nesta, 'it's none of my business really, but the way I see it, if the man can't be found, it's because he doesn't want to be.'

'Oh piss off, Julian,' said Holly wearily. But she knew he was right.

That evening, Holly plucked up what remained of her courage and went to the hospital to see Jess.

It wasn't that Holly didn't want to see her sister; it was just that she was in such low spirits that she was afraid of making her feel even worse. So it was with great trepidation that she pushed open the door of Jess's side room and stuck her head inside.

'Hi, Jess,' she said as brightly as she could, stepping in and closing the door quietly behind her. 'Can I come in?'

'You already did,' Jess pointed out, her voice muffled by the bedcovers she had pulled halfway up her face.

'Oh. Yes. Sorry.' Holly advanced a few steps. 'I brought you some ... er ... oh.' It was at that moment that she realised the room was crammed with flowers of every size, shape and description, from pot plants to massive bouquets and orchids with heart-shaped balloons floating above them. Her own modest bunch looked positively weedy by comparison, not to mention unoriginal. 'Oh ... bum,' she sighed. 'I never was any good at choosing presents.'

'That's true.' Jess let the bedcovers fall and reached out for the flowers with a sigh. 'Let's have a look then. Hm, well at least you didn't buy them at a petrol station. They'll do.'

Jess lifted her head to look her sister in the face for the first time, and Holly saw her bottom lip quiver with barely controlled emotion.

'He's won, hasn't he?' Jess whispered hoarsely. A fat, silent tear ran down her pallid cheek. 'Kev's won. He wanted my baby dead, and now he's won.'

Holly sat down on the edge of the bed and stroked her sister's tangled hair. 'You know, I think Kev's really sorry for what he said,' she replied. 'I honestly think he is.'

A flash of the old anger crackled through Jess. '"Sorry" won't bring my baby back, will it?'

Then her face crumpled and she fell, sobbing, into her sister's lap.

It was the night of the Cotswold General Hospital's grand charity performance of *Tarzan and Jane – the Musical,* and Cheltenham's Playhouse Theatre was full to capacity, give or take a sprinkling of empty seats. Two of those empty seats were next to Holly.

'It's not the same without Jess,' she said as she and Harry took their places.

'No,' agreed Harry with a sigh.

Or Phil, thought Holly, trying hard not to picture him sitting beside her tonight. He'd been texting her all week, asking her to meet him for coffee, but to date all his messages remained unanswered. I can't do it, she told herself. I can't trust myself. I daren't let myself love him until I've sorted things out with Murdo. And when will that be ...?

With her sister in hospital, Steve helping behind the scenes and Kev in the band, that meant the Bennett clan was reduced to just two representatives: Holly and her dad, plus Nesta as a sort of honorary sister. In happier, less complicated times, thought Holly, they would all have been here together – Mum too, of course – and after laughing themselves silly, they would all have gone down the chip shop, even Grace, since that was in the days before she became a part-time Neighbourhood Watch co-ordinator and a full-time snob. Tonight, it would probably be more a case of cocoa for two and an early bedtime.

How stupid I was, she thought; how stupid to think that I could find my birth mother and make her become part of one big happy family. She already has one happy family of her own, what would she want with me?

Nesta scanned the programme as they waited for the curtain to rise. 'Oh look, Harry!' She pointed in delight to a line in bold print, underneath the cast list. '"Props and special effects by Mr Harry Bennett"! You're famous!'

Harry chuckled. 'Let's see if the special effects actually work before you get on the phone to Hollywood,' he advised.

It was wise advice. Less than halfway into the first song and dance number, one of the elephants fell over and exploded with an enormous bang, briefly setting off the fire alarm.

'I knew I shouldn't have used helium balloons and papier mâché,' Harry lamented. 'I was just trying to make the costumes light to wear.'

'I wouldn't worry about it.' Nesta grinned and unwrapped a toffee. 'It got a massive laugh. It's not every day you see a

240

consultant rheumatologist explode on stage.'

Harry's wooden crocodile provoked a few good belly laughs, too, as – while engaged in a life-or-death struggle with a bravely singing Tarzan – it managed to lock its jaws securely around the hero's neck. It took two gorillas and Jane to free the king of the jungle, by which time he'd sung most of his big number down the crocodile's throat.

Despite her worries about Jess and Kev and Murdo, Holly found herself joining in the laughter. It certainly wasn't the West End. Frankly, it wasn't even Weston-super-Mare. Tarzan was a decade too old and his wig kept slipping; Grace looked sensational as Jane but couldn't sing to save her life; and the spectacular aeroplane crash in the jungle was so realistic that it had to be put out with a fire extinguisher. But it was obvious from the word go that the cast were having a ball, camping it up and flouncing around the stage like characters in some bizarre Victorian melodrama.

'We're going to have to find something nice to say to Grace afterwards,' Nesta pointed out as they ate their ice creams in the interval.

'She looks wonderful,' declared Harry. 'I think they've done her proud with that leopard-skin two-piece.'

'And her acting's not bad either,' said Holly, family loyalty winning out over honesty every time. 'I'm sure the other girl couldn't have done it half as well.'

'Well, I'm going to tell her she has a real gift for comedy,' said Nesta. 'I haven't laughed so much in years. Did you see that bit where she kissed Tarzan and his wig got caught up in her hair comb?'

'I'm not entirely sure that bit was meant to be funny,' ventured Holly, 'but you're right, it's a good show.'

'It must have raised bucket-loads of cash for the premature baby care appeal,' observed Nesta, scanning the packed seats.

A wave of sadness washed over Holly. 'Too late for Jess,' she said softly. And she wiped the beginnings of a tear from the corner of her eye as the curtains parted for the second half.

The after-show mayhem was so intense that it was almost impossible to get backstage to the dressing rooms. There were half-dressed elephants on the stairs, sharing a bottle of Cava; Tarzan was holding court in the wings, peeling bits of wig glue off the top of his bald pate; and they finally tracked down Grace in the dressing-room she shared with the other female members of the cast. They had already changed, and were heading off into town to sample whatever delights Cheltenham had to offer on a midsummer Thursday night.

Grace wasn't with them though. She was still sitting on a beaten-up old swivel chair in front of a mirror framed with light bulbs, three of which actually worked. She was staring so intently at her reflection that she didn't even notice when her father, sister and sister's best friend all filed into the dressing room behind her.

Nesta pushed Holly forward. 'Go on then!'

Holly cleared her throat. Why did she always draw the short straw? 'Congratulations, Grace! You were great.' She bent down, put her arms around her sister's neck and kissed her on the cheek. 'We've brought you a card. Jess has signed it too, see? And there's a lovely bouquet of flowers waiting for you at home.'

'There were lots of posh people in tonight,' observed Nesta. 'Plenty of the right sort for you to rub shoulders with.'

Nothing happened. Grace didn't move a muscle. She just sat there in her leopard-print finery, as motionless as a doll in a shop window.

'Where's Steve?' enquired Harry, looking around him as though Steve might be hiding behind the empty clothes rail.

It was only then that Grace made a sound. Just a small, quiet sound, as though even in her distress she wanted to keep up appearances. At first, Holly couldn't quite believe it. Not Grace, not her self-contained, almost haughty sister, for whom appearances were everything ...

'Grace!' exclaimed Holly, seizing her sister by the shoulders and swivelling the chair round to face her. 'You're crying ... Why on earth are you crying? The show was a huge success.'

'The show?' Grace wouldn't even look her in the face. She stared down at the floor, almost as if she was too ashamed to make eye contact. 'Do you really think I give a shit about the show?'

'But, Grace, love,' said Harry, 'you've been talking about the show for months, looking forward to your big night ...'

'Perhaps it's shock?' suggested Nesta. 'You know, the let-down after all the stress of being in the show?'

At last Grace looked up. 'For God's sake will you all shut up? I'm not in shock, OK? I'm just sitting here trying to ... to get things straight in my head.'

'Things? What things?' asked Holly.

'Money things. As in, we don't have any, not any more. Not a penny. Zilch. Everything's gone: the house, the business, the car ...'

'But ... that's ridiculous,' objected Holly. 'How can it all be gone?'

'Ask Steve,' Grace replied. 'Steve has a little problem, you see.'

'With the business you mean?'

Grace laughed humourlessly. 'Not exactly. You see, Steve thinks you can solve all the world's problems with a hand of poker, or a bet on the two-forty at Kempton Park. And once he discovered online gambling, he found he couldn't stop.'

'Steve's addicted to gambling? I can't believe it.' Harry staggered back, and was steadied by Nesta. 'You're telling me he's gambled it all away? Everything?'

243

'Every last penny, apart from the little trust fund I set up when Adam was born – and they'll probably take that off us too.' There was a weird, calm quality to Grace's voice now. 'It's been hard, keeping it a secret all these weeks and months. But at first I thought we could cope, you see. If I could just get a better job, with a bit more money . . .'

Holly gasped, suddenly understanding what had been going through her sister's mind for so long. 'So that's why you were looking at ward sisters' jobs? Because you needed a bigger salary to pay off Steve's gambling debts?'

Grace smiled sadly. 'You know me, Hol. I've never craved authority for its own sake. I just wanted to work with kids, and bring in enough money to keep the family going.' She grimaced. 'Keep the lifestyle going. But I was too thick to realise it was all just a stupid dream.'

'And all that charity work?' asked Holly. 'And hobnobbing with VIPs?'

'It never hurts to have contacts,' admitted Grace. 'I was desperately trying to get work for the business. The more worried Steve was about not having enough contracts to survive, the more he gambled. He just can't help himself.'

'You should have told us,' said Harry sternly. 'We could have helped you.'

'No you couldn't,' replied Grace with a firm shake of the head. 'Nobody could help Steve, not even me, not without proper training, and maybe not even then. But now all the pretending is over, and at least I can stop making out that everything is fine. Everything's over now.'

There was something doom-laden about Grace's tone of voice that made Holly's flesh prickle. She gripped her sister's hands. 'In what way is it over?' She was almost too scared to ask the question. 'What's happened, Grace? What haven't you told us?'

244

Grace freed one hand and used the back of it to wipe her eyes. 'Bankruptcy,' she replied, clearly determined not to break down again. 'Steve's filing for bankruptcy. It's the end, Hol. We don't own anything any more.'

Twenty

'Things aren't too good for you right now, I'll grant you that,' Nesta acknowledged as she and Holly ate lunch together in the staff canteen at the postal depot.

'Not good!' Holly eyed her friend and boss with incredulity. 'As an understatement, I'd say that was a prize-winning example. Let's see: I've got one sister who's had a miscarriage and isn't on speaking terms with her husband, who's moved out. Then there's the other sister, who's just informed me that her husband is a gambling addict, who's about to declare himself bankrupt. Oh, and I was forgetting: there's my not-quite-ex-boyfriend, who won't tell me where he is, and who – for all I know – may be slitting his wrists at this precise moment. Yeah, I'd say that wasn't too good.'

'There's no need to be overdramatic,' protested Nesta. 'Besides, it's not really your responsibility to sort all these people out, is it?'

Holly's fork paused halfway to her mouth, a piece of carrot quivering on the prongs. 'It's easy to see why you and your family don't get on,' she commented. 'In my family, we all try to help each other out.'

'Even really annoying relatives?'

'Yep, even them.'

'Sounds like a great system – when it works. Unfortunately all my relatives either loathe each other or are in prison, or both.'

Nesta continued eating, rather morosely. 'So what are you going to do about them all then?'

'Good question.' Holly had little appetite, and was mostly pushing the food round her plate. 'There's nothing I can do about Murdo, anyway; everything hangs on him getting in touch with me.' If he doesn't turn up dead somewhere in the meantime, she thought gloomily.

'So that's one you can tick off the list.'

'Nesta, why are you being so disgustingly bright and breezy?' demanded Holly suspiciously.

'I'm not,' Nesta assured her. 'It's just a nice summer's day, and for once we're not short-handed, that's all.'

'Hm.' Holly wasn't entirely convinced. 'Well, if you're in such a great mood, maybe you can think of a way to get Kev and Jess talking again, if only for the sake of little Aimee.'

Nesta's smile faded. 'Ask me the impossible, why don't you? Look, Hol, I get the impression Jess would rather cut her own leg off than let Kev anywhere near her – or Aimee.'

'So do I,' admitted Holly, 'but there's got to be a way to change that, if only I – we – can think of it. Do you fancy going for a drink tonight, and we can throw some ideas around?'

'Sorry, mate.' Nesta's expression metamorphosed from semi-glum into what Holly could only describe as coy. 'I've made ... arrangements.'

'Well, well.' Surprised, Holly looked her best friend up and down. 'Have you got a date or something?'

'Not exactly. And that's all I'm saying about it,' added Nesta, closing an invisible zipper across her lips. A few seconds later, she said: 'By the way, you've missed somebody off your list of people in distress.'

'Who?' asked Holly.

'Phil.'

'Phil's not in distress.'

'I bet he is now you've stopped seeing him,' retorted Nesta.

That blow hit Holly squarely below the belt. 'I haven't stopped seeing him,' she protested weakly.

'So why aren't you answering his calls or his texts?'

'I will ... when I get round to it.'

'Why not now? What's stopping you?'

Holly's cheeks burned crimson with the embarrassment of being found out. It was true; she'd been putting off getting back to Phil for a couple of days now, mostly out of terror because she no longer knew what to say to him. She couldn't just phone him and tell him that she yearned to be in his arms, could she, even if it was true? Now that they'd come to the end of their Great Quest for Holly's birth mother, the map they'd been following had petered out, leaving them no more guidelines for their relationship. Did they even have a relationship any more? Dared they dream of being together for ever? They needed to have a very long talk about that very subject, and they would ... just as soon as she'd sorted things out with Murdo.

'One or two other things are more important at the moment, that's all,' she told Nesta, silently begging her to change the subject. 'Now, do you fancy a pudding?'

Holly couldn't work out what was driving her as she stood on Kev's doorstep that evening. Was she trying to show everyone how kind and forgiving she was, or deliberately trying to upset her little sister? Or was it just, as she suspected, that she felt sorry for Kev because no one else would have anything to do with him?

She was still debating the whys and wherefores when footsteps inside the flat answered her knock and the front door opened.

'Wow, it's you,' said Kev, visibly pleased to have a visitor. 'Sorry about the security chain, only you know what the bad end of the

Bluebell Estate's like. Somebody in the next block got fire-bombed last week.

'It's cheap, though,' he added with forced cheerfulness as he led Holly into the living room, a sparsely furnished cube of a room with a single armchair, an orange box with a TV on top of it, and a selection of electric and acoustic guitars. 'Have a seat.' He pointed to the armchair.

'What about you?'

'That's OK, I'll sit on the floor.'

Dear God, thought Holly, Kev and Jess's flat was never paradise, but it was compared to this dump. It was pretty obvious that Jess had come out a lot better from the separation – which was doubtless right, with Aimee to consider – but Kev didn't seem to have even the necessities of life.

'Is Jess getting the money from my benefit cheques OK?' he asked.

'I think so. But ... you're not sending her all your money, are you, Kev?' asked Holly worriedly.

Kev looked at her in surprise. 'But it's for her and Aimee. Of course I am.'

'Then what are you living on?'

He shrugged. 'I get a few quid from busking, and the odd gig. And they paid me for playing in the band for *Tarzan and Jane*.'

Holly looked at his tall, angular frame, leaner than ever under his loose sweat top. 'But you're so thin; you're wasting away!'

'Don't worry about me, I'm fine. I just want to do the right thing by Jess ... and I'd do anything to see Aimee. Do you think there's any chance ...?'

'As yet, no, I don't think so. She's still getting over the miscarriage, and she still seems very angry.'

Kev groaned, and raked his long, thin fingers through his blond dreadlocks. 'Why the hell did I say what I said? I'd do anything,

249

Holly – anything – if I could turn the clock back and keep my stupid mouth shut.' He looked at her, his gaze urgent and full of pain. 'Is there anything you can do? Anything you can say?'

Holly felt like the worst, most useless person in the world as she replied: 'I don't see that there's much I can say that I haven't already said. The last time I begged Jess to let you see Aimee, she just accused me of siding with you. It's going to take time, Kev. I think you're going to have to be patient. That, or . . .'

'Or what, Holly?'

'You could see a lawyer. They have one at the Citizens' Advice Bureau who offers advice for free.'

Kev nodded. 'Yeah, I know. But I don't want to go down that road if I can avoid it. That's like, well, admitting defeat, isn't it? In my heart, I still love Jess and I think there's a part of her that still loves me. So there must be a way of getting through to her.'

'There might not be, Kev.'

'Well, if it comes to that I'll see the solicitor. But I'm not giving up just yet. I've got this really great idea. I want to—'

The doorbell rang three times, and then there was the sound of a key turning in the lock. Holly looked up at Kev in surprise. He grinned. 'That'll be my new lyricist. You always told me my lyrics were crap, so I found myself someone who can write decent ones.'

Footsteps came along the hall, and a figure appeared in the doorway to the living room. 'Hi, Kev,' said the girl, then she spotted Holly and stopped dead in her tracks.

Holly's jaw dropped. 'Nesta?'

Holly listened to the song with tears in her eyes. 'It's wonderful,' she said as Kev put his guitar back on its stand, 'but I still don't understand.'

'You know, for an intelligent woman you can be really dense,' said Nesta. 'Tear-jerking love song; great lyrics; a melody that could make an angel weep ...'

Suddenly, Holly realised what Nesta and Kev were getting at. 'You've written the song for Jess!' she exclaimed. 'So Kev can try and get her back. What are you going to do?' she asked Kev. 'Serenade her outside her bedroom window?'

'I would,' replied Kev, 'but it's on the second floor and I'm scared of heights.'

'We were thinking maybe he could sing it at Steve's birthday party next week,' explained Nesta. 'Assuming we can smuggle him in. Your whole family are bound to be there, aren't they?'

'Actually,' Holly said slowly, 'I'm not sure there's going to be a party.'

'Oh dear said Nesta, 'that would be a real shame if they had to cancel. I'm sure Grace mentioned that everything had been booked and paid for in advance, even the band.'

'Perhaps it will go ahead then,' Holly said, thinking aloud. 'No point in wasting money if it's already been spent.'

'Anyway,' Kev cut in, 'If you think "Sometime in my Heart" is good enough—'

'Which it is,' said Nesta.

'—I'll sneak into the party and beg the band to let me have the stage for a few minutes. What do you think?'

'It might work,' conceded Holly. 'After all, you've tried everything else. And it is a lovely song.'

'So you'll smuggle me into the party then?' asked Kev, brightly.

Oh shit, thought Holly.

'You could have told me,' said Holly, as she and Nesta drove home in Harry's van, with Nesta's bike slung in the back.

'Why?' demanded Nesta.

'Because it was kind of embarrassing, you walking into Kev's place and me not knowing anything about you writing songs together.'

'One song,' Nesta corrected her. 'And how could I refuse to do the lyrics for him when I knew what was at stake? He only wants one thing in the whole world, and that's to get Aimee and Jess back.'

'He used to want to be a big star,' Holly reminisced as they drove along.

'I expect he still does,' replied Nesta. 'Only now he's got higher priorities.'

Holly took a sideways glance at her friend. 'When did he ask you to help?'

'Oh, a couple of weeks ago,' Nesta replied airily, 'or thereabouts. He remembered that Holly's weirdo friend wrote poetry, and got my number from your dad.'

'Why didn't he ask me?' demanded Holly.

'You were in the Isle of Man with lover boy, remember?'

'He's not my lover boy! As a matter of fact, I haven't seen him since we came back.' A little sigh escaped from her lips. 'Not for days.'

'For pity's sake cheer yourself up and phone him,' urged Nesta. 'I don't know why you're putting yourself – and Phil – through all this. It's not your fault Murdo's hidden himself away and you can't tell him to his face that you've dumped him. Stop going around with a long face, telling everybody that everything's your fault.'

'Is that what I do?' asked Holly, embarrassed.

'All the time.'

'Really?'

Nesta let out a small, exasperated explosion of breath. 'Look – do you want me to film you on my mobile and play it back to you?'

'Sorry,' said Holly. 'I don't mean to be a miserable bugger.' They drove on a little further. 'How the hell am I going to smuggle Kev into Steve's party? Everybody hates him.'

'Oh, you'll think of something. Try snogging the bouncers or something.'

'What?'

'Needs must, and all that. Now, concentrate on your driving, madam, or you'll have us up the next lamp post.'

'It's a long time since I did this,' whispered Holly as Kev's legs disappeared into the old Tithe Barn. A popular – and expensive – venue for dances, exhibitions and private parties, it had an additional advantage beyond its spacious interior and olde-worlde ambience: it had a lot of windows at the back.

There was a muffled crash, and then silence. 'Are you OK?' hissed Nesta anxiously.

'I'm in the ladies' loo!' Kev whispered urgently, his face appearing at the window, this time from the inside.

'Then you'd better get out of there – fast,' recommended Holly, her head filling with visions of her and Kev being arrested on a charge of public indecency, should anyone actually want to use the loo. She answered Nesta's accusatory look with: 'How was I supposed to know which window it was? And you're the one who got me into this, remember.'

'I need my guitar,' Kev reminded them, reaching out an arm to take it.

There was only one problem: the guitar was wider than the window. It took several minutes of frantic jiggling to get it through diagonally, by which time it was hopelessly out of tune, but Holly would have felt bad about just tiptoeing away and leaving Kev to it. So she and Nesta stood there, petrified, and endured another five minutes of frantic twanging as Kev tuned up, until at last he hissed through the open window: 'Ready to go now. Thanks for everything, I really owe you both.'

*

Inside the Tithe Barn, the party was in full swing: Harry was sitting gloomily in a corner; Grace was being forced to make polite conversation by someone she'd met at Pilates classes; and Steve was quietly drinking himself into a coma. Not that any of the other guests seemed to notice. They were too busy hurling themselves around the dance floor, or helping themselves to copious quantities of free booze.

'Great party, Steve,' boomed some guy nobody recognised, thumping him on the back as he went past.

'Yeah,' agreed a girl from Steve's old office, 'you should have a birthday more often!'

Holly hugged the wall with a glass of tepid white wine, wondering what torments Grace and Steve must be going through tonight. It must be terrible enough just having to lose their luxurious lifestyle, but how much worse was it, having to go through with this party and pretend that everything was fine? She's on something, thought Holly as she took in Grace's expression, blank and bland; she must be, just to get through this. And just look at Steve: if he keeps on drinking like that, he'll be in the Cotswold General having his stomach pumped before the night is out.

And then there was Jess. She'd had a fair bit to drink, too, but still seemed in control. Holly had never seen anybody dance angrily before, or indeed thought that it was possible, but Jess was flinging herself about to the band's rather psychedelic cover versions like some demonic jungle queen, oozing sex appeal. Holly had meant to go over and ask how she and Aimee were getting on, but thought better of it, at least for the time being. She wondered nervously what Kev was doing, and when he was planning to make his big entrance.

Just then, the band came to the end of 'Wonderwall' and the lead vocalist whistled down the microphone for silence.

'Ladies and gents, can we have a bit of quiet just for a minute?'

Everybody stopped what they were doing, and turned to look at the stage.

'I've just been told that there's a guy here tonight who wants to sing a song he's written for his special lady. Isn't that romantic?' He beckoned towards the back of the stage. 'Come on, Kev, don't be shy.'

Holly's eyes weren't on the stage, they were on Jess. And as the band leader spoke Kev's name and he stepped up onto the stage, Holly saw her face turn a greenish shade of white. For a moment, she thought Jess was going to faint.

'What's your song called, Kev?'

Kev shuffled his feet nervously. 'It's called "Sometime in my Heart".'

'And who's it for?'

Kev's eyes searched the throng of party guests. 'It's for Jess. My wife, Jess. And my daughter, Aimee. To tell them how much I love them.'

Kev strummed the first chord of the song, and opened his mouth to sing, but suddenly a figure erupted from the crowd, pushed its way on stage and grabbed the microphone from the stand in front of him.

'Don't you dare do this, Kev!' snarled Jess. 'Don't you fucking dare!'

Kev stared at her, totally thrown. 'Jess, I—'

'Want to play happy families, do you? Well, let me tell you this. You lost the right to do that the day you told me to kill my baby. Do you understand that? Do you?'

Jess glared at Kev, her arm raised as though she might strike him with the microphone, then she threw it down in disgust, and pushed her way back through the crowd.

Oh God no, thought Holly, her heart in her mouth. What have I gone and done now?

Jess was standing by the free bar, throwing vodka shots down her throat. Holly hung back, not quite sure what to say but knowing that she had to say something: apologise for herself and Kev, and maybe – if she got a chance – try to explain.

Holly's attention was diverted for a moment or two by an old school friend, and when she turned back to look for Jess, the whole scene had changed radically.

Jess was still near the bar, all right, but she wasn't alone. She was all over some tall, brown-haired guy, kissing him as if it was going out of fashion, her mouth locked on his as though she was trying to suck the life out of him, pressing his body tight against the wall. Holly nearly fainted with realisation.

The tall guy was Phil Connell.

Twenty·One

Holly strode across the car park towards the main road, with no clear idea of what she was doing or where she was going. A single, agonised thought had pushed all others from her mind: why did he do this, why did he do this to me?

She didn't hear footsteps behind her, or sense the presence of another person, until a hand clutched the sleeve of her blouse and a breathless voice pleaded: 'Slow down, Hol, will you? I can't keep up with you.'

It was Nesta, her short legs trotting to keep up with Holly's long-legged strides.

'Go away,' said Holly. 'Please just go away; I want to be on my own.'

'No you don't,' Nesta assured her. 'And in any case, I'm not letting you.'

Holly stopped in her tracks. She would have screamed, but screaming had never been her thing. It was more the kind of thing Jess would do. She tried to chase away the mental image of Jess spitting fury at Kev, and turned her attentions to Nesta.

'Knock it off, Nesta,' she pleaded. 'It's been the crappiest of crap nights already, and the last thing I need is you trying to make me feel better. Just go back to the party and let me go, OK?'

'Go where?' Nesta enquired.

'I don't know ... home.'

'You can't drive,' Nesta reminded her. 'You've been drinking.'

Irritation was fizzing inside Holly, like the fuse on a stick of dynamite. 'So I'll walk!'

She strode out again, but Nesta was instantly by her side. 'Holly, it's miles and miles back to Cheltenham.'

'I don't bloody care!' Holly exploded. 'If I want to walk back to Cheltenham, I bloody well will!'

Nesta sighed. 'OK.'

'OK what?'

Her best friend fell into step beside her. 'OK, I'll walk with you. I can't possibly let you walk all that way in your state, can I?'

And they headed for Cheltenham along the long, moonlit road.

When Holly awoke, she had the sour mouth and carpet tongue to remind her that she'd been drinking the previous evening. It didn't take much, she mused resentfully. A couple of glasses of cheap wine could always guarantee a nice fat hangover the next morning.

That wasn't all Holly had. When she fumbled for her mobile on the bedside locker and switched it on, she found no fewer than seven text messages from Phil. Bastard. She turned it straight off again, without reading any of them.

It was twilight in the bedroom, and she glanced at the clock. Only eight o'clock in the morning; practically the middle of the night on a Sunday. Besides, what was there to get up for in a world where everyone turned out to be not what you thought they were? Grace and Steve, and now Jess and Phil: who would be the next disappointment?

As she snuggled down under the duvet, preparing to drift off into a pale-pink place where love was for ever, she heard the distant sound of somebody knocking at the front door, followed by her father's surprised-sounding voice: 'Oh, well, it's good of you to come but you can't really go up there now, she's still in bed ... I'd really rather you didn't ...'

She froze as Harry's voice died away and footsteps came up the stairs, not just one pair of footsteps either. Then there was a peremptory knock, and the next moment her bedroom door flew open and the light clicked on.

What the hell ... ?

Holly sat bolt upright in bed, blinking in the light, as a small figure shuffled in, followed by a taller, much more decisive one.

The duvet dropped out of Holly's hands. 'Phil Connell, what the hell do you think you're doing in my bedroom?'

'I'm sorry, Holly, but I – we – just had to see you, and you haven't answered any of my messages.'

'So what are you here for, Jess?' Holly enquired coldly, pulling the duvet back up to cover her embarrassment. 'Come to gloat, have you? You did put on a very good performance last night, I'll give you that.'

Jess raked a thin, white hand through her straggly two-tone hair. She looked awful, thought Holly. So at least there was some justice in the world.

'I think it's about time you did a little explaining, young lady,' said Phil, nudging Jess forwards.

'I've come to apologise,' said Jess gruffly. 'What I did last night ... it wasn't meant for you. I didn't mean to hurt you.'

'What makes you think you did?' demanded Holly. 'It's not as if he's my boyfriend or anything, are you, Phil?' Phil looked away, and Holly felt a brief flicker of satisfaction. 'In fact I don't even know what he was doing at the party,' she added haughtily. 'Because I certainly didn't invite him. What did you do to get in, Phil?' she enquired. 'Snog the bouncers as well?'

'What?' Phil groaned. 'Didn't Harry tell you? Your dad invited me, Hol. He said he thought "Cupid needed a helping hand" or something to that effect. I thought you knew.'

'Yeah, right.'

Jess took a deep breath and said: 'Look, Phil's telling the truth. And he had nothing to do with all that snogging you saw, OK? I just launched myself at him cause he was the nearest decent-looking bloke.'

Holly frowned. 'What? Why would you do that?'

Jess gave Holly a look that read: 'imbecile'. 'For Kev's benefit,' she replied. 'Why else?'

Holly's brain reeled. 'But I thought you didn't want anything more to do with Kev!'

'I don't.' A thin, rather unattractive smile spread across Jess's face. 'But that doesn't mean I don't want him to hurt.'

Holly hardly knew what to say: whether to be angry with her sister or sad for her. 'Don't you think you're taking this too far?' she suggested gently. 'Can't you just accept that things are over between you and Kev, and move on with your life? Do you have to be so ... vindictive?'

Jess's expression hardened. 'I knew you'd take Kev's side.'

'For God's sake, Jess, I'm not taking anybody's side! I just don't want people to suffer more than they have to,' said Holly. 'I'm really worried about you, Jess,' she added.

'Worried about me!' Jess's dark eyes flashed. 'Look, I've done what your lover boy here wanted me to do, and you've got your fucking apology. If that's not enough, well, tough shit. You may have gone through your whole life getting everything you want, Hol, but this is all you're getting from me.'

'I've what?' gasped Holly, thunderstruck by Jess's tirade.

'Oh ... fuck off!'

And with that, Jess pushed Phil aside and left, running down the stairs and banging the front door shut behind her.

Holly's head sank into her hands. 'What have I done?'

'You!' exclaimed Phil. 'You haven't done anything except want the best for everybody. Everybody except yourself,' he added quietly.

'I can't believe Jess would do that to Kev,' murmured Holly, shocked to the core.

'Neither could I,' said Phil. 'When she threw herself at me, I thought she'd lost her mind or something. For a few seconds I was too surprised to push her away – and that's the honest truth, Hol.'

Holly didn't doubt it. Jess might be bad at apologies, but she was no liar. 'My own little sister,' murmured Holly. 'She and Kev were so in love, you know, and when Aimee was born, well, I've never seen anyone happier. If only Jess hadn't got pregnant again so soon, and if only Kev had kept his stupid mouth shut.'

'Life is full of "if onlys",' said Phil. 'And people do change.'

Holly looked him straight in the eye. 'Will you change?' she asked.

'I might, I suppose,' he admitted. 'But my feelings for you won't. They're written in stone.'

Holly's heart pounded. 'You mustn't say things like that,' she protested. 'We agreed that we wouldn't talk about stuff like this until—'

'Until you've talked to Murdo, I know. But he's vanished off the face of the earth, Hol.' He reached down and took her hand. 'I'm ashamed to say this, but I'm afraid,' he whispered. 'Afraid that when this is all over, he could be the one you choose.'

Holly looked up at him in surprise. 'Why on earth would you think that?'

Phil let out a long sigh. 'Because from everything you've told me,' he replied soberly, 'I think Murdo's a better man than I am.'

Twenty-Two

When Holly got to Jess's flat, she wasn't at home.

'You just missed her,' said a neighbour who was outside, energetically washing her front windows. 'Popped in for about five minutes, then went straight out again with the baby. She didn't look very happy,' she added, clearly fishing for gossip.

Holly groaned. 'I don't suppose she said where she was going?'

'To the park, I should think. She likes to take the little one to watch the kiddies on the swings. She's not in any kind of trouble is she?' enquired the neighbour eagerly. 'Police involved, are they? I did wonder if that hippy husband of hers was into drugs ...'

'Thanks for your help,' Holly replied tersely, anxious to get away from the unsavoury neighbour before she said something she regretted.

Sure enough she found Jess at the local park, sitting alone on one of the benches that were arranged around the children's play area. Jess had taken Aimee out of her pram and she was bundled up in her mother's arms while Jess provided a running commentary: 'See that little boy on the swing? Look, he's going right up high in the air. You'll be able to do that too when you're a little bit older. See? Up and down, up and down ...'

'Er ... Jess,' said Holly, embarrassed at having to cut in.

'Oh great. It's you.' Jess didn't even bother looking up.

Holly sat down next to her sister and reached out to stroke her niece's face. 'She really is a lovely little girl,' she commented.

'Yes. She is. And I don't need you or anybody else to tell me that.'

Clearly this wasn't going to be the easiest of conversations. Holly decided to take a chance and aim straight for the heart of the matter. 'Jess,' she enquired, 'why do you hate me?'

At least this question grabbed Jess's attention. 'I don't hate you,' she said wearily. 'Don't flatter yourself. I haven't got the energy left to hate anybody.'

'Except Kev,' Holly reminded her.

'You know what?' laughed Jess. 'I don't even hate him either. Not any more.'

'So why are you doing all these things to hurt him?'

Jess curled protectively around her baby, rocking her from side to side. The motion seemed to comfort them both. 'I hate what he did to me,' she replied after a moment's thought, 'and what he said. And I really thought I hated him too. But today I just realised.'

'Realised what?' enquired Holly.

'That I don't have the strength to hate him any more. Only I feel I have to go on pretending I do,' she explained, 'otherwise I'll have no excuses left, and I'll have to let him back into my and Aimee's life.'

'You'll probably have to do that anyway,' Holly pointed out. 'Kev's talking about going to a solicitor and getting visitation rights. I really don't think he'd try for custody of Aimee, but—'

'No!' Jess clutched her daughter so tightly that she began to cry. 'I won't let him take her away from me!'

'He won't,' Holly promised, cursing her big mouth and sliding an arm round her sister's shoulders. 'Kev would never do a thing like that, I know he wouldn't. I'm sorry, I didn't mean to frighten you. I always seem to say the wrong thing, don't I?'

Gradually Aimee stopped crying, and Jess seemed less agitated. 'Yeah,' she said, 'you do screw up a lot, but at least you set out trying to do what's right, unlike most people. Just like Mum,' she added with a smile. 'She got things wrong too, sometimes.'

Holly was taken aback. 'I really remind you of her?'

'Oh yes. You look a lot like her, too, believe it or not. Maybe that's why Dad's always loved you the best.'

'He hasn't!' exclaimed Holly, horrified at the thought that her dad could possibly love any of his daughters more than the others. 'He wouldn't do that.'

'Oh for God's sake, Holly, open your eyes! You're Daddy's golden girl and you always have been: the image of Mum and brainy with it.'

Holly found herself laughing at the idea. 'Jess, stop saying that. How can I possibly look like Mum? I was adopted!'

Jess shrugged. 'Don't ask me. Fate. Coincidence. All I know is I was so jealous of you that I was desperate for you to find your birth mother, so you'd go away with her and Dad would take some notice of me instead. Only you didn't go off with her, did you?' She grunted. 'And the funny thing is, I'm kind of glad.'

'Jealous.' Holly sat and stared blankly at the children playing in the playground, shocked to the core, seeing nothing. 'I can't believe you were jealous of me,' she murmured. 'I just can't believe it.'

'Jeez, Holly. Think about it: hot boyfriend, hot London job – which you ought to go back to, you stupid cow – loads of money ... Who wouldn't envy you? Plus you were so close to Mum at the end ... I know that upset Grace a lot.'

Holly gaped. Her world of certainties was being dismantled around her again. 'Grace was jealous of me too?'

'Not exactly jealous maybe ... But she's a born nurse, Hol. She wanted to look after Mum when she was ill, only she was so poorly after she had that miscarriage. I think she feels sort of guilty about the fact that she couldn't do it and you could. Leastways, that's what I reckon.'

'Any other revelations while you're at it?' enquired Holly.

'I'll tell you if I think of any.'

They sat there side by side for a while, lost in their own thoughts.

'I'm sorry,' said Holly after a while. 'About everything.'

'Me too,' admitted Jess. 'Me too.'

Do I really know anyone or anything any more? wondered Holly as she drove home. Her head was still buzzing as she walked up the front path and slid her key into the lock.

Harry was in the hall as she came in, mending a wobbly leg on the telephone table.

'Hello, love.'

'Hi, Dad.'

'Are you all right? Only you look like you lost a pound and found sixpence, as my old Uncle Bill used to say.'

She half turned and threw him a reassuring smile. 'Everything's fine, Dad. I just had a little chat with Jess; it was very ... um ... yes, everything's fine now.'

Harry tapped his forehead just as Holly placed her foot on the bottom tread of the stairs. 'Oh, I forgot. There was a phone call for you while you were out. From the Isle of Man.'

The Isle of Man! Holly's heart turned cartwheels in her chest. Could it be? Could it?

'It was that nice Eileen Christian, just checking up to see how you are.'

'Oh.'

'And she says did you know you left a pair of socks tucked down the back of the sofa bed?'

*

265

It was a beautiful day, and Murdo had made good progress on his journey down from Scotland.

All the way down he'd been rehearsing what he planned to say to Holly. The only problem was that every time he went over it, it came out different. Perhaps that was because, deep down, he hadn't quite resigned himself to letting her go. For so long, he'd thought of her as his other half, his natural complement, that it felt like having an arm or a leg amputated, and it was no use pretending that he felt happy about it.

But he'd made his decision, and he was sure things would work themselves out once he saw her. They had to.

At the motorway services, his hand strayed to his mobile. Should he phone Holly and let her know he was coming?

No. Perhaps not. This was going to be hard for him, but he could at least make the whole thing as surgically swift and painless as possible for her.

Steve was very, very drunk.

As he lumbered across the elegantly furnished lounge of number seven, The Avenue, he sent Swarovski crystal animals scattering in all directions. Eyes wide, Grace clung to the wall like the heroine in an old-time horror movie, horrified and just a little afraid.

'Steve, please,' she begged, 'just sit down and let me make you some black coffee.'

He laughed, but there was nothing in the sound but pain. 'Coffee? D'you still think coffee's enough to sort this out? Do you?'

'It's a start.'

'Bloody hell, woman, are you a fucking saint or what? I've lost everything. Everything. Pissed it all away like yesterday's beer. I've destroyed our life, and all you want to do is make coffee.'

'There's always hope, Steve. The bankruptcy won't last for ever, and then we can make a fresh start.'

Steve roared like a wounded animal, and pounded his fist against the wall. 'You just don't get it, do you? It's over; there is no fresh start. I've destroyed it all, I've destroyed us, there's nothing left. Nothing left but me, and things would be a damned sight better for everybody if I wasn't here.'

'Please don't talk like that. And please don't shout, you'll wake Adam.'

Grace was in tears, but Steve couldn't see it. He was so deeply mired in his own misery and shame that he was no longer aware of anything else. 'Shut up, will you? I'm no use to you or the kid any more. No use at all.'

Grace moved towards her husband, attempting to take him by the arm and lead him towards the sofa. But he pushed her away, so violently that she fell back onto the sofa, hitting her forehead on the corner of the table as she fell.

'Get away from me, woman,' he pleaded, lost in the very depths of anguish. 'Just let me walk away, will you? There's only one thing left for me to do now, so just let me get on with it, for God's sake.'

Drowsy and slightly concussed from the blow to her head, Grace was only dimly aware of Steve leaving, and the front door banging shut behind him with an awful finality.

Twenty-Three

Holly lay on her bed, gazing up at the ceiling, her favourite detective novel discarded by her side. All she could think of was what Jess had revealed.

Was Jess imagining it, or had she really been her father's favourite all these years? The more Holly thought about it, the less she could imagine Harry having any favourite. He always talked about 'his girls' in the plural, was never happier than when they were all together.

Jess's grounds for envying her weren't so easy to dismiss, though. Holly felt ashamed when she thought of how easy it had been for her to succeed. She'd never had to struggle at school, or at work. Jess was right: her life delivering the post wasn't a life at all; it was an escape from real life. And if she wanted it to end, all she had to do was snap her fingers and Payne, Rackstraw and Bynt would take her back tomorrow. She began to feel incredibly ungrateful: all of this had been given to her on a plate, yet for some unaccountable reason none of it was quite right for her. And that went for Murdo, too: a man who had done nothing but love and respect her.

Sometimes I really hate myself, she thought gloomily. Rolling onto her side, she examined her features in the mirror opposite. Am I really like my mother? she wondered. But that's impossible – we're not even related! Yet in a strange way she could see what Jess

268

meant: a distant echo of Maureen's large, dark eyes under curving brows; the ghost of her mischievous smile, breaking through at the most inappropriate moments.

'Mum,' she whispered. 'Mum, I miss you so much. Why did you have to leave us? We're all miserable, and we're making a bloody awful mess of things without you.'

Holly was still busy feeling sorry for herself when somebody rang the doorbell – not once, but several times in quick succession. Oh bugger, she thought, it's Dad's night for his model-making class. I suppose I'll have to answer it, and I bet it's something and nothing. Maybe it's the pizza delivery man and he's got the wrong house.

She reached the door just as the doorbell went again. 'All right, all right, I'm coming,' she shouted, ready with a few well-chosen words for the pizza man.

But as she opened the door onto a rainy night, a bedraggled figure almost fell on top of her. If Holly hadn't caught her, Grace would have crumpled onto the hall carpet.

'Oh my God,' breathed Holly, taking in the trickle of blood down the side of her sister's face. 'What's happened to you?'

'An accident,' Grace said, her voice faint and frail. 'I fell and hit my head.' Suddenly she gripped Holly's robe so hard that the satin almost ripped. 'We've got to find Steve. Please, we have to find him before it's too late.'

Grace lay on the sofa in the lounge, while Holly dabbed at her forehead with some cotton wool dipped in antiseptic. Now that she was resting, some colour had returned to her cheeks, but she still looked half-drowned and not at all well.

'We have to get you to the hospital,' decided Holly, profoundly relieved that baby Adam was safe and sound at his grandparents' house.

269

Grace sat bolt upright. 'No! Not yet.' She winced and clutched at her head.

'There, I told you so,' said Holly.

'You don't understand,' persisted Grace. 'If we don't find Steve, he might—' she bit her lip '—do something to himself.'

'But Grace, you don't even know where he is,' pointed out Holly. 'He could have gone anywhere.'

'But we have to try! Whatever he's done, he's still my husband and I love him!'

Holly wavered. It was clear how distraught Grace was, but was she making things sound worse than they really were? And in any case, if it came to a choice between concern for Steve and concern for her sister, there was only ever going to be one outcome.

'Hospital first,' she said firmly.

Grace clutched her hand. 'He's beyond despair, Holly. I really believe if we don't get to him first, he's going to kill himself.'

As Holly opened her mouth to answer, the front door opened and closed again, and footsteps sounded in the hall. Dad! Thank God.

'Dad, I need you to get the van out again,' Holly called to him. 'It's really urgent.' Harry appeared in the doorway, his features tense with horrible anticipation. 'Don't panic,' Holly reassured him, 'but Grace needs to go to hospital right away; she's hit her head.'

'Will you come with me?'

'Of course I will.' Holly squeezed her sister's hand. 'Don't worry, I'll call the police; they'll find Steve.'

Tears flooded Grace's eyes. 'They're no use. How many "missing persons" do you think get called in every week? They'd be lucky to get round to Steve by Christmas. No, call Phil.'

Holly let out a startled, 'What?'

'Phil,' Grace repeated. 'If anybody can find Steve, he can. Promise me you will?'

270

'OK. I'll do it now. But what do I tell him?'

'Give me a pen and paper.' Holly scrabbled around and found a notebook and pencil. Grace scribbled down a few lines. 'These are all places Steve sometimes goes. I know it's not much, but it's the best I can do.'

As fate would have it, Murdo's Bentley turned into Holly's street just as Phil was emerging from the Bennett house. Murdo cursed and punched the steering wheel as the anger and pain surged through his body. It was too much, too much to bear – driving all this way, and then coming face to face with Him.

Murdo had always believed that he could take anything – even this – like a man. He'd planned it all so carefully and so calmly. It was quite simple. He'd just call on Holly, talk to her, tell her it was over between them and then leave for ever. End of story. End of them. But the sight of Phil walking out of her house like that, bold as brass, hurt so much that it unravelled something in his brain, clouding his rational mind and driving him into a blind, agonised fury.

As Murdo watched Phil get into his van and drive away, the rage that now controlled him grew cold and calculating. 'I'm right on your tail, you cheating bastard,' Murdo muttered to himself, wrenching the wheel and slewing the car into the van's wake.

I'm on your tail, and when I catch you I'm going to corner you like the animal you are, and teach you a lesson you'll never forget.

If Phil had been less preoccupied, he would surely have noticed the sleek black Bentley that always seemed a car or two behind him. But Phil's mind was on other things.

As he drove along, he glanced at the list he'd Blu-tacked to his dashboard. A pub, a park, another pub ... none of these places seemed like the kind of place you'd go if you wanted to end it all.

271

What kind of guy was going to top himself in the middle of the public bar at the Royal Oak on karaoke night? The park was a possibility, but Phil knew it well and at this time in the evening it would be full of courting couples – so again, not really a goer.

He tapped the steering wheel, asking himself the somewhat tasteless question: Where's a good place to commit suicide in Cheltenham? The Devil's Chimney on Cleeve Hill, perhaps, but that was a long way to go just to jump off something . . .

And then something in his memory clicked. He recalled a conversation with Holly and her dad about Harry's model train set, and Holly mentioning that Steve liked trains too, but preferred full-sized ones – that he'd been a fanatical trainspotter as a kid. For years the railway station had been like a second home.

It was only a hunch, but before his mind had even processed it properly, Phil's hands were swinging the steering wheel round and pointing the van's bonnet towards Cheltenham Spa railway station. He desperately needed to be right about this, as much for Holly's sake as for Steve's.

Summer evenings were intermittently busy at the station. From time to time, fat express trains from distant ends of the country disgorged waves of travellers, who filled the taxi rank for a little while, and then all was as quiet as the grave again until the next arrival or departure.

Phil parked the van in the car park, ignoring all the signs that warned him to buy a ticket from the machine, and half walked, half ran towards the station, slowing almost to a halt as he reached the square arch of the entrance. Now he was here, he felt very, very stupid. He was sure he was wrong. But now that he was here, he might as well go through with it. So he took a deep breath and walked inside, passing the ticket office on the left, and the tiny red postbox on the right, and then wondered where to go next. Platform 1? Platform 2? The station buffet? Well, perhaps not the buffet. The toilets? Lots of people killed themselves in public conveniences.

Then Phil realised that he was looking straight at Steve. Stretching ahead of him, an old iron bridge spanned the railway lines, perhaps twenty feet above the track. Not a big enough fall to kill someone ... unless they happened to be jumping in front of a train at the time.

Steve was standing in the middle of the bridge, gazing down at the railway tracks as he leaned against the balustrade, his chin resting on his folded arms. The occasional traveller strolled past him, completely unaware of the little drama unfolding just yards away from them. A goods train was rumbling past underneath the bridge, and Phil was able to creep to within a few feet of Steve before Steve noticed the detective and sprang away.

'Get the hell away from me,' he commanded, but softly so that no one else in the vicinity would hear and raise the alarm. Phil could see that he was shaking violently.

'OK, look, I'm not moving. I'll just stand here, is that OK?' Phil shuffled a couple of steps nearer and leaned on the balustrade.

'If you come any closer, you know what I'll do,' Steve warned. 'There's an express due in a few minutes.'

Phil sighed. 'You don't want to do something like that,' he advised. 'You're a nice guy who loves his wife and kid. Do you really want all these decent, innocent people to be traumatised by the sight of your guts spattered all over the track?'

'Stop it!'

'I've seen it a fair few times, when I was on the force, and believe me it's not pretty. I had to search for this man's head once. It was—'

'If you don't shut it ...' said Steve.

'Of course. I'm sorry. Me and my big mouth.' He watched

273

closely as Steve wiped his eyes on his shirtsleeve. 'I just wondered if there's anything I can do to help.'

Steve laughed, almost maniacally, and the elderly man walking past nearly jumped out of his anorak. 'Help? Well you could push me in front of the train, I suppose.' He lowered his voice to a despairing hiss. 'Do you realise what I've done? Do you?'

'Yes,' Phil replied simply. 'And so does Grace.'

'Don't talk about Grace.'

'She loves you and she wants you back home so you can sort things out.'

Steve's face crumpled as he wept. 'I've destroyed everything. How can I ever go home?'

In the distance, Phil caught a familiar sound: the faint clackety-clack of an approaching train. 'You can start again. Together.'

But Steve was shaking his head and, to Phil's horror, he hoisted himself up until he was sitting on the balustrade, with his back to the line. Bizarrely, nobody else seemed to notice. They were all far too interested in their own small problems, their timetables and their taxis, to take an interest in Steve's minor tragedy.

'Tell Grace I love her,' said Steve.

'Tell her yourself.'

'I can't.'

The train was getting nearer, and Phil's heart was in his mouth. He pictured Grace's face as he broke the news that her husband was dead. And then Holly's . . .

'Of course you can't, you little worm,' snapped Phil.

Steve froze at Phil's sudden change of tone. 'What did you say?'

'I said you're a miserable little worm, who's too scared to face his own wife so he takes the easy way out. That's the truth, isn't it, Steve? Take the easy way out and let everyone else take the shit.'

'You can't say—'

'Oh yes I can. And I'm telling you if you don't grow up, go home right now and face this like a man—' Phil was watching the approaching train out of the corner of his eye with gathering horror '—I will personally push you off this fucking bridge – got that?'

Steve opened his mouth, but his answer was lost in the tumult as the non-stop train to London headed for the bridge. And in the moment's hesitation as he turned to let himself fall in front of the engine, Phil pounced on him, hauling him back from the brink and holding him like a child as he wept on his shoulder.

An elderly lady tapped Phil on the shoulder as she walked by, pulling her suitcase behind her. 'You really should tell your friend it's very dangerous,' she said reprovingly, 'sitting on the edge like that. He might slip and fall off, you know.'

As Murdo watched, unseen and unheeded, a reluctant realisation stole over him; a realisation he had been refusing to contemplate for a long time.

Phil Connell was not a loser. Neither was he a monster, a two-faced cheating bastard or any combination of those descriptions. Quite apart from his other qualities, Phil Connell had saved a man's life, and in his heart Murdo knew that was something he probably couldn't have done.

Most importantly, he knew deep down that Phil Connell was the best man for Holly. He could see it clearly now. And that put an end to the argument.

Meanwhile, Grace had been admitted to the Cotswold General overnight with mild concussion, and there didn't seem much more for Harry and Holly to do at the hospital. All any of them could do was wait for news.

They were on their way back home in Harry's van when Holly's mobile rang. She recognised Phil's number immediately, and felt sick with apprehension as she answered.

'Phil?'

'He's OK. Upset, but OK.'

Holly let out a huge sigh of relief. 'Dad,' she said, 'Phil says Steve's OK! What happened?' she demanded.

'I found him at the train station. It's a long story.'

'I've got to tell Grace.'

'Already done. I called the hospital and they put me through to her ward. Steve's coming home with me tonight, just so I can keep an eye on him, and I'll make sure he goes down the doctor's in the morning. I'll, er, keep you posted, yeah?'

'Yes, of course. And, Phil ...'

'Hm?'

'Thank you. And I mean really thank you.'

A lot seemed to have happened in one evening, but that wasn't the end of it. As Holly jumped down from her dad's rusty orange van, she heard a car door slam and turned to see someone walking up the pavement towards her.

'Holly, it's me. Can we talk?'

'Murdo!' Holly was so startled that she couldn't move. It was a hot night, but cold perspiration began to pool at the base of her spine. 'I ... I don't know what to say. This is a bit of a surprise, to say the least.'

'I'm sorry. I didn't mean to scare you. I just thought it might be easier for us both if I didn't tell you I was coming.' He glanced towards the house. 'About that talk ...'

'Y-yes, of course. Come in.' Holly looked round. 'Dad?'

But Harry had dematerialised in that way only parents have, when their offspring are in awkward or embarrassing situations.

'In his shed, I should think,' said Murdo, who, after three years, knew Harry's habits almost as well as his daughters did.

Holly led the way inside, clicking on the lights. Suddenly, with

276

only herself and Murdo in it, the interior of the house seemed cavernously huge; to Holly it felt as if the two of them were tiny actors on some gigantic stage, watched by invisible gods who were looking down on them and laughing at their antics.

'It's good to see you're all right,' said Holly. 'I was worried.'

Murdo smiled. 'There was no need. I was just ... putting my life in order.'

Holly knew that if there was ever going to be a right time, this was it. 'I've been doing a lot of thinking,' she began.

'So have I.' There was a briskness to Murdo's delivery that had never been there before; a feeling that he wanted to say what he had to say as quickly as possible, and then leave. 'Over the last few months we've had our problems, I think you'll agree, and I feel I've treated you unfairly.'

'You?' Holly couldn't believe what she was hearing. 'You've done nothing wrong at all.'

'No, believe me, I've treated you badly. For some time now, I've felt that our relationship was coming to an end, but I, well, couldn't bring myself to tell you. You know how it is,' he went on, that smile returning like a glimpse of winter sunlight, 'when you've felt a lot for someone, it's hard when that feeling goes away.'

Holly blinked at him in amazement. 'You're saying that ... you've fallen out of love with me?'

'Well, put simply, yes, I suppose that's what I am saying.' Murdo took both her hands. 'And I'm so terribly sorry. I should have told you sooner, not kept you wondering.'

'But ... that's what I wanted to tell you,' said Holly. And tears began to trickle down her cheeks.

'No need. All said and done. I just think it's time we said goodbye and both moved on with our lives, don't you? I've had such wonderful times with you, you know,' he added, more softly this time. 'Times I shall never regret, not for a moment.'

At that moment, there was a part of Holly that was screaming, No! Beg him to stay, tell him you want to be with him for ever!, but she knew it was only the attraction of having what she could no longer have. Murdo had fallen out of love with her, silently, without her even realising, and at the same time she had found a new chance for love in Phil. Those were the facts, and it was no use disputing them.

'I really loved you, Murdo. I did.'

'I know.'

The moment was broken as Murdo checked his watch. 'I have to get away, I'm afraid. Business meeting. But I'll keep in touch.' He bent and planted a brotherly kiss on her tear-stained cheek. 'Take care of yourself, Holly.'

Then he turned and walked away, got into the Bentley and drove off into the darkness.

It wasn't until he was a good mile away, well out of Holly's sight, that Murdo parked the car and turned off the ignition.

And wept.

Twenty·Four

'I still don't quite believe it,' Holly told Nesta as they sat outside the Montpellier Wine Bar a few evenings later. 'All this time I've been terrified of telling Murdo that I didn't think I loved him in the right way, and trying to psych myself up to tell him it was over, and while I was doing that he was falling out of love with me.'

Nesta shaded her eyes against the setting sun. 'It still sounds a bit, well, convenient to me,' she commented.

'You think he was lying?' Holly had her suspicions too. 'But why would he do that?'

'To spare you the distress of dumping him? Oh, I don't know – ignore me. What do I know about men?' Nesta took a slug from her large glass of house red. 'I've given up thinking,' she declared. 'Whenever I try to do it, I just say stupid things. Shall we order some dinner? I'm starving.'

The food came as a welcome distraction to Holly. Murdo's out-of-the-blue revelations and Steve's breakdown had left too many black thoughts rattling around inside her head. It was good just to sit in the sun, drink wine with Nesta and eat too many crunchy, golden chips.

But the respite didn't last long. Before they'd got even halfway through their meal, Nesta returned doggedly to the subject Holly most feared: 'So, now you're young, free and single again, what are you going to do about Phil?'

'Oh Nesta!' protested Holly.

'Don't tell me that after all that you've gone off him!'

'Of course not!' Far from it, thought Holly.

'So what are you going to do then? Now it's all sorted out with Murdo, you can't keep avoiding him, can you?'

Holly squirmed in exquisite discomfort. She really didn't want to admit to Nesta that she was absolutely terrified for the first time since her very first kiss, aged fourteen, backstage at the school play. And terrified of what? Of her own spooky certainty that Phil was The One? Perhaps, deep down, she was afraid that he might turn out to be Mr Wrong, and if that happened, she was sure that she would never be certain about anything ever again.

'Perhaps I should do what the agony aunts always advise in women's magazines,' speculated Holly, neatly bisecting a slice of tomato.

'Namely?'

'Spend some time just being myself before I commit myself to another man.'

'Oh.' Nesta looked surprised. 'Yes, well, perhaps you should. But is that what you actually *want* to do?'

'Not really,' Holly admitted. 'In fact ... not at all.'

Nesta shook her head and smiled. 'Didn't think so. So get out there and rip his clothes off with your teeth, or something.'

Holly gave up on the rest of her dinner and pushed away her plate. 'I've got too much else to think about at the moment,' she admitted.

'Steve and Grace, you mean?'

'And little Adam. At least he's too young to understand what's going on. But poor Grace is going through hell, worrying about where they're going to live after the house is repossessed. They've only got a few months. And as for Steve ... Oh, Nesta, I wish there was something I could do to help.'

Nesta wiped her mouth with her napkin. 'Listen, Hol,' she said, 'I know it's hard, coping with the fact that Steve's been admitted to a psychiatric unit. But remember when I had that really bad bout of depression, just after my mum and dad got divorced? I spent a month in hospital then, didn't I?'

'Gosh, yes. I'd almost forgotten. And you were only – what – fourteen?'

'Thirteen,' Nesta corrected her, 'and my world completely fell apart for a while. Anyhow, that's all water under the bridge and I'm fine now. What I'm saying is that when that happened, all I wanted was to be somewhere safe and quiet, where somebody else would take care of everything for me. Steve's in the best place, Hol, believe me. And there *is* something you can do to help.'

'Really? What?'

'When I was ill, your visits meant everything to me. Why don't you go with Grace, next time she goes to visit Steve?'

'You really think he'd want me there?'

'I do. And I know Grace would.' Nesta leaned forwards, elbows on the table, fingertips touching. 'Now all we need to do is sort out you and Phil.'

A few days later, Holly was sitting in the lounge at home, soaking her tired feet and skimming the local paper when her dad came home from work and dropped an envelope on the coffee table.

'You know my mate Joe, who works down at the racecourse?' Holly nodded. 'Well, there's an exhibition of fashions through the ages there this weekend, and he got me a couple of free tickets for the preview on Friday. Apparently they've got Mr D'Arcy's breeches on display, if that means anything to you.'

281

'Thanks, Dad. I could take Jess – she loves costume dramas and all that stuff.'

Harry beamed. 'Exactly what I was thinking. It'd be just the thing to buck her up a bit.'

'Chuck me the phone would you, Dad? I'll give her a call right now.'

Holly dialled Jess's number and held the phone to her ear with one hand while drying her feet with the other. Just when she'd come to the conclusion that her sister was out, she answered.

'Hi, Holly. What's up?'

'Nothing's up, everything's fine. I just wondered if you fancy going to the preview for the historical fashion exhibition at the racecourse.'

'Yeah, actually I'd really like that. When is it?'

'Friday afternoon.'

'Bugger. I can't go. I'm ... seeing someone then.'

'Can't you rearrange it?' Holly cajoled.

'Not really. It's sort of complicated, and I don't really want to have to call him up again.'

Holly's ears pricked up. 'Him?' she enquired.

There was a silence, and then Jess sighed. 'Kev,' she admitted. 'I'm seeing Kev.'

For a moment, Holly could hardly believe her ears. 'That's ... great news,' she gasped. 'So you and he ... you're actually talking to each other again?'

'Yeah, all right, I know I've been giving him a rough time,' said Jess quietly. 'I know I've been a bit ... extreme. The doctor says it's some sort of hormonal depression, I don't really understand it but she arranged for me to talk to someone and it's helping.'

'That's brilliant,' said Holly. 'Look, if there's anything I can do to help, you know you only have to ask, don't you?'

'Yeah, I know.'

Curiosity got the better of Holly. 'So, you and Kev?'

'We're talking, Holly. *Talking*, got that? Nothing else. It's just that, well, I started thinking clearly again and I realised that it doesn't really matter what I think: Kev is Aimee's dad, and every kid needs a dad. I don't have the right to take that away from her. So we're getting together on Friday and taking Aimee out for the day, just to see how we all get on together.'

'For what it's worth,' said Holly, 'I think you're being really brave.'

Jess snorted derisively. 'Screw that. I just talked to the psychologist guy, and I started thinking, maybe this isn't all about me. There's more to life than what I want, and besides, I need to think about the future. Aimee's future, not just mine. That's when I realised I had to find some way of getting on with Kev.'

'But you're not actually, you know, getting back together?'

'No, Hol. We're not getting back together. But ... you remember that conversation we had, the one where I told you I thought I'd fallen out of love with Kev and I was trying to find excuses for splitting up with him?'

'Of course I do.'

'Well, let's just say I was in a bad state at the time. I believed every word I said, but now ... I'm not saying I think I could love him again, but there might just still be a spark of something left between us. I guess only time will tell.'

'Good luck,' said Holly, 'and kiss Aimee for me.'

As she switched off the phone, Holly felt her sister's words resonating inside her mind, striking up echoes she could not ignore. The time for excuses has passed, she thought. Now that she'd found her birth mother, and her relationship with Murdo was over, there was no excuse for putting her life on hold any more. She couldn't hide away in the sorting office for the rest of her life, that much was obvious.

But what was she going to do with the rest of her life?

A few days later, Kev got a break: a chance to play a mini-gig in front of an audience at the Flag and Whistle.

It was Sunday lunchtime, and the pub was crowded. Kev was probably dying with terror inside, thought Holly, but you'd never have thought it from the confident way he played. The new songs he'd written with Nesta were a big success, and 'Sometime in my Heart' went down an absolute storm. Jess tried hard not to look at him as he was singing, but it was obvious that the song was dedicated to her. Holly thought she caught the flicker of a smile on her sister's face, but it might have been wishful thinking.

At the end, there was genuinely warm applause and somebody put a pint of beer in Kev's hand as he stepped down off the makeshift stage. The landlord told everyone that they'd be hearing a lot more of Kev, now that a music publisher was interested in his songs.

His songs. Nesta stood next to Holly throughout the gig and clapped louder than anyone. The lyrics might be hers, but no way was she about to try to steal his hard-earned thunder. Nesta just wasn't that kind of girl.

And that's why she's my best friend in the world, thought Holly, lifting her glass to Cheltenham's new rising star but silently toasting Nesta too.

Holly was so deep in thought as she walked her mail round, MP3 player on full blast, that she almost walked straight into Phil, who had to dodge to the other side of the pavement to avoid her. It wasn't until he tapped her on the shoulder, making her jump sky-high, that she even realised he was there.

The unexpected sight of him left her momentarily lost for words, as a wave of mingled guilt and indescribable joy washed over her.

She had a sudden, powerful urge to throw her arms around him and make him dance down the street, but confined herself to an enthusiastic hug.

'Phil!' she exclaimed, as the broadest of smiles sneaked its way across her face. 'It ... It's really good to see you.'

'You too,' said Phil. 'I was beginning to think you'd emigrated or something.'

Holly cringed. 'I'm sorry, really I am. I should've got in touch straight away. It's just, well, I thought I'd wait a day or two and then when I wanted to, I realised I was too scared to do it.'

Phil laid a hand on her arm. 'You don't have to explain, you know. If you didn't want to see me—'

'But I did! I do!' Holly seized Phil's hands in hers and planted a kiss on each. 'You can't imagine how amazingly happy I am to see you now.'

Phil dared to venture a smile of his own. 'Does that mean you might want to go somewhere for a drink with me when you finish work?'

'It means I'd love to go with you right now,' Holly declared. 'And I would too, only I've got about half a ton of flipping double-glazing leaflets here and they won't deliver themselves.'

'That's OK,' said Phil with a grin, shouldering Holly's mailbag and only slightly buckling under the weight. 'I could use some healthy exercise. Come on, we'll deliver them together.'

Finding herself back in Phil's local, the grandly named Royal Shakespeare Tavern, took Holly right back to the first day they met.

'So you're still drinking in this dive,' she remarked as they chose a table by the grease-smeared window.

'Of course I am,' Phil answered proudly. 'The beer's cheap, and the ham sandwiches haven't poisoned me yet, so what's not to love about the old rat hole?'

She laughed along with him, and once again felt the power of the force that had always drawn them together. 'I really am sorry I haven't been in touch,' she said, fiddling with the stem of her glass. 'It's been difficult for me, this last week or two.' That at least was true, she mused; true in more than one sense.

'I know. How's Grace bearing up?' Phil enquired.

'Really well, all things considered. I don't know how she does it,' admitted Holly, 'rushing backwards and forwards to see Steve, especially with Adam to consider. And constantly trying to find somewhere to live ...'

'I wish I could help,' said Phil. 'I really do. I've been racking my brains. But the only person I can think of who might be of any use is a guy called Sanjeev who works for a housing association near Gloucester. I could have a word ...'

'Please. Anything. They've only got six weeks left before the house is repossessed. What if the council shoves them into some horrible hostel and tries to forget about them?'

Phil placed a steadying hand on her arm. 'If I know you, Holly Bennett, you won't let them. You know,' he added, 'I really admire the way you care about your family, but if you keep trying to carry the weight of the whole world's problems on your shoulders, you'll end up making yourself ill. Then you'll be no use to anybody.'

Holly looked at him in surprise. 'That's ... That's what Mum always used to say.'

Phil laid his hand on top of hers and their fingers interlaced. 'Well, maybe she was right,' he said.

It was strange sometimes, the way a kind of telepathy seemed to operate between Holly and her dad. One of them would think something, and the other would seemingly pick it up out of the ether. That was what happened when Holly arrived home from the pub.

286

'I was thinking,' said Harry as he dismantled an old clock on the kitchen table, 'have you decided what to do about Phil Connell?'

It was as if an electric shock had jolted through Holly. 'Ph-phil?' she asked.

'I think he cares a lot about you, and I know you care a lot about him,' Harry went on, happily making a mess as he spoke. 'But you don't seem to be, well, getting it together as we oldies used to say. I know I shouldn't have invited him to Steve's party without telling you, but I thought it would be a nice surprise.' He looked up and saw his daughter's crimson, embarrassed face. 'Sorry, I'm not very good at this. Did I say the wrong thing?'

'No, Dad, of course you didn't,' Holly assured him. 'It's just that … Dad, I'm scared. Too scared to make the first move.'

Harry nodded understandingly. 'I think he probably feels the same way.'

'I'm almost certain that I love him,' she blurted out.

Harry's eyebrows lifted a fraction. 'Almost?'

'Well, all right, completely certain,' Holly confessed. 'But then I get this horrible, creeping fear that I might just be on the rebound from Murdo, and I daren't pick up the phone.'

'Hm,' said Harry. 'Well, it's no bad thing to be cautious; I wouldn't want either of you to move too fast and end up getting hurt. But I don't think moving too fast is your problem, is it, love?'

'No, Dad.'

'And one of you is going to have to do something soon, love, or I'll be accompanying you up the aisle in a bath chair.'

Twenty·Five

Holly gazed at herself in the mirror above the telephone table in the hall, and gave herself a thorough talking-to, in the faint hope that it might do some good.

'Come on, girl, you're supposed to be an adult,' she scolded herself, 'not a quivering jelly with all the decision-making skills of a postage stamp.' She stepped back to consider her reflection at a distance. 'I *look* like an adult,' she concluded. 'I go in and out in more or less the right places, so why can't I behave like one?'

'Because you need practice,' replied Nesta, emerging from the downstairs loo. 'And you're only going to get that by taking a deep breath and going for it. I'll take you out for a couple of voddies first if you think it'll help.'

Holly eyed the telephone mournfully. 'You're going to make me do this, aren't you?'

'Make you? Don't be silly, I'm just here to offer encouragement.' Nesta sat down on the stairs, folded her arms and looked expectant. 'Don't mind me.'

Holly picked up the telephone directory and brandished it threateningly. 'If you don't stop winding me up, you'll be getting a thick ear with the *Yellow Pages*.'

'Just phone him, for goodness' sake,' urged Nesta. 'You had a drink with him yesterday – so what's the problem? It's only a phone call, not a proposal of marriage.'

'Oh ... all right! Just give me a minute.'

Holly knew it was just plain stupid to be so nervous about calling Phil, after all they'd shared over the past few weeks. They'd even slept in the same bed – though admittedly sleeping was all they'd done. But since they'd come back to Cheltenham, those days and nights they'd spent together on the island seemed to have belonged to a different world – a world in which they'd had a definite reason for spending time together, beyond simply liking each other. Now it was time to act on all those vague promises they'd made, all the things she'd said they'd talk about later, once she was a free agent. No more putting it off, no more –

The telephone rang.

'Shit,' said Nesta. 'Just as I was psyching you up.'

'Shush,' said Holly, picking up the phone and putting on her telephone voice. 'Holly Bennett. Oh.' Shock vibrated through her, to the tip of every bone in her body, making her quiver like a tuning fork. 'Phil. Hi.'

Out of the corner of one eye, Holly could see Nesta giving her a thumbs-up and mouthing 'Go for it.' She tried to ignore her, but it was like being fifteen again and trying to have an intimate conversation with her boyfriend in front of her mum. 'How are you?'

'Great,' replied Phil. 'I really enjoyed spending time with you yesterday. You sound a bit odd though – have I picked a bad time to phone?'

'N-no, of course not!' Holly gabbled hastily. 'It's great to hear from you.' The words 'Over the last twenty-four hours I've missed you more than you'll ever know' were forming inside her mind, but typically she didn't have the bottle to voice them out loud.

'Really?'

'Yes, really.'

'Well, I was wondering ...' Phil cleared his throat. 'Would you like to come round to my place tomorrow night? I could cook us dinner. But if you'd rather not ... I mean, it's not much of a place ...'

'Dinner?' Holly's mouth went sandpaper dry. Nesta was mouthing, 'Yes, yes, yes!' at her, and it wasn't helping her one bit. 'I'd ... um ... I'd ...'

Nesta jumped up, seized the phone and shouted 'She'd love to!' into it.

It wasn't until several moments after Nesta had triumphantly slammed down the phone that Holly realised she didn't know Phil's address.

The next evening, Holly found herself standing outside a rather grand house in Montpellier, not far from the Ladies' College.

Wow, she thought as she stood outside, clutching her bottle of white wine and gazing up at three Georgian storeys of golden Cotswold stone, I wasn't expecting this. I wonder if I should have worn my posh dress instead of this skirt.

She was about to climb the four steps to the massive front door when she saw a small wooden sign bearing shaky painted lettering. It read: FLAT 1 ROUND BACK and a right-angled arrow pointed to the murky alleyway that lurked behind the row of houses, through an archway that must once have been used for horse-drawn carriages but which was now full of wheelie bins and smelly dumpsters.

She picked her way between piles of litter generated by the row of restaurants nearby, squeezed through a gate that was half off its hinges, and finally reached a small, peeling door behind two large dustbins and a mountain bike, chained to a drainpipe. The doorbell had a little printed label underneath that read: FLAT 1: CONNELL, so she rang it and waited.

From somewhere inside came a crashing sound, followed by

swearing and the word 'Dweezil' at high volume, and then the door opened to reveal Phil, in shorts and T-shirt, carrying a cat covered in what looked like tomato spaghetti sauce.

'Holly!' Phil's face registered something between delight and absolute horror. Oh God ... didn't I say seven thirty?'

'It *is* seven thirty. Thirty-five, actually. I didn't want to be too early so I walked around a bit. Can I ... come in? Or do you want me to walk around some more?'

'You're welcome to come in, but it's a bit of a disaster area, I'm afraid. I was planning to clean up before you arrived.' Phil led the way into a small, low-ceilinged kitchen just about big enough for two people and one fat cat – as long as the cat breathed in. 'Dweezil decided to jump up and investigate what I was cooking, and of course he managed to upset the pan all over himself. Good job it wasn't too hot.'

'Indeed.' Holly giggled at the sight of a partially orange cat. 'What exactly is that stuff he's covered in?'

'Arabbiata sauce – and it's really hot. If he gets a lick of it, he'll go through the roof, poor little guy. Come on mate, it's bath time.'

Phil promptly dumped Dweezil in the kitchen sink and turned the taps full on. To his credit, Dweezil barely protested as he received the bath of his life, followed by a vigorous towelling down and a blast from an ancient hairdryer that left him looking like the feline equivalent of Johnny Rotten.

'I'm really, really sorry about this,' Phil went on, looking downcast. 'I must've got my times wrong. I had this amazingly cool designer shirt to change into, as well.' He sighed. 'Now I'll never impress you.'

'Oh, I shouldn't worry,' Holly reassured him. 'You look good the way you are.'

'You really think so?' Phil investigated a gooey blob in his hair. 'Are you sure there's nothing wrong with your eyesight?'

Holly laughed, happy and comfortable in Phil's company now that Dweezil had broken the ice for them. 'As a matter of fact, I have perfect twenty-twenty vision.' She placed the wine on the kitchen table, trying not to notice that one leg was sawn-off short and propped up on a copy of *Roget's Thesaurus*. 'I hope this is OK; it should still be chilled.'

Phil wiped down the table and chairs to eliminate all traces of Dweezil and spaghetti sauce, then they sat down and opened the wine. 'I'll have to make some more sauce for the meatballs now,' lamented Phil. He directed a laser-beam glare at Dweezil, but the cat simply yawned, rolled onto its back and started licking one of its feet.

'I'll help.'

'But you're the guest!' protested Phil.

Holly shrugged. 'So we'll do it together.' She rummaged in Phil's fridge and produced an onion. 'Here – catch. I'll do the chillies.'

Half an hour later, they were sitting down eating dinner and talking as though they'd known each other all their lives. Side by side on Phil's rickety sofa, with their plates on their knees, they recalled the time they'd spent on the island, searching for Holly's birth mother.

'Have you heard anything?' Phil asked Holly.

Holly shook her head. 'Not a thing. I do want to go back there sometime soon, though,' she went on. 'Knowing that it's where I was born makes me feel like I ... well ... belong, I guess.'

'There you are!' Phil grinned. 'I told you the island would work its magic on you.' Then his smile faded. 'But was it all worth it? All that money, and all that time?'

'Oh yes,' replied Holly. 'It was well worth it.' She wanted to say: 'It was worth it a hundred times over, because I met you,' but it sounded so cheesy, and she was too much of a coward anyway. So instead she said: 'At least I found out who I am, and that's really important to me.'

'But you didn't find out all the things you wanted to know,' pointed out Phil. 'The hereditary diseases, and all that kind of thing. 'And you didn't really get to know your birth mother – or at least, you haven't yet.'

'No,' admitted Holly, 'and I wish I had. But just having seen her and spoken to her means an awful lot to me. And I understand a lot of things better now,' she went on. 'I understand that you can't just bludgeon your way into someone's life after thirty years and expect to be welcomed with open arms. Not that I exactly expected that anyway ... but I don't think I quite understood that Denise is somebody else's mother now, not mine. Maureen Bennett will always be my mum,' she said, with a touch of sadness.

'All the same, you must have looked at your birth mother and seen something of yourself in her,' argued Phil.

'Honestly? Nothing,' Holly replied. 'I don't look like her, I don't sound like her ... It's possible that I think like her, but that's something I may never find out. And if I'm honest, I think that what I am now is the sum total of being brought up by Maureen and Harry Bennett. They taught me what was right and what was wrong, and a lot of the things that interest me are the things Mum and Dad loved. Jess even says I look a bit like Maureen,' she added, shaking her head wistfully.

'All I know is that you look beautiful,' said Phil softly.

Holly didn't know what to say, so she stared down at her knees instead, but a flood of happiness overwhelmed her so completely that she was sure Phil must have noticed. Surely it must be radiating out of her, lighting her up like a Christmas tree? In the end, she managed a feeble 'Th-thank you.'

Phil got rid of the plates and sat down beside her again. 'No, you mustn't thank me, Hol, it's true: you are beautiful. I've thought that from the moment I first set eyes on you.' He smiled.

'I know it sounds ridiculously clichéd, but you make my heart sing, you really do.' Startled, he reached out and gently turned her head so that she was looking at him. 'Holly,' he asked in alarm, 'are those tears? Did I say the wrong thing?'

How could she explain? 'No, no!' she exclaimed, laughing through the tears. 'Don't you understand? You said the *right* thing. A wonderful thing.' Then a pang of sadness gripped her. 'But I know I can't ever be Sita, and—'

'No, don't say that!' Phil silenced her, placing a finger to her lips. 'Please believe me, Holly. No one has ever made me feel the way you do. *No one*. And no one else ever will.'

She gazed into his eyes. 'Truly?'

He kissed her tenderly on the forehead. 'Don't you see? I'm in love with you, Holly. I always have been. More in love than I thought I could ever be.'

Holly closed her eyes and moaned softly as he ran his hands slowly, passionately, through her hair, making her arch her back with pleasure, making her suddenly want him more than she had ever wanted anyone or anything in her whole life. And as his hands slid lower, desire loosened her tongue, finding the words she had been too afraid to speak before: 'I love you too, Phil. I really, truly love you.'

His arms enfolded her and her lips sought out his as they sank onto the sofa cushions. And at last Holly Bennett understood what true love really meant: a combination of breathless, joy-filled ecstasy and perfect, companionable warmth that she and Murdo could never have shared; the feeling she had waited for all her life – until now.

The passionate fulfilment which she had found at last, in Phil Connell's arms.

'Well, well, well,' said Nesta, wagging the finger of junior managerial disapproval. 'I don't know what to say to you, young lady.'

It was the following morning and Holly was struggling not to yawn too much. After a night without sleep, it was extremely difficult to stay awake and listen to one of Nesta's lectures on flagrant employee misconduct. 'Oh come on, I was only half an hour late,' she protested, 'and it's the first time I've been late – ever!'

Nesta's eyes narrowed. 'Ah, but I know *why* you were late, Miss Dirty Stop-out!' She held the mask of disapproval for a few seconds, then it cracked, and she dissolved into schoolgirl mirth behind her office desk. 'So much for self-control and "taking things slowly"!'

Holly cursed her lifelong tendency to blush crimson at the smallest embarrassment. And this was a big one. 'Nesta, don't,' she pleaded.

'But I want to know all the details'

'Can't you just use your imagination?'

'Sorry, Hol. You know I've got no imagination.'

'But you're a poet!' Holly spluttered.

'Ah, but my stories at school were always crap. And besides, I'm your best friend. You know you'd be just the same if it was me,' she added, making a valid point. 'So come on, spill the beans – or I'm going out there—' she pointed towards the depot floor '—and telling all your colleagues exactly why you were late this morning ...'

From that first night with Phil, Holly's life began to change. The very fact of knowing that he loved her seemed to give her the strength to do things that might have frightened her before.

She had been apprehensive about going to see Steve in the psychiatric unit; in fact, to her shame, she had found one or two good excuses for not going. But the next time Grace announced that she was taking Adam to visit him, Holly volunteered to come along too.

'He's getting better,' Grace told her as they turned in through the hospital gates and parked, 'he really is. And the doctors think they can help him control the gambling addiction – if he can get the right treatment.'

'Is there a doubt about that?' asked Holly.

'Right now, there's a doubt about everything,' replied Grace sadly. 'There's an NHS waiting list as long as your arm, and as for going private ... hah!' She rested her forehead on the steering wheel. 'I just wish I had better news for him.'

Holly stroked her sister's hair. 'Hey, come on, we're the fabulous Bennett sisters, remember? We'll find a way.'

Grace removed Adam and his baby seat from the back of the car, and they headed for the clinic entrance.

Holly wasn't too sure what she'd been expecting, but it wasn't this: an airy, modern, well-laid-out living environment with a dining room and a comfortable lounge where people were sitting around in armchairs chatting. Admittedly one or two of the patients did unnerve her a little – especially the girl whose arms bore the scars from a thousand old knife cuts – but it was pretty obvious that, like Steve, these were just ordinary people with problems that needed fixing.

'Steve's in his room,' one of the nurses explained. 'He's been doing a lot of thinking.'

They found him standing by the window in his room, gazing out at the little garden which formed the centrepiece of the clinic development. Some of the patients were sitting outside in the sunshine.

'Shall we go outside?' suggested Grace, after kissing her husband on the cheek.

He shook his head. 'I can't take the sunshine at the moment. It's too ... I dunno ... I just prefer it darker. You must think I'm completely cracked.' He stroked Adam's silky hair. 'And God only knows what this little chap's going to think of his dad when he's older.'

'I think he'll be very proud of you,' said Holly. 'Both of you.'

Adam looked up at his dad, stretched out his arms and gave a cheerful 'Da-da!'

'Go on then,' said Grace. 'He wants you to pick him up.'

Steve looked uncertain. But Grace hoisted the little boy into the air, and placed him, giggling, in his father's arms. 'See,' she said softly, 'that's someone else who loves you.'

Steve clutched Adam to him, holding the little boy's head on his shoulder so that he couldn't see his daddy silently crying. 'How can any of you love me?' he demanded. 'I've destroyed everything.'

'So we'll build it up again,' replied Grace, putting her arms around the two of them and resting her face on Steve's shoulder.

Suddenly Holly realised how heroic her sister really was. For so long she'd cast Grace solely in the role of impossible, irredeemable snob, but all the time she'd been playing a part, networking with all the right people, trying to save Steve's business, trying to hold her family together.

'I think I'll just pop out for a breath of air,' said Holly, as she slipped out of the room without the others even noticing. 'I'll be back in a little while.'

As she turned to close the door behind her, she took a last look at the little family – Grace, Steve and Adam – and swore that if there was anything she could possibly do, she would somehow help Grace to keep a roof above their heads.

Twenty·Six

As summer slid seamlessly into autumn, so the relationship between Holly and Phil metamorphosed from friendship into love, and they took to spending every spare moment together, content just to be in each other's company.

There was only one problem: Holly was afraid to admit, even to herself, that she had never been happier. One false move, one wrong word, and this new happiness might melt away like a drift of autumnal mist. So mostly she just smiled when people asked her how things were going with Phil, and said: 'OK – I think.' Only Harry and Nesta really knew how much Phil meant to her, and they knew Holly so well that they could tell without having to ask.

One afternoon after work, Holly headed for the Bloodhound Investigations office to invite Phil to the next family Sunday lunch, and do a little routine paperwork while she was at it. Phil might mean the world to her, but he was still utterly rubbish when it came to administration. Anyone who could blithely allow his cat to shred his VAT return was clearly in need of a little help.

Letting herself in with the key Phil had given her, she ran up the stairs and was about to open the office door when she spotted the handwritten notice stuck to it. It read: GONE TO BANK BACK 15 MINS. Well, fifteen minutes wasn't long to wait, and he might already have been gone for ten, so she opened the door and went inside.

Dweezil was so excited to see Holly that he actually jumped down off Phil's computer keyboard, and farted impressively when she bent to stroke his furry back.

'You did that deliberately, didn't you?' Holly said, pointing an accusing finger at the cat. She could have sworn he was smirking.

As usual there were heaps of files and papers everywhere, though these had diminished somewhat since Holly had declared war on them. As Phil wouldn't be back for a few minutes, she supposed she might as well make a start. He really ought to get himself a secretary, she mused, but that was just pie in the sky. She knew he couldn't afford it and besides, she rather liked being au fait with what was going on at the agency.

The first pile contained several unbanked cheques, some dated several weeks previously; with a groan, Holly collected them all together with a paper clip and placed them right in the middle of Phil's desk, with a paperweight on top. When he got back to the office, she'd have to send him straight back to the bank. Then there was all the junk mail, which filled the wastepaper bin to overflowing, and a number of letters from clients which would need to be filed later.

Just as she was reaching the bottom of the pile, Holly came across an envelope marked 'Granley Stott, Solicitors'. The letter it belonged to lay underneath, spread out flat so that it was impossible for her not to read it. It began:

'Dear Mr Connell
My client, Miss Sita Yossarian . . .

Holly was still sitting there, staring blankly at it, when the door opened and Phil walked in.

'Why didn't you tell me? Why?' demanded Holly, pursuing Phil around the office as he attempted to make a cup of coffee.

'I . . . forgot,' he said, lamely.

'You forgot! How could you possibly forget that your ex is demanding her share of your business back? Come to that, how could you forget to mention that she still owns half of it?'

Phil squirmed with discomfort. 'All right, I didn't really forget,' he admitted. 'But I was trying really hard not to think about it. When you can't do anything about it, it's not the sort of thing you can think about for long without going insane. And what's the point of worrying you with it? How much milk do you want in your coffee?'

'Phil, stop this.' Holly took the mug out of his hand and replaced it on the counter, then did the same with the spoon he was holding. 'Please stop talking about coffee, and tell me what the hell is going on.'

Phil took a deep breath and let it out, visibly sagging as the breath left his body. His office chair groaned as he flopped into it. 'What's going on is that she wants her money and she wants it now.'

'The cowbag. Why now, after all this time?'

'I dunno.' Phil shrugged. 'Maybe business isn't so good in the Japanese sex industry. Maybe she just has an urge to make me suffer. Either way it's the same: I can't afford to buy her out.'

Holly sat down slowly, trying to stay calm despite her pounding heart. 'What about your savings?' she asked.

'I don't have any to speak of, not any more. Every penny I had, plus an enormous bank loan, went into setting up the business and fitting out the office. And, fool that I was, I let myself be conned into putting the bank loan solely in my name.'

'Oh Phil!'

He groaned. 'I know, I know. Spot the idiot.'

Holly battled to think of a solution. 'But what about your

income – the money you've earned from jobs … the money you earned from me?'

Phil sighed. 'The assignments are coming in,' he conceded, 'but it takes time before you can show much of a profit. Years. After overheads, loan payments and living expenses, there's never much of a surplus at the end of the month. Certainly not enough to pay off Sita.'

'And if you can't … what does that mean?'

'It means if I don't get the money within the next fortnight or so, which I won't, I'll have to sell the business to pay her off. Goodbye Bloodhound Investigations, hello nasty job in Birmingham.'

Holly struggled to take all of this in. 'Birmingham? What's Birmingham got to do with it?'

Phil drew invisible patterns on the desk with his fingertip. As if he knew something was up, Dweezil waddled over and lay down on his master's feet, promptly cutting off the circulation to his toes. 'There's a job going with a big agency in Birmingham,' he explained. 'A bloke I know there offered it to me when he heard what happened. But all I'd be doing is serving writs all day long, and the commuting would be hell. Unless …'

Holly filled in the blanks. 'Unless you moved there.'

'Which I'm not going to, because you're here.'

'Who says I wouldn't go there with you?'

Phil drooped visibly. 'Can we not talk about this, please?'

Holly perched on the edge of his desk. 'You're going to have to talk about it pretty soon,' she pointed out. 'Like, in about a fortnight's time. Oh, Phil, why did you think you couldn't tell me?'

'I didn't want to hurt you. I didn't want to … to spoil what we have.'

'You'd have to try an awful lot harder than that,' replied Holly emphatically. She got up and walked around the office. 'I wish I had some money left. Enough to buy Sita's half of the business. But

I sold my car to pay for the search, and I've given nearly all my inheritance money to Jess.'

'Holly, love,' Phil protested, 'even if you did have any money, you wouldn't want to waste it on a crap business like this.'

'If I had any money – which I don't – I'd waste it on whatever I liked,' Holly replied firmly. 'But as it happens I think Bloodhound Investigations is a bloody good investment.'

'You do?'

'Look, Phil, you're a skilled and experienced investigator, and if you're a little short on admin skills, well that doesn't really matter because I'm not, am I? And besides,' she added, turning back to face Phil, 'it just so happens that I'd quite like a stab at being an investigator too.'

'You? An investigator?'

'There's no need to look quite so horrified!'

'I'm not horrified, just … surprised.'

'Well,' demanded Holly, 'do you think I'd be any good? Honestly?'

'As a matter of fact, yes,' Phil replied. 'Honestly. But this is all hopelessly academic, isn't it? Seeing as I've got no money and neither have you.'

They looked at each other as the ridiculousness of the situation overwhelmed them.

'Would you really come to Birmingham?' asked Phil.

'Why don't you ask me and find out?'

'Well, would you?'

'Just try and stop me.'

'My God,' said Phil, through tears of laughter, pulling her towards him, 'you're as mad as I am.'

That night, Holly and Harry were watching a soppy drama on TV together, Harry sitting on the sofa and Holly cross-legged on the floor at his feet. Suddenly, for no apparent reason, everything welled up inside Holly and tears started pouring down her cheeks.

Harry was glued to the action, and it took him a few moments to realise what was happening. Panic overtook him and he scrabbled for the remote, extinguishing the heroine in mid-flow.

'Holly, love, is something the matter? Are you poorly?'

Holly shook her head. 'No Dad, I'm fine, really I am.'

'Fine! People don't cry when they're fine.' With a creak of middle-aged joints, Harry lowered himself onto the floor beside his daughter. 'Now, come on, tell your old dad what's up.' He stroked her hair, the way he used to when she was ill as a child. 'It's not your love life is it? I thought everything was going really well with you and Phil.'

'It is. I'm ever so happy, really I am.' Sobbing uncontrollably, Holly buried her head in her dad's ancient jumper. It smelled comfortingly of creosote, motor oil and chocolate, and of childhood days when everything had been so very simple.

Harry sat there looking baffled in a very masculine way. Despite living in a household entirely composed of women for so many years, he'd never quite got the hang of feminine emotions. 'It's not your ... you know—' he cleared his throat embarrassedly '—time of the month, is it?'

Holly's sobs turned to coughing and then laughter. 'No Dad, nothing like that.' She sat up and wiped her face with the proffered paint-spattered hanky, feeling rather silly and childish. 'It's just ... there are so many people who need help: Grace and Steve, Jess and Kev ... and Phil. And I can't help any of them, can I? I really, really want to, but at the end of the day I'm just plain useless because it all comes down to money and I haven't got any.'

'Hey, calm down,' urged her father softly. 'Of course you can help – you do help. You ask Grace, or Jess, and they'll tell you how grateful they are to have a sister like you. Money doesn't come into it.'

'But it does, Dad, it does.' Holly explained about Phil and Sita, and about Phil having to sell the business in order to pay off his ex-partner. And then she told him how she would have liked to buy into Phil's business herself, if only she'd had the means.

'Has Phil asked you for any money?' asked Harry.

'No,' admitted Holly. 'Not a penny. But—'

'But nothing,' said Harry firmly. 'Believe me, love, it's not money that lad wants from you, it's your love and your support. That's what couples do for each other, through good and bad.'

'Like you and Mum, you mean?'

'Like me and your mother, yes. And all the money in the world can't make things good if they're not meant to be that way.'

Like Murdo and me, thought Holly. The man with all the money in the world, and the girl who tried so hard to love him but failed miserably.

'So you're happy with Phil?' asked Harry.

Holly nodded. 'Very.'

'Then be content with that,' her father advised. 'It's more than most people ever have. And don't worry so much about his business. There's still time for things to work out for the best, and—'

'No, Dad,' said Holly sadly. 'I think time's run out for Phil. But what about Grace and Steve, and—'

'You can't sort everybody's problems out for them,' her father scolded. 'That's what I was always telling your mother, but would she listen? She used to worry about other people morning, noon and night. You're just like her, you know,' he added wistfully. 'Sometimes I look at you and I can see her in you.'

'Dad ...' began Holly.

'Yes, love?'

'All that money I spent looking for my birth mother ... Do you

304

think it was a waste? Should I have saved it and—?'

'No, love, I don't think it was a waste, any more than you do, deep down. It was something you had to do. The world doesn't all come down to pounds and pence, you know.' His kindly face crinkled into a smile. 'Now give us a hand up off this floor, love. I think my back's gone.'

The following Sunday lunchtime, Holly found herself back in the family kitchen with her two sisters, discussing the merits – or otherwise – of Jess's gravy.

'It's definitely lumpy,' declared Grace, shoving the gravy boat under Holly's nose. 'Are those lumps in there, or what?'

'They're just granules!' protested Jess. 'Undissolved gelatinous granules. Aren't they, Hol?'

Holly smiled to herself and carefully avoided taking sides. Things seemed to be getting back to normal at last. 'Oh, I'm sure it'll do,' she said. 'It can't be worse than the time Mum had flu and Dad tried to cook the Sunday lunch all on his own. Remember his attempt at gravy?'

Grace chuckled. 'Of course I do. It's the only time I've ever seen gravy you really *could* stand a spoon up in. And as for his custard . . .'

'I cut mine into cubes,' Jess reminisced, 'and fed it to the dog.'

'So now we know what killed poor Buster,' commented Holly, stooping to take the joint out of the oven. 'Do you think this beef's done?'

'Give it another five minutes,' advised Grace, the Bennett family's domestic goddess. 'And don't forget to rest it before you carve.'

Jess went across to the kitchen door and peeped out. The dining room was just across the hall, and the door was open, offering a glimpse of what was going on inside. 'Do you think Steve's OK?' she wondered aloud. 'The family can be a bit . . . intense.'

'He'll manage,' Grace said confidently. 'They wouldn't have discharged him for the weekend if that didn't think he could cope, and he told me he was really looking forward to having a proper Sunday lunch with the family, after so long in the hospital.'

'Your Phil's a bit of all right,' Jess informed Holly with a cheeky grin. 'I wouldn't mind throwing myself at him for real.'

'You do and you're dead,' Holly replied sweetly. 'Pass the carving knife will you, Grace?'

In the dining room, the guests were arranged around the Bennett family's sole heirloom: the big oval table that had been old even when Great-grandma Bennett was a girl. Like the family members themselves, it had suffered one or two knocks down the years, but it still stood firm, give or take an almost imperceptible wobble to the left.

Everyone was there, including Phil and even Kev, with the little ones babbling to each other excitedly in their high chairs. Steve was home at last, albeit temporarily, and there was a real air of celebration, though behind the smiles still lurked unanswered questions, such as: where was home going to be for Steve, Grace and Adam, once the bank had repossessed their house?

Kev, too, faced a few questioning glances. In the kitchen, Grace whispered to Jess: 'I thought you two weren't speaking.'

'We weren't,' replied Jess awkwardly, turning away to slap individual Yorkshire puddings onto enormous, oven-warmed plates. 'But we are now. Sort of.'

In the dining room, Steve turned to Phil. 'I'm glad you could come,' he said, fiddling nervously with the stem of his wine glass.

'I'm honoured to be invited,' Phil replied.

Steve opened his mouth to say something, closed it again, and then blurted out: 'I'm so ashamed. I don't know how to thank you for … you know …'

306

'No need,' said Phil, patting Steve on the shoulder. 'Tell you what – buy me a pint of best at the Bell and we'll call it all square.'

'Who's the extra space for?' asked Kev, who had been pretty quiet up till then. 'There's one more chair than there are people.'

Harry smiled. 'Because we've an extra guest,' he replied.

Holly's voice sounded from across the hall. 'Time to dish up, Dad.'

'OK, I'll come and give you a hand.' He winked at Phil and then disappeared.

'OK, Phil, you're the private eye,' observed Kev. 'What's he up to?'

Phil was spared the embarrassment of admitting he didn't have a clue, as at that moment Harry, Holly, Grace and Jess reappeared, laden with roast beef and all the trimmings.

'You carve, Dad,' said Grace, taking charge as usual.

'Just a moment,' replied Harry. Then he went back into the hall and called up the stairs. 'Lunch is ready, Eileen. You can come down now.'

Eileen?

Phil and Holly exchanged looks. Not *that* Eileen, surely?

'Eileen who?' demanded Steve. 'Do we know anybody called Eileen?'

Holly knew it was Eileen Christian, just from the sound her feet made on the stairs, well before Harry ushered her into the dining room. And it was lovely to see her. But what on earth was she doing here?

'For those of you who don't know Eileen,' Harry explained, 'this is Phil's grandmother, Eileen Christian, and she's come all the way from the Isle of Man to see us.'

Nobody actually said, 'Why?' but the question was hanging in the air as the polite introductions were made.

'Eileen and I have been having some interesting phone conversa-

307

tions lately,' Harry went on, 'ever since Holly and Phil went over to the island to carry out their investigations.'

Phil's jaw dropped. Holly gaped. 'You have?'

'Oh yes. And it turns out we have a lot in common, don't we, Eileen?' He drew back her chair for her to sit down.

Eileen nodded as she took her seat at the table. 'Absolutely. Though I can't quite see the appeal of model train sets. I had enough of those when Philip was a little boy. He was Hornby mad,' she reminisced. 'You even had your own little station-master's hat and whistle, didn't you, Philip? Have you still got them?'

Everybody laughed, Holly included. Phil looked as though he wanted the ground to swallow him up. 'That was a few years ago, Grandma,' he pleaded. 'I've grown up a bit since then.'

Grandma Christian dismissed this with a cheerful wave of her hand. 'Not to worry, I'm sure I have the photos somewhere.'

To Phil's evident relief, Harry stepped in and rescued him. 'Anyway, the reason why Eileen's here today is because we both have something to tell you.'

Every drop of blood drained from Grace's face. 'Y-you're not getting married, are you?'

There was a minuscule pause, and then Eileen and Harry burst out laughing. Eileen laughed so hard that Holly was afraid she might choke. 'Married!' she gasped. 'Good heavens, no. Once was quite enough, thank you. Not that your father's not a fine man,' she added hastily, 'but this has nothing to do with matrimony.' She looked at Harry. 'I think you should explain, dear. It was your idea, after all.'

Harry filled everyone's wine glasses, then sat forwards in his chair. 'When we adopted you, Holly,' he began, 'it made me think about the future and I took out an endowment policy. It's due to mature in a few years, when I retire, but I contacted the company and it turns out that I can cash it in now and still get a decent sum of money.'

Apprehension tautened the muscles in Holly's chest. She wanted to cut in, tell him that this was a bad idea, but knew she had to let him finish.

'Now, over the past few months you've all had your problems, and that's been a big worry to me – which is why I've decided to cash in the policy and divide the proceeds equally between you: Holly, Grace and Jess.' Dipping into his shirt pocket, he took out three cheques and handed them to his daughters. 'It's not a massive amount, as you can see, but it ought to help.'

'Dad!' protested Holly, shocked almost speechless by her father's actions.

'This isn't right,' said Jess.

'No, Dad, you can't do it!' exclaimed Grace.

Harry smiled. 'I already have, love, and I feel all the better for it. Anybody fancy another roast potato? I'm starving.' While his family stared back at him, hardly knowing what to say, he pointed his fork at Eileen. 'Your turn.'

Eileen dabbed at her mouth with her napkin. 'Lovely roast beef,' she said, dimples appearing in her plump cheeks as she smiled. 'Now then, as Holly will have told you, Philip has been having a little trouble with an ex-girlfriend of his who still owns half of his business and wants it back – the only problem being that since my dear grandson has no chance of finding the money in time, he'll have to sell up.

'Well, if there's one thing I can't stand, it's a young woman with a nasty streak, and that one's bad to the bone, I can tell you. You really do have terrible taste in women, Philip,' she added, with a gimlet stare at her grandson that sent Holly's heart plunging into her boots. 'Or at least—' her eyes lighted on Holly and suddenly they were twinkling '—you used to.

'Now, my Charlie left me a decent pension which is quite enough for me to live on, and my savings are just sitting around in the bank. So what I'm proposing to do is buy that awful woman's share of your business, Philip. But ...'

Eileen paused. She certainly knew how to work an audience, thought Holly, she had them hanging on her every word. But what? wondered Holly, already dazed from her father's sudden largesse, and ready to expect just about anything from Philip's grandma.

'But,' Eileen continued, 'I intend to put it into your name, Holly.'

'Mine?' Holly looked from Eileen to Phil and back again. 'B-but ... why?'

'Because Philip has always needed someone in his life who could take care of him, organise him and teach him a little sense – and you see, Holly, I think he's finally found that person in you.'

'What on earth did you say?' demanded Nesta, hanging on Holly's every word as they shared a morning cup of coffee in the staff canteen.

'What could I say?' replied Holly. 'I said, "Thank you," and then I burst into tears.'

'You big, soft ...' Nesta threw up her hands in despair. 'What did you go and do that for?'

'I was happy! You know how much I've wanted to help Phil and learn the business. And Eileen just gave me a chance to do both, in one fell swoop. What with Dad giving us all that money as well ...' She fixed Nesta with one of her hard stares. 'OK, what would *you* have done?'

Nesta munched reflectively on her cheese and pickle sandwich. 'Probably go straight down town and bank that cheque before Harry changed his mind,' she admitted.

'You cynic!' exclaimed Holly, spluttering coffee everywhere.

'And there I was, thinking you had the soul of a poet.'

'Well, it's not every day people give you free money,' Nesta pointed out. '*Especially* when you're a poet. Anyway, go on, tell me what happened next. You can miss out the blubbing and the heart-felt thank yous.'

'We all ate a lot and had too much to drink,' Holly recalled, 'and Grace asked Dad if he'd hold on to her money until Steve's discharged as a bankrupt, just in case it got taken off them. It'll be a real help to them when they're starting out again.' Holly sipped what was left of her coffee. 'Steve was saying that the council would probably rehouse them on the Bluebell Estate, so they'd be right back where they started out – and do you know what Grace said?'

'I will when you tell me.'

'She said, "I lived there for six years, and I can live there again. Actually there are some really nice people on the Bluebell Estate." Can you believe she actually said that?'

'She's changed, has your sister,' remarked Nesta. 'Mind you, it was about time. Then what?' she demanded.

'And then Jess and Kev made their big announcement,' Holly went on. 'They've decided to get back together, for Aimee's sake.'

'Oh,' said Nesta. 'That doesn't sound very ... romantic.'

'Not on the face of it,' conceded Holly, 'but Kev did say they're going to try to make a real go of it, and if you ask me, Jess still has a thing for Kev even if she's not admitting it.'

'Ah well. At least Aimee will have a daddy again,' mused Nesta, 'and that's no bad thing. And Kev can get out of that cockroach-infested hovel he's been squatting in.'

'Exactly. Oh – and then I had a light-bulb moment,' Holly announced. 'When Grace was talking about the Bluebell Estate, I suddenly realised that there was no need for her and Steve and Adam to go back there at all. And there was something I could do to help.' Holly's eyes brightened with excitement. 'All I have to do is leave home, find a place of my own, and they can all move in with Dad. It's the perfect solution – and it's the perfect house for a child to grow up in.' She smiled wistfully. 'We should know.'

'Hey, aren't you forgetting something?' suggested Nesta.

'What?'

'It's all very well going on about moving out, but you don't actually have anywhere else to go, not now Murdo's off the scene. Unless of course you're thinking of moving in with darling Phil?'

'He hasn't asked me,' sighed Holly. 'I think he's scared.'

'What of? You? You're hardly Arnold Schwarzenegger.'

'Not me. Her. Sita – or the ghost of Sita.'

'But you said he swore he was completely over Sita!'

'He is. It's just . . . Well, the last time he asked a woman to move in with him it was her, and we all know how that turned out.'

'Great! So the guy's mentally scarred as well as short of dosh. So what does that mean for you?'

For a moment, Holly felt the lure of Nesta's brand of cynicism. It was true: she was dating a man who – although she knew that he cared for her deeply – seemed in thrall to the past, terrified of taking the final, symbolic step to commitment because if he did, fate might step in and destroy him all over again. But Holly couldn't live her life the way Nesta saw it, tinged with bitter loneliness. Things were going to work out for her and Phil, deep down she knew it.

'It means,' she replied, 'that Phil and I are going to take things one day at a time. Oh, and by the way, you're coming flat-hunting with me tomorrow night. OK?'

Twenty·Seven

After that Sunday lunch events moved swiftly, and suddenly Holly had difficult decisions to make: decisions that couldn't be put off any longer.

On that particular Monday morning, Holly was first back from her round, and the sorting office seemed unnaturally quiet as she walked across the vast space to Nesta's poky little office in the far corner. She'd made that same walk hundreds of times over the past couple of years, but this time her legs felt like jelly.

She knocked, didn't bother to wait for a summons, and walked straight in. 'Morning, Nesta. I've come to hand in my resignation.'

Nesta stared at the long, white envelope in Holly's hands.

'You're kidding me. You are, aren't you?'

Holly shook her head. 'Not this time, Nesta. It really is time for me to move on.'

'Oh my God.' Nesta sprang out of her seat and started pacing up and down. 'Are you really sure about this?'

Holly laid the envelope down on the desk, right in the middle where Nesta couldn't ignore it. 'You know it's strange,' she said, 'I thought that when it came to it I might not be sure, but now it has, I couldn't be surer.'

'But I don't *want* you to hand in your notice,' protested Nesta, pushing the envelope away with a fingertip.

Holly pushed it right back again. 'Sorry, mate, but I already did.'

They looked at each other for a long, reflective moment, and then Nesta sat down, slowly and mechanically. 'Somehow, I never thought you'd leave,' she said. 'I must've been crazy. I thought that now you'd come back home, I could keep you here – get you promoted, maybe, so you wouldn't want to go back to London.'

'But I'm not going back to London,' Holly reminded her. 'I'll only be just up the road, at Bloodhound Investigations.'

'It won't be the same though, will it?' lamented Nesta. She sniffed, and to Holly's amazement wiped away a tear. She hadn't seen Nesta cry since she fell head first off the climbing frame, aged six. 'It's been brilliant having you here; just like the old days.'

'You make us sound like a couple of old grannies,' laughed Holly. 'But you're right, it has been great working with you and being back home. The thing is though, everybody has to move on eventually or else they sort of . . . fossilise.'

Nesta threw her a sceptical look. 'Fossilise, my arse,' she said. 'Admit it, Hol: you're only going because you've fallen for Mister Love-pants Connell.'

'And because I need more in my life than sorting letters and being chased by vicious chihuahuas,' retorted Holly, surprised by the vehemence of Nesta's tone. She took a good look at her friend, hunched miserably over her desk. 'Oh, Nesta, please don't be jealous of me.'

'I'm not jealous,' Nesta insisted. 'Why on earth would I be jealous?'

Oh Nesta, please don't make me spell it out, thought Holly. But Nesta just went on eyeing her defiantly, daring her to say it. 'Because,' Holly began. 'Because you don't have anyone to love, and I do.'

'Thanks,' said Nesta flatly. 'That makes me sound like a complete saddo.'

314

Oh dear, trust me, thought Holly, I've just made things worse again. 'I didn't mean anything of the sort,' she protested. 'I just—'

'No, it's OK, you're right. All in all I'm a bit pathetic really. I should grow up and ... and enjoy being single, like all those crappy American life gurus are always saying.'

Holly thought for a moment, choosing her words carefully. 'Circumstances can change, Nesta,' she said. 'That's what you're always telling me. Tomorrow you might meet the man of your dreams.'

'Or not,' retorted Nesta, ever the realist. 'Look Hol, I've got a pet spider and a half-share in a vintage traction engine; I'm hardly Miss Average. Be honest: what kind of bloke's going to want to end up with me?'

'A lucky one,' declared Holly. 'He just doesn't realise it yet, that's all.'

Luckily Nesta never stayed down for long, and by the end of the week she was her usual energetic self. In fact, when Holly reported for work on Friday morning, she found Nesta in a state of high excitement.

'Look, Hol! Look!' Nesta was practically dancing with elation as she dragged Holly into her office and thrust a letter at her. 'Kev got this yesterday – read it!'

Holly skimmed the contents, and found herself almost dancing with her friend. 'You and Kev have been nominated for a song-writing prize! Oh Nesta, that's amazing!'

The two of them bounced around Nesta's office like seven-year-olds.

'We probably won't win,' commented Nesta.

'Why not? You deserve to. "Sometime in my Heart" is an incredible song.'

'It would be great to win,' Nesta admitted, her thoughts flying

315

high. 'Red carpet, a big dress ... We might even get on TV! And look!' She pulled open a desk drawer to reveal piles of scribbled notes. 'I've written lyrics for at least another twenty songs. All Kev has to do is come up with some groovy tunes, and he's brilliant at that.' Her eyes sparkled. 'Do you think I can make Kev a star?'

'Why shouldn't you both be stars? The words are just as important as the music.'

'Ah! Talking of words ...' Nesta reached into another drawer and took out a notebook. 'Can you think of a rhyme for "greenhouse"?'

Holly wrinkled her nose in puzzlement. '"Greenhouse"? Er ...'

'No? Well what about "triple spiral fracture of the ankle" then?'

'Why?' demanded Holly, ever so slightly suspicious.

'I can't find a rhyme for "rabid chihuahua" either,' went on Nesta.

Holly grabbed the notebook, but Nesta grabbed it back again before she could read what was written in it. 'What the hell are you up to, Nesta?'

Nesta chuckled naughtily. 'Oh, I've just been collecting a few anecdotes about you from your colleagues,' she replied airily. 'Some really good ones, I must say. I particularly liked the one about the vicar and the bomb squad.'

'The parcel looked dangerous!' protested Holly. 'How did I know they were going to blow up his new cassock? And what do you need these anecdotes for anyway?'

'For the poem I'm writing for your leaving card,' Nesta replied merrily. 'No previews I'm afraid, but I promise you it'll be a good one.'

Time moves so fast, thought Holly as she sat at her dressing table, finishing off the letter. It hardly seems like the blink of an eye since I was five years old and Grace was just a screaming baby in the next

316

room. Jess didn't even exist ...

And now I'm leaving home for the second time, probably for ever.

She knew it was silly to make a fuss about it really, since she was only moving to the other side of town, but she had a feeling in her heart that this room would never again be hers. And that was only right and proper. This was a house for children to grow up in, not for a woman pushing thirty who was still trying to find her life's direction.

I think I've found it now, she said to herself. I really do. Please let me be right this time ...

Finishing off the letter, she addressed the envelope to the Catholic priest in Port Erin. She'd felt she ought to write to him, giving him the address of her new flat just in case her birth mother wanted to get in touch sometime. Not that Holly really believed she ever would, not now.

Sealing and stamping the envelope, she slipped it into the pocket of her jeans and ran downstairs, where Phil and her father were deep in conversation about the bogeys on 1960s' diesel locomotives. They looked like two schoolboys playing Top Trumps, she thought with a smile, happy that Harry was as fond of Phil as she was.

'Sorry to spoil the fun, boys,' she said, 'but I'm ready to go.'

Phil leaped to his feet and so did Harry, scrabbling around for his favourite cap. 'I'd best come along too,' he said, 'in case you can't find the stopcock or something.'

'I'll be fine, Dad,' Holly assured him as his warm, strong arms enfolded her and she tried to hold back the tears. 'It's only a couple of miles away and I'm coming back for lunch on Sunday, remember?'

For all her upbeat words, she felt more than a twinge of sadness as she walked down the front path towards the box van which Phil had hired to move all her stuff to her new flat. Everything was loaded up and ready to go. There was no excuse for her to linger a moment longer.

'Bye, Dad,' she called through the van's passenger window as Phil turned on the ignition.

'Goodbye, house,' she whispered. And although she was excited about moving to a place of her own, it felt like saying goodbye to a part of her own soul.

Holly and Phil had hardly driven half a mile when Phil stopped the van by the side of the road.

'Why have we stopped?' asked Holly anxiously. 'Is there something wrong with the van?'

'No, there's something wrong with me,' said Phil, thumping the steering wheel. 'This is ridiculous.'

'What is?'

'You moving into your own flat.' He turned to face her. 'Why the hell don't we just turn this van round and drive the whole lot round to my place?'

Holly swallowed hard, afraid to believe that she was hearing what she'd so wanted to hear. 'Y-your place?'

Phil took her hand in his. 'You've been spending most nights round at my place anyway,' he reminded her with a kiss. 'I know it's not a palace, but it just doesn't make any sense for you to be paying out all that extra money on a place of your own, does it?'

'Not really,' Holly whispered.

Then Phil drew back, as if something awful had just struck him. 'U-unless you'd *rather* have a place of your own,' he stammered. All his bravado evaporated, leaving the overgrown schoolboy Holly had fallen for. 'I mean, you might want the privacy. Oh.' Another thought struck him. 'And you've already paid a month's rent in advance ...'

She silenced him with a kiss, and slipped her arms around him as best she could in the van's cramped cab. Traffic poured past. Somebody honked their horn, but she didn't care. This was a moment of pure happiness, a capsule insulated from the rest of the world and its cares.

'No, Phil,' she replied. 'I would *not* rather have a place of my own, and I don't care if the landlord keeps my deposit. I don't care about anything but you.'

'So you'd like to move in with me?' Phil looked as if he couldn't believe his luck. The truth was, neither could Holly. 'You really would?'

She sat back in her seat, closed her eyes and felt a huge grin spread across her face. 'Shut up and drive, Phil. We're on double yellow lines.'

When they got to Phil's flat they unloaded most of the boxes containing Holly's stuff and piled it into the only available space: the middle of his living room.

Phil eyed the miniature Everest with alarm. 'Hey, I hope you're going to unpack this sometime soon. We won't be able to watch TV unless we're standing on the sofa.'

Holly laughed at the look on his face. 'Do you really think we'll be spending much time watching TV? I sincerely hope not.'

He grinned and cuddled her close. 'Sorry. Automatic man-reflex. You know what we're like with our gadgets.'

'Are you quite sure you want me here?'

'Holly!' He flung the pair of them onto the sofa, almost knocking over a box of wine glasses. 'Don't you realise? Having you here with me is a dream come true. I-I never believed you could care about me enough to want to live your life with me.'

'Well, I do, OK?'

They snuggled up on the sofa, ignoring the unpacking and the autumn rain thundering down outside, because frankly they didn't matter. *This* mattered.

'Holly,' said Phil.

'Hm?'

'There are so many other men out there – better men than me. Richer men than me. Men like Murdo. What have I got that they haven't?'

She looked into his sea-green eyes and whispered: 'My heart.'

That evening, as Phil was preparing dinner, Holly suddenly remembered the letter.

She pulled it out, somewhat flattened and crinkled by its journey in the back pocket of her jeans. Good job I didn't post it, she thought, carefully opening the envelope.

Taking a pen from her handbag, she crossed out the new address she'd given the priest and replaced it with Phil's. I won't mention that I'm actually living in sin with Phil, she thought, he might not approve. Then she wrote out a new envelope, popped the letter inside and slipped out to post it.

As she dropped it into the postbox, she wondered fleetingly if there was really any point. After all, her birth mother would probably never enquire after her, and even if she did, she probably wouldn't bother getting in touch. The stakes were too high for a woman in Denise's position. An illegitimate daughter might lose her votes – and her husband.

Ah well, thought Holly, you never know. And she turned and walked away from the postbox, sure in her own mind at least that if Denise never contacted her, she could live with it. She didn't need her any more, because now, Holly Bennett finally knew who she was.

Epilogue:

Cheltenham, eighteen months later

It was a wonderful spring day, the kind that poets write about. Poets and song lyricists, thought Holly as Nesta bounded up the path to Holly and Phil's new house, armed with wine and a card with a special welcoming verse.

It wasn't a very big house; in fact as houses go, it was more of a cupboard. But Holly and Phil loved it and its tiny garden, and more to the point it had an extra room for the baby they were expecting.

A small house was all they could afford, since all their spare money had been going into the business. There was a long way to go, but already Bloodhound Investigations was making a name for itself as the most professional detective agency in town. And the clients were coming in thick and fast: so much so that they'd had to take on a junior, Eddie, who held the fort while Holly was out of the office on cases. She'd passed her private investigator's course with flying colours, thanks to tuition from Phil, who kept telling everyone he was the proudest boss in Cheltenham.

And he'd be the proudest husband too, when they got married at St Mungo's in the summer.

'Hiya kids,' chirped Nesta, embracing Holly and Phil with her free arm. Then she patted Holly's swelling stomach. 'How's Junior?'

Holly grimaced. 'Kicking penalties for England.'

Phil grinned. 'That's my boy!'

'Girl!' Holly stuck her tongue out at him. Then they both laughed and hugged.

'Who cares?' said Phil. 'We just can't wait for it to arrive. I wonder if it'll be a great detective?'

'Of course it will; its mum and dad both are.' Holly took the wine and card from Nesta. 'Come inside, the others are already here.'

How so many people had managed to squeeze into the living room, Holly would never know. But they were all there: aunties, friends, neighbours and even Dweezil, who had at last reached a state of uneasy détente with Holly and Phil's new kitten, Holmes. Eileen was there too, resplendent in huge crystal earrings and a patchwork skirt, and chatting to everyone about the benefits of reiki; and Harry was there with Grace, Steve and Adam, who was now toddling about furiously and leading his mum a merry dance.

Jess was there too, fresh from her new job as a junior in a local hair salon, but there was no sign of Kev. There was a good reason for that though ...

Phil glanced at his watch. 'Quiet, everybody – it's nearly time!' He turned on the TV with great ceremony, and everyone tried to find a seat or a perch in the tiny room.

Holly held her breath as the presenter waffled on about the show, the competition, the performers ... Would he never get to the point? Then at last he introduced the star of the show: 'the winner of *The Star Factor*: Kev Thompson, with "Sometime in my Heart" ...'

Jess cried buckets as Kev sang her song live on air. To everyone's relief the two of them were now completely reconciled, and were

322

even talking about having another baby. Holly glanced at Nesta, who was smiling broadly, radiantly happy to see her song performed on television and doubly delighted to see Kev making a success of his musical career. There was another reason for her happiness though, mused Holly: the handsome young music publisher who'd been taking more than a strictly business interest in a certain flame-haired lyricist from Cheltenham. I knew it, Holly thought to herself. I knew there had to be a man out there who loves spiders, bad poetry and traction engines as much as Nesta does.

'A toast!' declared Harry, raising his glass as the song finished. 'To Kev – and Nesta of course – and to Holly and Phil, wishing them every happiness in their new home.'

Glasses were topped up and raised. In the midst of it all, the phone rang in the hall.

'I'll get it,' said Phil, squeezing past Holly's enormous Great-aunt Gladys.

A minute later he reappeared, with all the colour drained from his face. 'Holly,' he announced slowly, 'it's for you.

'It's someone ...' He swallowed hard. 'Someone who says he's your father.'

Read on for a sneak peek of

SPECIAL DELIVERY

a wonderful novel
by Zoë Barnes
that is completely unputdownable!

Ally and her sister couldn't be more different. While Ally is
happily married to Luke, has two young children and a cosy
home life, Miranda is child-free, has a millionaire husband and
lives in a show home that wouldn't be out of place in the pages of
House & Garden. Ally gave up trying to compete years ago. But
she is shocked when Miranda asks her if she'll help provide the
one thing that is missing from her perfect life: a baby.

Ally has every sympathy for Miranda's infertility problems, but
can she really have a baby and hand it over to someone else?
Especially as that someone else is Miranda ...

978-0-7499-3902-1

Praise for *Special Delivery*:

'Zoë Barnes does justice to this sensitive subject' *Daily Telegraph*
'A real page-turner, pack it in your beach bag' *Reveal*

Prologue

One very ordinary Monday morning at the unfashionable end of Cheltenham ...

One very ordinary Monday morning at the unfashionable end of Cheltenham ...

'Mum, I can't find my pants,' wailed a young male voice over the din of the cartoon channel on the kitchen TV.

Ally Bennett half-turned her head towards her son as her hands automatically went on filling the two plastic lunch boxes on the counter, while keeping one eye on the ancient toaster that could go from anaemic to carbonised in a nanosecond. There was a smear of margarine in her hair, but that was nothing new.

'Which pants? I left some for you on your bed.'

'Not those, my Little Britain ones!' replied seven-year-old Kyle, in an exasperated tone that implied no other pants in the world were worth wearing. 'My *best* ones.' He was standing in the kitchen doorway wearing his school shirt and jumper, twinned with a pair of half-mast pyjama bottoms.

'Well they're not in the wash,' replied his mother, 'so I haven't a clue what you've done with them. You'll just have to wear the ones I put out for you.'

'But I want *those*—'

'Sorry, Kyle.'

A hint of red-faced obstinacy was entering the conversation. 'But I *want*—'

Calmly, Ally turned back to her sandwich assembly line, effectively cutting her son off in mid-flow. When you had a young son, a toddler daughter and a husband to sort out by half-past eight, nothing could be allowed to disrupt the daily routine. Not even your son's favourite underwear. 'Pants,' she intoned with her back to him and just a soupçon of menace. 'Now. Or no chocolate pudding tonight.'

With much muttering, her eldest child shuffled off upstairs, while his three-year-old sister Josie liberally splashed her cereal about, some of which found its way into her mouth but most onto the floor.

It was chaos every morning at number 22, Brookfield Road, but Ally took it all in her stride. Or to be scrupulously honest, she loved it. Some people might accuse her of having no ambition, but this had always been her own personal dream: a husband she loved, a house of their own, and two important jobs – part-time teacher and full-time mum. OK, so a little extra money wouldn't go amiss, and they'd never be in the same social league as her elder sister, but did that really matter? They managed. And she wouldn't have changed places with toffee-nosed singleton Miranda for anything.

Luke Bennett yawned as he entered the kitchen, still pulling on his work shirt, a lock of sandy-gold hair slipping down over one eye. He was quite good-looking really but in a decidedly crumpled way; no matter what Ally did to them, his clothes looked perpetually unironed. Luke was one of those men who could have five o'clock shadow at seven in the morning: no matter how often he shaved, he invariably looked as if he hadn't bothered. Thankfully, outreach workers for homelessness charities weren't generally judged on their personal grooming, and besides, Ally loved him just the way he was. She'd never really fancied the slick, City type; or the 'metrosexual' who was forever pinching his wife's moisturiser, for that matter.

'Hi darling.' He gave Ally a squeeze and a tickly little kiss on the back of the neck. 'What's up with Kyle? He's got a face on him like a slapped backside.'

'Lost underpants.'

'What – again? How can a boy *lose* underpants?' Luke stepped in a puddle of milk and shook his soggy, slipper-clad foot. 'Josie!'

The little girl held up her spoon up to her dad and smiled.

Luke contemplated the sodden remnants of his slipper as Nameless the cat trotted over to lick it clean for him. 'Oh well, never mind. At least it's only milk!'

'And let's try and get some breakfast your tummy please,' instructed Ally (who, like all mums, had eyes in the back of her head). With one deft movement she whisked away Josie's bowl and spoon and handed her some toast soldiers. 'Have some toast instead . . . you like toasty soldiers. Kyle! Breakfast. Now!'

Luke extracted a few envelopes from the back pocket of his cords. 'Post's come. Mainly junk mail. Oh – one for you though.' He waved it in front of his wife's face. 'Ooh, look: a Wiltshire postmark.'

Ally groaned. They only knew two people in Wiltshire, and one of them was currently working in Dubai. The other one was Miranda.

'Tell you what, you open it,' she said, adding jam to Kyle's toast as he raced into the room. 'I've got sticky fingers.'

'Coward.'

'Guilty as charged.'

'Is that a letter from Auntie Miranda?' piped up Kyle, his interest peaking. 'Is she coming to see us? When's she coming?'

Oh dear I do hope not, thought Ally, instantly feeling guilty for having such unsisterly thoughts. I don't think my inferiority complex has quite recovered from the last visit yet. But rich Auntie Miranda was always welcome in Cheltenham as far as the kids were concerned. There couldn't be many other kids whose aunties showered them with presents as expensive as Miranda's.

Luke didn't answer. He was too busy reading the contents of the envelope, and chuckling. 'Well, well . . .'

'Well, well, what?' demanded Ally, her curiosity aroused.

'What do you reckon to Mr Fancy-Pants then?' Luke handed her a photograph of a dark-haired, lean-jawed, smart-suited guy whose almost peridot-green eyes seemed to reach right out of the picture and draw Ally in. Not classically handsome, that much was true; but striking. And he had that certain magnetic something that made a woman want to look and keep on looking.

She affected an unimpressed shrug. 'He's . . . OK I guess. What is he, another one of Miranda's actor-friends or something?'

327

Luke chuckled. 'Believe it or not, that guy there is a big-time property developer who owns his own polo team. Oh, and he's also the future Mr Miranda.'

'What!' Ally's eyes widened in disbelief. 'She's never ...?'

'That's right, darling, it's time to buy a hat. Your ever-loving sister is finally getting hitched.'

This was going to be the mother of all engagement parties, and there were hordes of well-heeled, designer-clad clones in the Overbury Suite; but Ally's sister stood literally head and shoulders above the whole lot of them, like a six-foot beacon of loveliness.

Miranda Morris was the sort of woman who glided through a room as though she were on invisible wheels. Endowed with effortless elegance, she was the irritating kind of woman who never tripped over things, ate with the wrong fork or looked anything less than stunning – with or without make-up. The type of woman, as Ally's best mate Zee had once quipped, who'd eat crisps with a knife and fork. Oh, and she had enough of her own money to keep her in Manolo Blahniks for life.

It wasn't too difficult to guess what a bloke might see in her, but all the same Ally couldn't help feeling a wee bit sorry for Gavin. After all, she'd spent all her childhood years sharing a bedroom with Miranda, and it had been ... well ... an experience, and not one she'd care to repeat. Gavin Hesketh must be quite a guy if he fancied attempting it on a permanent basis.

After years in her shadow, Ally ought probably to have hated her elder sister, but the curious fact was that nobody hated Miranda. Ally suspected it might be genetically impossible. And yet this was the woman who'd had every damn thing she demanded as a child; never showing a hint of gratitude towards her hard-up parents or her hard done-by sister. Then she'd breezed into medical school, junked it after a couple of years in favour of an international modelling career, and promptly posed and pouted her way to a Coutts bank account that was exponentially bigger and fatter than her über-pert backside.

Nowadays, at the ripe old age of thirty-seven, the girl who couldn't sew a button on or boil an egg was playing at being an

328

interior designer and filling the rest of her time doing 'charity work', which (as Luke had noted) seemed to consist mainly of going to posh dinners with local celebrities. Everything in Miranda's life was so, so easy. Ally wondered if things would be any different for her now that she had somebody else to think about. Knowing Miranda, probably not.

Ally finished adjusting her make-up, straightened up and looked at her reflection in the powder-room mirror. Not too bad for a thirty-year-old mother of two: half-decent boobs, nice shiny golden hair and not too much of a jelly-belly; but all the same it was hard not to feel outclassed when you were wearing last year's skirt and top and everybody else was in this season's Prada. And Ally hadn't quite got to the stage where she was desperate enough to accept her big sister's hand-me-downs. It wasn't only the fact that Miranda was twice as tall and half as fat. It would just have been too much like history repeating itself.

All her life Ally had felt like an afterthought. Her mother and father had been trying for a baby for eight years when Miranda made her dramatic appearance; and right from day one Miranda had always seemed like the 'special' one in the family. It helped of course that she was the most beautiful baby anybody had ever seen, the cleverest child in her year at school, and brilliant at any and every activity she'd ever tried her hand at, from macramé to driving a tank. But most of all, she was the golden child; the baby Maureen and Clive had feared they'd never have.

Not surprisingly, when Ally unexpectedly popped out seven years later, just after her mum had given away all the baby clothes, the excitement was noticeably more muted. It wasn't that there was anything wrong with Ally, far from it. She was healthy, perfectly presentable and above-averagely intelligent. But compared to her big sister she was, well, a bit ... ordinary. How could she be anything else, compared to Miranda?

One final blot of her lipstick, and Ally headed back towards the party. But she'd only got a few yards down the hotel corridor when a voice called out her name.

'Alison?'

Surprised, she stopped and looked round.

'It is Alison, isn't it? I haven't quite got the hang of everybody's names and faces yet.' The tall, dark and kind-of handsome Gavin Hesketh was walking towards her. 'Sorry if I startled you,' he went on. 'I just wanted to thank you for your engagement present.'

Ally fidgeted, curiously uncomfortable in the light from those almost spookily luminous green eyes. They gave her the shivers. Nice ones, though. 'Um. Great, that's fine. No problem.'

'Only I thought Miranda was a bit ... well, let's face it, much as I love her she can be a little thoughtless sometimes.'

Ally raised an eyebrow. Perhaps the beauteous Gavin hadn't been entirely blinded by lust then. Generally, Miranda's besotted suitors didn't take the trouble to figure out the real Miranda until some time after they'd been dumped. 'You think so?' she asked, with a touch of amusement.

He laughed. 'I know so. And you're her sister, so you do too. I'm guessing you've been on the receiving end of Miranda's "directness" more times than you can count. Anyhow, I thought she was very rude about your present. Those hand-embroidered tablecloths are absolutely beautiful, and they must have taken forever to make. Thank you.'

He had hold of her hand, just for a few seconds, and she just couldn't decide if she was desperate for him to let go of it, or desperate for him not to. All she knew for sure was that she didn't dare look him in the face, because then those green eyes might perceive the truth: that she was thinking about him in a way that a future sister-in-law really shouldn't.

'I – I'd ... er ... better go,' she said eventually; and as she looked up their eyes finally locked, and she felt the delicious spark zap between them.

'Yes, I think you had,' Gavin replied after a moment's silence.

And then she knew that he had felt it too.